PRAISE FOR
CLAIRE DELACROIX

"Ms. Delacroix is a master storyteller of medieval romance."
—*Old Book Barn Gazette*

"Claire Delacroix makes the Middle Ages glow with adventure, love, and beauty."
—*Bell, Book, and Candle*

"[An] engaging tale of lost love found."
—*Booklist* on *The Rogue*

"An ex   es up to its title. A wond   expected from the gift   *Rogue*

"If ever a novel spurned the conventional trappings of the romance genre in favor of a strong narrative voice and a lushly rich historical setting, *The Rogue* would be it. This medieval romance has the ability to transport readers to a time and place of dark mysteries, heraldry, and quiet romanticism."
—www.RomanticFiction.tripod.com on *The Rogue*

"An enchanting tale—just what readers expected from the talented author."
—**Romantic Times Book Club** on *The Rogue*

ALSO BY CLAIRE DELACROIX

The Rogue

CLAIRE DELACROIX

The Scoundrel

WARNER BOOKS

An AOL Time Warner Company

WARNER BOOKS EDITION

Copyright © 2003 by Claire Delacroix, Inc.

Cover design by Diane Luger
Cover illustration by Alan Ayers
Hand lettering by David Gatti

Warner Books, Inc.
1271 Avenue of the Americas
New York, NY 10020

Visit our Web site at www.twbookmark.com

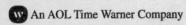 An AOL Time Warner Company

Printed in the United States of America

First Paperback Printing: August 2003

10 9 8 7 6 5 4 3 2 1

*With heartfelt thanks to all my editors,
past and present, for so generously sharing their
insight and experience.
Particular thanks to Karen Kosztolnyik
—an editor both past and present!—
for her continuing support and enthusiasm.*

The Scoundrel

Prologue

Inverfyre, Scotland—All Hallow's Eve, 1371

When darkness fell and the shadows in her chamber took vaguely human shapes, Lady Elspeth of Inverfyre understood that the dead had come to add her to their company.

It was a night that might have come from an old tale. The sky was blacker than black, the stars obscured, nary a sound carrying through the windows but the murmur of the wind in the trees.

It was the festival Samhain and, though the church had forbidden the celebration, the land heeded its ancient rhythms. On this night, legend told that the veil betwixt the worlds drew thin and that the dead came to visit the living. Elspeth, come to this land from the court of Burgundy, had never given much credence to local tales, not until now.

Indeed, she had no choice—she could see the dead, clustered 'round. Their phantom whispers rustled in the darkness, telling her a truth she did not want to hear.

Elspeth took a painful breath, relieved that it was not quite her last. She still had one deed to perform, one she had avoided in the hope that she would not be required to do it at all. Exhaustion filled her every sinew, just as pain racked her very bones. It would be blissful to be free of the agony, and Elspeth did not care at this point whether hell or heaven was her fate. No pain could be more fearsome than what she had already borne.

Still she would have borne it longer, if that might have made a difference. She closed her eyes and listened to the sounds of her daughter arguing yet again with Fergus.

"You should release Aphrodite," Evangeline said, referring to the gyrfalcon recently granted to Fergus as a gift. Her daughter's tone was precisely right, in Elspeth's opinion, neither pleading nor insistent. Fergus could take no insult from such reasonable speech. "She yearns to return to her nesting site. It will only drive her mad to deny her instincts, and a mad falcon is of no value to hunter or falconer."

It was a reasonable argument, one Evangeline had presented with respectful persistence. Elspeth held her breath, as she listened for the reply, though she suspected already what it might be.

Fergus laughed, his manner mocking. Elspeth winced. Had there ever been a man more given to ignoring good sense?

"Oh, you have a whimsy, Evangeline," Fergus said in the manner of one indulging a stupid child. "Only a woman could believe it wise to cast away a prize such as this!"

"But . . ."

"I will never let Aphrodite fly free—what fool would spurn a bird fit for a king? You may rest assured that whatever her instinct, she will learn to prefer my hand."

"She will lose heart." Evangeline persevered, though Elspeth guessed that her daughter understood the battle to be lost. "A falcon is most clever, more clever than a hound. A haggard falcon, taken long after its infancy, is never a good captive. This is why we have never captured haggards at Inverfyre."

"You capture *no* falcons at Inverfyre, to my knowledge. That is why it is so delightful to be granted a gift such as this bird."

"Aphrodite must be permitted to return to her nest, wherever it is, there to meet with her partner."

"And who are you to grant me counsel?" Fergus mocked. "Remember your place, Evangeline. You may be a beauteous woman, but beauty is less pleasing when accompanied by a viper's tongue."

There was a pause and Elspeth suspected that her determined daughter had to grit her teeth. "I think only of the value of the bird to you, Fergus," she said with a deference that must have been feigned. Truly, Elspeth had taught the child well! "I would not have your prized gift wither—how impressed would the donor be if Aphrodite died?"

"She will not die! What do you know of gyrfalcons?"

"I am the daughter of the Laird of Inverfyre, baron of the greatest falconry in all of Christendom," Evangeline snapped. Elspeth averted her face, disliking that her daughter's pride could not be better confined. Fergus would take affront. "I am born to a centuries-old lineage of falconers. It could be said that I know something of falcons."

"To be born at Inverfyre does not grant one innate knowledge of falcons or falconry," Fergus retorted. He was wrong, more wrong than he could know, but Elspeth knew this man could be taught nothing. "Fear not—Aphrodite will be smitten with another male."

"Falcons mate for life."

"No, Evangeline, they do not. That is the kind of whimsy I expect to hear from a woman prone to chattering nonsense."

Elspeth grimaced at Fergus' dismissive tone. The pain chose that moment to revisit her, and she gasped at the vigor of its bite.

Immediately, her daughter was leaning over her, eyes filled with concern. "Mother? How do you fare?"

"Not well." Elspeth coughed and caught her breath. She laid a hand over her daughter's hand, so much younger and smoother than her own. "This night will be my last."

"Do not say as much!"

"It is the truth, Evangeline."

"Nonsense! A healer comes from Edinburgh even now. Do not lose heart so readily as this."

Elspeth sighed, knowing she could not persuade her daughter of what she knew to be unassailable. "Then, aid me to sit up, if you please."

Evangeline pushed pillows behind her mother's back and smoothed the hair back from her brow. Elspeth noted that Fergus lingered in the doorway, the gyrfalcon Aphrodite perched upon his gloved hand, though he clearly wished to be elsewhere. He stroked the bird's back with a bejewelled hand, his gaze assessing. The bird's hood was splendidly wrought of green leather, embellished with gold and topped with a crest of peacock feathers.

Fergus himself was finely attired as well, seemingly every gem of Inverfyre's treasury stitched onto his clothes. Fergus' fine garb, however, could not hide his age. He was elderly, vain, and not terribly clever. Not for the first time, Elspeth wondered why Gilchrist had chosen Fergus as his successor. Her husband had had many failings, but she had always admired his ability to judge character.

Until Fergus and his honeyed tongue came to Inverfyre.

"Evangeline speaks aright," Elspeth informed Fergus, uncommonly bold in her last moments. "If you do not release the bird by midwinter, she will be useless in the spring. It is always thus with birds snared after their second moult. They are captured too late to avoid their instinct becoming habit."

"More counsel from women," Fergus said with a roll of his eyes. "How fortunate I am this night to be privy to such *wisdom.*"

"Fergus!" Evangeline whispered, but Elspeth waved a hand.

"Go then, and leave us to our womanly whimsy." She yearned to say more, but bit her tongue. There was oft a glint in Fergus' eye that made Elspeth wonder whether he was as weak as she believed.

He left, with nary another word.

"I am sorry, Mother. He does not know what he says."

Elspeth smiled and touched her daughter's cheek. Here was the one jewel she had wrought in all her days. Evangeline was a beauty, with the blue eyes and fair skin of her father and the black tumbling curls of her mother's younger days. There was more than beauty to Evangeline though, for she had a will of iron, not unlike that of Gilchrist and his warrior kin.

What a leader Evangeline could have been!

"You should have been born a boy," Elspeth murmured, before she could halt herself. "If you had been shaped as a man, your father would have died at ease."

"I doubt that I should have met his standards even then," Evangeline said with unexpected bitterness.

Their gazes met for a heated moment. Then Evangeline smiled primly, as if she had made a jest. Her eyes had revealed the truth, though, and Elspeth was ashamed.

"All couples yearn for a son, Evangeline. There is no sin in desiring an heir and stability."

Evangeline lifted a brow and looked away. She stroked her mother's hand, her gaze searching the shadows.

"Do you see them, too?" Elspeth asked hopefully.

"Who?"

"The souls in the shadows."

Evangeline smiled, as if she believed Elspeth to be losing her wits. "Be calm, Mother. There is no one in the shadows."

"You should speak more with Adaira. She will teach you things I failed to teach you."

"You said she was mad. You always forbade me to speak with her!"

"I was wrong. Ask her."

"Ask her what, Mother?"

Elspeth was distracted by one shadow separating itself from the others, then astonished when she discerned its features. It was Gilchrist, yet not Gilchrist, Gilchrist as if he had been touched by the wand of the frost elves.

Her heart nigh stopped as he paused beside her bed, his gaze searching her own. Gilchrist always had looked into her eyes before he spoke, had done so with a marvel in his own expression, as if he could not believe she was his bride. It was this gesture that persuaded her of this shade's identity. Silver glimmered along his silhouette, shone in his beard, crested his hair and spiked his eyelashes. Only his eyes remained the same vivid sapphire she knew so well.

Elspeth caught her breath, for she knew full well why he had come. He reached out to her and she hesitated to take his hand, fearing he would be displeased that she had not fulfilled her old pledge to him.

She turned back to Evangeline and was surprised to spy tears forming in her daughter's eyes. The first fell like a gem, glittering in the lamplight until it splashed upon their hands.

Elspeth reached for her daughter and caught her close, closing her own eyes as Evangeline began to weep. "I can linger no longer, Evangeline."

"I would never have asked you to endure the pain for so long as you have. But I shall miss you sorely."

"And I you." Elspeth stroked the dark silk of Evangeline's hair, remembering all their former embraces, remembering the babe, the child and the young girl that this woman had been. This would be the last embrace they shared and she never wanted its sweetness to end.

"I never wished that you were aught other than you are," Elspeth confessed softly. "Not once you were born, not once you smiled at me. Do not imagine otherwise."

Evangeline wiped her tears and might have said something, but Elspeth hastened to tell her tale while she could. "I have waited five years for the right moment to share a tale, but this moment shall have to suffice. Promise me that you will share this revelation with Fergus when the moment is right, that he may act upon it."

"Of course."

"In all your lessons of birds of prey, did you learn of the lammergeier?"

Evangeline shook her head.

"It is a sheep vulture. It is not a noble hunter like the peregrine, the falcon or the gyrfalcon. It is not even of the lesser predators like hawks. The lammergeier is a scavenger."

Elspeth could not help but sneer. Her life at Inverfyre had made her as discriminating about birds of prey as Gilchrist had been. "The lammergeier feeds upon plunder and carrion. It will not kill its own prey—it prefers to steal a kill from another, or to consume what has been discarded. They are to be reviled."

"I have never seen one."

Elspeth smiled, for she knew this was not quite true even if her daughter did not. "Do you know how your father died?"

Evangeline patted her mother's hand, clearly certain that Elspeth's thoughts flitted from one subject to another. "He took a fit and fell down the stairs. It is five years in the past, Mother."

"And what caused his fit?"

Evangeline shook her head. "It is not of import. Do not excite yourself with this matter now, Mother. . . ."

Elspeth held her daughter's hand more tightly. "A man by the name of Lammergeier—an apt choice on the part of his forebears—sent a missive, offering the *Titulus Croce* for purchase."

Evangeline's flicking gaze revealed that she did not know what to say. "But the relic is in the chapel," she began cautiously.

"No, it is not. We lied to you, your father and I lied to all of Inverfyre."

Evangeline sat back, but Elspeth would not be halted now. "The *Titulus* was stolen years ago. Your father knew that he had failed his people and his forebears in allowing such a theft to occur."

Evangeline was curiously aloof, but no one liked to learn that she had been deceived.

"What choice had we had but to guard our secret closely?"

Evangeline arched a brow. "Then, surely Father would have paid any price to retrieve the *Titulus*."

"So thought Avery Lammergeier." Elspeth swallowed.

"And the price he set was more, far more, than your father ever could have paid. It infuriated Gilchrist beyond belief, for as a matter of principle he believed he should not reward a pirate to return his own birthright."

"Yet still he desired the *Titulus*."

"He believed its return was the sole thing that could save Inverfyre." Elspeth held her daughter's gaze steadily. "It is far more cruel to be offered a solution to your failure at a price you cannot pay, than simply to have failed in the first place. Your father's fury overcame him when Avery wrote that another nobleman would pay double the price he had initially asked."

They watched each other in silence for a long moment, Evangeline's grip tight upon her mother's hand. "And his fury prompted his mis-step, and thus his fall," Evangeline guessed quietly. Elspeth nodded. "You never said as much."

Elspeth frowned. "Further, it is the responsibility of your father's successor to avenge his death."

"You will wait long for Fergus to do as much."

"I have waited as long as I can. The burden now lies with you. You are the bough, Evangeline, the bough that will bear the prophesied fruit of the seventh son. You must ensure that your son has his due, that the *Titulus Croce* is here to legitimize that son's suzerainty and bring prosperity to Inverfyre."

"These are the workings of men, Mother. A relic, however holy, will do little to aid in such a goal."

"Is that so, daughter mine?" Elspeth spoke sharply as seldom she did. "Tell me then: why are the falcons barren? Nary an egg is there to be found since the *Titulus* was stolen. The *Titulus* was granted to your forebear, Magnus Armstrong, by divine favor and brought with him to found this keep. His holding prospered, because he kept his bargain with God. The relic must be here, the grace of God must be upon us, or Inverfyre is doomed forevermore."

She fell back against the pillows, exhausted by this tirade. Evangeline looked down at her hands, her expression solemn. Fergus' laughter rose from the hall below, the cries of the gyrfalcon tied to his wrist making both women wince.

"It may be too late," Evangeline said quietly.

"You are the vessel!" Elspeth said fiercely. "You cannot lose faith or fail in your responsibility!"

Evangeline shook her head. "It has been five years, Mother. Even if I told Fergus of it now, even if he departed this very night, the relic could have traveled to any place in Christendom."

"No. No, this is not true." Elspeth mustered the last of her strength and sat up, despite her daughter's attempt to urge her back against the pillows. "Avery Lammergeier died, not long after your sire. Murdered, he was, murdered by his own son, this I heard, and a more fitting fate could not have been found for that wretch. There have been no tales of such a relic being transported, and one would hear of it for it is a prize worth the bragging. The relic is still there, still at the Lammergeier abode of Ravensmuir."

"Ravensmuir." Evangeline rolled the name across her tongue.

"Ravens are carrion-pickers and foragers." Elspeth fell back again, exhausted. "This felon named his eyrie well. The son must not know what he has, or he would have sold it by this time. Perhaps God favors our cause, I cannot say. But Fergus must go to Ravensmuir to retrieve the *Titulus,* and you must persuade him to do so."

"You have seen how he heeds my counsel—not at all!"

"Promise me!" Elspeth felt the pain rise anew and feared the end came too soon. She seized Evangeline's hands and her tears rose, so fearful was she that she would fail Gilchrist. "Promise me that you will find a way!"

Evangeline's lips set to a firm line. She looked not unlike a peregrine now, her carriage proud, her gaze intensely blue. Even her pupils dilated and her lips thinned almost to naught. Her black hair gleamed like a bird's plumage and she held her chin proudly.

The similarity to her father was startling. Gilchrist had taken this pose when he would not be swayed from his course, and the sight reminded Elspeth of an old legend. It had been whispered through the years that there was a curious kinship betwixt Magnus Armstrong, the forebear of the lairds of Inverfyre, and the falcons. Indeed, it was rumoured that he had taken flight with them on moonlit nights, that he was one of them, that they had prospered in his holding because they were among kin.

Certainly, Elspeth had seen an echo of the bird's savage determination in her husband, though this was the first time she had glimpsed it in her daughter.

"I promise that the *Titulus* shall be returned to Inverfyre," Evangeline vowed. "No matter what I must do to see it so."

Elspeth had no time to reply. The pain redoubled and seized her innards with sharp talons. She writhed, parted her lips to scream, and then saw the silver shimmer of Gilchrist's proffered hand. She seized the shadow, welcoming whatever he offered.

A coolness like a spring stream flowed over and through her flesh, filling her with quicksilver, sweeping all earthly sensation away. It was like walking into the shade or dipping into a cool river, effortless and soothing. She saw a thousand shades of grey and silver that she had never imagined before, then drank of the gleaming sapphire of Gilchrist's gaze. She slipped from her flesh as easily as she might have shed a garment in her mortal days, shaking off her pain like an old chemise.

One touch and all she had known, Elspeth abandoned. Her earthly life became no more than a distant dream. Inverfyre, Fergus, even her beloved Evangeline, was forgotten. Deaf to her daughter's sobs, blind to the watchful presence of an old woman in the woods below the keep, Elspeth surrendered her past to embrace her future.

She held fast to Gilchrist's hand, watched the wings unfurl from his back, then took flight at his side, as free as any falcon to ride the mists forevermore.

An Unwitting Pawn

Gawain

I

December 29, 1371

Only a fool rides at night in these times, especially with a burden so precious as mine. The sky was darkening as the shadowed walls of a burg rose beside the road. It was York, not far enough from Ravensmuir to my thinking, but the darkness gave me pause.

It seemed that Ravensmuir breathed at my very back. Though my brother was dead, I had stolen from him and I half-expected his specter to demand some grisly compense of me. Though I am not a superstitious man, I would have preferred to have all of England and half the continent betwixt Merlyn's corpse and myself. The ominous shadows lurking on either side did little to ease my trepidation.

The rain began while I tried to recall how far it was to another settlement, let alone one I might find hospitable to my tastes. Certainly, I could not reach London in less than several days and my horse needed a respite. Night fell, swallowing what little light there was with that northern haste I find both astonishing and daunting.

The rain began to fall in gusts, a surly kind of weather

and one to which this hostile land seems inclined. That made my decision for me. To be dry and cold was far better than being wet and cold. I conjured some tale of being a merchant on the road for the complacent gatekeeper and he waved me onward with indifference.

York is a muddy burg, and the dirt hides whatever charm it might possess. I suppose it is large enough and prosperous enough for those who choose to inhabit it, but one glimpse of its churning river, filled with mire, and its dingy streets, thick with another manner of mire, and I was repulsed.

I chose the tavern simply because I saw it first. It was no meaner and no cleaner than any of the others that were its neighbors.

The demanded price was exorbitant, but both steed and I would be sheltered from the rain that now drove against the shutters. I grit my teeth and paid, then tended my own horse as they seemed disinclined to offer any service in exchange for my coin.

The meat served to the guests was sinewy, the gravy thin, the bread tough enough to break a tooth. That the stew was the same hue as the muck in the streets did little to encourage a man to clean his bowl. It is, however, oft said that hunger is the best sauce. As I was nigh starved, I ate the swill and called for more ale to rinse the taste of it from my mouth.

"Ale" I say, for I know no other word to use. They make a brew in these lands that they ambitiously call ale, but which bears no resemblance to any ale of my acquaintance. By the third cup, the taste of the brew improves considerably, and so it did that night. Even the cold, which is enough to freeze a man's marrow, began to retreat from my flesh.

It could be no coincidence that she appeared at that very moment, just as I might take interest in a comely wench, if only to prove that I still lived.

She ducked through the portal and shook back her hood, scattering raindrops to the floor. Every soul glanced up at the gust of wind and rain she admitted, every complaint was silenced afore it was uttered.

She was a beauty, of that there could be no mistake. The sight of her fairly stopped my heart, and it certainly stopped the chatter in the common room. She shone, like a polished gem, all the more glorious for the humble setting.

Her hair was as black as ebony and hung in loose waves over her shoulders. It was long and thick and tempted one's fingers to tangle within it. Her eyes were a sparkling clear blue, her lashes and brows as dark as soot. Her face was heart-shaped and her fairness gave her the appearance of being carved of alabaster. I had the sense that a fine sculpture drew breath, pinkened slightly, then stepped daintily from her pedestal.

She was finely boned and tiny, but there was a fire in her eyes when she lifted her chin to survey her surroundings. A slight smile curved her ripe lips, the glint in her eyes telling every man there that she would choose her companion.

Ah yes, there could be no doubt of her trade. More than one man in that hole caught his breath hopefully. The keeper frowned and might have made his way toward her, but she spied me and her smile broadened in a most inviting way.

I smiled in my turn, not averse to a little companionship. She waved her hand, as if we were acquaintances well met, and called something I could not hear.

The keeper stepped back to his place by the ale with a shrug. Most of the men returned to their cups, but I did not care.

There was solely the demoiselle for me. She cast her hair over her shoulder and loosed the neck of her cloak, easing her way through the crowd to my side. The man beside me nudged me and muttered some manner of congratulations beneath his breath, but I had eyes only for her.

Every graceful step she took made my blood heat yet more. Every pace fed my desire—I fairly simmered when she finally halted before me.

I thought it Providence at the time that she chose me so readily, or perhaps her ability to assess masculine potential. I was the best dressed of the sorry lot gathered there and certainly the most handsome. No doubt I also had the heaviest purse. In my experience, whores are quick to assess such practicalities.

She tipped her head back to meet my gaze, her secretive smile tempting me to taste her lips. Her eyes twinkled, as if she had just heard a particularly amusing jest.

"Good evening, my lord," she murmured, her voice low and luscious, then drew her cloak open with a fingertip.

I inhaled sharply at the view she covertly offered me. She wore nothing beneath the garment. I could see her creamy throat and the pale curve of her breasts. Her nipples stood erect against the shadows of the cloak, and at my reaction, she chuckled.

"You rode with such haste that I thought you lost to me forever," she said, then winked.

I realized that she meant to let others believe that we were acquainted. Her manner was so intriguing that I decided to support her ruse, if only to see what she desired of me.

I had my hopes.

I took her hand in mine, then kissed her knuckles. "It was never my intent, my lady, to lose such a prize as you." Her skin was surprisingly soft, considering how difficult her life must be. Perhaps whores fared particularly well in this burg.

I met her gaze, noting again how she seemed to be amused, and considered that a good portent.

She smiled, then plucked the cup of ale from my hand, ensuring our fingers brushed leisurely in the transaction. She stood so close that I could smell her skin, some sweet perfume mingled with her own scent and the smell of the rain.

And I lusted for this bold beauty, as I have seldom lusted for a woman before.

I watched hungrily as she ran the tip of her tongue around the rim of the cup, then paused where I had placed my mouth. Her gaze darkened as she licked there, and the thought that she savored the taste of me made me adjust my stance. It was cursedly warm in this place, to my thinking, and there were too many curious souls in proximity.

Mischief danced in her eyes as she raised her voice. "I feared that you tired of my company, my lord," she said, her words carrying to the attentive men surrounding us.

"Never."

She eased closer, her hand landing companionably upon my upper arm. "I feared to slumber in a cold bed this night."

I smiled and slipped my arm around her waist. "I can ensure that you do not." She was finely wrought, small and light, and I knew that I could easily lift her against me.

But I had no need to do so. The bold wench stretched up and brushed her lips across mine, her touch so achingly sweet that I closed my eyes.

Her next words I felt as well as heard, her breath falling against my lips. "I miss you too greatly when we are apart, my lord."

I should have guessed what she intended to do, but I was beguiled.

She pressed the cup back into my hand, locked her hand behind my neck and, stretching to her toes, kissed me boldly upon the lips. She tasted of ale and her own sweet nectar. Her breasts pressed against me, the knowledge that she was nude beneath her cloak enflaming me. I caught her more tightly around the waist, drawing her closer and drinking deeply of her kiss.

She purred, a gorgeous deep purr that had my tongue easing between her teeth. Her fingers twined in my hair, her tongue danced with mine, the scent of her deluged me. I was lost, oblivious to the hoots of the other men, and might have taken her there if she had not pulled away.

She was flushed and disheveled, her eyes sparkling so that I yearned only to finish what we had begun. I took a deep breath, wondering when I had ever come so close to losing command of myself.

Her fingertip traced a seductive path around my ear and down my throat. I swallowed, tried to slow my racing heart, and smiled with all the gallantry I could summon.

There was rather less of it than might have been hoped.

"My lady, I meant no offense by my haste."

She chuckled, clearly unoffended.

I ran my fingertips down her cheek in a caress I could not have forgone. She turned her face into my palm, pressing a hot kiss against my flesh even as she closed her eyes.

My next words were uncommonly thick. "Perhaps you will allow me to compense you for your disappointment on this night."

"Compense?"

I smiled. "With pleasure, of course."

"I shall be difficult to persuade," she teased, fluttering her eyelashes playfully. Her eyes danced with merriment and fetching color touched her cheeks. The men hooted and elbowed each other as they watched us, doing so more overtly with every passing moment.

"It is fortunate that I feel most persuasive this night." I pulled her close and bent her backwards as I claimed her lips. I kissed her, so possessively and thoroughly that she made a little growl of satisfaction. I felt her grip in my hair tighten to a fist, felt the wild flutter of her pulse against my fingertips, and knew she was as aroused as I.

Her passion made the kiss sweeter than sweet, the sordidness of our surroundings irrelevant.

When we parted, breathless, her eyes were dancing. "I suppose it would only be polite to permit you the opportunity," she whispered wickedly.

I gave her no chance to reconsider. I swung her into my arms and made for my humble room, knowing there would be little sleep for either of us this night.

I did not care. I was not so distracted that I forgot to sling my saddlebag over my shoulder, but its contents were hardly at the fore of my thoughts.

The demoiselle ensured as much, for she kissed me with fervor even before we left the common room. She had my chausses loose and her legs locked around my waist by the time I reached the summit of the stairs.

I lunged across the threshold of my chamber, distracted as I seldom am. I placed her upon the pallet, then locked the door and stowed the bag. I turned to find her nude upon my shabby pallet, her dark cloak pooled beneath her creamy curves. Her welcoming smile was all she wore and all the enticement any man could need.

When she reached for me, I could do nothing but surrender to the magic she wrought.

I am only human, no matter what is said of me, after all.

What a night! There was something about this woman, a mingling of ardor and innocence that snared me in her amorous spell. Every kiss she savored as if it was both her first and her last. She embraced my every suggestion like a virgin greedy for knowledge, but responded to my every touch like a whore who knew how to prolong each pleasure. It seemed she anticipated me, as I did her, as if we had loved a thousand times before.

Yet this was no mating burdened by habit or ennui. There was a spark of discovery along with the ease, and I could not fathom the combination.

Save that I could not have enough of it, or of her. We moved together so well and so effortlessly that I was half-persuaded that she had been wrought for me alone. I do not recall how many times we mated that night, I recall only that each time was more splendid than the last, that each release made me yearn for another.

I dozed when it was impossible to continue, but came fully awake in the midst of the night when my passionate companion stirred. I am inclined to sleep like a cat, even when alone, for mine is a life that requires one to be vigilant. I schooled my breath, as I am wont to do, letting her believe that I yet slept.

She rose from the hard straw pallet, and my flesh chilled where she had nestled against me. I listened to her soft footfalls as she crossed the dark chamber. I parted my eyelids slightly, and watched her pale silhouette. She paused before my saddlebag and I stiffened, well prepared to leap to the defense of its precious contents.

But she did not touch my belongings. Instead, she reached up and unlatched the shutters. She flung them open, then leaned her hands upon the sill to regard the sleeping town. It still rained, though the sky had turned to such a hue of pewter that it was brighter outside than inside, despite the hour.

She stood there nude, her hair cascading to her hips, and when she turned slightly, I saw her smile. There was satisfaction in that smile, as well as a measure of pride. She looked like a woman sated, which made me smile in turn, and I was reassured as to her intentions.

"You are pleased," I said softly.

She pivoted in alarm at the sound of my voice, then laughed as she leaned back against the lip of the window again. I liked that she did not hasten to cover herself or feign shyness after all we had done. "I did not know you were awake."

"How could I not awaken, with the night's chill spilling through the window?" I patted the pallet and shivered elaborately. "Come back to bed that we can force the cold from our bones."

She laughed again, genuinely amused by my words. "But it is not cold on this night! I can smell spring in the wind."

"In December? I think not. Spring may never touch this savage land again, for all that is in the wind."

She laughed again, then strode across the room, perching on the side of the pallet. "And where are you from, my lord, that your blood is so thin as this?"

"From the south," I said with characteristic evasiveness.

"The south of where?"

"England, of course."

She laughed again, though this laughter was knowing. "You are not of these isles. I can hear as much in your voice. Tell me, from whence did you come? Where is it so much warmer than here?"

I reasoned that it mattered little whether I told part of my tale to a pretty whore. I sat up and donned my chemise beneath her amused gaze. "From Sicily. It is an isle in the Mediterranean."

"Where the Normans ruled in times past and now law-lessness ensues," she said, surprising me with her knowl-edge. "Where Frederick II, the Holy Roman Emperor and marvel of the world, did reign so nobly."

"How could you know such a detail?"

She smiled coyly though I fancied that her cheeks pinkened, as if she had said more than she intended. "I knew a man who had an interest in the emperor's writings."

I said nothing, for I knew little of that man's treatises save for one composed upon the art of falconry. Such a sport of kings could not be of interest to any soul in this remote place, certainly not to a common whore. Of this I was cer-tain, and I had no desire to either challenge her certainty or insult her.

She took my silence for astonishment, which it was in part, and tapped my nose with a chiding fingertip. "We whores are not so stupid as that, even in these cold, cold lands."

I was startled that she mocked me, even though she did so gently and with charm. That spark of intellect I had glimpsed in her eyes earlier was there again, shining as if in challenge. There was devilry in her smile, devilry that should have given me pause, if I had not been distracted by the perfection of her breasts. I raised a hand to cup one and she arched her back, casting her hair over her shoulders.

"You do not know who a whore like me might have wel-comed between her thighs. Perhaps the king himself has vis-ited me and told me of his travels."

A chill passed through me then, and my hand fell away from her flesh. How much did she know of me? In hind-sight, I know that she noted my response, for she moved quickly to set me at ease again.

And this she accomplished by the simplest means. She

wrapped her arms around my neck and eased onto my lap, caught my face in her hands and kissed me as if her very soul depended upon it. I could not think, let alone be suspicious, with my arms full of this tempting wench—though later I would curse the fact that she had known precisely how to distract me.

"Tell me of this Sicily," she demanded when her lips left mine. Her hair fell around me, her buttocks were in my hands, and her smile rivaled the radiance of the sun.

"Why? Do clever whores not know all about its charms?"

She laughed, then her expression turned coy. "Because I am curious. Because I would know why you favor a place that others curse." She kissed my ear with such beguiling expertise that my eyes closed. "Because I cannot imagine a place warmer than this one."

Three good reasons they were, and reassuringly feminine reasons as well. I sighed and considered where to begin. "First, you should know that any lawlessness is not so fearful as men here would have you believe."

"Then, there is a ruling king?"

"One in Spain, which suits all in Sicily well enough." I smiled wickedly and she laughed, chiding me with a fingertip.

"You are not fond of having the eye of justice upon you. Is it possible that your coin is gained by nefarious means?"

"Sicily suits me." I merely winked and smiled when she might have asked for greater detail, then guided her gaze to the window with a sweeping gesture. "Imagine that we sit upon the top floor of a house, with solely the stars of the night above us as canopy."

"Your home?"

I ignored her query. "Imagine that the air is warm but not

hot, that the breeze is pleasant. Close your eyes and you can smell jasmine flowers in bloom. . . ."

"Jasmine?"

"A flower which emits a perfume beyond sweetness." She seemed skeptical of this detail, but I resumed my tale. "Imagine that the vista before your eyes is not the muddy grey of York, but the splendid Mediterranean sea—it is as blue as turquoise in the daylight and as the midnight sky at night. Before you is spread the entire town, for we are outside the city walls. There is the palace, surrounded by a lake which gleams in the moonlight and surrounded by orange trees. . . ."

"Orange trees? Trees are green, as every fool knows!"

"No, no, trees bearing the fruit called orange." She arched a dark brow at this, her doubts clear. "It is a small fruit, red-orange when ripe, green when not. These blossoms too are redolent with sweetness. The leaves, which are indeed green, are dark and glossy, as if polished to a shine."

"This sounds most fanciful."

"A veritable paradise upon earth. These trees were first planted by the Saracens, along with those of lemons and limes, both tart small fruits, one yellow and one green. The entire town is wrought of fine stone houses, with verdant gardens surrounding them. Here, on our loggia, we cannot see the distant isles called the Aeolian Isles, but we know they are there."

"How?"

"There are nine of them, two in perpetual fire. Although smoke rises from them during the day, at night you can discern solely red flames licking at the night sky from further down the coast. We can see the plume of smoke and know its import."

"This loggia sounds to be at the very gates of hell."

"No, no. The mountains are filled with fire there, though they seldom spill their lava and never into the town of Palermo."

"How reassuring." Her tone was wry, but she was intrigued.

"Our loggia is paved with interlocking stone, in a pattern wrought of red and green and gold. The walls are covered with glazed tiles of yellow and blue, and if you peer over the edge, you will spy a fountain on the ground floor. Fresh water runs from the aqueduct wrought by the Romans into the main room, then is channeled to a pond. The pond is filled with great golden fish and lilies grow around its perimeter."

"Water flows in the house itself?"

"Its coolness, and that of the stone, mitigates the day's heat. And the sound of it soothes the spirit."

"It would freeze in winter."

"There is no winter in Sicily, at least not as you know here."

"How hot *is* it there?"

"The sun shines most fiercely and there is a hot, dry wind from the south in summer which makes matters hotter."

She ran a fingertip across my jaw and down to my tanned chest. "Which is why your flesh is of such a hue." She followed her fingertip with a teasing line of kisses, but before I could return her embrace, she ruffled my hair. "Do all people there have hair as golden as the sun?"

"No. In fact, most have hair the hue of your own, though their eyes are dark."

"Then how did you come to abide there?"

I ignored this inquiry as well. "Close your eyes and imagine the sound of the night in Sicily, the hum of night insects, the distant ripple of laughter."

"You know this villa well."

"I intend to make it my own, for it is lush and elegant, a respite from the woes of the world." I slid down the pallet with her weight atop me. "Close your eyes and imagine. Smell the jasmine and the greenery, feel the heat of the air upon your flesh, hear the play of the water in the fountain. Look, there is red wine and fine cheese, fruits to tempt any palate. Choose a pomegranate. . . ."

"A pomegranate?" She braced her elbow upon my chest, her expression skeptical.

"A most uncommon fruit, both sweet and sour, and so delicious as to be sinful."

She shook her head then, as if impatient with me. "There can be no such fruit, as there can be no such paradise as this Sicily. You lie!"

"I do not!"

She laughed and swatted my shoulder playfully. "I do not believe that this Sicily of yours exists. I think you concoct a tale for my amusement." Her eyes narrowed. "Or perhaps for your own, that you might measure the gullibility of a simple whore."

The heat between us suddenly chilled.

"No! Sicily is precisely as I tell you."

She was unpersuaded. Indeed, she rolled away from me, convinced that I made a jest at her expense. I was not yet prepared to see this demoiselle leave my bed, however, so I leapt to my feet.

I recalled that I yet had two pomegranates in my saddle-bag, so loathe had I been to eat the last of those I had brought. I rummaged in the bag for one, refastened it so that she might not spy its contents, then turned to confront her proudly with the fruit. "A pomegranate."

She lounged on the pallet, her weight braced on one elbow, her expression inscrutable. "A painted ball."

I sat on the side of the bed and took my knife to the rind. The distinctively sweet scent of the fruit had her sitting up behind me. I smiled, noting her curiosity, then let her examine it.

"It smells sweet, yet tart." She turned the red fruit in her hands, her curiosity clear, then removed one of the glistening beads and rolled it between her fingers. A pomegranate, as you know, is filled with such beads, each containing a juicy red pulp and a seed. She marveled at it, then slanted a considering glance to me. "You did not lie."

"Of course not. This one has lingered long in my saddlebag, so is not at its prime. They are larger and more filled with juice when freshly plucked. See how the flesh has dried and tightened."

"And these can be eaten?"

I loosed the beads, then offered her several upon the blade of my knife. Her uncertain gaze flicked from it to me, then to the bead she yet held between finger and thumb. I took several and ate them myself under her scrutiny, then spat out the seeds.

"Your lips are stained, as with carmine," she said with a merry laugh.

"Every pleasure has its price." I winked and she smiled, then shook her head.

"There is a truth that cannot be denied." There was a sadness in her eyes at that moment, but I caught only a glimpse of it before she popped the bead of pomegranate into her mouth. Her eyes widened when it evidently burst in her mouth, then she gasped with pleasure at the taste of the fruit. She spat the seed into her hand with all the grace of a noblewoman, then her tongue made quick work of the juice upon her lips.

"It is delicious!" Her eyes lit and she reached for more.

But I held the fruit beyond her grasp, knowing my own smile was wicked. "And what," I mused, "would you be prepared to do for more?"

She chuckled, her eyes dancing with mischief. She feigned submissiveness in a way that prompted my own laughter. "Anything, my lord. Anything at all."

Which was precisely what I had hoped she would say. That fruit, I assure you, was well savored and the linens were as sticky with its juice as we were.

Indeed, I had never tasted a sweeter pomegranate in all my days and nights.

II

I never sleep in the company of a whore. It is folly to do so, for it is their trade and their inclination to see themselves better compensated than any man might feel was warranted. But I slept that night and that was my first error.

Or perhaps it was the second, after the taking of this alluring whore to my bed.

Either way, the bells were pealing from York's cathedral, summoning the faithful to prayer, when I awakened in a far finer mood than should have been possible in such a locale. It was raining and the shutters hung open, the better to admit fully the damp onslaught of morning. I smiled all the same as I stretched a hand across the mended linens.

I found nothing.

Or rather, no one. The cause of my fine mood had fled. I frowned, disappointed, though it is usually easier to avoid the faltering conversation of the morning after such a night as we had shared. I would, though, have liked to look upon her beauty in what passed for daylight in this country.

But then, maybe it was better to have the perception than

the truth. Perhaps she had not been as fine as I had believed. Perhaps the ale had been more potent than expected. Certainly, my head ached.

I rolled over, discontent, then realized that I had never asked her price.

Worry had me on my feet in a heartbeat and checking my belongings. Amazingly, my purse not only remained, but was as fat as it had been the night before. I smiled as I jingled its weight, delighted that she had been so uncommonly pleased by my caress as to forgo her fee.

It *had* been a fine night. That we shared the sentiment was enough to put a whistle upon a man's lips. I dressed in haste, anxious to be upon my way. I had retrieved the relic, the *Titulus Croce,* which was owed to me, and had spent an unexpectedly delightful evening. It was time for a repose in sun-baked Sicily, red wine upon my lips, soft whores in my lap and sweet fruit upon my tongue.

That thought only made me yearn anew for my lusty partner of the night before. How sweet the pomegranate juice had been when laved from her nipples! It was unfortunate, truly, that she had fled so quickly. I could have offered to show her that Sicily existed in truth.

But what was done was done. No doubt, her allure would have faded with time. I pulled on my boots and flung my cloak over my shoulder, shivering despite its thickness. I would never leave the south again, I vowed, then bent to heft my saddlebag.

It was not as I had left it. My heart lunged for my throat, even as I guessed what I would find. I flung open the flap, a curse crossing my lips at the void within the bag. I ran my hands around the clean chemise there, dumped the few fripperies, dropped to my knees in the filthy herbs strewn across the floor and ran my hands under the bed.

Nothing. Nothing but dust and the waste of vermin.

The *Titulus* was gone.

So too was the last of my pomegranates.

The whore had had her price, after all.

I swore then, swore loudly and thoroughly as I seldom do, kicked the pallet that had been the site of her deceit, then cast myself out of the humble room. I had been beguiled and cheated and it was the fault of no one but my own cursed self.

I knew with utter conviction that my brother Merlyn's faithful servant, Rhys Fitzwilliam, must have been at the root of this deed. Merlyn alone had known the value of the religious relic I had carried—though he was dead, he might not have held his tongue when he had yet lived. If his widow had told Fitz of my deceit of her, then loyal Fitz would have fetched the relic back.

I had to concede that Fitz's strategy had been a clever one. No man would suspect a whore of such a scheme, though her uncommon beauty and her determination should have warned me. There had been moments when I had wondered, but she had been clever enough to distract me from my own suspicions.

I admired that, even if it irked me. Fitz might be loyal and he—or his consort—might have outwitted me once, but I would triumph in the end.

I always do.

The fat keeper and his fatter wife were breaking their bread in the common room, both half-rising to their feet at the sight of me.

"Too many bites from the bed for a fine lord like yourself?" the keeper asked. He smiled amiably as he spoke, but his flicking gaze revealed his uncertainty.

Perhaps he was complicit with Fitz and the thieving wench. "Where is the whore?" I demanded more sharply than I might have preferred.

The wife sniffed and sat straighter. "We have no whores in our tavern."

Her husband held out a hand to her in caution, and if anything, his smile broadened. He was fretful and well he should be. "Lightened your purse, did she? You are not the first, sir, to not see past your prick, nor will you be the last."

"She cheated me." I took a steadying breath. "I would speak with her and see the matter corrected."

The keeper shifted his weight uneasily. "Understand that I want no trouble, sir, but whores are what they are and there is little an honest man can do. . . ."

"Where is she?"

"Will you have a cup of ale, sir?" His manner was intended to placate me, but instead it infuriated me. "Upon the house. Nothing sweetens the morn better than a draught of ale."

"Drives out the damp," the wife added and rose to fetch a cup.

I leaned my fists upon the board and spoke through gritted teeth. "I want the girl."

The keeper chuckled though the sound was not merry. "Oh, it is a young man who can think solely of rutting so early in the day."

"Or a fornicator," the wife muttered, setting the cup down before me with a bit too much force. She spared me a glance. "If you forgive me speaking so bold, sir, it is a priest you should be seeking this morn, that you might fall upon your knees and beg forgiveness for your sins. You should not be seeking to repeat them."

"I thank you for your counsel." I spoke so tersely that she flinched. "You evade the matter with such diligence that I am persuaded that you are part of her scheme. How much did she render to you?"

The keeper flushed scarlet, bounced to his feet and jabbed a finger through the air at me. "This is a reputable tavern! There are no whores in my alehouse, upon that my name rests."

"Perhaps you merely turn a blind eye to what is evident to all others, for clearly there was a whore in your common room last night."

"I never saw that girl afore!" he roared, well and truly insulted now. "I thought she knew you."

"No."

"But she . . ."

"She played a game and I indulged her." Too late I saw that my clever wench had known that this keeper would not have tolerated her presence, had he been certain of her trade.

She was wily, nigh as wily as me. Her scheme had ensured that nothing was left to chance—and I had to admire that, if grudgingly. Fitz's strategy had been brilliant, and his partner uncommonly bold.

"Mark my words," the keeper huffed, "had I known her intent, I would have cast her back into the streets. She will not be welcome here again, upon that you may rely."

"You must know her, or at least have seen her before. York is not so large as that."

"Never has she crossed this threshold," the keeper insisted stubbornly. "Never. I have never seen her, this I know to be fact." He met my gaze. "She is a woman any man would recall."

His wife drew herself taller, but I believed him.

The keeper must have guessed that my complaint was no longer with him, for he sat down heavily and took a swig of his ale. "I am sorry that you were robbed, sir, though there is little to be done. You can hie yourself to the sheriff and he may tell his men to seek her, or he may mock your folly, but I doubt he will find her."

"It is true enough." I lifted the cup of ale grimly, not in the least bit consoled.

The wife harumphed, her expression making clear her opinion of fornicators and whores and their ultimate fate.

I cast my glance around the rough hall, thinking. The road was not safe for women traveling alone, especially when darkness fell. Even if Fitz had accompanied my whore this far, she had entered the tavern alone. I had to admire her audacity. Any foul fate could have befallen her—and she was not witless, so she had known the risk.

She had taken that risk, because she had also known the value of the prize. I felt an unwelcome kinship for this woman, though I pushed such sentimentality aside. I drained my cup and set it down upon the board, determined to find her myself.

I could do no less. The relic she had stolen was not only mine by right and by pledge, but it alone could see my future secured. It is the mark of a good thief to not leave without the item that thief has come to retrieve.

I am an excellent thief, let you have no doubt of that.

When I turned away, the keeper caught at my sleeve. "The wench left a missive for you, sir, I nigh forgot. There are days when I would forget my own name, and that is the truth of it, sir."

I assumed this would be a gloating message from Fitz,

one that told me little other than that he had triumphed and deservedly so. I was tempted to not collect it. Still, I dared not risk ignoring whatever clue he might unwittingly surrender.

The missive was mine for a penny and it was worth every morsel of silver.

> *My dearest Gawain Lammergeier—*
>
> *So you think yourself a thief beyond compare! It seems you have competition for that honor. Not only have I proven your estimation of your talents to be undeserved, but I have reclaimed what is rightfully mine own.*
>
> *Retrieve the* Titulus Croce, *if you dare.*
>
> *I thank you, by the way, for the generous gift of your steed in compense for your poor performance abed. In truth, I had expected a better ride, given your reputation, but we both know that reputations are oft finer than the truth. You need not fear for my welfare while riding such a costly and large destrier, for I am adept in the taming of spirited stallions.*
>
> *Yours in dreams alone—*
> *Evangeline*

Evangeline?

I read the missive twice, so astounded was I by its contents. Not only was Fitz not responsible, but I had been cheated by a stranger. I knew that I had never before met this Evangeline who had spent the night so delightfully wrapped around me.

But she had not confused me with another. There was my name, writ in her hand. She was lettered. I had the unfamiliar sense that I had been neatly targeted.

I had been prey, I who was always predator. You will forgive that it took me some moments to reconcile myself to this unwelcome truth.

She was no whore, this Evangeline who could write and who taunted me to retrieve my due. She not only knew who I was, but she knew precisely what she had stolen from me.

Sadly, I did not know who she was—not until I tipped the missive in the slanting light and studied the imprint of its seal. The crest was oval, the falcon within it clearly discernible. Understanding dawned with my recognition of the mark.

Inverfyre! So much that had previously puzzled me now made sense. I welcomed another cup of ale from the keeper, now so anxious to please me, and considered this unexpected circumstance.

You see, I knew Inverfyre, if not well then well enough. It had been fifteen years since my father and I had stolen the religious relic known as the *Titulus Croce* from that very keep.

Yes, the very relic that Evangeline had just stolen from me.

You see the matter more clearly now. Though still I did not know her association with Inverfyre, the very fact that she had one told me a great deal.

I folded the missive carefully, then tapped it upon the board. I saw Evangeline again in my mind's eye, her confident swagger as she made her way toward me across the smoke-filled tavern, the sparkle of challenge in her eyes and the audacious smile upon her lips.

There is something seductive about a woman who knows what she desires and is unafraid to confess as much. Even the recollection sent heat through my loins. And there is something rare about a woman prepared to take a risk to win her desire. I smiled despite myself, recalling the splendor of our nigh sleepless night. Hers was a noblewoman's name, so I had not erred in thinking her too fine to be a common whore.

But I had erred in trusting her. And I had erred in assuming that Fitz was somehow behind this deed. Evangeline had surprised me twice in one morn, a considerable feat. Now, this bold woman taunted me to confront her again, to collect what she had stolen while I slept, exhausted by her passion.

The very prospect quickened my pulse.

I was not fool enough to imagine that she would not be expecting me to take her bait. No, a woman of Evangeline's intellect dared me only because she was certain she would win the successive encounter as well.

I tucked her missive into my chemise. Aye, she would be ensconced behind Inverfyre's gates, waiting to spring a trap upon me. A dozen stalwart men no doubt defended her, and iron bars must already surround the relic I would make mine again.

Inverfyre, I remembered dimly, was remote and secured with high walls, perched upon a cliff better suited to peregrines than to men. Indeed, it existed solely because of the hunting birds that could be found there—there was not a hunting man in Christendom who did not burn for a falcon from Inverfyre's famed mews.

I would not hasten to arrive there, nay, I would give Evangeline time to conclude that I did not pursue her. I would grant her time to become confident and more bold.

More bold? The very prospect was tantalizing.

The prize at stake was, of course, the *Titulus Croce*. Do not be troubled if you do not know it: few know it by its

Latin name. Recall, if you will, the scripture in the Gospel of John regarding the crucifixion of Christ:

> *And Pontius Pilate wrote a title, and put it on the cross. And the writing was JESUS OF NAZARETH, KING OF THE JEWS. This title then read many of the Jews: for the place where Jesus was crucified was nigh to the city: and it was written in Hebrew, and Greek and Latin.*

That is, incidentally, the only scripture that I know. Mine is not an occupation that allows one to rely overmuch on divine providence, or to enjoy pondering the rewards of sin. My father taught this verse to me all those years past, when we waited to spring our plan upon Inverfyre, and still I remember it.

What Evangeline had stolen from me was a part of the whole, the sole part known to yet exist. There is speculation among those who fret about such things that the *Titulus* was severed, that part was granted to the eastern empire and part to the west, back when the Romans yet ruled Christendom.

The relic itself is believed to have been discovered by the party of Helena, mother of the emperor Constantine. Ah, you do recall—he was the emperor who not only became Christian, but severed the Roman Empire into two halves, establishing a city in his own name in the east. Constantinople remains a place of considerable refinement and many pleasures.

(Perhaps I should acquire a villa there with my reward, instead of Sicily. Courtesy of Evangeline, I had plentiful time to consider my options.)

Is the *Titulus* real? Who is to say? And, more importantly, why should I care? It is the sole fragment with a claim to such ancestry, and as such, it has a remarkably high value. This is why I covet it. It is my reward, my release from the company of crude men and vulgar locales. It is the compense I should have had a hundred times over for my services, a compense that I ultimately had to steal. Always I was known as the thief in the family, but in securing every last speck of my father's property, Merlyn proved to be the more agile thief.

He did not live to savor his triumph long, but still it irks me. After my years of cunning, after my irreplaceable contributions to the building of my father's trade—one cannot, after all, trade in religious relics without having such relics in one's possession—after years of loyalty, I was left with not one crumb from my father's table.

Is the wound bitter? No longer, but I know better now than to believe the pledge of any living soul. A man can rely upon himself alone. I relied upon my father and even that was too much. The lesson has been learned.

Indeed, I believe it was uncommonly generous of me to settle this debt with solely one relic of the thousands Merlyn inherited. This fragment of wood, sold with care, will enable me to repose in luxury in that Sicilian villa for all my days and nights.

And no whore—or even a thief pretending to be a whore—would cost me the sole prize I desired.

I finally took the road to Inverfyre on the morn of January 25, the very day that Saint Paul's conversion is celebrated by the devout. It had been three weeks since Evangeline and I had so thoroughly sampled each other's wares.

I had lingered. I had drunk and I had slept and I had eaten and I had ambled from one village to the next, with no clear destination in mind. I had listened, because I cannot cease to listen, and I had watched, because that is a habit of my trade.

And I had thought rather too much about a woman who had met me touch for touch. Evangeline haunted my dreams by night and dominated my thoughts by day. No whore had ever reveled in every caress as she had, no virgin could have been so awed by the passion betwixt us.

A more whimsical man than I might have said there was a curious magic between us, perhaps an attraction greater than mere lust. I knew that I had simply not had enough of Evangeline to be sated. Another night between her thighs, I was certain, would loose me from her spell.

I whistled at the dancing snowflakes as I finally took the road to Inverfyre. The day was dancing bright, though it had begun to snow soon after I and my recently acquired horse left the last village's walls. The snow was pretty, my mood improving with each step I took closer to Inverfyre.

As the road climbed, however, the snow began to fall in earnest. This snow tumbled from the sky in fat, wet clumps that accumulated with alarming speed.

The horse, a short shaggy beast, proved itself worth every silver penny it had cost me. It bent its head against the wind and strode onward with heartening fortitude. By midday, however, the road was so slippery underfoot that the horse stopped, obstinately refusing to go on.

I dismounted, intending to lead the horse, and was halted by the press of silence. I heard nothing at all, not a bird, not a footstep, neither a rustle nor another footstep. I fancied I could hear the snowflakes landing on the barren tree branches all around me. I glanced back to find that our footsteps were already being obscured. I realized belatedly that I had not seen another soul since the morning.

And dread began to tickle my belly.

I am a man of villages and towns, a man accustomed to the murmur of conversations just beyond earshot. I am a man who endeavors to accomplish his labor without awakening those who sleep within dangerous proximity. I am a man who sits on the periphery of the assembly, but is part of it nonetheless. To be utterly alone, save for a horse, was a new experience for me and not an entirely welcome one.

I could die in this woods and none would know of it.

Fewer would care.

Have you been to Scotland's shores? If not, I suggest you forgo the dubious pleasure. Not only is the weather foul and the fare scarcely better, but the land itself seems wrought by some sorcerer.

It has *moods*.

Oh, I have not lost my wits. One glimpse of these valleys piled with mist and these peaks shrouded by low clouds, and one realizes why the Celts have always insisted that the world of unseen matters is woven tightly with our own. To be sure, there are rocks and mosses and hills and dales much like any other land, but in this one, every leaf and stone seems alive.

Watching.

Waiting.

This is a land occupied by wraiths and shadows, a place of dreams, an abode of nightmares. The people's tales are filled with mournful ghosts and vengeful specters, of mischievous imps and malicious faeries, and not because the Celts are whimsical. No, I have never seen more stern and pragmatic souls in all my days, nor any more accurate to the measure.

No, it is the place itself that provides the wellspring for these stories. Tales abound of the fey seizing mortals for their own pleasure and entertainment, of ghosts luring mortals to their demise, of wayward travelers disappearing forever into the mist. The stories are as old as the hills and perhaps not untrue. I had heard a thousand variants upon these themes in the taverns I had frequented these past weeks, though not a one of them haunted me.

I carry my own nightmares. Indeed, in some corner of my thoughts, I believe I knew from the moment I set foot on Scotland's shores that a wraith was stalking me.

It found me here.

"Gawain!"

I jumped, so certain was I of my solitude. I looked back in alarm, desperately seeking the boy who had shouted my name.

Oh yes, I knew it was a boy. I knew his name, I knew the look of him, I knew how his wavy chestnut hair hung long on his neck and tumbled into his eyes, how he shoved it away with his grimy knuckles to no avail. I knew the agility of his fingers and the speed with which he could run.

I turned slowly, seeking his running figure in the snow, his clothing stained and tattered, his arms and legs too thin. I sought his running figure between the trees, darting from shadow to shadow.

But I could see only snow cascading from the sky. It fell relentlessly, filling the air with tumbling white flakes as far as the eye could see. It devoured the footprints left by the horse and myself, it burdened the trees, it disguised whoever might wish to hide. My heart thundered and I was breathing heavily.

Silence. There was not a sound beyond those I made myself.

The cry had been nothing, I assured myself, a trick of my own thoughts. Yet the hair stood on my nape. He was not here, that imp, for he was dead. He could not be here. He could not have called to me, not as he did that fateful day. . . .

I pivoted and plunged onward, leading the horse at a reckless pace. Desperation made me heedless, even as I knew I could not outrun a specter.

Yet I tried.

Mountainous crags rose on either side of the road, their summits lost in the low clouds, the chill that emanated from the stone enough to make me shiver. The road plunged and climbed, jammed with snow in its depths, icy at its heights.

I heard that phantom cry half a dozen times, and each time I redoubled my pace. I had no need for the stories of locals to taste fear. I yearned for the pungent heat of those taverns and their more pungent guests, the swill they offered as an excuse for fare and ale, the muttering of peasants seizing a moment of pleasure.

There was, however, no question of turning back. Inverfyre was my sole chance of salvation, for it was at Inverfyre that the *Titulus* was held captive.

My scheme to infiltrate Inverfyre, my plan to approach with caution, was lost in this mad flight. I was consumed with thoughts of warmth and companionship, of heat and sustenance and shelter. I did not know the hour or the day, I did not know how long I had persisted in this folly of fighting the snow. All was white and I had made so many guesses as to where the path lay that I feared I was utterly lost.

The horse and I were encrusted with the snow, nigh as two drifts ourselves, when night began to tighten its cloak about us.

"Gawain!"

Did I but imagine that the voice was fainter, as if weakening, as if realizing that I would not heed his cry? Guilt prodded me but I would not look back. I dared not.

Indeed, I had not looked back when it mattered.

I peered desperately into the flying snow before me, hoping I did not imagine the distant silhouette of a tower against the sky. I lunged toward it with new vigor, nigh running when I spied the gates before us.

Laughter carried to my ears, the laughter of men, the voices of women, the chatter of children. Surely, there could be no sweeter sight than those fortress gates opened wide, golden light spilling from the homes sheltered within!

I had no time to compose myself, to temper my haste or hide my relief, before a man cried out and pointed directly at me.

My heart clenched, though I could not discern his words. There was no place to which I might flee. He beckoned to two other men, the three immediately turning their steps toward me. The entire company within the walls turned as one to gawk at the newcomer, a stranger identified and singled out.

My heart sank. Evangeline had indeed prepared for my arrival.

But there is nothing to be gained in flinching from one's fate. I gripped the reins and strode onward as if I had expected to be met at the gates.

Bravado can oft yield unexpected rewards, after all.

III

"Connor, you old fool!" the first man roared inexplicably, then strode toward me, his arms wide. I glanced behind myself, but I was his sole potential target.

In a flash, I understood that I had been mistaken for a man known here. My spirits began to lift. This was the manner of moment that makes me question whether divine providence might exist after all. It seems absurd that I could be so fortunate, but fortunate I have been in the past, and fortunate I clearly was again.

"What possessed you to take the old road on a day so wretched as this?" this stranger demanded, before enveloping me in a hug so hearty that he nigh cracked my bones.

I laughed, then punched his shoulder as if we were familiar. I had listened enough these past weeks that I could make a fair approximation of their manner of speaking. "Old habits die hard. You know as much."

He was a tall man, roughly dressed. His grip was strong, revealing that he was well-muscled, and I felt a pair of blades hanging from his belt beneath his cloak. I liberated one of them, just because I could, and slipped it beneath my cloak and into my own belt without his noting my deed.

Habits do indeed die hard.

"Too stubborn by half, that is what you are, Connor Mac-Doughall," a second, more heavyset man, declared gleefully as he too granted me an embrace. "You insisted there was no need of a new road, nor of the tax collected to pay for it. Trust you to prove your own claim, whether the deed killed you or no."

The three men, all crudely dressed, gathered round and laughed at my folly, ale vibrating in their voices. The third punched me amiably in the shoulder—evidently he and Connor were not so intimate. They all sounded of an age with me, but their faces were etched with harsh lines from the fierce clime. Swords and daggers hung from their belts, ice crusted their brows and capped their heads. They were virtually indistinguishable from each other, save by their relative sizes, all looking like the spawn of Winter himself.

I realized that if I looked as they did, my own mother might not have recognized me. Therein lay the root of their error.

The horse nickered as the third man scratched its ears with unexpected affection. "I would never have sold Mathe to you, had I known you would try to kill the beast."

It seemed remarkable that he might have owned this steed before, but I had seen with my own eyes that horses were few in this land and it was not far from York if one rode directly to Inverfyre. To be sure, I was not in a mood to ask many questions: I had made a life of seizing what opportunity presented and I seized it now.

"He fares well enough by me," I declared, my thoughts racing. Perhaps by the time the snow melted from the lot of them, they would be too drunk to realize that I was not their comrade.

Perhaps I should ensure their drunkenness.

"And this is the greeting I get, after all this time?" I demanded in mock outrage. "Not a cup of ale nor a wench to be seen, just a grousing by way of greeting, even though the beast is fatter than when you sold him to me."

The men laughed, even the one who had previously owned the horse. He nudged me, a familiar gleam in his eye. "There is ale, but they are wanting a rich price for it on this night. If you have enough coin to fatten the horse, perhaps you have some to share with your comrades."

"Perhaps I do." I peered into the village, noting how it had changed since last I was here. Poverty and hardship showed in faces that had once been plump with prosperity. "Where *are* my comrades? I see only a company of rogues intent upon emptying my purse."

This was met with much laughter and back-slapping, and we moved as one toward a hut. A crowd clustered outside its open door, the lantern light from within spilling out upon merry faces. The alewife herself was a sharp-faced older woman with little flesh on her bones. There was a blue glaze across her eyes and she held her head at an angle that indicated at least partial blindness, though she moved with such surety that I immediately wondered.

Her prices were high, but I could not blame her for making the most of what opportunity she had in this remote place to better her circumstances. A baby cried from the hut behind her as she ladled out four cups of her brew at my request and her hand shook as she glanced back over her shoulder.

"It is no weather for a sick child," I said as I deliberately folded her hand over the coins I paid. I knew the moment she realized that there was one too many in her grip. The corners of her tight mouth lifted for a heartbeat, then her fist disappeared into the folds of her cloak.

She peered at me, as if unfamiliar with kindness from strangers, and I wondered again how much she could see. The weight of her gaze made my flesh creep, so odd were her eyes. I had the sense that she could read my very thoughts, that she knew my identity and my intent. I feared for a moment what she might say.

"No, sir, it is not," she said. "I thank you for your trade." She nodded and turned to her next patron.

We stepped away, clicked our pottery mugs together and drank deeply. It was even worse swill than that in York, but I was so glad to have reached my objective that it might have been the richest mead. I drained the cup in one grateful gulp.

"Woho! You will be beggared before the night is through, at such a rate," teased the first man.

I took a closer look at my companions now. The man who had greeted me first was dark and the tallest of the company, his bushy brows supporting a ledge of snow. Since our greeting, he seemed inclined to listen to the others more often than speaking himself. Indeed, his gaze oft strayed over the village, as if he sought someone. He was a handsome man, in a rough way, and more than one damsel tried to flirt with him while passing. I silently named him "Tall."

The second was stout, robust apparently in both appetite and manner. He was fair, and his cheeks bloomed with healthy color. His laugh rang loudly and frequently, and he seemed a merry companion. "Fat" would serve as his name.

The third—he who had owned the horse—was quieter and darker, a small, sinewy man who was probably much stronger than he appeared. His eyes were dark and his nose sharp. He seemed to regard all around him with a certain grim pessimism. In keeping with the other names, I called him "Dour."

"Too many have come to see whether the laird can work a miracle," said Tall, then drank of his ale.

Miracle? My ears pricked, though I said nothing. Talk of miracles oft indicates that I am in the vicinity of a religious relic worthy of my attention. I wondered . . . but peered into my cup as if uninterested.

"And thus the ale is in short supply," added Dour. "Rural folk have no ability to plan for such matters."

"True enough," concurred Fat. "Were we in London, or even Edinburgh, the alewives would have made triple their normal batches to ensure supply, but not here."

Dour frowned into his cup. "Though the town prices would have been no lower than the prices here."

They laughed together at this truth, then acquired another round from the alewife, each paying for their own this time. Again, I was generous, and this time, she spared me a smile. I asked after a stall for the horse and we walked toward the home of the villager most likely to accommodate me.

In the course of conversation with these rural louts, I learned a considerable amount of useful information.

Item the first: The old laird of Inverfyre had died some five years past and, being without a son, had chosen a comrade of his named Fergus of Balquhidder as the new laird.

Item the second: Approval of Fergus' leadership had not been universal, and that approval had been eroded by Inverfyre's failing fortunes after the old laird's death. Fergus lived lavishly while those beneath his hand suffered poverty.

Item the third: There had been whispers that Fergus' lairdship was cursed. It had long been held that the Lairds of Inverfyre were divinely favored as custodians for the relic of the *Titulus Croce.* Fergus had not displayed the relic upon Christmas and Easter, as tradition demanded, thus feeding speculation that he had lost both it and divine favor.

(I shall spare you the tedious and heroic details associated with this custodianship, as they were typical of this ilk of tale. I endeavored to not yawn, knowing full well that Inverfyre's first laird had simply pilfered his prize from some Outremer shrine. Not unlike others engaged in such deeds, he had then embellished his thievery with tales of portentous dreams, divine favor, and miracles that flowed as a result of his own extreme piety.)

Item the fourth: Challenged openly by my newfound comrade "Tall" some weeks ago, Fergus had insisted that he would display the *Titulus* upon this night—the feast of Paul's conversion—that the dissenters be converted to the truth, just as Saint Paul himself was said to see the light.

I had inadvertently arrived at the perfect time.

Further, if Evangeline was associated with Fergus and the maintenance of his suzerainty, her motives in stealing the *Titulus* were very clear.

I sipped of my ale with satisfaction, intrigued that there had only been speculation upon the absence of the relic for the past five years. I knew that the true *Titulus* had been at Ravensmuir for fifteen years.

I stifled a smile at the unexpected cunning of these barbarians. Evidently the exalted dead laird had seen fit to do a little forgery of his own after my father and I had visited his keep. How interesting. How enterprising. How uncommon.

Perhaps Evangeline had participated in his ruse. Perhaps she was *responsible* for the ruse and had to recover the genuine relic to hide her guilt. She certainly had the wits for it.

I confess that I found myself even more intrigued with my lovely thief than before.

I looked up at the keep looming high before us. It was built into the side of the hill and had the advantage that it would be spectacularly easy to defend. Why anyone would trouble to defend a sorry piece of turf in this wretched clime was beyond my comprehension, but I can appreciate good construction.

It oft provides boon or bane to my missions. I looked now, assessing the chances of slipping unknown into the stronghold of the keep. It would be difficult, for only one gate broached the wall, and the wall rose high on either side. Behind the main gates and the tower that must be the hall, a pointed roof was starkly etched against the snowy sky. A crucifix graced its summit, just as I recalled. My pulse quickened in recognition of my ultimate destination.

How sweet that the relic was in the same reliquary from which I had stolen it before! I had half-feared that Evangeline would have hidden it elsewhere, but even if she had, on this night it would be in the chapel.

One night was all I needed, after all.

"The truth is that it matters little whether the relic is there." Tall spoke with such vigor that we all fell silent to listen to his words. He looked suddenly taller, more regal, a man with something to prove. He spoke with the ferocity of a man convinced of his view. "Fergus is a poor leader, either way, a man too far into his dotage to lead Inverfyre."

"The old laird chose him, Niall," Fat reminded him.

"The old laird was wrong," Niall, or Tall, said flatly. He looked both grim and determined. "We should seize whatever tools we must to oust Fergus afore it is too late, and you know it as well as I do, Tarsuinn."

Tarsuinn, or Fat, looked uncomfortable, and so he should for this was traitorous talk. "He has agreed to produce the relic on this night," he said, new caution in his tone.

"So he has. What we must decide, comrades, is what we shall do when he fails." Niall flung aside his cup. "Or what we shall do if he claims to have succeeded."

The men shifted uneasily, the other two clearly not at ease with Niall's rebellious tone.

"We owe no less to Inverfyre and the memory of our old laird." Niall looked fiercely at each of us in turn, seeking support he did not find. I held his gaze for a moment, surprised by the fury in his eyes, knowing that he must be puzzled by the indifference in mine. The chapel bell began to toll and Niall spun away from the group, striding toward the chapel without glancing back.

Tarsuinn cleared his throat. "It will be a relief to know the *Titulus* is where it belongs. Even Niall's worries will be set to rest." Dour nodded vigorous agreement to this and Tarsuinn was obviously encouraged. "Indeed, Inverfyre has been blessed as no other holding in all the lands of the King of Scotland."

I bit my tongue at that. To be blessed was clearly a question of perspective. Sicily is blessed, in my opinion, as are Venice and Constantinople. They are blessed with sunlight and prosperity. No place where a man had to endure such cold as this and such hardship as could be seen in the faces of these residents could be called blessed, not to my thinking.

"It would be a sorry day that its laird proved himself an incompetent custodian of God's trust," Dour intoned, and the pair looked to me.

I smiled. "Let us pray that none are disappointed on this night."

"There is trouble in the wind this night," Dour said beneath his breath and even Tarsuinn looked uneasy. I stifled a smile.

Trouble, in fact, had bought them each a cup of ale.

* * *

The chapel was of goodly size and solidly built. I pulled my hood over my head as I crossed the threshold, hiding my features in its shadows. Though still damp, the chapel was warm enough to melt the snow and light enough to reveal that I was not in fact Connor MacDoughall.

Whoever that man might happen to be.

He might even be here. How strange a prospect!

I found myself conveniently near the altar, surrounded by fighting men who were clearly sworn to the lord. Niall was not alone in his dissatisfaction, apparently, for there was more than one skeptical expression in this company. The doors were closed behind the assembly of villagers and warriors, allowing a meager warmth to gather. Prayers were murmured all around me, but I did not pray.

Instead, I seized the chance to study the chapel that I would have to raid again without anyone realizing what I did.

The hewn stones that formed the walls were huge but expertly fitted. None of them would be loose, I knew. There was solely one door and the sanctuary itself was simply a large room. There was not so much as an alcove in its walls and no shadow where one might hide. The floor was stone, and I guessed that no crypt was carved out of the rock below.

There was only one window, high above the table that served as an altar. It was small and filled with a colored glass depiction of the crucifixion. The window was quite splendid, if small, and could fetch a goodly price. I was certain it had not been there before, as I had used that opening to fetch the *Titulus* the last time.

Of course, I was not quite as lithe and agile as I had been in my youth. I studied the window, surprised to find such artistry in such a remote place, though it was common enough in the great cathedrals. These lairds had either been far wealthier than I had imagined or fools with their coin.

They might be devout. I would have to remember that. This beleaguered Fergus might seek to quietly replace the *Titulus* with a greater treasure if his suzerainty rested upon such trinkets.

Other than the window, now obstructed with glass, the sole access to the chapel was the door, which would surely be locked or watched or both.

I peered through the haze of incense and smoke from the candles at the altar, seeking to confirm the relic's location. I was uninterested in the richly embroidered cloth covering what appeared to be solely a table, and spared only a brief assessment for the chalice and charger wrought of pounded silver.

They might be worth taking along, although they were not particularly remarkable. It would depend upon their weight and how much time I had.

There was no sign of the relic upon the altar. The reliquary that I had once robbed no longer lurked there, nor was it in the hands of the monks standing solemnly behind the altar. The four monks began to chant as the two on either end swung the brass censers.

"Let the festivities begin," I muttered to none in particular.

My eyes narrowed as the company of monks parted and moved to either side of the altar. A wooden door was revealed in the back wall of the chapel, directly below the stained glass window.

It had not been there before.

I almost smiled that my theft had prompted a more secure reliquary for the relic—or whatever they had shown in its stead. One monk held a great brass key, I saw now.

I dearly love brass keys. They are so large and solid that they inspire confidence—yet their tumblers are clumsy and easily encouraged even without the key. The keys themselves are easily borrowed, hooked and dropped precisely where one wishes to drop them, because of their weight.

I was much reassured. I scanned the company unobtrusively, seeking Evangeline, but she was not present. I must have been more overt than I thought, for I glanced up to find Niall's assessing gaze upon me. He looked away as soon as I noted his perusal of me, leaving me wondering what conclusion he might have made.

Or what suspicions he might have. Surely I had played their game well? The monks' chanting grew in volume as I grew uneasy, and the chapel doors swung open once again.

"The laird Fergus," whispered Tarsuinn with either awe or reverence as the entire company turned. A cold gust of air swirled around my ankles, though my shiver halted when I saw the woman whose hand rested upon the laird's elbow.

Evangeline.

But not Evangeline. This woman looked sufficiently like Evangeline to be her twin, but was so lifeless that she could not have been the Evangeline I knew.

This woman did not radiate confidence, she did not glow or swagger, her eyes did not sparkle. There was no flush in her cheeks and no swing to her hips. She was demure, her complexion pale, her eyes downcast. Her hair, which I knew to be dark and wild, was tightly secured beneath a veil and demurely fastened with a circlet.

She looked so severe and bloodless that she might have been wrought of ice. Her gaze was fixed upon the floor before her feet and even when peasants bowed before her, she did not smile. Still, that curious awareness tingled within me, the same that had made me note her entry into the ale-house.

I knew a moment's doubt. Was this my Evangeline? Did she have a sister? A twin? Or had I seen a side of her she preferred to hide from others? I was doubly intrigued.

There was, of course, only one way to be certain of the lady's identity. I awaited my chance.

The laird was far older than I had expected, given that he had held his position for only five years. His hair was grey, his features careworn. He was not a handsome man and never had been. He was solidly wrought and so richly dressed that he seemed to have stolen the garb of another, more noble, man. The tightness of his lips and the rapid flicking of his gaze revealed his uncertainties all too well.

He wore a falconer's glove upon his right hand and surrendered the hooded bird to a servant at the chapel door with evident reluctance. He was momentarily uncertain what to do with his hand then, until Evangeline gently laid his right hand atop her own. He nodded before beginning their procession down the aisle.

As he walked, he looked neither to the left nor to the right. Here was a man who knew he was challenged by his followers. Here was a man who knew this night to be the test of his suzerainty. Here was a man who was not the leader his predecessor had hoped he might be.

I looked to the lady, then back to the laird, and supposed that there was something noble about showing loyalty to one's own father. I had done it myself, for all the good that had come of it. If this was my Evangeline, I could appreciate that she had fetched the relic that might make her father's title more secure.

Three men who were younger than the laird yet showed some resemblance to him in their features strode behind him, their countenances as hard as stone. Their hair was ruddy, their faces tanned, their eyes narrowed. Two were men fully, while one was yet a youth. These, clearly, were his relatives and allies, perhaps Evangeline's brothers.

But Fergus was outnumbered and he knew as much. His color rose with every step. His gaze was fixed upon the altar ahead as if all his woes would cease once he reached that haven. More than one warrior shifted his weight, flicked his glance away from his laird or murmured his greeting so low as to be inaudible. Niall turned slightly away as his lord drew alongside, checking the buckle of his scabbard with undue care so that he would not have to even incline his head.

The laird's daughter stood steadfast beside him, her spine as straight as a well-wrought blade. I noticed that she squeezed his fingers once, a subtle sign of support that none would have noted who were not watching her as avidly as I. The laird seemed to lean upon his straight and determined daughter, a woman who resembled my Evangeline only in her resolve.

The pair reached the aisle beside me and I had my chance. The lady was on my side, though Tarsuinn was on the aisle between she and I.

"My lord. My lady, you look more splendid than could be imagined," Tarsuinn murmured. She spared him the thinnest smile of acknowledgement, her gaze flicking past him.

I smiled boldly as she glanced into the shadows cast by my hood, and winked when her eyes widened ever so slightly. She took a quick breath, a spark lit in the depths of her sapphire gaze and color blossomed suddenly upon her cheeks.

My own heart skipped. This was Evangeline, my Evangeline.

She was not entirely surprised to find me here, that much I knew, nor was she disappointed. A flame kindled in the depths of her eyes as she held my gaze, one answered by the fire she awakened in my loins. I felt warm from head to toe, warm as I had not been since we lay entwined abed.

Before any others could note her response, she abruptly averted her face. I noted the line of her shoulders, the sweet curve of her cheek, the indent of her waist beneath her kirtle and knew that night could not come soon enough. I felt the weight of Niall's disapproval without even looking his way, and understood that his ambitions were extensive.

Not that any such nuptial matters concerned me. Niall was welcome to wed the laird's daughter—just one more night in her bed would sate me, and then I would be gone from this foul land forever.

Indeed, I understood so much of the lady now, though it changed nothing. Evangeline had stolen the relic so that her father could prove that the grace of God blessed his suzerainty. Fair enough. There was, however, no reason for the *Titulus* to remain here after its showing upon this night. It would be a waste to lock such a prize away.

Just as the lady was wasted in this remote citadel. No doubt, her father could not find a fitting suitor for her here. I understood suddenly why she had left such a telling clue of her identity and location—perhaps she contrived to resolve the matter of nuptials herself.

I swallowed my smile, for I have never had an inclination to do what is honorable, or what is expected of me. I had no need for a wife and even less desire for one.

Evangeline could drive the heat from my bones afore she knew that detail.

The trick would be to slip between her thighs without her father guessing my intent. The prize was sufficient to risk far more than I might have risked otherwise. This, after all, would be my last theft.

I had best make the night worthy of remembrance.

IV

Evangeline was so quiet and still that she might have been a statue, some pagan goddess wrought of stone, had she not been so modestly attired. Her father lifted the *Titulus* high to the sound of prayers, but I watched Evangeline. Her gaze came to me seemingly of its own accord, perhaps because I alone knew that her small smile was less for her father's triumph than her own.

Her smile warmed and color touched her pale cheeks anew as our gazes locked. A song of desire began within me, heating me as naught else had done in this land.

Save Evangeline.

The procession filed out but I lingered, shaken by my response. I hovered in the chapel's shadows while countless peasants filed past the altar to brush their fingertips across the relic. I was protective, concerned that one would be so bold as to touch it too hard or even try to steal it. Only when it was safely locked away and the key hung from the monk's belt did I follow the company to the hall.

The mood in the hall was raucous and celebratory. Fergus had proven the legitimacy of his suzerainty with the presence of the relic, and his subjects seemed intent upon drinking themselves into a stupor in their relief.

I could barely glimpse Evangeline, let alone draw near to her, for she sat demurely beside her garrulous father. That man held his prized gyrfalcon again upon his fist and fed it morsels from his own trencher, more interested in it than his own daughter.

My three companions hailed me and summoned me to their corner. They were so besotted that there was little risk that they would question my identity now. The ale flowed, the meat was plentiful, the peasants and warriors fell upon the meal ravenously.

"Such a plentitude of eggs," I muttered. I have never had a fondness for them and it seemed each dish passed to me was wrought of them. Eggs in mustard sauce, poached eggs, scrambled eggs and stuffed eggs—who would have guessed they could be prepared so many ways!

"Fergus favors them so we are blessed with many at the board," Tarsuinn confided, helping himself to an ample measure of civet of eggs. "Do you not recall that he installed his own cook here at Inverfyre, solely because of that man's gift with an egg?"

I shook my head as if I had forgotten this detail. Tarsuinn passed the dish to me and I passed it on—if the ale was as foul as it was, then the wine could not be worthy of crossing a conscious man's palate. It would be no better with eggs in it.

"He has even filled the old falcon mews with chickens, so great is his lust for eggs," Niall added with evident disapproval.

Dour nudged me and winked. "Though it is said that

eggs preserve a man's potency. Perhaps that is why he favors them!"

He and Tarsuinn laughed heartily together, though Niall spared a dark glance to the head table and said nothing. To my relief, there was a haunch of venison that managed to make its way to our table and I served myself amply.

The meat was good, as were the noodles with gravy that followed. The hall filled with smoke and laughter that grew progressively louder. Their merrymaking was not unpleasant.

And the monk with the key was becoming soundly drunk.

When the trenchers were cast to the dogs, I glanced through the high windows and spied a clear night sky beyond, the stars glimmering brightly. The storm had ended then, the snowfall halted.

Were my mission accomplished, I could depart this night while all slumbered drunkenly. Indeed, there would not likely be such a prime opportunity to be away without questions as this night offered.

Which meant that I had several matters to resolve.

I took a pause, purportedly to relieve myself outside. En route, I "tripped" over the robe of the drunken monk and claimed the brass key to the reliquary in the process of getting up. How dreadful that I was so drunk as to lose my balance time and again! The monks were amused then—if not later.

After an interval in the chapel, fetching my due, I returned to the hall to discover that the lady had retired from the company. The laird had removed the hood from his gyrfalcon, a particularly large and fine bird. He spoke to it and stroked it with all the tenderness of a lover, though it seemed to me that the bird was skittish.

I sat at another table, joining the men there in a hearty toast to the laird's good health, scanning the hall all the while. Stairs wound upward at the other end of the hall, the sole flight obviously leading to the laird's solar and lady's chamber.

I understood Evangeline's retirement as both an invitation and a challenge. The invitation was obvious. The challenge lay in climbing those open stairs unobserved by such an enormous company. Any could witness me and cry an alarm—if they were not sufficiently distracted.

There is nothing more readily done than beginning a fight within a company of drunken warriors. I carry a few tools for precisely this purpose. Do you know the herb angelica? It has a sweet scent, pleasant enough, and thus is unremarkable to carry among one's possessions. Indeed, many men chew upon it when a rich meal gives their innards distress. I carry a dried length of stem, about the width of my hand, as well as a handful of dried peas.

Angelica stem, you see, is hollow. I can hide this piece within my cupped hand and discreetly create trouble.

I targeted Niall with the first pea, for he seemed inclined to be volatile. Thrice he was struck, and each time he turned more angrily to the man at the table behind him. Niall's flush rose as the man protested innocence again and again.

I embellished matters by striking Niall's supposed assailant twice, once in the temple and once in the corner of his eye. Another missile was fired at Niall and the battle began.

Niall rose to his feet and roared, while the other man took advantage of the moment to punch Niall in the nose. Men immediately took sides and made wagers, their shouts rising from all corners of the hall. A trestle table was kicked over, lanterns spilled, crockery shattered, meat and ale fell to the floor. The hounds were there in a heartbeat, devouring scraps even as they dodged feet. Niall and his assailant began to fight in earnest, grappling with each other as they shouted insults.

I slipped back into the shadows, launched a dozen more peas into the melée, and watched with satisfaction as more fights broke out. Tables fell and the seneschal called vainly for order. The gutted candles plunged the hall into greater shadows.

Fergus stood on the high table and cried out for discipline. He looked like an old woman, and more impotent than most elderly women of my experience. His gyrfalcon screeched and flapped its wings helplessly—it was, of course, held fast by its jesses, so could not flee the chaos.

A few more peas and the high table itself set to fighting. Food was flung from one corner at the laird, then some hardy soul pushed the head table over as well. Fergus screamed as he fell headlong into the throng of men. He loosed his grip upon the jesses as he fell and the freed bird flew upward with incredible speed.

"Aphrodite!" Fergus cried plaintively.

His courtiers nigh stepped upon each other to retrieve the bird, which circled the upper reaches of the hall, its jesses trailing behind it. When it found a hole near the rafters large enough to accommodate its wingspan, it swooped through the opening and disappeared into the night.

A cry of anguish rose from all assembled, the distraught laird himself nigh screaming. The tinkle of the bell tied to the bird's ankle grew fainter and fainter. The eyes of all who were not fighting fixed upon the dark gap through which the bird had disappeared.

"It is your fault!" Fergus cried, then pointed a finger at the seneschal. That man paled as Fergus's kin stepped forward to have compense from his hide. A trio of men tried to intervene—including Tarsuinn—and the lot of them fell to fighting with renewed vigor.

I deemed my work to be done. I darted up the stairs on silent feet. I was, of course, completely unobserved.

Or so I thought at the time.

There was a door at the top of the stairs, but to my relief, it was not locked. I slipped around it as noiselessly as a shadow, closed it and leaned back against it, muting the sounds from below. There was a marked contrast between this silent darkened corridor and the chaotic great hall.

Here I could be discovered.

I stilled my breathing so it was nigh silent and willed my heartbeat to slow. I waited for my eyes to adjust to the darkness and listened—a moment taken to observe is never wasted.

A pair of crude torches flickered upon the wall to my right, but the corridor was irregular, creating far too many dark corners for my taste. I lingered, listening for the breath of another, fearing that my flight had been too easy to not have been facilitated.

Who, truly, would have left two torches burning unobserved on the timber upper walls of a hall? Were these barbarians as witless as I suspected—or had some clever soul set a trap for me?

There were three portals, each tucked back into an elaborate niche, two on the left wall and one on the right. At the end of the hall was a window, framing a square of night sky. The snow had stopped falling, though a bit of it graced the lip of the window, for I could see the glimmer of stars. The air was crisp.

I eased to the door upon my right, hesitating there for

only a moment. No candle or lantern burned within, for I could not smell a flame. The wooden floor did not creak and betray the presence of another beyond this portal. I could hear no man's breath as he lay in wait for me.

The second door opposite seemed similarly quiet. I considered this, waiting for any assailant to reveal himself. It has long been said that I have uncommon patience and can out-wait any foe. None revealed himself—which meant either that there was no foe, or that he was as skilled as me.

I watched the sliver of light beneath the first door on the left for a long time. Finally, I slid across the corridor, making no sound as I progressed. I eased into the nook of the portal, listening avidly.

Here I smelled lamps and felt heat. I heard a muted splash, like a smoothed cube of soap slipping into water. I smelled something floral, as a noblewoman will use to scent her bath, something that awakened a memory in me of a night in York and a woman's sweetly scented flesh. I faintly heard the sound of humming.

I smiled. There was no trap. My arrival was simply anticipated. I made to ease open the door.

"Leave me, Fiona," Evangeline said tersely from within and I froze, my fingers just above the latch.

"But, my lady . . ."

"Leave me." Steel echoed again in Evangeline's voice.

Footsteps creaked upon the floor behind the door and I darted back into the shadows of the second door in the nick of time. A plump older maid whisked out of her lady's chambers, disapproval tightening her lips.

She marched toward the door at the top of the stairs, clearly intending to tell Fergus of his daughter's crimes. I shrank back into the shadows as she flung open that door, my luck holding when she did not look back.

Indeed, she gasped when she looked out upon the hall. "Sweet Jesus!" she cried, then picked up her skirts and hastened down into the fray.

What a marvel of a woman to believe she could halt such mayhem!

I returned to the door to the lady's chamber, delighted that Fiona had not closed it as firmly as she should have done, and eased my wand of angelica into the crevice between door and frame. A flick of the wrist and the door swung silently inward, granting me a fine view of Evangeline's bare back.

The sight of her stopped me in my tracks and brought a lump to my throat. Indeed, I could not breathe for a moment, so potent was my desire for her.

Her dark hair was pinned atop her head, though tendrils fell enticingly onto her fair shoulders. Her flesh was as smooth as alabaster, a rosy glow touching her buttocks. She was slick and wet, more curvaceous and tempting than any woman I had known.

"For a man said to be skillful in moving unobserved, it took you half an eternity to find your way up one flight of stairs," the lady said, without so much as a glance over her shoulder.

I blinked.

"Close the door, if you will, for there is a draft," she said, her voice husky. She glanced over her shoulder at me, that tiny coy smile curving her ruddy lips. The lantern light gilded her cheek, but left her eyes fathomless and dark. I had the uncommon sense suddenly that she hunted me and not the other way around.

Again.

I flicked the door closed with my fingertips, recovering some of my usual manner. "And I had thought you might greet me with less enthusiasm," I said, then winked. "Perhaps I underestimate my own charm."

"Hardly that!" The lady's smile stole the sting from her words. "Perhaps there is still something I would have of you." She gestured, effectively distracting me from the import of her words, for I saw that the bed was turned down, the linens fresh, the candles lit.

It is not all bad to be expected.

Nor is it all bad for a lady to be so desirous of your caress that she puts her argument aside, at least for the moment. I was certainly amenable to her scheme.

I smiled as I sauntered toward her, my thoughts filled with what we shortly would do, and gallantly offered her the length of linen left to one side. I held the cloth for her, just slightly out of reach so that she would have to step toward me to claim it. "I lingered in the hall as ladies, in my experience, prefer not to be hastened in their preparations."

"I would rather hasten my preparations than hasten my time abed." She stepped from the bath with no shyness, her hands brushing mine as she accepted the linen. She stood, not an arm's length before me, her gaze locked with mine. I could smell the rosewater upon her, feel the steamy heat of her wet flesh, see the tightened buds of her nipples.

She watched me look and smiled as she cast the linen aside unused. "Unless your thoughts are not as mine?" she teased, her arms slipping around my neck. I was deluged with the scent of her and caught her close, more than willing to repeat all we had done before.

"I thought myself summoned to a dire fate. You did invite me to pursue you, after all, and mocked my prowess as well."

Evangeline laughed lightly, the sound rich in her throat.

"Indeed, I did. What better way to ensure that you accepted my invitation?"

"By insulting my abilities?"

Her brow arched high. "By daring you to try again. You are a man, I think, who likes a dare well."

I chuckled. Anxious to begin our play, I bent to kiss her, but she lay a hand upon my chest.

"But I am not truly the prize you came to claim. Be honest with me in this, at least. You came to retrieve the relic."

My heart skipped that she saw my objective so clearly. "Did I? Perhaps I am glad to be rid of its burden. Perhaps I came to thank you." I nuzzled her neck, loving how she caught her breath beneath my caress. "Perhaps I came to claim you as the greater prize."

She chuckled. "You, come to seek a bride? I think not."

"Perhaps not a bride, but another merry night abed," I said, wanting to make this matter most clear. I took her hand and pressed a kiss into her palm, liking how her gaze darkened.

"No, I would not expect you to be a man anxious to wed," she mused, tilting her head to regard me. "I suspect that you like to live unfettered by obligations, responsibilities and expectations."

I should have been daunted that she already understood me so well—such was her charm that I was delighted. "There is nothing amiss with that."

She smiled, seemingly in agreement with me. "Or perhaps you came because you heard of my abilities at chess." She laughed low.

I might have laughed in turn, but her lips were upon mine and our discussion at an end. Evangeline cupped my head in her hands and rose to her toes, pressing her sweet heat against me and making me forget all else but the magic of her touch.

Hours later, we lay wrapped in each other's heat, exhausted by our lovemaking. It had been as marvelous and exhausting as before. Evangeline slid from my embrace to blow out a candle close to gutting itself. I watched her, as beguiled by her grace as ever.

Her lips tightened into a rosebud as she blew, her brow tightening slightly as she concentrated on her task. She was so serious about whatsoever she did, giving it every vestige of her attention—including lovemaking. Yet, she could be playful and uninhibited, as mischievous as a fey maiden sent to torment mortal men with desire.

Beyond the lust she awakened in me was something more, something deeper, something that made me curious to know more of her than mere touch could confide. The demure demoiselle in the chapel and the wanton I met abed were facets of the same woman—and I could not yet discern how the two were reconciled in the woman she was.

I knew that I should leave, but I could not bring myself to do so. Not yet. Indeed, I have always had an uncommon affection for puzzles. Evangeline nestled against my shoulder again and smiled up at me, looking so flushed and disheveled—yet also sweetly innocent—that my heart clenched. It was impossible to face the prospect of never seeing her again after this night, of never learning more of her mysteries.

"You should come with me." I made the invitation impulsively, but as soon as it was uttered, I knew this to be my desire. I had never traveled with another, but for Evangeline, I was prepared to make an exception.

She twisted to regard me, her eyes filled with the sparkle

of laughter. I bristled slightly that she found my invitation amusing. "Come with you where?"

"Away, to the south." I dared not tell her more than that. I pulled her closer and kissed her shoulder, hoping to persuade her to join me. "You could see with your own eyes that marvels exist."

She propped herself up on her elbow, her dark hair cascading over her bare shoulder. I dared to hope that she considered my proposal. "As does this home you described to me afore?"

"I will possess it soon." I was disappointed that she asked after such details, but in my experience, women find much joy in the dispensation of coin. I smiled for her, willing to allow her this concession. "Indeed, if you accompany me, you can aid in its furnishing." I was surprised that her expression turned wry.

"And there would be a place in your home for me as what? A courtesan?"

"You will live in splendor and have every frippery you might desire."

Evangeline almost laughed, then pushed away from me. She sat up, and stared down at me, her features shadowed. I felt whatever bond existed between us stretch thin, though I knew not what I had done. "Until you tire of me and cast me out?"

"I would not do that!"

"And who would aid me if you did?" she asked, rather more harshly than I thought the issue deserved. She had changed, not unlike the chameleons I knew from the south, changing hue even as I stared directly at her.

It was a kind of magic, for she had once again become the distant and cool lady, a woman who might have been wrought of ice.

"I have never treated a woman unfairly. You would live in luxury, admittedly for so long as we found each other agreeable. It would not be a common life." I reached out to touch her cheek, liking that she shivered slightly at my caress. It was encouraging that my touch could recall the side of her that most appealed to me. "And indeed, we might never tire of each other."

Evangeline pulled her chin away with a jerk. "And if we did?"

"If we parted ways, you would leave with a heavy purse and no need of anyone else. . . ."

"No need?" Now, her eyes flashed with fire. "How can a person have no need of a family, of friends, of a home to call their own? How can a person have no need of tradition, of legacy, of roots?"

She got to her feet and retreated from me, the lack of grace in her movements revealing that she was sorely angered. With every step, the welcoming woman with whom I had just shared such intimacy seemed more distant, more a figment of my own wishful thinking. "How can you imagine that I would leave all I call my own to live as your *whore*?"

I got to my feet in turn, discomfited as much by her charge as by the change in her. "That is too cruel a word!"

"What then?" Evangeline propped her hands on her hips and flung her hair over her shoulder, her pose so splendidly indignant that I had a mind to continue what we had begun. Her eyes snapped though, a warning that she would not be readily seduced.

Still I tried. I ventured closer, extended a hand. "We would be lovers, Evangeline, and our partnership would be untainted by petty pledges and words with no meaning. We would be together . . ."

"For so long as you wished to rut with me, or until I carried your child, and then you would cast me aside like so much offal. I may have been raised upon the edges of Christendom, but I know well enough how a man such as you treats a woman."

"Do you?" Now, I was angered. I pointed to the bed. "And by your own experience you know that I would treat you so poorly?"

She had the grace to flush, though she did not change her stance otherwise. I closed the distance between us with a single step and framed her face in my hands. She caught her breath, her eyes darkening, and I brushed my lips across hers, loving how she shivered.

"What is of import is trust between us, Evangeline, and this magical passion that we coax from each other. What is important is that we remain together." I kissed her again and she trembled, her hands landing upon my shoulders with evident reluctance. Her mouth softened beneath mine, though, and I thought the battle half won.

Until she tore her lips from mine and retreated, rubbing her hand over her mouth. "You cannot change the truth with kisses."

"The truth is that we should live well. . . ."

"Of course." Her words were bitter. "You are clearly acquainted with the fair treatment of harlots. A woman would be a fool not to accept your offer of hours abed and coin in exchange for her favors, so long as you had a desire for her."

Her arch tone infuriated me. I had never felt the need for the ongoing presence of a woman before, I had never made such a proposal, and she spurned my offer as insufficient.

I would not be so foolish as to repeat the proposal, or

worse, to fatten it. I understood that I had been rejected, though I doubted her stated reason was the genuine one.

I donned my chausses, lacing them with haste, then my chemise and tabard. It was clear that she would not see sense in this, though I was more annoyed with her than I knew I should have been.

"You make much of little," I informed her when I was fully dressed. She stood like a warrior queen, arms folded across her chest and features set, unashamed of her fury or her nude splendor. It was clear that my touch was no longer welcome and my tone sharpened as a result. "You have already met me abed. What difference if you do so again?"

"The difference is that I am here, among my own people and in my own home." She jabbed a finger through the air in my direction. "If I followed you, when you abandoned me in some distant land, as undoubtedly you will, I would be left to beg for kindness from strangers."

"You have a low opinion of me, based on so short an acquaintance."

Evangeline laughed, though the sound was not a merry one. Then she spoke with a harshness I had not known she possessed. "Tell me that you are not a man who sees to his own pleasure first. Tell me that you are not a man who cares solely for his own gain."

I glared at her. "It is only natural to ensure one's own needs are met first."

"And there is a sentiment to warm a woman's heart."

"You have no grounds for criticism," I appealed. "I came in pursuit of you!"

"You came in pursuit of the *Titulus Croce* and do not pretend to me otherwise."

"A man might be persuaded that you had taken the *Titulus* to ensure that you were pursued."

She smiled, her gaze knowing. "A vain man might, perhaps."

"Then, why did you take it? Why did you welcome me to my bed with such gusto?"

"Perhaps I had my own reasons for accepting what you offered so readily, reasons you need never know."

I had then the odd sense that she toyed with me, though I could not imagine how or why. She was enigmatic again, her expression inscrutable. "Surely, the *Titulus* was not so necessary as that for the ceremony this night? The old laird clearly found some acceptable substitute, if he showed a version of the relic twice yearly until five years ago."

She said nothing, her darkened gaze fixed upon me.

"I know," I added with deliberate care, "that the genuine *Titulus* has been gone from Inverfyre for fifteen years."

Evangeline turned her back upon me and donned a chemise. She tied the neck with such finality that I knew we would not meet abed again this night.

Or ever.

And that troubled me far more than I liked.

V

"Why now?" I demanded. "Why did you seek the *Titulus* after all these years?"

Evangeline granted me a sly glance. "If I were a man, what would you speculate?"

I smiled. "Mercifully, you are not." She scowled at me, so I folded my arms across my chest and pondered the question. "If you were a man, I would suspect vengeance of you, or perhaps some scheme to ensure my disadvantage. I would suspect that you had stalked me apurpose, perhaps followed me from Ravensmuir, specifically to steal the *Titulus*. I would speculate that you seduced me to distract me from your intent. Were you a man, however, that particular strategy would have been less successful."

She smiled coolly and arched a brow, her expression telling me that I had guessed aright. My heart chilled, for I had never met a woman capable of or desirous of planning such a feat. I was both troubled and fascinated.

"Do you know what is the root of our fortunes here?"

I recalled both Inverfyre's seal and its reputation. "Hunting hawks. You trade in peregrines."

"We did, because the cliffs around this keep have always been rife with them. For centuries, the falcons have returned to nest at Inverfyre, and their eyasses have been collected by our falconers, trained and sold to dukes and lords and kings."

I waited, for this could not be all of the tale.

Evangeline met my gaze. "Fifteen years ago, the falcons became impotent."

"What is this?" I was astounded.

"They still return, they still nest, but their nests are barren. It is the mark of divine disfavor and the root of our poverty. Without young falcons, we have naught with which to trade; without trade, we have no coin, no food, no garb." Evangeline's shoulders sagged slightly. "Few crops flourish at Inverfyre, even sheep disdain these hills. Without the *Titulus,* the Lairds of Inverfyre and even Inverfyre itself shall fade to a distant memory."

To say that I was somewhat skeptical of this conclusion would be a vast understatement. "You cannot believe that the absence of a relic is at the root of your woes. Evangeline, this is the manner of superstitious nonsense believed by peasants. There must be another reason."

She folded her arms across her chest, as if willing me to persuade her. "Name it."

"I do not know. Perhaps their favored prey has become scarce."

"The rivers are choked with waterfowl, which the falcons favor, simply because the predators' numbers have dwindled so far."

"Perhaps the nests are not so attractive as afore. Wild things oft are dismayed by the close presence of men."

"We are fewer than before, and the perimeter of our village has reverted to wilderness. By your logic, there should be more falcons."

"I am no falconer! I cannot name the reason, but to blame the absence of a religious relic makes little sense. I say there is an earthly reason."

"And I say you are wrong. As I now possess the *Titulus* again, your opinion is of little merit."

I was reluctant to comment upon that assertion. Indeed, I thought a distraction would be timely, lest she ponder the matter overmuch.

I caught the end of one tie of her chemise and pulled her closer, liking how her eyes widened in awareness of me. "And what would you pledge to me if I should prove you wrong?" I kissed the side of her neck lingeringly.

"Why should I pledge anything to you?" She caught her breath and, encouraged, I urged her closer to the bed.

"You could grant me the *Titulus* as my reward for discovering the true reason for your misfortunes," I suggested.

Evangeline pushed me away. "You have no shame, do you? You have had your desire of me and of Inverfyre." She lifted her chin. "Perhaps it would be prudent for you to leave."

I was stunned. I had never been told to leave, certainly not without a threat at the portal or without a parting kiss. "You have had your desire of me, as well!"

"Perhaps so."

"But you cannot spurn me so easily as this!"

"I just have."

"Because you are irked with my invitation to Sicily," I guessed. She lifted her chin, her pose telling more than any words could, and my frustration with both her and my unruly desire redoubled. "And what would you have of me instead? Would you have me *wed* you? Would that make it sweeter to part ways? How is it more admirable that those wedded remain together for all their days, even if their nights are spent apart? It is honest, at least, to cleave one's path to another's for solely as long as the destination of both is the same."

"Honest?" She shook her head as if she could not believe my audacity. "It is remarkable indeed to have *you* tout the merits of honesty!"

"And what is that to mean?"

Evangeline turned upon me, her eyes gleaming, and I saw that I had goaded her into telling me a truth of some kind. To be sure, I heeded her every word. "It means that I know who you are and what you have done, Gawain Lammergeier. I know that you are a thief, perhaps an uncommonly talented thief, but a thief nonetheless. You are a man with no scruples and no concern for others. I know this, for I have witnessed it with my own eyes, and I dare not believe otherwise, especially not if the only evidence for another claim is your own sweet words."

"But I had the *Titulus* when you sought me out. Who is the thief here? I witnessed your theft of that relic from me, without a care for *me*!"

"I reclaimed what was mine own," she said with vigor.

"But what did you witness with your own eyes? Never a theft of mine. You have witnessed no deed of mine, save those abed."

"Have I not?" Evangeline's eyes snapped with a new fire. "Fifteen years ago, you came to Inverfyre. I remember your golden hair and gilded tongue. I remember how fine and foreign you and your father seemed. I remember being enthralled that such men had come to our gates."

I desperately tried to place Evangeline in my memories

of this place. "But there were only men in the hall. There were no women—indeed, my father remarked upon it."

Evangeline must have been a child, perhaps of eight or ten summers. Her beauty would have been evident, even then, and I knew I would have recalled her.

If I had seen her.

"My mother forbade me to come to the hall. Perhaps she knew my curiosity to be unhealthy. Perhaps she simply knew more of men than I."

"But . . ."

Evangeline almost smiled. "In those days, I was not one to do as I was bidden. I watched from the top of the stairs as my father entertained his guests. I listened and I learned and I became enamored with a certain young man who spoke with unholy charm."

Her gaze held mine as she watched me understand her inference.

"Me. You were watching *me*." It did my pride no harm to know that the lady had found me fetching then, and indeed, if I had guessed that she lurked within these walls, perhaps I would have stolen more than an ancient piece of wood.

She smiled, if coldly. "I was smitten. You were as unlike the young men that I had met afore as any soul could be. You had grace and good looks and wealth and so many tales of distant lands! It was not fair that my mother had forbade me to meet you."

A determined gleam lit her eyes. "I could not let the moment pass. When all retired, I crept down to the chapel, the better to entreat God to grant me one chance to speak with you. One chance was all I desired, a single moment to impress upon you that I was here, that I could be the maiden of your dreams, that we were undoubtedly destined to be together."

Her lips twisted wryly and I saw that she believed this childish whimsy no longer.

But wait—she had come to the *chapel* all those years ago. I understood suddenly what she had seen. "You saw us in the midst of acquisition," I guessed.

"Acquisition? Is that what theft is called in these sorry times? Or in that lawless land of Sicily that you so favor?" Her gaze was cold now, her expression so grim that she might have been the woman I had seen in the chapel, not the one I had met abed. "But yes, I saw you steal my father's pride and joy. I saw you take the *Titulus*. I saw you laugh when it was in your grasp."

Bitterness tinged her words. "I saw you revel in the fact that you had deceived the host who had treated you with honor. It was only later that I realized your cleverness in charming every detail of our relic from my father's lips without seeming to do so." She took a step toward me and I retreated, uncertain what she would do.

"It is only a piece of wood, Evangeline," I reminded her. "It might not even be a genuine relic."

"That does not matter!" she said with unexpected ferocity. "My father believed it to be genuine and that was sufficient."

"Evangeline . . ."

"You stole more, far more, than a mere piece of wood. You stole the fortune that had blessed Inverfyre, you stole the unity that secured the rule of my family, you stole my father's pride and confidence, you stole my mother's faith."

"You know that this cannot be responsible for the impotence of the wild birds . . ."

She jabbed a finger into my chest, driving her argument home, but I dared not retreat further. "Worse, your theft sowed dissent in Inverfyre, and launched the slow rot that has brought us to our current sorry state."

"Evangeline, I . . ."

"To sustain his suzerainty, my father was compelled to lie about his possession of the *Titulus*. He had always been a man of honor, a man upon whose word one could rely. After he lied, my mother never looked at him the same way again. Indeed, he never viewed himself the same way. And the people smelled that there was rot at the core, even if they knew not what it was."

"But . . ."

"You can spew no pretty words to heal this wound. Be gone. Be gone afore I say too much."

And the lady turned her back upon me. I raised my finger, intending to argue the matter further, but a bird cried at close proximity.

A white gyrfalcon landed on the window sill, the bell upon her ankle tinkling with her movements.

"Aphrodite!" Evangeline cried with delight. Both I and our argument were dismissed.

I was not disappointed, you may be assured, that she was one to give vent to her temper and then be shed of its burden. My brother was like this, as was my father, and I suspect it is far more healthy than festering a slow burn for years and years.

Evangeline eased toward the bird and I assumed she would capture it anew for her father. She began to sing to it, to my surprise, even as she donned a leather glove and coaxed it to take her wrist. The bird was disinclined to do her bidding, but the song seemed to be an allure that could not be denied. It reluctantly stepped to her gloved fist as Evangeline continued to sing.

It was a stunning creature, its large-pupiled gaze alien and wild. It was so large that it could only be the one loosed from Fergus' fist in the hall. I was all too aware of the sharpness of its talons and beak, the prowess with which it could stalk and kill. Indeed, some deity had designed this bird to be a perfect creature for hunting.

Yet Evangeline was unafraid of it. I edged closer, intrigued.

"Why do you sing?" I dared to ask.

She granted me a hot glance, as if annoyed to find me still present, then deigned to explain. "It is her feeding song."

"I do not understand."

Evangeline sang another verse before replying. "Each falcon has a song which she is taught to associate with fresh meat offered from the hand. It is the sole way to tame them. Aphrodite remembers her song."

"You sing the same song each time it is fed?"

"She," Evangeline corrected even as she nodded. "All hunting birds of merit are female." I chose not to explore this particular detail. "She associates the song with food, thus will always allow herself to be captured when she hears the song."

I was impressed that a wild bird could be so astute as this. I had known hounds less readily trained. As she sang again, Evangeline untied the bird's jesses and removed the bell.

"But you have no meat for her," I observed belatedly. "Will she not be dismayed to have no treat with the song?"

Evangeline's smile flashed. "I have a better gift." To my astonishment, she cast the bell and jesses to the ground, then leaned out the window and jerked her fist upward so that the bird would take flight.

Unfettered.

Aphrodite needed no second invitation. Her great wings unfurled and flapped with a vigor that lifted her away from Inverfyre's tower with a trio of beats. She never looked back. Indeed, her cry was one of triumph and pleasure, if a bird could be imagined to feel such sentiments.

"What are you doing?" I sprang to the window, but Evangeline laughed with delight.

"I am setting Aphrodite free." She pointed skyward, her features alight. "Look at her flight! She is so powerful, so graceful. Look at her! She knows her destination." Indeed, the bird wheeled and turned like an arrow, flying north with uncommon speed.

I was woefully confused. "But I thought you traded in falcons here."

"Indeed we do."

"Then why . . ."

Evangeline turned to confront me, folding her arms across her chest even as she smiled at my confusion. "No falconer of sense takes a bird after its first moult. Aphrodite was sent as a gift, a poor gift, for she was captured after at least two moults. She knows her wild ways too well to be trained to hunt at a falconer's command."

"Where is her destination, then?"

Evangeline looked out the window and I imagined that she could yet discern the bird. "I do not know. She has mated already, it is clear, for she has been anxious to meet her partner."

I did not understand and my expression must have revealed as much.

Evangeline smiled. "Falcons are noble birds, possessed of admirable traits. They take but one mate for their entire life. Each year, peregrine and tiercel meet at the same nest to breed. And each year, they part after their young are raised, to hunt alone until spring comes again." Evangeline met my gaze steadily. "Aphrodite has bred at least once—she has found her partner. It would be beyond cruel to deny her urge to mate by keeping her captive."

"But she was captive, upon Fergus' fist. Surely Fergus understood this?"

Her lips thinned. "Fergus knows nothing of falcons."

"And listens to no counsel," I guessed, though Evangeline did not reply.

She turned away and crossed the room, keeping her back to me. "I do not know how she came to be unfettered, but it was good fortune that she came to my window. None other would have defied Fergus." It was curious that she called her father by his Christian name, but I assumed he was indulgent of his daughter, as men with beautiful children oft are. She glanced quickly at me, her expression unreadable. "Have you not departed yet?"

I was not prepared to leave without a parting token from the lady. I coughed delicately. "I must confess that I had a part in Aphrodite's timely escape."

Evangeline turned to study me, the chill melting from her gaze. "Why?"

"I needed a distraction to ascend to your chamber." I bowed with studied elegance. "I can only be gratified that my unwitting release of the bird pleased you."

Evangeline's lips parted but before I could decide whether she meant to curse me or kiss me—perhaps she too was undecided—there was a shout from the corridor outside the door.

"Aphrodite was here!" Fergus cried. "Find her!"

We both froze at the echo of approaching footsteps.

"Quick!" Evangeline seized my sleeve with brutal force.

She shoved me toward a door I had not glimpsed earlier, one hidden beyond the pool of light cast by the candles. She pushed me unceremoniously from behind, urging me to greater speed. "You must leave and you must leave this way. No one can find you here."

Her fervor amused me, especially given her earlier tirade. I halted and smiled, pausing to catch her chin in my hand. "So you would protect me, despite your supposed animosity. Your barbed words do not come from the heart, after all." I bent to kiss her but she pushed me away.

"Fool!" She shook off my grip, though flushed prettily. "You see nothing beyond your own pleasure."

I winked. "I would see to yours, as well. Hide me, Evangeline, for the night is yet young."

"I thought you were one to protect your own hide first."

"Of what import is that?"

She smiled coolly. "My husband will not be gladdened to find you in his place in my bed."

I gaped at her. "Your *husband*?"

"Do not imagine that I save you, Gawain Lammergeier." She sternly shook her finger at me. "I protect myself. We all know it is the woman who pays the price for adultery."

I still could not accept her claim. "But you have no spouse! If you had a husband, he would have sat with you at the board, beside you or your father. . . ."

"My father is dead. Do you not recall what he looked like, the man you betrayed and deceived?"

I did not, but I dared not admit as much before her quelling gaze. It seemed I had erred yet again.

The lady's dark brows arched high in feigned surprise. "Perhaps you noticed Fergus, my father's chosen heir? He was the one who lifted the *Titulus* high in the chapel."

I recoiled from the implication of her words. "But he is *old*! You cannot be his bride!"

Her eyes narrowed. "I am his bride."

"But this is a travesty!" The very idea revolted me and I guessed from her expression that she too found her marriage less than pleasing.

A shred of chivalry awakened in me, for I knew that I could save this lovely lady from her fate. "You cannot be condemned to bed that old man. This cannot be your desire."

"My desire is of no import." Her words were cool but already I understood that she hid behind a mask of measured calm when she was most agitated.

"Evangeline, do not be a fool! Do not discard what rises between us! Can you not see how circumstance favors us? Come away with me. . . ."

"You must go!"

"You cannot wish to be wed to this man. Leave him! Come away with me. I know what you truly desire and I will ensure that you are happy."

"You know nothing about me," she said savagely.

I planted my feet against the floor. "I know that I will not leave without you."

A knock came at her door and Evangeline glanced back, fear in her magnificent eyes. I was tempted then, sorely tempted to stay and have a reckoning from this aged husband who had taught such a lady to fear him, tempted to fight for her with my fists.

I had never felt such an urge before. The lady wakened some madness in my veins, of that there could be no doubt.

Evangeline caught at my sleeve. "Go now, or have my blood upon your hands!"

"For a kiss I will depart."

She made a vexed sound beneath her breath and would

have pressed her lips chastely against mine, but I kissed her soundly. I loved how she made a frustrated sound, then leaned against me, as if reluctant to succumb. But succumb she did, only the pounding of fists upon her portal forcing us breathlessly to part.

The sight of her reddened lips and sparkling eyes made my heart clench tightly. "Remember me," I bade her, for some foolish reason.

Sadness clouded her lovely features before her expression set to stone again. "I have already forgotten you."

Because she had to. I understood now the burden that she bore, but still was frustrated by her insistence upon clinging to it. I offered a hand, she shook her head with resolve. I held her gaze for a moment longer, until the men shouted at her. Only when she left me, crossing the floor with purpose, did I do as she had bidden me and duck through the low portal.

I had a moment to be heartily discontent, to be sorely disgruntled at Fergus' lusty greeting in the chamber behind me and Evangeline's demure reply. It was no more than a moment, before I perceived that once again, I had been tricked.

I was not alone.

They were waiting for me in the darkness. Too late I realized where the second door upon the left of the corridor led—it led to this dark chamber, no greater than the height of a man in any direction.

It was occupied by three men who encircled me like hungry predators.

"What manner of guest troubles the Lady of Inverfyre in her chambers?" growled one. I recognized Tarsuinn's voice, though it was now filled with menace.

I knew a relief that weakened my knees.

"Well met, my comrades!" I whispered gaily. "Shall we seek out another cup of ale?"

"We do not know you," Niall said grimly.

"What madness is this? It is me, your old comrade, Connor MacDoughall. Perhaps you do not recognize me in this light."

Tarsuinn chuckled. "You are not Connor."

"But . . ."

Dour shook his head. "Connor would never buy an ale for another, even if he had all the riches of Croesus."

"Do you think us fools?" Tarsuinn demanded. "Do you think us so dim of wit that we cannot recognize our own friends?"

"But the horse . . ."

"Never seen the nag," Dour insisted. "But I shall tell you this: whatever you paid for him, it was too much."

"The lady bade us watch for strangers," Niall murmured, his words menacing. "And that if a blond man appeared alone, we should feign knowledge of him. It appears that she was expecting you."

Once again, Evangeline had outwitted me, and now that I knew the reason for her deceit, I doubted I would survive for a third chance at being outwitted.

I surveyed the men, then the room itself. There was no visible means of escape, the door to the corridor being blocked by two of them.

I smiled, as if untroubled. "I suppose that was not the sum of her request."

"She does not wish you killed, more's the pity," Niall confided as he pushed up his sleeves. "Otherwise, you are ours."

My heart quailed. One against three is not odds I prefer.

"Be reasonable!" I urged with false cheer. "You have no complaint with me. If the lady wishes me gone, I shall leave and you can consider your task complete." I smiled as engagingly as I was able. "There is no need for violence."

"Ah, but there is." Tarsuinn said softly. "You are man in need of a lesson."

"Consider it learned," I said amiably, even as I took a step back. "I can be away from Inverfyre in a matter of moments. We can forget this entire exchange."

They followed, not so readily dissuaded as that.

"You aimed to trick us," Tarsuinn said, with a sad shake of his head.

"You took us for fools," Dour added.

"You mean ill to the lady," Niall said.

"Not I."

"Indeed?" Niall's gaze was hard. "Why then were you in her chambers at this hour and unchaperoned? She cannot have invited you, for to do so would bring scandal and the weight of her husband's hand upon her." He smiled coldly as his voice dropped. "We cannot permit some vermin to sully our lady's name."

"How fascinating this all is. Unfortunately, I have just recalled a critical appointment in London, on the morrow, in fact . . ."

"Indeed you will depart immediately." Niall stepped forward. "But not without a few bruises to remind you never to return. Count yourself fortunate, *friend*, that your chausses are laced, for otherwise the lady's insistence that your life be spared would have been forgotten."

They closed in and I knew that this would not be a pretty incident. I shall spare you the gruesome details, save that I was given a hearty thumping, with little chance to defend myself. I am good with my fists and fast upon my feet, but to face three bent upon pummelling me was a losing proposition.

Indeed, I found myself wondering whether the lady, with her laird heaving atop her in the adjacent chamber, could hear what transpired.

Then I wondered whether the sound gave her pleasure.

That was a most troubling prospect.

I finally collapsed, certain Niall had lied about not intending to kill me, for surely my every bone was shattered. I could not open one eye at all, so quickly had it swelled shut after the first blow landed there. My jaw ached, my knuckles bled, and I was fairly certain that at least one of my ribs was shattered.

A boot poked my gut and I groaned but did not roll away. It would have hurt too much to do so. My pride too was sorely injured, not so much by the beating as by fact that I had miscalculated the intellect of these barbarians.

Not to mention, the lady's affection for me.

These were mistakes I would not make again, if I had the fortune to live long enough to learn from them.

Someone grabbed my ankle and I did not care. A quick command and the other ankle was seized, then I was hauled to the far wall. Dirty rushes dragged beneath my tabard, an indignity beyond belief, but I did not care. If I was meant to die, I hoped it would happen soon—at least then the pain would stop.

I felt a sudden breath of chill air, then my wrists were seized as well. I swung helplessly as they lifted me off the floor, only fighting once I realized what they meant to do. A door or window had been opened in the exterior wall, and I was about to be cast through it.

"No!" I hollered with sudden vigor.

"One!" intoned Niall as I was swung backward.

"Two!" I was swung higher, gaining momentum.

"No! Halt this madness!" I was not quite ready to die, especially now that my demise seemed imminent. I struggled madly, but to no avail. Their grasp was merciless. I had a glimpse of a starlit sky before I swung back into the darkness of the keep again.

"Three!" the barbarians cried in unison, then flung me into the night. I roared, determined to not go quietly to my death. No doubt I made an inelegant sight as I flailed through the air, but I had little time to fret about the matter.

I fell like a rock.

VI

My heart nigh stopped when I shattered a thin layer of ice and plunged into the black lake below the keep. The water was cold and I sank so low that I thought I might never find the surface again.

But I am a strong swimmer and instinct did not fail me. I lunged for the surface, straining for air and life. I broke the surface with a gasp, then took a deep gulp of air so cold that a thousand knives seemed to stab from the inside of my chest.

The laughter of rough men carried through the darkness, but I ignored their petty glee. There was the more critical matter of survival before me. The shore was not far, though the shadows of the forest came directly to the edge of the lake.

I shook back my hair, then broke the ice between myself and the shore with my fist. It shattered easily around me, but got thicker as I progressed toward the shore. Finally, it did not break so readily and I dared to hope it might support my weight. The difficulty lay in getting a grip upon it. I was already shivering, the winter air fairly turning my flesh blue.

I thought resolutely of Sicily, of heat and sun-baked tiles and the languor wrought by a merciless sun, and tried again. After no success and three or four plunges back into the icy water, I glanced around for a way to pull myself out of the lake.

The end of a rope was not far beyond my reach.

I blinked but it did not disappear, as incongruous as it was. I followed its snaking trail into the forest on the shore.

Was this another trick? I looked further and spied the alewife. She bent and wiggled the rope so that the end nudged toward me.

"It is tied to the tree," she said. "I have not the strength to pull a man of your size from the water, but you can save yourself."

I eyed her warily. "Do you trick me?"

"You were kind with coin, Connor MacDoughall, as few have been kind to me. I owe you some debt."

In truth, I had not the option of entertaining suspicions. I knew I had to get out of the lake before my marrow froze. I seized the rope and hauled myself onto the surface of the ice. I took a deep breath, wincing at the aches that awakened in my body, then crawled toward the shore.

"There is a fire here, and some garb," the alewife said, her tone flat. "It is not so fine as that you wear, but it is dry."

In other circumstance, I might have been astonished by her generosity. For the moment, I was simply grateful. And who knew what grievances she had against those who had assaulted me? "I thank you for your kindness."

She busied herself hauling in the rope as I quickly peeled off my clothes and dried my flesh. I struggled into chausses that were somewhat too short for me, then hauled a coarse peasant chemise and tabard over my chest. The wool cloak was roughly wrought, but warm, as were the thick socks. I hunkered down beside the small fire, my teeth chattering, as I wrung water from my hair and tried to empty the water from my boots. There was no sign of the rope by this point, no hint that any had aided me.

"You were prepared for me." I smiled encouragingly at the alewife. "How did you know?"

She shrugged. "When I was a child, we came to this place to watch the laird's whores cast into the lake."

"The laird who died five years past?"

"No, the one before him. That laird, he was a lusty man. His wife was cold as the fishes, but still she did not like him sharing his affections with others. She had that chamber and that portal built, sent her men to seize the damsels who shared the laird's bed, then had them cast into the lake. 'Twould cool their ardor, she said."

"This is a cruel country you inhabit."

The alewife smiled secretively. "There is no cruelty in seeing those who believe themselves better than others face a reckoning." Her tone was so odd that I was not entirely certain she spoke only of the whores.

"I have no coin with which to compensate for your trouble," I said. "They cut away my purse."

"Fear not, I shall have my compense." She laughed then, a throaty chuckle that put me in mind of the ravens at my family abode of Ravensmuir.

I frowned, uncertain what she meant, but she rose to her feet with surprising speed. Perhaps it was payment enough that she foiled their plan. I could not say.

She abruptly kicked snow over the flames and extinguished the fire, much to my disappointment. "They will be seeking you," she said. "You had best be leaving." She pointed further down the lake. "Follow the shore to the great cedar that hangs over the water. It is as tall as three men. Turn there and take ten paces through the woods, and you will find the road. A day's hard riding will take you to the lands of the Comyn and the first of their villages."

"A day's riding upon what?" I asked. "My horse is yet in Inverfyre's stables."

"Is it?" The alewife pointed into the shadows of the trees ahead and I dared to hope. "Begone quickly, if you mean to survive."

"I thank you for your unexpected aid," I said.

"Oh, I shall have fair compense, Connor MacDoughall," the alewife said with unexpected intensity. "For I shall not have to watch another woman die as my daughter did."

I frowned in confusion.

She seized my sleeve in her bony grip and shook it. "I heard nothing from her until the very end, nothing but how fine her man was, nothing but how he would keep his promise to return for her." Her tone was bitter. "But fine Connor MacDoughall never did come for my bonny lass, even though she was ripe with his child. She died, heartbroken and without you. For this sin, you will have to face your maker, Connor MacDoughall. But I, I will not watch the light fade in the eyes of another girl."

I had no chance to ask what she meant by her last comment before she disappeared into the darkness under the trees. Did she have another daughter, one she would save from the lusty eye of Connor MacDoughall?

I strained my ears but could hear no hint of the old woman's passage. I peered about myself but all signs of the fire were gone, and the rope had vanished. It was almost as if the alewife had not truly been by my side.

This land, as I have told you, plays tricks with a man's thoughts.

The distant echo of men's voices told me that she had been right about one matter—I had not the luxury of lingering, even to sate my curiosity. I fled through the woods as she had indicated.

To my profound relief, my saddlebag was still fat and lashed to the saddle of my horse, just as I had left it. The sole difference was that I had left horse and bag in the village. I flung my wet clothes over the bag, then led the beast along the shore as the woman had instructed. I reached the tall cedar and turned into the woods, finding the road just as she had foretold.

Much reassured, I swung into the saddle. A clatter of hoofbeats and a shout far behind me hinted that Evangeline's thugs had found me out. I gave the horse my spurs, anxious to be away, and leaned over the beast's neck just as a baby cried.

A *baby?*

I pulled the horse up short and stared at my saddlebag. The child cried again, its location obvious, and my heart sank to my toes. I threw open the bag to find a baby nestled there, its face twisted as it cried lustily.

My innards tightened with the certainty that this child was not only the same child I had heard crying in the alewife's hut, but that it was a girl.

The alewife's daughter had died in the delivery of Connor MacDoughall's child—and her mother had seen fit that the father himself be blessed with the result of his seduction. Only now I saw the logic of her thinking, and the reason why she saw fit to ensure that I lived.

Except, of course, that I was not Connor MacDoughall.

I glanced back at the thunder of hoofbeats and knew there could be no chance to plead my case. Perhaps that had been the old alewife's intent.

I had no more time to ponder the matter.

Horses galloped around a distant curve in the road, Niall leading the trio. He stood in his stirrups when he spied me and waved a blade over his head, the others fast behind.

I lifted the child to my chest, slapped my horse's rump and rode away from Inverfyre as if the demons of hell themselves were at my heels. The child bellowed in protest, eliminating any possibility of a covert escape. Any fool could have followed and found me, unless he had also been deaf.

Fortunately, my pursuers fell back, clearly having been instructed not to follow me further than the perimeter of their laird's lands.

I was only to be chased away.

As I rode with the wind in my hair, my spirits lifted. My bruises would heal, my ribs would mend. I would find some haven for the child. I was free and alive, which was more than I might have hoped just hours ago.

More, Evangeline would have a surprise of her own. She had not had the last victory in this matter, for there was weight in my saddlebag beyond that of the babe.

The lady might have skill at chess, but I had the *Titulus Croce*.

And that, despite the squalling baby in my arms and the swelling of my eye, made me smile.

My triumphant mood did not last long. I know nothing about children, nothing beyond the fact that they are not overly interesting. This child, however, was clearly a demon in human guise. She looked soft and sweet, but her demands were ceaseless.

And they were loud.

I had previously had no idea that babes wept so much. Indeed, I could have happily lived out my days without learning of my error. My teeth were on edge from the babe's relentless wails. I did not know what she wanted, if indeed she wanted anything, or whether she howled simply to torment me.

That possibility seemed more and more likely the longer her protests continued. The woods and rocks echoed with her lament. The snow had melted a bit, so the horse found his footing more readily. The sky was clear and the wind biting.

I thought—foolishly!—that the babe might exhaust herself in time, that I had only to outwait her, but this small girl had the strength of a hundred men. I had no respite, but this creature did not care.

Remarkably, I was in the company of a soul more selfish than I.

I halted to let the horse rest just before the dawn, and the babe cried with greater vigor. I rocked her, thinking she perhaps missed the rhythm of the horse's gait.

But no. The babe gathered her small hands into fists, strained backward and hollered until her face was crimson. I whispered nonsense to her, I bounced her vigilantly, I even danced. I made a blessed fool of myself and I did not care.

If it would silence her, I would do it. Suddenly, I recalled that lullabies were sung to children. I cleared my throat and sang with gusto a song created on the spot.

There was a maid of Inverfyre
With blue blue eyes and golden hair.
So fair was the maid of Inverfyre
That knights came courting from afar.

It was a poor rhyme, as those made under duress could oft be, but she did not seem overly critical.

Indeed, she halted her crying. The horse snorted, but I had no care for his approval. The babe hiccuped, studied me, and sniffled. She cried again, but less vigilantly, her bleary gaze fixed expectantly upon me.

I am not unused to young maidens being intrigued with me, so I found her response reassuring. I composed another verse, contorting my features as I acted out the parts.

> *There came courting to her abode*
> *A man with a wart on his nose.*
> *Other suitors laughed at this node*
> *They told the maid this was no rose.*

To my astonishment, the baby smiled. Relief nearly took me to my knees, then she reached toward me. Her dimpled hand wavered in the air, uncertain, and I lifted one hand to steady her. A tumble would only make matters worse, and she seemed to have no more bones than a sack of wriggling kittens.

She grasped my finger in a surprisingly strong grip, then put its tip in her mouth. Her gums did not hurt as she clamped on to my finger and sucked, though I thought I could feel a tooth emerging.

But she was quiet. I heaved a sigh and sat down for a moment's reprieve beneath her adoring gaze.

Truly, she was an attractive child when she ceased to scream. She might have been called angelic. It was hard to reconcile the demon who had tormented me all night with this adorable creature.

Her eyes were as blue as the Mediterranean, her lashes long and dark and thick. Her cheeks were plump and rosy, her brows fair. Her hair was short and fine, golden curls that were softer than the finest down. She released my finger to smile and I was smitten.

But what should I do with her? I could not keep her, I knew that. She was not my blood, so I supposed I had no obligation to her. I could leave her on the porch of a church, or outside the door of some wealthy merchant.

She sucked on my finger with greater vigor, her tiny nails digging into my flesh, and I felt fear for her. What if no one claimed her? What if she was left to die? What if some hungered dog assaulted her before she was found?

No, that would not do.

I could find Connor MacDoughall, the man who was her father in truth. I could not help but consider that a poor option. What little I knew of Connor—that he was tight with his coin and lied to the pretty wenches he bedded—was scarcely an endorsement. And clearly, I could not return her to Inverfyre.

But I *could* take her to Ravensmuir.

I brightened at the prospect. It was perfect. My brother's widow, Ysabella, already had a young brother. Why not another child underfoot? The prospect of seeking aid from my brother's widow was daunting, since I had shamelessly deceived her when last we met, but surely she would feel compassion for a babe.

The sorry truth was that my past deeds could affect this adorable child's future, just as they had recently affected my own. That was not a comforting thought.

Perhaps I could abandon the girl at Ravensmuir's portal. She released my finger and gave me another toothless yet utterly charming smile. No, no, I would have to have Ysabella's sworn pledge to raise this infant with care. No less would do.

Perhaps the babe was hungry. I did not know what young children ate. Oh, babes suckled, I knew this, but I was not able to offer that particular choice.

How long could she survive without food?

How fast could I ride to Ravensmuir?

As I watched, the babe tightened her face again, though this time she did not cry out. She wrinkled her nose in a most delightful fashion and her cheeks pinkened. Her eyes closed tightly, as if she considered some philosophical matter deeply. I studied her, sensing that something was afoot, but did not comprehend the small sound that I heard emanate from her.

She smiled at me sunnily as a fetid smell rose from her swaddling. I choked on the fumes. Indeed, my eyes watered. I peeked and nearly lost whatever was in my own gut. I had not realized that a babe could make such a mess. I was not certain what to do about it.

Riding with all haste for Ravensmuir seemed the best course.

It took four days to reach the coast, and they were the four longest days of my life. The babe cried and fussed for the first day, straining against my grip. When we reached a river, I tried to clean her bottom, but she only made another mess before I was done. In the end, she looked worse than she had afore I tried to clean her—at least she had begun with her swaddling neatly arranged.

At first light in a tiny village, I charmed a maid who perched on a stool milking a stoic cow, then stole the bucket of milk when the maiden looked away. I sprinted back to the hidden babe and horse, and galloped several miles before halting to feed her. To my relief, the babe suckled heartily from the cloth I dipped into the milk.

Then she vomited upon my shoulder.

The second meal she seemed inclined to keep. She burped and hiccuped and howled the second day away, miring herself and taking solace solely from sucking upon my finger. I took the open road, uncaring whether any pursued me now or not. I had need of haste. I managed to get some water into her every few hours, and the occasional cup of milk.

Everything seemed to erupt into her swaddling in doubled quantities and with astonishing speed.

By the time I washed her on the third morning, her flesh was covered with an angry red rash. I was nigh mad with lack of sleep and worry for her survival.

The last time a child's fate had depended upon me, I had failed completely. I was determined not to repeat that particular sin.

When the babe ceased to cry at all, I realized that silence was far worse than her weeping. She would not even take my finger that afternoon. Her tiny face was pale and her eyes remained closed no matter how I sang or cajoled her.

Terrified that this soul entrusted to my care could be lost through my incompetence, I abandoned any thought of respite for the horse and rode through the night.

We reached the coast north of Ravensmuir just before the dawn.

Uncaring who saw me, I raced the horse along the cliffs, then dismounted before the furthest entry to the labyrinth that snaked beneath the keep. I led the horse into the darkness, whispering reassurances to it when it balked. There are a maze of tunnels beneath my family abode, a maze that I know as well as the shape of my own hand. It is disconcerting to step into dark tunnels, though, and more so for a horse. I nestled the silent child against my shoulder, and coaxed the horse onward.

The babe was a mess, I knew this, and would do little to charm Ysabella into accepting responsibility for her. I still had no idea how to best make this proposal, which was most unlike me. I like to be prepared, but the babe had consumed my every thought.

I carried her to a chamber directly below the keep where a warm stream trickled from the rock. The oil lanterns and flint were hidden where they always were, and I lit one lantern. I peeled off the babe's clothing gently and whispered to her, telling her tales of how fine a life she would have here at Ravensmuir even as I feared that Ysabella would refuse me.

"You must smile," I bade her. "Smiles soften hearts and yours could melt a stone. You must open your eyes and smile, just as you did to me."

The babe was despondent. Her flesh looked so swollen and sore that I almost wept. I swaddled her when I had washed her as best as I was able and lifted her to my shoulder again, touching her cheek with a fingertip. "You can charm them, I know this well. Come, grant me one small smile to show that you yet can."

I sang the ditty to her, but this time, she made no response. She settled her face against my palm and sighed, a single tear leaking from the corner of her closed eye.

"Sweet Jesus," I whispered in dismay as I gathered her closer. "What have I done?"

"I should think it quite evident what you have done," Merlyn said quietly from the shadows behind me.

I would have known my brother's voice anywhere, no less his ability to move as quietly as a cat. I struggled not to jump, though I knew Merlyn to be dead. I turned slowly, as if unsurprised by his presence, fearing that madness had claimed my wits in my exhaustion.

How much worse could it be to face a vengeful corpse?

Merlyn stood there, wreathed in shadows, and looking remarkably solid and hale for a specter.

My eyes narrowed at his smug smile. "There is nothing amusing about this."

"On the contrary, there is much amusing in finding you snared finally by the fruits of your own deeds."

"She is not mine!"

Merlyn smiled with disbelief.

"And you are said to be dead."

"Not yet, though I fear that truth may disappoint some." Merlyn gave me a quelling glance, but I held his gaze. He strolled closer, then frowned. His gentle touch had the babe's eyes opening so quickly that I was jealous of what he knew of children.

Merlyn looked at me, his gaze dark with accusation. "This child is gravely ill, Gawain. From whence did she come? Where is her mother, or did you cast her aside for the sake of the child?"

"The mother is dead."

"How charming," Merlyn said wryly. "I shall hope that you had no involvement in that." He plucked the babe from my grasp with enviable ease, as if I were incompetent beyond belief. His was the annoying manner of an older brother who knows best, and it irked me no less than it had when we were small. His frown deepened as he studied her. "God in heaven, Gawain, what have you done to this child?"

"Nothing!"

"Clearly. It is unlike even you to be so thoughtless."

"I did not know what to do with her or how to care for

her, so I brought her here." I straightened. "I hoped Ysabella would see fit to take the babe beneath her care."

Merlyn's quick glance only fortified my own doubts. "After your last deceit? My lady has a considerable dislike of you since you lied to her and deceived her."

"But surely, for the sake of the child . . ."

"If Ysabella agrees, she will accept the child from you, not for you."

"I do not care."

Merlyn studied me. "Why did you even seize the babe? What advantage did you hope to secure?"

"I did not seize her, nor was there any advantage I hoped to gain." I was disgusted by my brother's skepticism and my voice rose. "The grandmother mistook me for the child's father. I had no choice."

"You could have abandoned the child."

I spoke with resolve. "No, I could not."

Merlyn spoke carefully, as if testing me. "Of course you could have done so. People abandon children all the time. Babes are left at monasteries and churches every day of the year."

"Nonetheless, I could not do it." I felt him watch me as I lifted a finger to the babe's cheek. "Will she recover?"

Silence grew between us as my brother studied me. "It has been said that it would be a cold day in hell that you gave a care for any other than yourself," Merlyn mused.

I shivered elaborately, then met his gaze in challenge.

He smiled. "Do you not think it somewhat harsh to refer to our family abode as hell?"

"It has been no heaven to me."

"Whose deeds ensured as much?"

"The past is of no matter now, Merlyn. What is of concern is this child. She could have perished. She is so small and fragile." The babe made an effort to smile at my touch, the expression wrenching my heart. "Do you think she will survive?"

Merlyn watched me, apparently incredulous.

"I do not know," he said finally, his voice softer than it had been before. "But what of Michel? Does he not yet trot at your side like a loyal hound? Or did he become disenchanted with you when he learned you had not hung the stars and the moon?"

I looked away, my mood newly grim at this untimely and unwelcome reminder. My words were tight, my voice unfamiliar to me. "Michel died."

Silence stretched long between us, and I felt the urge to fidget beneath Merlyn's gaze. I had heard others complain that his stillness made them believe that he could read their very thoughts, though I had always been immune to Merlyn's ploys.

Until this day.

I thought I might scream in frustration by the time he finally sighed and shook his head. "Another casualty of your fleeting interest?"

"Leave it be!" I snapped.

Merlyn's eyes widened briefly at my rare show of emotion before he shrugged. "Michel's death is most unfortunate. He was a charming boy, if somewhat untrustworthy."

I flinched and I have no doubt that Merlyn noted that he had found a wound. When I said nothing further, he turned and walked toward one of the tunnels, the babe cuddled against his chest. "Extinguish the lanterns and bring your horse."

"Then you will aid her?"

"The choice is not mine and you know that well." He disappeared into the shadows, sure-footed and silent.

Belatedly, it seemed somewhat of a poor idea to have tricked my tempestuous and outspoken sister-in-law.

"I would make a wager with you, Merlyn!" I cried impulsively. It seemed suddenly critical to somehow win his favor, at least. I had no doubt that he could sway Ysabella if he so chose. "For your pledge to raise the babe with care, I would return the *Titulus Croce* to you."

It was not what I had intended to say, but once the words passed my lips, I had no desire to rescind them. Merlyn must have pivoted, for I heard the grind of his boots upon the stone. He stepped briskly out of the shadows and halted before me, his gaze searching mine.

"Let me see it," he said crisply.

"We should make haste. . . ."

"Forgive me, but I doubt that you even possess it any longer. You have been known to concoct a lie to suit your own needs, Gawain."

My fingers must have been cold, for I fumbled with the flap of my saddlebag in my haste to open it. I grasped the bundle there in both hands and offered it to my brother, like a supplicant before a vengeful deity.

Merlyn's expression was stony. "Unwrap it," he said.

I did so, my hands shaking. The wrappings fell away and I stared in shock at my so-called prize.

Merlyn made a sound of disgust, then turned upon his heel once more. "Even now, you would try to deceive me," he said with undisguised annoyance. "At least, you might have offered a decent forgery. What manner of fool do you take me to be?"

Then Merlyn was gone, leaving me holding this remarkably crude forgery of the *Titulus*. I had not stolen this, this *thing*, I knew that well. I had checked the wrapped relic when I removed it from the church's sanctuary and it had been the genuine *Titulus*.

My prize had been exchanged while the bag was out of my possession, either by the thugs or by the old alewife.

Undoubtedly the exchange had been done at Evangeline's command. How galling that she had distracted me with mere lust, the oldest trick known to man! I was disgusted with myself far more than I was with her.

Indeed, I felt a shred of admiration for the lady's cunning.

I swore, flung the useless piece of wood aside, then hastened after Merlyn. The exchange was a trick worthy of one of my own deceptions! How humiliating to have the jest played upon me—how untimely to have Merlyn think my estimation of him so low. Had there not been a child's survival at stake, I might have found it amusing that Evangeline had outwitted me so adeptly—again.

But I had to ensure the care of my ward, and quickly. Ysabella would have no qualms in refusing, simply because I was the one who asked for her favor, and Merlyn would certainly now be less inclined to argue for me. I would need all my charm.

And perhaps one of my babe's endearing smiles.

My lips set grimly as I marched toward the keep. Matters were not resolved betwixt Evangeline and I, that much was clear.

A Cornered Queen

Evangeline

VII

March, 1372

I stand in the small cemetery outside of Inverfyre's walls. A glistening half moon pours silver light upon the ground and the carved stones. I can see my objective clearly. There is only one stone I visit, one stone that draws my footsteps in sleep.

The tree boughs are barren overhead, black veins against the deep blue of the sky. A wind begins to gust as I walk and the branches clatter above me.

Like bones rolling in a grave, fighting to rise anew.

It is cold, colder than Hell could ever be, as my father used to say. He had a vision of Hell not as fiery torment, but as relentless cold. He spoke of Hell's denizens slowly turning blue, losing digits and then limbs. Immortal but doomed, they were condemned to suffer frostbite and cold for all eternity.

His was a vision wrought of a lifetime in a northern clime, of grey winters, of empty larders and emp-

tier bellies, of bloodless fingertips and lost toes, of falling asleep so cold that one half wishes to never awaken.

I hear his dire predictions once again as the chill permeates my bones, as I make my way to his grave. Surely my father never learned whether his vision was the truth?

Or is Hell to be compelled to endure one's own worst fear forever, each to his own as it were?

A peregrine cries—inevitably, for this is Inverfyre—the shadow of her outstretched wings passing over me. I shiver and hasten on, nearly falling into the hole before my father's stone.

His grave is open. It is always open in my dreams, not as if freshly dug but as if my father forced his way out of his dark prison. I recoil as always I do, stepping back into some soft mire that nigh stops my heart. A scream sticks in my throat. Being struck mute in the face of disaster is my deepest terror and I taste it yet again.

I spin, intending to flee, and halt at the specter come silently to stand behind me. I recognize it immediately.

It is my father, or some rotted replica of my father. The fine garments in which he was buried hang from his flesh, nay, the flesh hangs from his very bones. The bones themselves glow in the moonlight, discernible through the gaping flesh. Clumps of dirt hang from his hands; soil is embedded beneath his uncommonly long nails.

But despite the similarities, it is not my father. The eye sockets of his skull are filled with yawning emptiness. There is not a spark of his soul here, in torment *or otherwise. Bile rises in my throat as this half-rotted obscenity, this man dead but not dead, raises a hand toward me.*

I almost take a step back, then check myself, recalling the open grave in time.

He laughs with my father's laugh, and I shudder that the familiar merry sound should emanate from this monstrosity. His teeth rattle in accompaniment to his laughter, rotten flesh slides further from his temple.

"No," I whisper. "No." I edge sideways, for this cannot be the fate of my beloved father.

He pursues me, without appearing to move. "Wicked Evangeline, wicked child," he whispers, his voice echoing from all sides. He grows impossibly larger, his voice increasing in volume. Condemnation resonates in every word that issues from the foul hole of his mouth. "I know what you have done!"

I turn and run, stumbling over my feet, my hem, the stones, the tufts of winter-deadened plants. I feel the cold of his pursuit, feel his darkness embrace me, hear his words echo inside my very skull even as his dank chill engulfs me. I choke on the fetid air of rotted flesh and wet soil. I seize the portal of the keep with desperate fingers.

"I know what you have done, daughter mine!" he cries, the words raising to an unearthly howl. "And for this sin, you will pay!"

I awakened abruptly in my own bed, heart pounding, sweat trickling down my back. The stone portal in my dreams proved to be no more than my linens, my knuckles white from the tightness of my grip upon salvation. The rasp

of my uneven breathing filled my achingly familiar chamber
and I realized with relief that I was alone.

A pale sunbeam made its way through the window and
gilded a square upon the cold floor. The hunting horn
sounded again in the distance, awakening Fergus' men, and
I heard the falcons cry out in anticipation of fresh kill.

It was early, early enough that only hunters and hounds
were stirring. Fergus was gone from my bed because he had
left the morning before to hunt for three days.

I lay back, closed my eyes and fingered my lip. It stung
still, though was not as swollen as I had feared.

It would seem that men, alive or dead, left me with few
choices, then condemned me for whatever solution I found.
This was my thanks, for showing the decisiveness of a man,
for doing the labor of a man, for collecting the due that
should have been collected by a man.

I had had two recurring dreams this winter, and I far preferred the one featuring a golden-haired scoundrel with lust
in his eye and seduction in his touch, even if it did leave me
red with shame upon awakening.

Just the thought of Gawain forced me from the bed, the
site of my deception. I washed with haste, relieved to be able
to avoid Fiona's attentions. No doubt there was a bruise
upon my lip and she—as Fergus' cousin—would delight in
telling me that I had gotten solely what I deserved. She had
left the basin of water in my chamber the night before,
because she was too lazy to do any deed in the morn, and for
once I was glad of its icy chill.

Still my father's accusation of sinfulness echoed in my
thoughts, condemning me.

And yet unfair for all its core of truth. How I yearned to
argue with him, to persuade him that my choice had been no
choice but the sole chance of fulfilling his and my mother's

expectations! But my father had heeded no challenge to his conclusions while he lived, and I heartily doubted that death had changed that trait.

Still, I was irked. I had been taught from the cradle that the greater good had to prevail, that the needs of the many outweighed the desires of the individual. How dare my father haunt me for heeding his own counsel!

Had he not been the one to teach me to play chess, to teach me that one sometimes must sacrifice a lesser piece in order to protect the king?

And what lesser piece was there than a daughter who had not had the wits to be born a son? I flung down the washing cloth impatiently, restless with my lot, chafing with the tedious rota of duties that lay before me this morn.

Every morning. From the morn of my tenth birthday until the day I breathed my last, I was responsible for an endless array of tasks, none of which were important enough to merit praise when well done, all of which contributed to the sustenance of this keep, every one of which kept me as busy and fettered as a falcon tied to its post with a bone to worry.

When I rummaged discontentedly in my trunk for a clean chemise, a finger of sunlight touched the pomegranate forgotten in the corner, burnishing its leathery skin to a gleam.

It was as if my thoughts had coaxed the fruit into sight. I stared at it. I had not truly forgotten about it—although I had tried. It seemed a portent that it came to light on this day, on this day that I felt reckless and unappreciated. The pomegranate was smaller and harder than it had been, and I wondered whether it had spoiled.

I fetched my knife and sliced it open, gasping at the spill of glistening ruby pearls. They were as dark as blood and shone like jewels. I ate half a dozen off the blade of the knife, the pungent taste making me close my eyes and revel in a forbidden memory.

Gawain. I saw again his golden skin, the ripple of muscle beneath his smooth flesh, the sun-drenched spill of his hair. I saw the mischievous glint in his green eyes, the quirk of his lips just afore he smiled, the rumble of his laughter when my fingertips lay across his chest.

And I smiled. He was an impossibly handsome man, his wit quick, his charm dangerously engaging. I had never met the like of him—and though I knew him to be a scoundrel, I had not been able to resist his allure. I had been enchanted when he spoke with such passion of the home he desired in Sicily. I had liked that he asked me about Aphrodite as if a woman could know something of merit. I had told myself that I seduced him the second time solely to suit my greater scheme, but the truth was that I could not have resisted his touch once he stood in my chamber.

My plan to distract Gawain in the most primitive way imaginable and thus retrieve the *Titulus* had been simple, hastily concocted, impetuous and for the greater good of Inverfyre. It had been unspeakably bold, and I had felt a wicked tide of delight in my own scheme's success. I had not, however, expected matters to become so complicated.

More to the point, I had not expected to *like* Gawain Lammergeier. I had not expected desire to unfurl within me when he caressed me. I had not known that any woman could feel such ardor. I had never imagined that matters between a man and woman could be so sweet, so tender, so exhilarating. I had not known that I could be so wanton, so bold and so unrestrained in my response.

I had briefly been another woman, one without cares, one filled with passion, one I could envy even as I disapproved of her comport. It was no wonder he had invited me to be his harlot—I had behaved as one with astonishing ease.

Indeed, I was yet amazed that this wanton and I were one and the same. The taste of pomegranate recalled—with unwelcome clarity—the rasp of Gawain's tongue upon my nipples, his kisses upon my belly, the sweet stickiness of the fruit's juice upon my flesh. I caught my breath in memory of the loveplay we had made and my mouth, despite the fruit within it, went dry.

He had made it so easy to forget that I had no right to have any desires beyond those demanded of me by my birthright. He had made it so easy to believe that my fate was unfairly cast.

And still, I could not shake my conviction of that. Three months I had listened and watched for him, knowing I should not. Three months I had expected a reckoning over my last victorious possession of the *Titulus*, three months I had hoped for a rousing conclusion to our game.

But he was gone as surely as the previous summer's fruit. Worse, I knew that I should have anticipated as much. Did I not understand the manner of man he was?

The juice found the cut inside my swollen lip and stung mightily, reminding me to use the wits with which I had been born. Men like Gawain Lammergeier saw only to their own pleasures and their own rewards. He was a thief and a scoundrel, a man whose absence I should not mourn and whose temptations I should not heed. Our interval had been sweet solely because it had been short, solely because I had wanted nothing from him that he had not been prepared to give.

I cast the pomegranate from the window, newly vexed by men. I tried to clean the ruby stains of fruit juice from my fingers, but to no avail. Like Gawain himself, its stain was not so readily shed as that.

I reached into the chest of garments, but my hand strayed away from my fine wool gown, seemingly of its own accord, and landed upon my old homespun kirtle with its faded woad dye. It was the most ancient and disreputable gown I owned. Fergus loathed it. I loved its softness, but ceded to his demand.

Not on this day. Defiance rose hot within me, rebellion and recklessness fast on its heels. The truth was that I felt somewhat disloyal to my spouse this morn. I touched my wounded lip with the tip of my tongue, then donned the kirtle.

Its weight upon my back seemed to feed my defiance. It was true that I had made unconventional choices, it was true that the men in my life had left me cornered, it was true that I was yet convinced that I had served the greater good.

I would visit Adaira and ask her counsel, she who made only choices that defied convention, she who was reputed to be able to see the future, she who my mother had bade me seek out.

It was an impulsive thought, and one I knew I should forget. But the prospect was too deliciously forbidden for me to resist on this morn. It was early, too early for lazy Fiona to stop me.

Further, the snow had melted away and I could leave no trail in the snow to condemn either Adaira or me. Fergus could not disapprove of what he did not know. His male kin had all ridden to the hunt with him, and they were the ones most inclined to whisper in his ear of my transgressions.

It seemed Dame Fortune was on my side. I braided my hair and tucked the braid into my chemise, for my midnight tresses would be readily recognized. I wound my homespun cloak around me and left my chamber on stealthy feet.

To my delight, there were few souls in the hall, all of them taking advantage of the laird's absence to sleep late. I slipped through them unobserved and darted down the path to the woods.

As I ran, my heart began to sing. I was free of Inverfyre's walls, free without approval or a chaperon. The sun shone with vigor, the sky was the cleanest blue imaginable and there was a promise of spring in the wind.

I fairly danced along the forest path with an abandon I had not felt since I had welcomed Gawain between my thighs. Though I was late to defiance, I liked it well.

The forest spreads like a carpet below Inverfyre's high tower, and appears endless to one who gazes down upon it from the high walls. In truth, it is riddled with paths and streams. It is here that old Adaira makes her home.

There was a time when my mother and I came often to see the old wise woman, a time when I knew the path to her abode as well as the lines in my own hand. That had changed one day, changed so suddenly and with such finality that even as a child I had known better than to question it.

Adaira's is a hut in the deepest shadows of the forest, a shadow itself which any soul could easily walk past without seeing it. I had not been here in at least a decade, not for two decades with my mother, so was uncommonly pleased when I found my way directly there.

I hesitated just a step from the door, my hand already raised to knock. Perhaps, Adaira would not welcome me. Perhaps, my absence had insulted her.

I wondered at the wisdom of my visit, but it was too late.

"My lady?" she said softly, the sound of her voice making gooseflesh on my skin. Though I have known her since my childhood, she never calls me by my name.

My mother always said that the blind see more than the sighted, for their vision is in another realm. So it seems with Adaira. Her eyes are glazed with that bluish hue of thin milk and she holds her head oddly, but she always faces the person she addresses, even when the person has moved silently. When she fixes her blind stare upon me, her lips twisted in a cunning smile, I feel that she can see the secrets of my heart.

It is a most unsettling sensation.

My mother had also said that Adaira had been an uncommon beauty in her youth. I could recall none of this, for she had been blind and old even when I was a child. Her eyes still fascinated and repelled me.

I stood on the threshold, reluctant to invite myself into her abode. "I would ask for your counsel, Adaira."

She nodded but once, then stepped back into the hut, leaving the door open between us. After a moment, I chose to enter, though I was uncertain how welcome I was. I shut the door of the hut and the shadows closed around me like an embrace.

Adaira said nothing, but stirred the contents of her old iron pot, which was set over the glowing coals of an old fire. The hut smelled of precisely the same pleasant mix of earth and damp and nameless herbs as always it had.

Not for the first time, I had the whimsical thought that there was no passage of time in this hut, that I interrupted her at the same moment over and over again. Adaira was waiting for me, as always she had been. Time might not have passed in this place. That was foolery indeed, for I knew that I was both older and taller, that at least a decade had slipped away since last I stood here.

"Counsel, from me?"

"Perhaps wisdom is a better word," I said. "I have been compelled to make uncommon choices, as you oft have done, and am uncertain."

Adaira chuckled at this, then bent over her pot. "Come here and take a deep breath."

I did as I was bidden. It is pointless to defy Adaira's commands and even more pointless to ask her any question outright.

I inhaled the rich scent of what seemed to be a rabbit stew, then stepped back to regard her with surprise. "I have never known you to eat meat."

"And still I do not."

"Where is Annelise?" I asked, peering again into the hut's shadowy but vacant corners. "Does she yet abide with you? Or has she wed and moved away?"

Adaira's lips tightened. "Annelise is dead."

My lips parted, though no sound came forth. The old woman seemed to watch me struggle with this news, her expression shrewd. "I am sorry. I did not know. . . ."

"A year ago, she died birthing a child got upon her by a man I will not name."

"He did not wed her."

Adaira shrugged. "It is of no import. My daughter is dead either way."

Her manner was so final that I guessed the baby must have died as well. "You should have come to the village. . . ."

"And to what purpose? That others could mock me, the finest midwife in all of Christendom, yet one unable to save her own child? I would not give them the pleasure." She abruptly turned back to the stew. "I have prepared this for you," she said, her words so measured that I understood we would speak of Annelise no more.

Then I realized what she had said. I had never before eaten in Adaira's abode. "You knew I would come, even afore I did?"

"Some events are less a matter of personal choice than we would like to believe." She fetched a carved wooden bowl with the surety of one who knows her surroundings well, ladled a generous portion of stew into it and pressed the bowl into my hands. In truth, it smelled delicious, the meat stewed with wild onions. I had eaten nothing this morn and my belly growled.

She smiled thinly. "Sit. Eat."

I did as I was bidden, making short work of the unexpected feast. Adaira stirred the cauldron with such concentration that she might have been alone or unaware of my presence. I guessed that she mourned her daughter, for she and Annelise had been close.

When I put down the spoon, well sated, she spoke.

"Have you bled since Christmastide?"

I caught my breath. A child was both my greatest hope and my greatest fear, but Adaira spoke as casually as one might when discussing the hue of a cloak. I sat forward, desperate for whatever she might tell me, but spoke with care. "I seldom bleed in the winter, and have had false hope before."

Adaira smiled coyly. "Perhaps the hope is only false when you plant a withered seed."

How could she know of my digression? I swallowed before I could speak, and even though I decided she could not know the truth, my voice was strained. "I do not understand what you mean."

Adaira laughed and I understood then that she knew about Gawain, though still I could not imagine how she could be so certain.

Instead of asking what she would not answer, I asked what I most wanted to know. "Are you certain that I carry a child? Is it a boy?"

She snorted, then shook her head. "You and your mother. A son, a son, a son. It was all she asked of me when she ripened with you." Her voice turned harsh. "Whether it is a son or a daughter is of less import than if the child is hale."

I was duly chastened. "Of course, I did not mean to imply otherwise. . . ."

Adaira interrupted me with the old verse, her tone mocking.

When the seventh son of Inverfyre,
Saves his legacy from intrigue and mire,
Only then shall glorious Inverfyre,
Reflect in full its first laird's desire.

To my astonishment, she then spat into the embers of the fire.

I sat straighter, affronted. "Do you deny that it is time for the seventh son of Inverfyre? It is my duty to be the vessel for that prophesied child. . . ."

"You stole a man's seed to beget the boy you carry." Adaira clicked her tongue to chide me. "It is an ominous beginning to a life, to be the product of a woman's deceit."

"No one needs to know. . . ."

Adaira laughed harshly. "Will they not guess? I, an old madwoman living in the woods, have guessed the truth! Do you think that no one will whisper if the child is born fair of hair?" My heart leapt in terror. "You are all dark, all of you of Inverfyre."

"Fergus' hair is ruddy. It may have been fair when he was

a child," I argued with resolve. "All will be too relieved to ask questions."

"People *always* ask questions," she said tartly. "It is in our nature to not believe whatsoever we are told to be fact."

"What else was I to do?" I demanded in frustration. "Five years I have been wed, and five years I have been barren. I saw a chance to conceive a child and I took it, though it is true that I did not consider the hue of the man's hair."

"Was that your sole reason to couple with that stranger?"

I flushed, though she could not see it.

Adaira laughed harshly. "You thought to use a man, as men use women every day, to use him, achieve your ends and then discard him. Do not deny that you thought to indulge your curiosity as well. But you are no fool, my lady. You cannot have believed that there would not be repercussions for your deed."

"I thought all would be relieved. . . ."

Adaira cleared her throat and interrupted me. "Do not mistake my warnings for more than what they are. I intend only to counsel you against folly. There are those who despise you, who would find pleasure in ensuring your fall."

That was more true than I would have preferred.

"There are those who would hurt you apurpose," she said, then touched my wounded lip with a gnarled fingertip. She moved so unerringly that I could not evade her. I do not doubt that she felt me flinch. "Why did Fergus do this?"

I was not surprised that she knew who had granted the blow. "I touched him more boldly than is my wont," I admitted grimly. "I thought we might find pleasure together."

"And so your deed already shows its price. You have had a taste of what can be, and it has spoiled your appetite for what you have."

I averted my gaze. It is true that men go to whores to find

pleasure. It is unseemly for a noblewoman to enjoy her bedding.

I knew all of this, though Fergus had reminded me after he struck me. I had forgotten my place, he had said, and my place was upon my back, with my legs spread wide. Submissive, silent and supine—the cut from his ring would remind me of what I should not have forgotten in the first place.

I could blame Gawain for teaching me of matters I would have been better not to know. But no. I was glad to know that lovemaking could be sweet, even if it gave me another reason to loathe my spouse.

"I grow no younger, Adaira."

"Nor does Fergus."

Her tone was so ominous that I suspected she knew something I did not. I leaned forward and caught at her hand. "Can you see the future, Adaira? What do you know? Tell me what you glimpse."

She was silent for so long that I feared she would not heed me.

"I see that you have erred," Adaira finally said. Her words fell so softly that the hair upon my neck prickled. "You have meddled in matters beyond your comprehension, you have done what no other might have anticipated you would do. You have loosed something that should not have been loosed—and like a scent released from a stoppered vial, it will not be readily recaptured again. With your choice, you have added a new thread to the tapestry being woven at Inverfyre."

"What tapestry? I do not understand."

She wove her fingers together, mimicking the warp and weft of cloth. "All of our deeds and words weave together to shape the future. Each choice changes what will be, just as each new thread changes the final appearance of a tapestry."

"But . . ."

"Long ago, you were wild and carefree, a girl so bold she might have been a boy. Then you were taught your place, as a wild colt is taught to bear the saddle willingly. The impetuous child disappeared, some would have said forever. Some, more observant perhaps, would have glimpsed that your willingness to defy convention was but thinly veiled. You came to be quiet, dignified, solemn and demure. As your mother was, on the surface, but without her serenity within."

I cast my gaze down to my hands, guilty.

"It is not your fault, my lady, that you are wrought as you are. The blood of your forebear, Magnus Armstrong, courses strong in your veins—he was said to accept no obstacle to his ambitions. I warned your mother about this when you were young, for a rebellious woman is doomed to woe, and perhaps she labored overmuch to eliminate this facet of your nature."

I recalled my mother's sudden ferocity that I behave with decorum and understood her intent as never I had. "She never understood why I could not be more docile, more like her."

Adaira shook her head. "What lies within must show without. It is only a matter of time. Against the expectations of many, you have found the willful child in the woman. Your goal is noble, but your choice has opened the portal to many possibilities."

"You make it seem most dire."

She sighed. "Your heart is good, my lady, though you underestimate those around you. You see the goodness in them and neglect the wickedness, even when you do spy it."

"I do not think . . ."

"I cooked the hare for you for a reason," she said firmly, her tone brooking no interruption. "It is not my habit to consume meat, but this morn I found a hare outside my door. It had been sorely wounded some time ago, probably last evening, and still it suffered from the two arrows embedded in its flesh."

I looked up at her then, horrified. "But it was still alive?"

"Still alive, still filled with pain." She grimaced. "They come to me for aid oft times, the creatures of the woods, but I could not aid this one. The wounds were too grievous and too old. I spoke with it, then killed it quickly with its consent, rather than leaving it in anguish. I would not waste anything of this world, so I wrought a stew and a lesson of it."

The meat felt to be curdling in my innards, for I sensed that this lesson was for me and that I would not like its teaching.

"You have found a voice within yourself that you did not know existed. I would have you realize that others may also hide secrets. I would have you know that nothing is ever as it seems."

Adaira left my side and fetched something from the far side of the fire. She pushed bloodied arrow shafts into my hands, not caring how I recoiled from their familiarity.

Fergus took great pride in enumerating his kill, though it often was a feeble count, and had his arrows wrought distinctively so that there could be no mistake in the tally. The tuft of pheasant feathers and circles of red paint upon the shafts in my hand could have graced an arrow from no other quiver but his own.

Adaira's lips set to a thin line. "I would have you know what manner of man you have wed, my lady."

VIII

"You do not know that Fergus loosed them!" I leapt to my feet and flung the arrow shafts to the ground. "Some other hunter might have used his arrows."

Adaira snorted. "Does your lord share his weaponry?"

I said nothing. He would not do so willingly, not after he expended such pride and coin upon having them made thus.

"What manner of a man, my lady, turns his back upon the suffering of an innocent creature that he has maimed, one that he has wounded for no better reason than his own amusement?"

"Many men hunt," I said woodenly. "Many men bring meat to the board in this way."

"An honorable hunter finishes what he has begun."

"The hare might have fled into brush where it could not be pursued," I argued. "You do not know what happened."

"Do I not? Perhaps the hare told me that they made sport of it, that they laughed at its wounds and the prospect of its slow death." Adaira turned her back upon me, overwhelmed with her anger.

I did not doubt her word for a moment. Still, I felt compelled to defend my spouse against her lesson. "Fergus savors comfort and the hunt, a hind of meat and a cup of ale. He is a harmless old man so long as he has comfort. You do not know him at all."

"I know all I need to know." She turned to her cauldron. "You should be aware that you know less than you need to know."

"Fergus is old and feeble and weak, but he is not cruel," I insisted.

Adaira spun and touched my lip again. "How many times must you have the lesson?"

"He was vexed with me. . . ." My words faded and I fell silent, unpersuaded but knowing she would not be swayed.

"You are graceless to argue this matter, my lady. I only give you a warning." Adaira picked up the arrow shafts and pushed them back into my hands, then her voice fell to a whisper. "What would such a man do if he learned that his wife had made him a cuckold?"

"But Fergus wants a son!"

"Perhaps you are right." Adaira smiled coolly. "But once he has his son, what need has he of a faithless wife?"

I stood there for the longest time, but she clearly had nothing more to say to me. And I feared that if I parted my lips I would utter something even more disloyal than what I had already said—that I loathed my spouse, for example, or that I was glad to have conceived a child by Gawain.

Would the babe be as fair and as finely wrought as its sire? My senses flooded suddenly with the recollection of Gawain, as if his touch had been seared into my flesh. I remembered how he had accepted all I offered and willingly granted all that I had demanded, how he had no expectations of how I should demurely lay back and provide only a repository for his seed.

I heated from head to toe in recollection, then made the mistake of glancing at Adaira.

"If you are as clever as I know you to be, you will drink this afore you go to sleep this night." Adaira pressed a vial into my hand that did not clutch the arrow shafts.

The vial was wrought of heavy green glass, its surface mottled. The glass itself was unevenly blown and filled with bubbles. Some murky viscous liquid swirled within it.

My stomach roiled again, even though I did not remove the stopper. This dark juice would smell of earth and rot, of darkness and shadows, of matters of the forest best left unobserved. My tongue would recoil from its rank perfume, my innards would roil at its approach.

I knew well what its effect upon me, upon my child, would be.

"No!" I tried to give it back to Adaira, without success. "I will not kill my child!"

Instead of heeding this laudable sentiment, she shook her fist at me. "Then perhaps you condemn it instead. Is that more kind, my lady? To bring a child to life only to watch its demise? Perhaps you and your spouse have more in common than I believed. Perhaps you both prefer to see a matter half resolved, to leave the difficult labor to another. Who will raise this child if your spouse sees fit to kill you? Who will warn this child of all the dangers ahead?"

I was suddenly cold then, as cold as if I stood knee-deep in snow, and my arms stole around my still-flat belly. "No one will kill me. No one will kill my child. No one would dare. I am the daughter of Inverfyre."

. "You are so like your father! You refuse to see the audacity of others. This child should not be born, not now. You summon a soul to life and breath before his time and the repercussions for him will be more dire than you can believe."

"You said 'him.'" My heart skipped.

Adaira snorted. "Of what import? This son comes too soon."

"Inverfyre has need of a son now," I whispered.

Adaira turned her back upon me, leaving the chills running up my spine. I waited for a long moment, fingering the vial and the arrow shafts, but she did not acknowledge my presence, or the righteousness of my choices.

"You will see yourself proven wrong in this," I insisted. She did not reply. I turned without another word and left.

No sooner had I crossed her threshold than I dropped the vial into the undergrowth, knowing I would never consume its contents. Indeed, my hand cupped my stomach once again and I smiled to myself. I did not doubt Adaira's assertion.

I would bear Gawain's son. For that, I had no regrets.

I reached my chamber without being noticed, only realizing once I was there that I still clutched the two cursed arrow shafts. I hastened to the window and cast them toward the forest, glad to be rid of them. I watched them tumble through the air until they were out of sight as I wiped my hands upon my old kirtle.

I turned at some small sound and froze when I saw Fiona standing just inside the door. She had not spared a knock to announce herself and her expression was sly, as if she had caught me in the midst of some crime.

Irritation rose within me at her presumption. "Fiona, I have asked you often to knock afore you enter."

She smiled coolly. She was of Fergus's kin and owed her

role in the household to him. She knew as well as I that I could do nothing to evict her—and we both knew that there were times that we could have been happy never seeing each other again. Fiona always had a disapproving air, as if the failing fortunes of Inverfyre were the fault of the weaknesses of its ruling family, as if all would come aright if Fergus and his family could rid the halls of the last of the Armstrongs.

If they could rid themselves of *me*. I was very aware of Adaira's warning as I met this older woman's gaze. I had always assumed that no one shared Fiona's attitude toward me, but could Adaira be right?

"Have you secrets to hide from a loyal servant, then, my lady?" Fiona asked archly.

Events of the morn sharpened my tongue. "Of course not. I am simply surprised that with your wealth of rules to be followed that such a simple gesture of respect is not among the list."

She marched into the room, reaching to lift my cloak from my shoulders. "You are shrewish this day. Were you plagued by bad dreams?"

"No."

"But you have been out of your chambers without an escort. Fergus will not be pleased to hear of it."

"I donned the cloak because I was cold," I lied, then looked her straight in the eye, fairly daring her to recount this bit of news to Fergus. "I am certain my husband would find such a morsel unworthy of his attention. He has many more compelling matters to attend these days than the temperature of his wife's flesh."

Her eyes narrowed slightly, but she tightened her lips as if biting back a retort. She might have said nothing, but her gaze dropped to my robe and she gasped aloud.

I glanced down and saw that the pomegranate juice was still upon my hands. Additionally, there was an arching russet stain across my hip from wiping my hand there.

"I stumbled," I lied. "It is nothing."

"Let me wash your wound."

"Do not trouble yourself. It is nothing, as I said." I hastened to the pitcher of cold water still upon the floor from my morning wash and poured some of the water out into a bowl. The cursed juice would still not come from my hands.

I recalled belatedly that I had extinguished the brazier when I left this morn. It was cold in the chamber by this point, which probably fed Fiona's skepticism that I had been here all this time.

The juice and rabbit blood in the wool was difficult to coax from the fibers. I could fairly taste Fiona's curiosity but I was determined to share no secrets with her.

"Perhaps you should change, my lady, that I might wash your kirtle."

"I can see to it, Fiona, though I thank you for your offer." To my relief, the stain slowly loosened from the wool.

"If you stumbled in the solar and managed to injure yourself so badly, I am certain that my lord Fergus would wish to know of it," she said slyly.

"Just as I am certain he would not wish to be troubled by such meager woes." I granted her a cool glance. "Was there a reason that you sought me out, Fiona?"

"Of course, of course." She bowed now, a rare show of respect which roused my own suspicion. "A missive came for you and the messenger insisted that it be delivered with all haste. In fact, he wished to see it into your hands himself, but I forbade such familiarity from a stranger." She inclined her head, offering a bundle tied with a scarlet ribbon.

It was a package wrought of parchment, a cleverly folded

square clearly intended to secure something within the missive itself. It had weight and an ungainly lump in its center. I turned it in my hands, mystified, especially as it was addressed to me.

Lady Evangeline of Inverfyre.

The script was bold. I had no doubt that this confident stroke of ink had been wrought by a man. The folding roused further suspicions, as did the ribbon and the parchment itself. This was a fine package, one wrought with the uncommon flair of one who had traveled far and wide.

One who was accustomed to ensuring that his packages surrendered their secrets to the recipient's eyes alone.

The hair upon my nape prickled and I fancied that I could feel the warmth of a certain man's fingers still upon the parcel.

"Is it a missive from a lover, my lady?" Fiona teased, a gleam in her eye.

"Of course not!" I granted her my most confident smile. "I cannot imagine who would dispatch such a missive to me, or why."

She eased closer. "Perhaps you should open it, for the answer might lie within."

I knew that she wanted to know what was within the parcel—in truth, I was surprised that the seal upon it had not already been broken in some supposed accident. It was a testament to the folding of the parchment and the precise knotting of the ribbon that the parcel could not be opened without evidence being left of the deed. I yearned to open it in privacy.

I knew, however, that if I banished Fiona from my presence while I opened this, she would spread a fabricated tale of its contents, a tale that would better suit her than me.

Thus I smiled, and cut the ribbon with my knife. "Indeed, you speak the truth," I said. I unfolded the parchment before her very eyes and only just snatched the jewel from the air before it fell to the floor.

Fiona gasped, but I simply stared at the marvel cradled in the palm of my hand. My blood ran cold for the second time this morn.

It was a crucifix, wrought of amber stones, each the size of my thumbnail and of almost identical hue to each other. Seven of them formed the vertical axis. The third from the top was the juncture, two more added on either side of it to form the horizontal arms of the cross. The stones were set in silver, a garnet mounted on either side at each place amber met amber. The piece was a marvel, not because I had never seen the like, but because I knew it well.

It had been my mother's most prized possession.

I would have known it anywhere. There could not be two. This crucifix had been my mother's dowry from her own parents, a legacy of a long family tradition. As eldest daughter, the ornament had been promised to her and she had pledged in turn to continue the tradition.

I recalled with painful clarity the day that she had draped its chain around my own neck, letting me touch it as the sunlight danced in the amber.

"This will be your dowry, Evangeline," my mother had whispered. "When a man claims your heart and your hand, you shall wear this for your wedding day."

I blinked back unbidden tears and closed my fingers tightly over the ornament. For it had not graced my neck when I wed Fergus. By then, it was long gone. This gem had not been seen in Inverfyre for fifteen years.

My mother's pride had been stolen, on the same night as my father's pride, the *Titulus*, **rode** south in the saddlebag of a guest and his son.

No thief could have planned to steal the lifeblood of my parents so adeptly. The loss of this heirloom had removed the color from my mother's cheeks, it had shaken her faith in my father's ability to protect her, it had made her question the divine goodness of the deity to whom she prayed daily.

I released a shaking breath, only then realizing that I was shaking with anger at one man's audacity.

"What a gift!" cooed Fiona.

"It is no gift to return what was the recipient's own," I said fiercely. When she glanced to me in surprise at my fervor, I glared back at her. It was shocking how readily Gawain could coax my blood to boil. "It is a taunt, no more than that."

"But who . . .?"

Even my words shook, falling in tremors from my lips. "A thief and a scoundrel sent this to me, upon that you can rely."

"But what of the missive itself?"

In my dismay, I had forgotten that there might be a message inscribed on the parchment as well. I unfurled it hastily, my eyes narrowing as I read the text.

> *Never let it be said that I failed to understand the secret desire of a lady's heart.*

The shameless cur!

"Where is the messenger who brought this missive?" I crumbled the message in my fist, then stood as tall and frosty as a queen. I was outraged that I should be mocked like this, but I knew with sudden certainty that Gawain would have entrusted this errand to none.

Why else would the messenger have asked to deliver the missive himself? No, he had brought it himself, so confident was he that his deed would escape repercussion, so certain was he that he could outwit any soul who confronted him.

I intended to prove his lofty assessment of himself wrong.

Again.

"He takes a respite at the board."

"Bring him to me." I turned to change my garb, dismissing Fiona with a gesture, then thought better of it when she inhaled in disapproval.

"My lady, it would be most improper!"

I almost laughed. There was little improper that Gawain and I could do together that we had not already done, though Fiona knew nothing of that. Her objection, though, made me think better of my course. Knowing Gawain, he might have seized an opportunity to collect the *Titulus*, and this time, I had not been prepared for his presence.

I pivoted, giving her the appearance of a concession, and forced a thin smile. "How kind of you to remind me of such details. Truly, I forgot myself in my annoyance."

"You know this piece?" Fiona eased closer, her expression revealing her lust for gossip.

"Clearly." I strode past her, savoring her dissatisfaction with my reply. Her gaze flicked over me, her curiosity roused by my heated response.

I reminded myself of the cool decorum I should exhibit, but could not make enough haste to the hall even so. As irked as I was, I had to admit that something crackled to life within me at Gawain's proximity. I felt vibrant as I had not of late. My thoughts were as clear as a spring lake, my reflexes alert, my body taut.

Indeed, I felt like a woman awakened from a long slumber, refreshed, invigorated, and prepared to whatever challenge this unpredictable man might cast my way.

If I had thought Gawain might don a disguise to visit the very abode he had robbed once successfully and once less so, I had called the matter wrong. Similarly, if I had expected him to cower in the shadows, I would have been disappointed. He sat, nay, he *lounged*, in Inverfyre's hall, his back against the far wall, his gaze locked upon the stairs to the solar.

He dressed with the flair of one accustomed to fine garb: his tabard was of emerald silk and I had no doubt that the color had been deliberately chosen to match the hue of his eyes. His chausses were black, his boots blacker still and even from a distance I could discern the fine quality of foreign leather.

His cloak was a marvel, wrought long and full, cut from wool so dark that it seemed he had the midnight sky thrown across his shoulders. The shade made his hair gleam brightest gold in contrast and showed his tanned skin to advantage. The cloak was lined with miniver, silken silvery pelts that looked thick and soft.

Gawain was as magnificent a man as I recalled. His shoulders were broad, his legs long, his languid ease not disguising his strength and vigor. His hands were elegant, long-fingered and tanned, and he held a cup of ale with easy grace. His golden hair gleamed in the light of the hall, a smile teased his firm lips, his eyes twinkled with barely contained amusement as he watched those around him.

Lust lit in my innards like a flame, startling me with its

intensity. Three months of coupling dutifully with an old man had seemed an eternity. Three months of feeling heat kindle deep within me at just the memory of what we had done, three months of savoring the fading scent of Gawain's flesh upon my linens had left me starving for more of his touch.

There is something glorious about a man with confidence, a man who can sit in the midst of his enemy's lair with the ease of one with no concerns, a man indeed who has the audacity to invite himself fearlessly into the very core of that lair. It was not because Gawain was a fool—on the contrary, it was because he had a scheme, and doubtless a brilliantly conceived one.

Something had required that he be gone for three months. I was ridiculously pleased that he had returned to match wits with me—then annoyed with myself for forgetting the provocation of his taunting me with my mother's own jewel.

Gawain paused in that moment, in the act of lifting a cup of ale to his lips, and his gaze found mine. We both froze. It seemed to me that a cord drew taut between us and the hall grew warmer from the heat of our locked gazes.

There was a glimmer in his eyes, one that resonated of the same vigor I felt in his presence, and the realization that we held this awareness in common brought a flush to my cheeks. My mouth went dry as I greedily sought changes in his appearance.

His hair had grown slightly. He had found sun wherever he had been, for his skin was more golden a hue than it had been when last we met.

Sicily was my immediate thought. Was it possible in so short a time? I thought of the fruits he had spoken of, of

sweet juice on hot tongues, and licked my lips without any
intent of doing so.

He arched a fair brow and sipped casually of his ale, his
gaze still holding mine. He seemed to read my thoughts,
unsurprised by my response to his presence and perhaps
even bemused by it. I felt my pulse flicker in my throat.
When he smiled, his expression was so knowing that I
feared that even the slowest of wit in this hall would guess
what had passed between us.

Then I was mortified that I could so forget my place. I
was the Lady of Inverfyre. I was an heiress and a noblewoman and no ruffian from Sicily's shores would make me
lower myself to the conduct of a common whore! I forced
myself to recall Gawain's transgressions and added to his
crimes that of embarrassing me before all the vassals in my
hall.

Heart thumping, I marched down the stairs and crossed
the hall with decisive strides. Even in this, I betrayed myself,
more than one whisper beginning at my high color and my
haste.

And my garb. I had never appeared in the hall in such
informal attire, never descended without my hair neatly
arranged and my features composed to banality.

Worse, I had not even thought of it when I heard that
Gawain awaited here. Adaira had spoken rightly—some-
thing had been loosed that would not be readily recaptured.
I made an effort to behave with my usual poise.

"Who is this foreigner?" I demanded.

Gawain's lips quirked with amusement that I should
feign ignorance of his identity. I hoped for a moment that he
would choke upon his cursed ale.

Our elderly castellan came forward and bowed deeply.

"He is but a messenger, my lady, who brought a missive to you. . . ."

"She knows who I am," Gawain murmured, his voice so low and certain that all fell silent at his words.

Every soul in the hall looked betwixt he and I with undisguised curiosity. I cursed the heat that suffused my face, for it launched a bevy of new whispers.

"I know who he is in truth," I said firmly, my gaze unswerving from Gawain's. "I asked only which lie he had told you to gain admission to Inverfyre."

"My lady!" Fiona huffed. "It is not seemly to call a guest, even a messenger, a liar."

"It is seemly to call matters as they are," I said with vigor. The castellan looked to me with surprise. "I received his missive and it tells his identity more clearly than anything else could." I opened my palm, showing the castellan what I held.

Hamish caught his breath, his fingers easing toward the crucifix before he halted and pulled them back. "But it cannot be . . ."

"But it *is*, Hamish. It most certainly is."

He touched it with a tentative fingertip. "But how can this be? Your mother lost it in the forest." He fumbled with his words for a moment, his brow furrowed as he tried to make sense of this gem's presence.

Gawain unfolded himself from his seat and sauntered closer. He propped his hands upon his hips when he halted before me, the scent of him nigh weakening my knees, the twinkle in his eyes telling me that he knew the fullness of my lust. "How pleasant to discover that this trinket is welcome here."

"It was stolen from here," I snapped.

"My lady!" Hamish's eyes were wide with shock and dismay.

"My mother did not lose this gem in the forest," I informed Hamish. "It was stolen from her, stolen by a man and his son who came to Inverfyre some fifteen years ago. My father asked her to hide the truth to ensure that strangers still found hospitality as guests in his hall."

Hamish's expression turned thoughtful. "Avery Lammergeier was here at that time," he mused. "Indeed, his visit was one unlikely for any to forget. Such tales he told! Such coin he had!"

"Indeed," I agreed sourly, holding Gawain's unrepentant gaze. I had a sudden urge to shock them all by kissing the smile from the lips of this cursedly confident man.

He winked at me, as if guessing my thoughts. Curse the man, he made me blush with renewed vigor! Two impulses were at war within me, neither one consistent with the cool demeanor I should show.

Curse him and curse him again!

Hamish appeared oblivious to the crackle of heat between the guest and myself. "I remember thinking how odd it was that Avery and his son departed so early and that they wished for no aid with their steeds. But they were foreigners and one cannot know what to expect from foreigners." He turned his gaze upon Gawain, studying him now as he had not before. "Avery's son was fair, and surely must have grown to manhood by now."

"I assure you that he has." Gawain smiled, knowing every gaze was upon him and surely reveling in it. He claimed my hand, then bent low over my fingers. "Gawain Lammergeier, at the service of my most beauteous lady Evangeline. I look forward to *sampling* the hospitality of Inverfyre yet again."

Gawain kissed me with the leisure of a man with no need for haste, boldly letting his lips linger on my knuckles. The assembly gasped that he would be so audacious. I felt Fiona bristle behind me, but took longer than I should have to pull my hand away from his teasing lips.

Clearly, Gawain intended to make trouble for me and just as clearly, he enjoyed that he succeeded.

"This man is a thief!" I said, then Gawain began to chuckle. "What makes you smile before such a serious accusation?"

Gawain leaned closer, dropping his voice to a merry whisper. "What have I stolen, my lady fair?" he asked, his eyes dancing with merriment. "Even if the locale of this crucifix has been in doubt, it cannot be argued that I am the one who returns it to your own hand."

I opened my mouth and shut it again when I realized the truth. I could not reveal that Gawain had stolen the *Titulus*, not without revealing that my father had shown his people a forgery for years afterward. I could not even claim that he had tried to steal the *Titulus* the last time he was here, as I had anticipated him and the relic was precisely where it belonged.

Gawain and I knew his crimes, but I had not a scrap of evidence to prove my accusation. Worse, any claim on my part would prompt questions as to how I knew so much of this handsome stranger and his deeds.

He had me cornered and the ruffian knew it.

So he smiled, his gaze knowing, challenging me to condemn him.

"Fifteen years of holding a stolen gem is no prompt return," I said, disliking the sense that he commanded this situation, not I.

Gawain shrugged with an ease I envied. "Perhaps I found

it in the forest on my way here. Did your mother not say that she had lost it there?" He stepped closer, eyes gleaming. "Perhaps I should be greeted with that reward, instead of rude accusations. A kiss from you, my lady, would suffice to ease the affront of your words."

His gaze dropped boldly to my lips.

The assembly whispered, but Fiona had no need to intervene. I slapped that smile from Gawain's face with one crisp strike, the crack of my blow loud enough to echo in the shocked silence that followed.

IX

"He lies," I said in a low voice. When Gawain smiled coolly, I could have cheerfully shredded the meat from his bones. "This man is not only a thief, but insolent as well."

"Indeed, I have never seen you so agitated, my lady, so your accusation must have some grounds." Hamish spoke soothingly, then inclined his head slightly. "Of course, you would find this matter troubling, as women are wont to do."

"My accusations have *every* ground," I informed him, my tone so fierce that Hamish flinched. "By all that is holy, Hamish, I swear to you that this man stole this jewel fifteen years past and must be punished for it!"

"The laird will decide his fate," Hamish said, again speaking to me as if I were a difficult child. "Perhaps you should retire to your chamber, my lady, and see to your attire."

I was being dismissed by the castellan! I should not have been so shocked. For five years, Fergus had undermined the authority that my father had allowed my mother and I to exercise, and I, trapped in the shell of passivity I had been taught to don, had never protested.

My days of docility were now behind me, though only Fergus himself could command that my word have weight. It was ironic, for he was only laird because he had wed the heiress, while I, who carried the blood of Inverfyre in my veins, was powerless in my hereditary hall. By wedding, I had ceded all authority to my spouse. I fumed at my own impotence. I was not so angry that I did not realize that any word I uttered would only make matters worse.

My father would have been appalled by this change.

Perhaps he would take to haunting Fergus instead of me.

A flick of Hamish's finger and two guards stepped out of the shadows to seize Gawain's elbows. To my astonishment, he did not struggle. His gaze was fixed upon me, his expression somber. I felt that he alone realized what a blow I had taken this day.

I averted my gaze. I did not want the sympathy of a renegade.

When the guards tugged at Gawain, he seemed insulted. He pulled one arm from a guard's grip and had time only to fastidiously brush his sleeve before the guard seized his arm again, this time with greater force.

"And what of Inverfyre's famed hospitality?" Gawain asked.

Hamish waved the two men out of the hall. "We would be remiss to not let you savor the delights of the Hole, at least until the laird's return."

"The Hole," Gawain repeated. "Why does such a chamber not sound alluring?" When no one replied, he accompanied his captors with apparent willingness, only breaking one arm free to blow me a jaunty kiss as they left the hall.

"Until later, my lady fair," he called gallantly and I flushed as I turned my back upon him.

I was shaken that Hamish would cast Gawain into the vile dungeon that had been my grandfather's pride, even though I wanted him to pay for his crime. I ran a hand across my brow, shocked that my feelings could be so mingled as this.

What if Fergus demanded that the father of the child in my womb be executed? The very prospect made me fear that Adaira's rabbit stew would soon be scattered at my feet. I felt hot, then chilled, then unsteady upon my feet.

"He is bold beyond belief," I said firmly, but was dismayed to note assessment in more than one pair of eyes.

I turned, intending to retreat to my chamber to change my garb—and smooth my roiled emotions—but there was no opportunity to do so. I was not halfway across the hall before a shout carried from the courtyard.

"The laird is wounded! Clear the way!"

My heart stopped cold.

Fergus? Fergus could not be wounded!

Indeed, Fergus was not wounded.

He was dead.

I raced to meet the party bearing his body and fell to my knees beside him when they lowered the litter to the ground. The men stood around me in awkward silence, for they knew it was too late to aid their laird.

Fergus was so still and grey that there was no doubt.

I whispered my husband's name in shock. Three arrows were driven deep into his neck, and the blood had run profusely from the wounds, staining his tabard and flesh. The flow had slowed now and the blood was drying. His skin had taken an odd pallor but still I searched for his pulse. The hue of his flesh, the lack of blood within him and his stillness made him look ancient and frail, as he had not looked in life.

Or had he?

I sat back on my heels, for there was nothing to be done. The rest of the household had come on fleet feet and edged closer for a glimpse of their fallen laird. Already the whispers had begun.

"Did anyone see this transpire?" I asked, alarmed by the flutter of my heart. Although I had never wished Fergus dead, although I would never have wished for this death for him, I could not deny the relief that flowed through me.

He would never heave himself atop me again. I would never avert my face from the smell of ale and meat upon his breath, never have to listen to the rasp of his quest for release, never dread that he would strike me the next time with more force than ever he had.

And I was ashamed to find myself glad of that.

My childhood friend Niall, tall and stalwart, answered me. "He spurred his steed in pursuit, and left us in his dust. I am sorry, Evangeline. We heard him shout, but thought he cried at the capture of the boar, or the retrieval of his falcon."

"Then there was only silence," grim Malachy said with a shake of his head. "If he had only shouted again, we might have found him in time."

"Were you all together?"

Niall shook his head again. "We parted ways, for we were near the lowlands and feared he would ride directly into the marsh."

Fergus had done as much once before, so ardently did he follow his falcon's course. He gave not a glance to the land below his own feet and his steed, in a most uncommon fashion, was scarcely better. The beast was loyal to the point of stupidity—it would run wherever it was bidden to run, despite nigh fatal mis-steps in the past.

I looked down at Fergus, and my heart clenched that his life should end so ignobly as this. To be mistaken for a boar or a buck charging through the woods was no dignified way for a man to pass from this world. Fergus' pale blue eyes were open, bulging slightly now, as if he too was incredulous of his own fate.

A bird cried in the distance and I was certain that it was his falcon, mourning the loss of its master. Though he had not been as fond of this peregrine as of Aphrodite, still the bird was much indulged.

"He must have seen the bowsman," Niall said gently, his hand falling upon my shoulder in a familiar fashion that made Fiona inhale sharply.

I was startled by this assertion. My shock must have shown when I looked up, for Niall shook his head.

He spoke softly but with resolve. "The arrows could not have gone so deep, not unless fired from close range. Half a dozen paces, at most. He must have seen the bowsman."

I stared in horror at the arrows lodged in the front of Fergus' throat, then stumbled to my feet. No man could err in identifying the soul before him at such close range, and certainly could not do so thrice.

"But that means Fergus was killed deliberately," I said. "You cannot mean that he was murdered!" My gaze danced from one grim face to the other and I saw now that the men had long ago reached this conclusion.

I gaped at my fallen husband. That Fergus had let an armed man come so close to him could mean only one thing: he had felt no threat.

Because he *knew* the bowsman.

Again, I feared I would swoon, though it was uncommon

for me to do so. I realized that there was dissent in our hall, but I had never guessed that it might come to such treachery as this.

But if everyone had returned, as indeed they had, then I must be in the company of Fergus' killer! I retreated again beneath Niall's watchful gaze and fought against my rising bile.

Of the six men surrounding me, I knew three quite well, for they had served my own father. Niall, Tarsuinn and Malachy had sworn to support Fergus and had served him since my father's death—though they also had undertaken the occasional favor for me. All three men had been at my father's court for at least a decade before his demise.

The others were Fergus' own kin—his younger brother, Alasdair; his cousin, Ranald; his nephew, Dubhglas—and I did not know them well. They were of an age with me, save for Dubhglas who was yet a youth. They were quiet, gruff and disinclined to speak of much at all, sturdily built, their hair ranging in hue from Alasdair's dark auburn to Dubhglas' brilliant red.

And what did I know of my father's men? Always fastest, tallest, boldest and most outspoken, Niall stood with his eyes narrowed, his posture sure. He had been filled with bold ambitions for as long as I recalled and frequently expressed discontent with Fergus' lairdship. He was the most obvious choice of a killer, though he returned my gaze so steadily that I was ashamed to suspect a man I had known so long—a man who had once asked my father for my hand in marriage—of any ignoble deed.

There was dour Malachy, a man prone to venting discontent at the world but one I had not thought inclined to do much about the matter.

Doughty Tarsuinn was not his usual merry self, for his

eyes were filled with some shadow. I wondered whether the loss of the customary twinkle in his eye was due to something he had witnessed, then he flicked an accusing glance at me.

Of what was I guilty? Of not loving the man I was compelled to take to husband? If that was a sin, eight of ten women in Christendom were destined for hellfire. Every maiden wed the first time for duty and only the second—if she was sufficiently fortunate to have the chance—for love.

"And so we stand in the company of a murderer," Niall said, voicing the thought we all must hold. "The question is not who of us would have found Fergus' demise convenient, but who was bold enough to do something about the matter."

"Or sufficiently wicked," I retorted, not liking his tone. No one had done a good deed in this.

"No one could wish my brother dead," Alasdair said. "He was a good and kindly man."

"An incompetent ruler," Niall added.

"And the sole obstacle to your own ambitions, Alasdair," Tarsuinn said.

"What of Niall's ambitions?" The three men of Fergus' clan stepped forward as one, bristling for a fight.

The two I knew stepped behind Niall supportively. As the men glared at each other, I watched the household divide ranks behind them, each soul allying with either the newcomers of Fergus' family or the old guard of mine.

I had never realized the animosity between the two families had such deep roots.

I had never realized how outnumbered we had become by the MacLarens, Fergus' own kin.

"I suppose you think that you should be laird in your brother's place," Niall said, as if the idea was folly.

"I have a greater claim than any of you," Alasdair insisted.

Niall fixed his gaze upon me and I knew a moment's dread at what he might say. "It is the lady who carries the blood of the lairds of Inverfyre, thus whosoever takes her hand should be the new laird. Fergus held the title of laird solely because he wed Evangeline, after all."

I guessed immediately what Niall implied, for I recalled my father denying the younger man's offer for me. I straightened then, fearing that once again I would become a trophy to lend dynastic credibility to a man's ambitions.

Alasdair laughed. "You can cherish your petty traditions all you like. I have no care for them, or for my brother's barren wife. If she were not so cold, Fergus would have had two or three heirs by this time. I need not indulge your desires at any rate. Look at you pathetic lot! You could not defend Inverfyre from us if we were to claim it."

"What we lack in numbers, we make up in boldness," Malachy said grimly.

"There are far more of us, and no less bold," Dubhglas observed.

"Aye, you would overrun Inverfyre with MacLarens, given half the chance," Niall sneered. "What manner of men find themselves bereft of their ancestral lands?"

"The king claimed title." Alasdair stepped forward, his brow dark.

"Because you are weak and worthless, unfit to rule." Niall clenched his fists. I was certain that a fight would erupt over Fergus' body.

Fiona's cackle of laughter halted the men. "While the Armstrong clan is so untouched by sin?" she demanded, then flung out a hand toward me. "What of your fine lady herself? Was she not outside the keep this very morning?"

I felt the company's attention land again upon me. "I had an errand, no more than that."

"Where? With whom?" Alasdair demanded.

I lifted my chin, tired of lies and demanding men. "I visited Adaira, as is the custom of the women of this abode."

Fiona snorted. "An old mad woman said to reside in the woods since time out of mind. An old woman who does not truly exist." She spat into the rushes. "Spare us your lies. You went to rut with your lover, the same lover with whom you rutted on the feast of Saint Paul's conversion, the same lover you savored before welcoming your legal laird to the same bed." The company gasped. Fiona stepped forward, eyes gleaming. "The same lover who brought you a trinket this very morning."

The crucifix suddenly burned in my palm and the missive that was still balled in my fist prompted a dozen whispers. "I . . ." I began to protest, even as the men who had aided me in encouraging Gawain to depart regarded me with dawning suspicion.

"Lover?" Niall asked softly and to my shame, I could not hold his gaze.

"I have done nothing wrong!" I cried. "You would simply be rid of me that you might seize claim to Inverfyre."

"Your fine lady of Inverfyre is no more than a whore!" Fiona declared. "No doubt, she conspired with her lover to be rid of her husband. Is it not convenient that he arrived on the very day that Fergus was struck down in the forest?"

"You have no proof of this," Niall protested, though his words seemed fed more by duty than conviction.

"No?" Fiona's smile turned sly. "Then why did the lady return to the keep with blood upon her hands? And why did she cast something from her own window in the hope that I would not see it?"

All eyes turned upon me, condemnation in most of them. "I did not kill Fergus! This accusation is outrageous!"

"She is struck mad," someone whispered in the assembly though I could not discern who uttered the words. "Look at the wildness in her eyes."

"Who speaks?" I demanded, glaring at each of them in turn, to no avail. "I am no killer and you should all know the truth of it." They did not recognize the outspoken woman I had become as the cool and demure lady who usually graced their hall.

And they condemned me for the change.

Alasdair raised a finger toward his cousin Ranald. "Go and look beneath the lady's window."

"I will go with him," Niall said, and I appreciated that none should be able to contrive evidence against me.

I looked down at Fergus and saw only now that the arrow shafts had been broken off. Had Fergus tried to remove them from his wounds? Or had his assailant snapped them off to remove the mark of their owner?

An ominous weight claimed my belly and I feared as I had never feared before. We stood silently, straining for the sound of the two men's return, my ears filled with the pulse of my blood.

Niall looked grim when they reappeared, Ranald triumphant. They carried the two arrow shafts that Adaira had forced upon me and I nigh fainted that they had found them so readily.

Niall bent, all eyes upon him, and held the broken shafts against the arrows still jutting from Fergus' flesh. It seemed that none breathed in the hall.

Niall looked up at me, his expression woeful. I knew he did not like what he had found, just as I knew he would not lie for me or any other.

"I am sorry, Evangeline. Two of them match," he said quietly.

It was absurd. It was madness. It could not be true, and even if it was true, there had to be a reasonable explanation. Niall must be mistaken! I had no time to express the thousand arguments that jumbled my thoughts.

I was seized before I could take a single step, let alone flee. Alasdair roared that justice would be served and I fought then in terror, fearing for my very survival.

I demanded a chance to explain, I demanded that Adaira be brought to the hall. I shouted that I was the daughter of the sixth son of Inverfyre and the last of my lineage, that such treatment of my person was unacceptable.

My words fell upon deaf ears.

Indeed, I was flung, despite my struggles, into the black abyss of the dungeon. I flailed as the darkness swallowed me and I screamed outrage as I fell. It is a goodly drop into the prison that my grandsire named The Hole. The floor is the height of two men below the threshold of the door and there has never been a single soul who managed to crawl out.

I knew the distance, yet it seemed I took an eternity to hit the dirt floor. They laughed, the wretches, when they heard the crunch of my bones and my grunt of pain.

I was mightily bruised, but too angry to care. I bounced to my feet, more than prepared to fight for what was mine own. "This is not justice! You cannot steal my legacy so readily as this!"

"No one can murder without repercussions," Fiona said, smacking her lips with satisfaction. "Not even the lofty Lady of Inverfyre."

"But someone *has* escaped justice! I did not kill Fergus! His killer still stands among you."

Niall stepped forward, his familiar silhouette making me hope for leniency. "I cannot blame you for your anger, Evangeline, but the evidence is irrefutable."

"It must be refuted, for it is wrong!"

"Do not compound your sins with lies," counselled Niall. Had he been within reach, I would have boxed his ears. How could someone who had known me so long believe me capable of such a foul deed?

But he evidently did believe it, they all did, and I was infuriated by their low estimation of me.

"You will pay for this!" I shouted, shaking my fist at their silhouettes far above my head. "I am the heiress of Inverfyre!"

"Sleep well, Evangeline," Alasdair said smoothly. It was significant that he called me by name, not by title, for we were not old friends and he had no right to use such a casual address. What would have been impolite just this morn was now a sign of my fallen status. There was more than one snort from the watchful company above, then the door was closed with finality.

The damp shadows folded around me and I wrapped my arms around myself, shivering. I stared hopefully at the faint sliver of golden light, outlining the door far above me, my heart sinking to my toes when the key turned resolutely in the lock. I refused to consider how long they would leave me here.

Or what they would do to me once they plucked whatever remained of me out of this place.

I had little chance to fret over this prospect, for a voice cleared at close proximity. I nigh jumped out of my own flesh.

"Well met, my lady fair," Gawain said as calmly as if we met at the king's own board.

"You!" I peered into the darkness in the direction of Gawain's voice and could faintly discern his silhouette. He seemed to be leaning against the far wall and my heart thumped in a most painful way that I shared this imprisonment with him.

"I meant to compliment you, by the way, not only on your cleverness in retaining the *Titulus*, but for the burden of the child," he said, confusing me utterly. "It was a masterful touch, a grace note if you will, to redouble the insult. You must indeed be a formidable chess player."

That he should mock me now with riddles, in this moment when all had gone awry, was too much. "What child?"

"The child forced upon me at your command."

I was prepared to argue the matter with him, for I had decreed no such thing, when the words of his missive filled my thoughts.

Never let it be said that I failed to understand the secret desire of a lady's heart.

I gasped in sudden understanding. Gawain had insisted when last we met that my secret desire was to be free of Fergus.

"God in heaven! It was *you* who killed my husband!" I retreated hastily, flattened myself against the cold wall and screamed. "I am trapped in this dungeon with a murderer! Release me!"

X

Perhaps it had been unwise to make such an accusation when trapped with the criminal in question. I clapped my hands over my mouth, cursing my own newly impulsive tongue.

But Gawain, far from stalking me and choking the life from me, began to laugh. His laugh was merry and deep, the kind of infectious and hearty laugh that rolls effortlessly from a man's gut and sets all other lips to twitching.

I straightened. "There is nothing amusing about a man's death."

"There is much amusing about the thought of me killing another." A thrum of amusement echoed beneath Gawain's words, then his tone sobered. "No, not any other, but your *husband*."

The word hung betwixt us, heavy with accusation. I fidgeted, though I knew I owed this scoundrel nothing. "I did not intend for you to know."

"Clearly."

"I could not see that it mattered, not to you. . . ."

"How could such a detail not be of import, even to *me*?"

I stood straight. "How was I to guess that a thief would have some concern for his immortal soul?"

"I have no care for my immortal soul." Gawain dismissed the very thought. "But it is well known that in this corner of Christendom, a husband who finds another man abed with his wife may exact whatever punishment he sees fit . . . and that, contrary to custom elsewhere, the due is oft exacted of the man not the woman."

"But Fergus is not vengeful. . . ."

"You assume much of your deceased spouse. *All* men are vengeful, Evangeline, when they discover they have shared through no choice of their own. I would not be so foolish as to bed the wife of any man in this land, not if I had the benefit of knowing her true circumstance."

"Indeed? You did not ask any questions when we met afore."

"The onus was not upon me to mention such a significant detail! Had I been wed, I would have told you."

"I heartily doubt that!" I propped my hands upon my hips and glared in his direction, vexed that he blamed me for all. "Who could I have been, other than the laird's wife? What did you imagine *was* my circumstance?"

"That Fergus was your father!" Gawain was irked by the pitch of his voice. I should have liked to have seen the look of him when he was agitated for I imagined it was a rare sight. "Fergus was sufficiently aged to be your sire, was he not?"

"That is no uncommon situation! Even so, how could you believe that seducing the unwed daughter of the laird would bring no repercussions?" I scoffed. "You know less of men than myself if you believed such folly!"

"You *deceived* me, Evangeline, and I could have paid for

our deeds with my hide. That may be of no merit to you, but I am rather fond of ensuring my own survival." Gawain took a breath as if steadying himself. "I have risked my life a thousand times and more, but always, *always* by my own choice." He cleared his throat slightly. "And for the prospect of reward, of course."

"Of course." Coupling with me was apparently not such a reward, and I had no qualms about revealing that I was insulted. My back straightened and my chin rose. "Did you kill Fergus, then, to save your sorry life?"

Gawain's chuckle sounded again, so deep that it must have been coaxed from some secret refuge. "Did you?"

I was shocked. "What reason had I to kill my spouse?"

"What reason had you to let him live?" my companion asked. "Perhaps he discovered the truth of our liaison. Perhaps he kept you from wedding a lover true. Perhaps he abused you. Perhaps . . ."

"I did *not* kill him."

"Then what stains your hands?"

I felt my color rise. "The juice of a pomegranate."

"A pomegranate?" Gawain's tone turned thoughtful and I had no doubt he would believe I had yearned for him. "I had no inkling that they could be found so far north."

I heard him saunter closer and took a step back. "They cannot," I admitted breathlessly. "Save in exceptional circumstance."

Gawain's laughter was a mere exhalation, a sound of surprise and pleasure. His voice dropped so low as to make me shiver. "It was indeed exceptional circumstance, my lady fair."

I averted my burning face, too mortified to summon a word to my lips.

"Perhaps you imagine that I killed Fergus to win your

favor." The very prospect set Gawain chuckling again, a fact that no lady could find flattering.

Understand that I had had what I desired of this man, that I had no maidenly fantasies of our living in nuptial bliss forevermore. I merely considered it graceless for him to boldly state that his sentiments were the same as mine.

And I was insulted that he did not at least desire to bed me again, if you must know the truth of it. He was supposed to be consumed with lust for me. Men were always supposed to be consumed with lust for women above their station, and this affliction should be the worst for charming, handsome scoundrels and thieves of no good repute.

I glared in Gawain's direction, indignant that he did not think I was worth murdering another, then furious with myself for even desiring that a man should think as much.

What a talent this man had for addling my wits!

Gawain cleared his throat, apparently sensing my hostility. "Would you prefer that I lied to you?" His voice hardened when I said nothing. "Would you have me tell you sweet lies of how I love you, how I yearn for you, how no other woman's beauty can compare to yours?" I heard him step closer, even as my traitorous heart leapt. "Would you have me fill the air with nonsense, with worthless pledges intended to coax you to my bed again?"

"Of course not." I was cross that he made me so aware of the muddle of my expectations.

"Yet you bristle when I tell you the truth."

"You do not know how to tell the truth."

"Indeed?" Gawain leaned against the wall beside me and my pulse leapt at his cursed proximity. I struggled to keep from glancing his way, though I shivered when his voice dropped to a low caress. "I shall tell you a truth, Evangeline.

You seduced me as no other woman has ever done and our nights together were both sweet beyond compare."

My heart lodged in my throat so I could say nothing.

Gawain's words heated. "I will not sully that truth with a lie, a lie that I seek to wed you or to win your heart for my own. I have no such quest. I never have sought and never will seek a bride."

I looked toward him, for I could not restrain my curiosity any longer. "Then, what do you seek?"

"Companionship and pleasure, for so long as matters are magical for both parties and not a moment longer."

"Marriage does not necessarily become burdensome."

His smile flashed in the shadows. "You can say this to me, given your own marriage? Do you not feel in some corner of your heart a measure of relief that ancient Fergus is dead?"

I turned away, hating that he had guessed my secret. "I feel shame that I did not love him enough," I said, for this too was true.

"Your heart is your own, Evangeline," Gawain said softly, his words all the more persuasive for being whispered in the shadows. "And so it should be, as mine is my own. One's heart can never be commanded to love another, by duty or vow. I will never be shackled to any soul by a pledge, by a lie that tender feelings will never change." His tone became harsh. "People change, circumstances change, feelings change. I will not let some foolish optimism trap me within the sentiment of days long gone."

I was more intrigued than I should have been. "You were wedded before," I guessed. "And unhappy."

"No, not I. I have never stepped within the nuptial noose, for I learned young to avoid it."

I waited for a long moment but he told me no more.

Indeed, he seemed to have become somewhat melancholy, as if an old, unhappy memory gripped him. I was curious. I wondered whether Gawain had once loved a woman trapped in a loveless match and had never had the chance to win her hand for himself.

Indeed, I sighed quietly at the tragic romance of it all, for such a history could have made him the apparently carefree scoundrel that he was. I felt a strange unwelcome sense of companionship with him, as if we were kindred souls instead of adversaries.

Perhaps that was what prompted my impulsive confession.

"I will grant you then a truth that you deserve to know," I said. "I seduced you because I wished for a son and my husband got no child upon me in five years." I felt Gawain's scrutiny upon me, as if he assessed both me and the tale, but I did not look up.

"Fair enough," he murmured. "And did you succeed?"

"Adaira says as much, but it is early days to be certain."

"If it was of such import that you bear a son, then why did your father insist that you wed so ancient a man as Fergus?"

"My father believed that he owed Fergus a debt."

"Why?"

I sighed, then reasoned that we had nothing but time. "Fergus came to Inverfyre some three summers after the *Titulus* was stolen. The falcons were without issue and food was scarce. Fergus came to pledge himself to the Laird of Inverfyre, if the laird would have him, for he had been driven from his lands by the crown. All he had to surrender as a gift were forty chickens and a cock."

"A rich gift by any accounting."

"A richer one still given the emptiness of our bellies. We

have never grown many crops at Inverfyre, for the land is steep and ridden with stones. And we always had coin from our trade in falcons to acquire much of what was needed. Without trade in the birds, our treasury emptied with startling speed."

"The arrival of Fergus was timely, then," Gawain mused. "And your father deemed this so great a favor that he pledged his sole daughter to this keeper of chickens?"

I flushed. "To save my father's vassals and his pledge to sustain them was no small thing. Fergus served my father for many years after that, too. I suppose my father respected his counsel."

"And you?" came his quiet but relentless question. "Did you respect Fergus?"

I caught my breath and turned away, even though I knew he could not see me. "He was my lord husband and his word, my command."

My declaration hung between us, unpersuasive even to me. I licked my lips, but could add nothing more compelling to what already I had said.

The truth was that I savored this unexpected honesty between us and would not destroy it with a lie, however well-intentioned it might be. I spoke with impulsive haste. "In this spirit of sharing truths, will you pledge to never lie to me?"

Gawain sounded amused. "Why?"

"It is good to have one person to rely upon for the truth." I half-laughed. "It might not be so onerous a pledge, for we may not survive long."

"You can only rely upon me for the truth if you can believe my pledge." He came to lean his shoulder against the wall beside mine.

I was unable to read Gawain's expression in the shadows

though I felt the weight of his gaze. I had difficulties drawing a full breath. "Assume that I can," I whispered.

I felt him study me, felt the intensity of his stare. He hesitated so that I wondered whether anyone had ever said they would believe him before. "Fair enough," he finally said, his words husky. "You have my pledge of honesty, Evangeline, for whatsoever you decide it is worth."

"Swear it."

Gawain caught my hand in the warmth of his, then planted a kiss in my palm. He folded my fingers over the heat of his touch, then lifted my hand to his chest. I could feel his heartbeat beneath my hand and I caught my breath, even as the passion stirred within me. "I swear to you, Evangeline of Inverfyre, that only truth shall pass from my lips to your ears."

He bent then and kissed my ear with delightful languor. His heartbeat skipped beneath my fingers when his lips touched me and I found my face turning, to welcome his embrace upon my lips. There is something about darkness that encourages intimacy, something about shadows that makes one bolder than might be possible beneath the sun's bright eye. I could not resist his touch, for with a simple caress he summoned the wanton in me.

I had been taught to surrender nothing to a man, taught that my own desire was not of import, and yet Gawain could make me forget all I knew.

And worse, I did not care.

I finally summoned the will to step away from the temptation he offered, snatching my hand from his grip. I asked what I most wished to know, thinking this truth would cool this dangerous ardor between us. "Did you kill Fergus?"

I heard Gawain's smile in his words, but he spoke with a

compelling certainty. "I am a thief, Evangeline, perhaps a rogue and a scoundrel, perhaps a forger and one to make much of opportunity . . ."

"A formidable list of talents."

Gawain ignored me. ". . . but I am not a killer. In fact, I have only once killed another, and even then did not do so with my own hands. You may rest assured that my victim was not your recently deceased spouse."

I wished that I could discern his features clearly. This confession should have frightened me, I suppose, but I have lived all my life in the company of men unafraid to mete justice with their own blades. The weight of the king's hand is light in these territories, and even my father's justice had only prevailed without contest inside the high walls of Inverfyre's keep. Honorable men could be relied upon to do what needed to be done to ensure peace and justice.

On the other hand, a murderer—or so it always seemed to me—is another manner of man, one with a thread of viciousness or evil, a reckless man. Gawain was not reckless or vicious, it was clear, nor was he inclined to violence.

You may think it odd, but I found his confession reassuring. I had thought Gawain carefree and frivolous, a man concerned solely with his own survival and comfort. I was glad to know that he was a man, as I knew men—that he was unafraid to wield his blade but did so with temperance.

Gawain continued in that casual manner. "The repercussions for murder are too dire for my taste so, as a rule, I avoid it. Murder tends to agitate the common people, as you have witnessed this very day, which interferes with my labor."

"But if you did not kill Fergus, then what did your missive to me mean?"

"Ah!" I heard the scuff of his boots upon stone as he

paced the width of the chamber, paused, then sauntered back to my side. "In the name of chivalry, I grant you the chance to rescind your demand for honesty, for you may not like my reply."

"I would hold you to your pledge."

"Very well." Gawain tucked a strand of hair behind my ear, his touch sure and warm. "I have dreamed of you, Evangeline." His voice was low and intimate, seductive. I shivered anew at his sudden proximity.

He was a thief, I reminded myself, an untrustworthy scoundrel even if the most alluring man that ever I had met. Despite my own reminder, my mouth went dry.

"I have remembered you over and over again." Gawain seemed as surprised by this as I was, and I guessed it was not common for him to think of a woman once he had savored her charms. A dangerous thrill went through me, though I knew such a man as he was not wrought for me.

He might have been the serpent in the garden, beguiling Eve with what she most wished to hear, with false promises of what could be. I knew this, knew I should not listen, but could not halt myself.

Then Gawain's fingertip touched my cheek and a shiver roiled over my flesh. As much as I would have liked to step away, I found myself powerless beneath the caress of that single finger. "I was convinced that you could not possibly choose to abide here," he whispered. "I was certain that you merely wished to be persuaded to leave this wretched place. . . ."

"Inverfyre is beautiful!"

"If cold and impoverished and lacking in what some might consider essential amenities," he added, clearly unpersuaded. "I thought that you protested overmuch at my offer to take you south when last we met." That fingertip traced a beguiling path to my ear, then down the side of my throat. I leaned my head back, suddenly unable to draw a full breath, and he traced the outline of the hollow of my throat.

I swallowed and he quickly kissed that hollow, his kiss searing my flesh. My resolve wavered. It seemed foolish to protest his amorous assault.

"I merely intended to return to Inverfyre and repeat my offer," he whispered, his lips somehow having landed on the tender place beneath my ear. "Perhaps somewhat more persuasively." He kissed my earlobe and my knees nigh melted at the sweet heat of his touch.

His words only gradually made sense to me, and when they did, I ducked the caress of his fingertip and lips. "You meant only that I should flee to be your whore until you tire of me."

Gawain clicked his tongue. "It sounds so vulgar put thus."

"It is a vulgar offer."

"While death in Inverfyre's aptly named Hole is so much more civilized?" He was close enough that I could see his brow arch high. I spun away from his wry tone—and the temptation he offered—to pace the width of the cell and back.

"Dungeons are not meant to be hospitable places," I informed him. "If I could only escape, I could fetch Adaira and have her tell the truth of what happened. If only she granted her testimony, the true murderer could be uncovered. . . ."

"Why would any heed her pledge?"

"What would they not? She would be telling the truth!"

"Ah, Evangeline." Gawain chuckled and I imagined that he shook his head ruefully. "If I understand correctly, this

Adaira is an old woman who lives in the woods, perhaps a healer."

"Yes, a healer, an alewife, a wise woman. What matter?"

His chuckle came again, though this time it was low and affectionate. I could find no mockery within it. "Can you not see, Evangeline, how very convenient it is to be rid of you?"

"No!"

"Releasing you, or giving credence to any evidence that you might muster, could only put any man's claim to Inverfyre in jeopardy. I predict that you will be left to rot in this charming chamber."

"They could not," I fumed. "They would not."

"They *have*," Gawain interrupted flatly.

Indeed, they had. I was trapped in the dungeon of my grandsire's construction and unlikely to ever be invited to depart it alive. They would let me die. Alasdair and Fergus' other kin only wanted Inverfyre, a holding to which they had no right but one they could make their own by force.

Without me, without my inevitable protest to the king, they possessed my family holding without contest.

My son would die before he even came to light.

"But that is not fair!" I cried, knowing how little that mattered but vexed all the same.

"Perhaps you now understand why I have little interest in what is right and legal—it is seldom fair."

I clenched my fists in outrage, not liking my powerlessness a whit. "If only we could escape! Then justice could be served. I could send word to the king. I could muster troops. I could . . ." I scrabbled ineffectively at the rock face, but it was impossible to catch a grip, precisely as my forebear had planned.

I spun upon Gawain in annoyance. "What pathetic manner of thief are you that you cannot steal us away from this place?"

Again I heard the smile in his voice. "It is not a question of whether I can pick that excuse for a lock, my Evangeline, it is a question of when it would be best to do so. Captors, in my experience, like to gloat."

He could pick the lock.

I stared in Gawain's direction, aghast, even as the lock was turned and the door high above flung open. The finger of light that fell into the Hole gave me a glimpse of Gawain's confident smile—and no doubt he had an eyeful of my gaping astonishment—before Fiona shouted with glee.

"I have a gift for you, my fine lady," she sneered, then hurled the contents of a bucket into the dungeon.

Gawain moved like lightning. He seized my wrist and pulled me out of the way, when I might have stood there like a startled hare. He folded me against his heat and backed me into the wall beneath the door.

The slops splashed noisily against the far wall, the smell enough to curdle milk. I buried my nose in Gawain's shoulder and inhaled hungrily of his scent instead.

I forgot completely about the slops.

Fiona laughed and locked the door with gusto. She whistled merrily as she left us trapped, no doubt swinging her bucket as she trudged back to the hall.

I did not push Gawain away. The tickle in my belly that had awakened with first sight of him grew to a roar. I could feel the muscles of his back beneath my hands, feel the strength of his thighs against mine. My battle against temptation was well and truly lost.

"Evangeline," Gawain whispered, a throaty purr that melted the last of my resistance. There was desire in his whisper and in his chausses. Perhaps he found his desire for me as unexpected and fathomless as I found mine for him.

I felt gloriously, vibrantly alive, as I had when we met afore. I turned my face slightly and let my lips graze Gawain's neck, boldly touched my lips to his mouth. He shivered and I could not have cared less about Fiona.

"It never serves one to be absent when the captor comes to check on their prey," Gawain murmured into my hair. His breath made my flesh tingle and the heat that only he could kindle spread through me. "Escaping too soon can oft lead to unfortunate results."

"Like?"

"A more doughty prison, one which cannot be so readily conquered when the time is right."

I shivered despite myself, though more from the antics of his tongue than the import of his words. "My grandfather used to execute criminals who survived a fortnight in the Hole."

"Ah," Gawain breathed, kissing me in a most satisfying way. He was thorough about his kisses, as if there was naught else of any import in all of Christendom. He did not hasten, he savored each kiss as if it might be the very last he ever tasted.

Indeed, when he finished his languid kiss, I was persuaded to his perspective. I felt rumpled and sampled, awakened and not nearly sated.

I dared in the darkness to caress him. Gawain caught his breath and I chuckled, even more delighted with my effect upon him when he spoke in a strained voice.

"In my experience," he said carefully, "a public execution is quite difficult to escape."

I unlaced his chausses slowly, teasing him all the while. He was neither shocked by my audacity or disapproving of it. He merely let me do as I would with him. It was exhilarating. "But you have escaped one?"

"Only once." I could see the shadow of his features and guessed that his eyes were twinkling with mischief. "I have learned caution since my younger days."

"Indeed?" I lifted my skirts and pressed myself against his nakedness. He caught my buttocks in his hands and lifted me against him, backing me again into the wall.

"Indeed." Gawain kissed me soundly then, surprising me with his ardor. I found myself arching closer, knotting my hands in the golden silk of his hair. The darkness gave me license to unleash my desire.

"Indeed," he whispered. "For example, I do not, in general, seduce married women."

"You seduced me."

"No." Gawain chuckled as his wicked fingers worked the laces loose on the sides of my kirtle. One hand slipped beneath the wool and I gasped as his hand closed over my breast. "You seduced me, Evangeline. Twice, and most satisfactorily on both occasions." He teased my nipple to a peak with ease.

I arched my back toward him. "You clearly intend to seduce me now," I teased.

His smile flashed. "But you are a widow now, Evangeline, not a wife," he murmured, his lips hovering the breadth of a finger above mine.

"Suddenly, you are a man of principle?"

"I have always been a man of principle." Again, the breath of his laughter touched my cheek. "My principles, however, are not always those shared by other men."

I was seized by an abrupt curiosity about his life and his principles, his loves—beyond sun-baked Sicily—and his deepest desires, but Gawain kissed me with such expertise that I said nothing. I could do nothing, nothing but gasp into his kiss, nothing but surrender to the ardor between us.

"We must do something to pass the time until they are sleepy with confidence and ale." Gawain murmured against my throat, then his lips closed over my nipple. I moaned at the caress of his tongue and gathered his hair into my fists. He halted, tormenting me, and I heard the teasing laughter in his voice. "Unless you have another suggestion?"

"A game of chess, perhaps?" I suggested mischievously.

He seemed to ponder the prospect, then I felt him shake his head. "Too dark. And I suspect I would lose. I could not bear to lose a game on what might be my last night alive."

"Then we should choose some deed in which we both shall win."

"Precisely. As I was suggesting . . ." He caught me closer and kissed me so soundly that I fair forgot my name.

When he lifted his lips from mine, I held him close, suddenly fearful. "We could fail to escape, despite your confidence, or their plans could be other than you anticipate," I said, wishing he would argue but knowing he would not. "We could be caught while escaping and killed immediately."

"We could indeed. Our scheme is not without danger."

I was not so cavalier about this as he sounded. "This truly might be the last night that ever we face, Gawain." I caressed his cheek as he had so oft touched mine, tracing the line of his jaw with my fingertip. "What better way to spend it than in pleasure?"

"I knew you were a lady in pursuit of my own heart," Gawain said with approval. He kissed me again and I responded in kind, welcoming all he had to share.

XI

I awakened to the sound of rushing water. I was disoriented for a moment, so lost in a haze of pleasure that I did not remember where I was. The darkness did little to aid my orientation.

Then Gawain swore close by my ear and I remembered everything. It was the silky fur lining of his cloak that cosseted me, the strength of his arm that surrounded me.

"There is water pouring into this cursed place!" he cried, then I felt him shift beside me. He leapt to his feet, then scooped me up into his arms, his cloak still wrapped around me. My feet were wet, as were my hips and the wool of my kirtle that had lain beneath me. I could smell the dank water gathering on the stone floor, hear it running, feel its chill.

"It must be raining," I said as calmly as I could. My heart was racing, for I knew very well what fate lay ahead. Panic would serve us poorly, for only our wits could save us now.

"Raining?"

"The keep is wrought so that the rainwater from the roofs

and from the courtyards is led to the Hole. It acts as a drain for all of Inverfyre's rain."

"How?"

"There are two walls in this dungeon." I warmed to my theme, having been coached in the marvels of Inverfyre's construction since I could toddle. "The outer is of fitted stone, smooth and without pores. The inner wall, which is what we see, is made of stones fitted with tiny gaps between them. No one can grip the wall with any success, for the spaces are too small. But the water sluices over the lip of the outer wall from all sides . . ."

"And filters through the inner wall, filling the dungeon from the bottom." His tone was sour.

"Precisely."

"And why is it not always filled with water?"

"There are several small holes at the bottom of the outer wall, so the water flows out gradually."

"But it flows in far more quickly than it can drain?"

I nodded, though he could not see my gesture. "Especially when the rain falls with vigor."

Gawain considered the matter as the sound of rushing water brought goosepimples to my flesh. It was turning colder in the Hole by the moment. Mercifully, we had not completely disrobed, merely eased aside whatever garments obstructed our lovemaking. We were yet garbed, if unlaced and disheveled.

Gawain's tone was wry when he spoke. "I assume that no one will aid us?"

"It seldom rains enough that a man standing upright will drown in the Hole." I heard my father's words being uttered in my voice, a most curious circumstance. "A prisoner will, however, be chilled and wet and inclined to develop any manner of illness, which will ultimately shorten his confinement. Prisoners generally are left here for a fortnight before any soul looks in upon them."

"And if they survive, an execution in the square awaits."

"It was my grandfather's contribution to local justice."

"How charmingly barbaric." Gawain moved and I heard the water splash around his boots. I guessed from the sound that it had risen nearly to his knees. "This would seem to be a most opportune moment for our departure."

His easy tone made it sound as if we planned a court's journey to Edinburgh, complete with servants and carts. I laughed despite myself, but then he put me upon my feet and the cold of the water nigh stopped my heart. It was past my knees and swirling as it flowed into the space. I had to grip his upper arms for a moment to find my balance. He had caught his cloak from my shoulders and held it above the water.

"I apologize for my lack of gallantry, Evangeline, but there is no other way to accomplish our escape. I would not have the cloak get wet, for it may be the only source of warmth we have after escape. I shall need your aid, if you will."

I guessed his intent immediately. "You need me to hold you up that you might foil the lock."

He leaned closer, his hand resting upon my shoulder. "Can you do it?" His concern warmed me. "I am not a small man."

"Nor am I a delicate woman." I spoke with resolve. "I can do any deed, if it means my survival."

"Good!" I caught a glimpse of his smile, then he seized my elbow and guided me to the wall beneath the door. "I will be as quick as possible. Fit your hands together as if to boost me into a saddle."

I did as bidden, bracing myself against the wall to bear

his weight. Gawain put his wet boot in my locked hands and moved with lithe grace.

One boot landed on my shoulder, then the other. I braced my back against the wall and closed my eyes as I held the ankles of his boots, locking my knees and gritting my teeth. I was determined to hold his weight for as long as was necessary, though I felt as if I grew shorter with each breath.

Stabbing pains erupted all too quickly in my knees, and it was too soon to say whether the cold of the water was a boon or a bane. The water roiled around my hips now, chilly and—I imagined—filled with vile, sucking creatures.

The weight of Gawain was suddenly diminished and I looked up even as a scattering of small rocks fell upon me. He apologized for the scree which splashed into the pool, though I did not imagine what else he could have done.

"I have found a toe hold," he whispered. "It is not as solid as I would like, but it will do."

And it took much of his weight from my shoulders. I was disproportionately pleased that he had shown concern for me while focused on his task. I heard the tinkling of metal tickling metal and held my breath.

Something fell, metal landing against metal. Gawain muttered something grim beneath his breath that I was glad to not fully hear, then the tinkling began again. Again came the sound of metal falling, but the sound was deeper and I heard Gawain blow a kiss.

To me?

To the lock?

"Beautiful," he murmured, his choice of word confirming neither option.

Before I could ask—or decide whether I wanted to—the door swung open far above me, letting a pale wedge of light fall into the Hole. Gawain's weight was suddenly gone. I looked up to see his hands braced on the threshold, his boots swinging above my head. He hefted himself up and through the door with more agility and grace than I had ever witnessed. He landed as silently as a cat, out of the range of my sight.

I was so delighted that I could have laughed aloud or applauded, but instead I stretched to my toes. I reached up, straining for the hand I knew would be there, and fought for some toehold upon the submerged wall.

Nothing.

There was no strong male hand reaching to grasp mine. I peered upward, but there was no shadow, no silhouette, no rope coiling down from the threshold.

Had Gawain been discovered?

Assaulted?

Killed?

But it was so quiet above. It was impossible to believe that any struggle could have ensued with no noise whatsoever.

"Gawain?" I whispered, but there was no response.

The Hole was abruptly plunged into blackness again. The lock set with a clatter as I stared upward, aghast in sudden understanding.

Gawain was leaving me here.

The cur had used my aid to ensure his own escape, then abandoned me to my fate! This was the merit of his pledge to tell no lies?

Too late I realized that he had warned me that his word was worthless, but still I had trusted him.

How could I have been such a fool?

I had just tipped back my head to shout every foul name I had ever heard after Gawain—having no care whether it foiled his escape—when the door opened suddenly above me again.

I blinked in the sudden light, half-convinced that the rope that dropped toward me could not be offered by Gawain. What trickery was this?

"Hurry!" Gawain whispered.

"You came back for me, after all." I made no haste to grasp his offering, my ire undiminished by his apparent change of heart.

"Evangeline, take my hand," he said urgently. "There is not a moment to waste."

I sneezed, for the cold water touched the bottom of my breasts.

"Evangeline, *now!*"

I seized the rope and was delighted to find knots in it which aided my grip. Though I am agile and strong, my wet wool skirts ensured that I could not pull myself from the water. I struggled and strained, but the weight pulled me backward as if the Hole would not willingly relinquish me.

"Hurry!"

Fortunately, my laces were not fastened securely. I held fast to the rope with one hand and tore out the loose laces with the other, then wriggled out of the sodden garment. Its cold weight fell from my back and I nimbly climbed the rope in no more than my chemise, pleased despite myself at Gawain's smile.

"A lady of resource," he murmured with satisfaction as his hand closed over mine. He hauled me over the threshold of the door, cast his fur-lined cloak over my shoulders, then seized my hand to flee.

I resisted, my feet rooted to the floor. My husband's nephew lay limply beside the doorway to the Hole, his blood running between the fitted stones of the floor. His eyes were open, cast to heaven, and he was still beyond still.

"You killed him," I whispered in horror. My first thought was that if this had been the reason for Gawain's delay, then I was a wretch to have doubted him.

"He is not dead, though he will not stir for a while. He insisted that I choose betwixt the two of us, so I did." Gawain's manner was chilling, as if he had done nothing more troubling than rid the keep of a rat. In this moment, he looked as determined as the warriors I had known all my life, as resolute and as determined.

And I, daughter of a warrior, lusted for him with a vigor that made my blood sing.

Gawain arched a brow when I made no move, his usual light manner restored so suddenly that I doubted what I had glimpsed. "Do you mean to linger and mourn the injury of this boy? Or shall we seize this opportunity to depart Inverfyre?" He gallantly offered his hand, but I hesitated for a new reason.

"Depart? I thought we would seek out Adaira."

"You thought incorrectly."

"But this is my home and my legacy. . . ."

"No longer."

I caught his sleeve in my hand, trying to make him understand. "If I could only explain, if I was only granted a moment to defend my actions, then my innocence could be proven to all."

Gawain visibly grit his teeth, then glanced over his shoulder. "I have told you that none will listen, Evangeline."

"But Inverfyre is mine by right and by blood!"

"You will not be granted any semblance of justice here." Gawain seized my hands and stared into my eyes. "If you would win back Inverfyre, your best course is to ensure your own survival first."

I knew he spoke aright, just as my every instinct fought his advice. The keep slumbered around us, the light revealing that it was just before the dawn. Rain drummed steadily against the stone, dampness rising from the very floors, silvery light turning the old stones to pewter.

I could smell the rushes in the hall, the meat that had been consumed the night before, the ale that had been spilled. I could smell the warmth of sleeping bodies, many of whom had not washed since Christmas, mingled with woodsmoke and wet forest. A peregrine cried from a high perch and the river that fed the lake below the keep could be heard faintly gurgling.

These were the smells and the sounds of home. It was the only home I had ever known and the only one I had ever desired.

And it should be mine. It was obscene that the MacLarens would steal it from me, unspeakable that I should have to flee to save my own life.

"Think of the child you bear," he said quietly and I knew he spoke aright. There was more than my own life to preserve, though this child was owed more than what I could grant him from outside Inverfyre's walls.

Gawain's hand was tanned and strong, the hand of a man unafraid to do what had to be done, unafraid to choose his own life even if it meant leaving what he loved. I supposed that if I had never known a home like this one, if I had been as rootless as he, then I might think such indecision as mine foolish.

I met his gaze and saw both sympathy and conviction there. He knew my instincts warred within me, just as I recognized that in another heartbeat, he would abandon me here with those instincts without a backward glance.

Had he not warned me as much?

Gawain might not look back when our ways inevitably parted, but I understood that I would remember him for all my days and nights.

And not with regret.

When I took Gawain's hand, I had a heavy heart, but more for knowing my import to him than the prospect of leaving my abode. And so, I tugged him in the opposing direction to the portal.

"I cannot leave my mother's crucifix," I whispered, letting him think it was sentimentality for my family that prompted this choice. That was not my reason. I had to have the crucifix because Gawain had returned it to me, because the thief had defied his instincts and his own advantage.

Gawain might never care for another, but he had made a concession to me. That gesture was one I would long cherish. Before he could protest further, I tugged his hand, releasing his grip when he resisted me, and strode back into Inverfyre's hall.

I would have one keepsake to show when I told our son of his father, Gawain Lammergeier.

Fiona would have claimed the gem, of this I was certain. I had seen the greedy gleam in her eyes when the crucifix fell out of the package. She would have let no other lay a hand upon it.

I had only to find her. Gawain muttered a curse behind me. I smiled to myself when his footfalls echoed softly behind me, liking that I had not misread the gallantry he liked to hide.

I tiptoed through the hall, looking at this face and

another, dodging dogs and bones left upon the floor. It was disgusting that the hall had been reduced to such squalor in a single night. My temptation was to rouse the lot of them and set them to cleaning their own mire.

I restrained myself with an effort, well aware of Gawain silently stalking me. He exuded exasperation and I feared his thoughts alone would wake those around me.

One man snored and rolled over, flinging his hand across the floor before me. I halted, heart hammering, fearing he was not truly asleep and meant to seize my ankle. A dog rose and shook itself, regarded us with disinterest, then trod circles in the rushes and went back to sleep with a sigh. The man slumbered even as I stepped carefully over his arm.

The sky had lightened and I knew I had not much time. Fiona was not in the hall. I glanced up the stairs, wondering whether she had been so bold as to take my own bed. She had made comments aplenty over the years as to the softness of its mattresses, always compared with the meanness of her straw pallet.

And why not? Who would halt her?

"No," Gawain whispered urgently, evidently guessing my intent. I felt him snatch at my wrist, but I was gone, dashing up the stairs as quickly and quietly as I could.

I dared to glance back from the summit, and found him fast behind me, eyes flashing with rare anger. He caught me against him from behind and hustled me through the doorway at the top of the stairs, his words against my ear.

"Would you prefer to die?" he demanded. His arms were tight around my waist and we huddled together in the shadows pooled in the corridor. "I cannot believe you are so witless as to not understand the peril of our situation. There will be prices upon our heads as soon as our escape is discovered."

"I must have the crucifix," I repeated stubbornly. "I

know Fiona will have it and I would wager that she has claimed my bed, too. If she wears the gem, you will have a challenge to steal it."

"Ah." Gawain smiled at the prospect, his eyes bright, then held up a finger to caution me.

We stood motionless for what seemed an eternity. Gawain left me, my back chilling with his absence, and moved with silent grace to the portal of what had been Fergus' solar. He listened intently, then held up two fingers and made a gesture to indicate someone sleeping.

"Alasdair and Ranald?" I mouthed the words, guessing that Fergus' brother and cousin would have taken his quarters.

Gawain shrugged, indicating with a lewd gesture that he guessed those two occupants to be men. I bit back my laughter and he winked at me.

He was across the hall at the portal to my former chamber in the blink of an eye. I was startled that he could move so quickly, then watched as his eyes narrowed.

He held up one finger, then indicated the occupant's gender by cupping his hands before his chest.

Fiona. I wondered how he could be certain, then reasoned he had eavesdropped upon many a sleeper over the years. There might be a different timber to breathing between genders, or simply a greater tendency to snore. I could not say.

But I believed him.

Gawain beckoned me with a flick of his finger, pointing disapprovingly to a floorboard I knew was inclined to squeak. That he remembered such a detail from his last visit impressed me until I realized it was part of his trade. I reached his side so silently that he gave my fingers an approving squeeze as our shadows melded together.

He opened the door as quietly as he had when I had awaited him in my bath. The hair on the back of my neck prickled in recollection of that meeting—and the night that followed—and I wondered whether he savored the sweetness of that memory. I glanced to his expression of concentration and guessed that I would never know.

I further surmised that that might be best. The truth might not please me, not in this case.

The shutters were open, letting the morning's first light touch the room's contents with pearly grey. Fiona slept upon her back in my bed, every pillow plumped beneath her head, her mouth open and her chin wobbling. We eased closer, like two malevolent faeries at the crib of a babe in an old tale, then leaned over her.

The amber crucifix glinted upon her chest. She had found a heavy but humble chain of some dull grey metal and used it to hang the jewel around her neck. Her fist was knotted around the lower arm of the cross, as if she guessed that some stalwart soul might covet her pilfered prize. The light danced in the stones, taunting me to reclaim it.

I felt defeated, knowing that it could not be had without awakening Fiona but still not wanting to be without it. I reached out a hand, thinking that I could simply seize it and run for lack of a better plan.

Gawain restrained me with a touch and a disapproving look.

Truly, this was his art. I nodded and hovered closer to watch. He shook a finger in warning and gestured me back to the door, touching his ear so that I knew to listen for any arrivals.

I did as I was bidden, but still I watched him, fascinated.

He stood there, as motionless as a statue, for longer than I could have believed possible. His gaze darted over the room, over Fiona, as if he memorized every detail. He leaned over her, assessing the problem from all sides.

I nigh screamed with impatience. He was the one who counseled that we flee with all haste!

Just when I might have chided him, Gawain bent slowly and pursed his lips. I thought he meant to kiss Fiona, but instead he blew gently upon her cheek. She brushed at the first touch of air with her fingertips, releasing the crucifix as she did so and turning her face toward him. To my surprise, she smiled, perhaps greeting a lover in her dreams.

Then she locked her hand around the ornament again. I frowned in frustration, but Gawain was undeterred. He breathed her name, the sound so low that it seemed to come of another world. He blew again and Fiona's smile broadened.

"Tarsuinn," I whispered. Gawain granted me an enquiring glance. I clasped my hands together and tried to look like a besotted maiden dreaming of her lover true, then pointed to Fiona. "She adores Tarsuinn," I mouthed.

He nodded once, then bent closer. "It is I, Tarsuinn, come to tryst with my lady love," he whispered and Fiona smiled.

"Tarsuinn?" she mumbled.

"Yes, Tarsuinn." He blew again, gently, his words a perfect whisper of desire. "Do not reject me, fair Fiona."

Her fingers unfurled from the crucifix, then she tentatively reached a hand toward Gawain.

He gallantly kissed her fingertips.

Another gentle breath, another lover's murmur, and Fiona sighed as she turned fully toward Gawain. She rolled from her back to her side, whispered Tarsuinn's name. She tucked one hand beneath her cheek and left the other upon the mattress, as if she would whisper secrets to another sharing her pillow, then pursed her lips for a kiss.

I clapped my hand over my mouth at Gawain's chagrined response.

Then I saw that her move had made the crucifix land upon the mattress, the chain coiled in the fold of flesh between her breasts.

Gawain did not look my way, so completely did he concentrate upon his task. He opened the purse that hung from his belt and removed two pieces of metal. I craned my neck to see. They were not quite awls and not quite nails from a horse's shoe. Indeed, I would not have picked up either from the ground even if I spied them.

But evidently they were sharp upon the sides. He slipped one into a link of the chain, then pressed it together with the second, the link snapping between the two tools.

He bent to touch his lips to Fiona's puckered mouth, whispering her name for good measure. As she arched toward him, he adeptly slipped the crucifix from the broken chain, increment by increment. He moved so slowly that I feared I would scream with the uncertainty.

"Tarsuinn!" Fiona's noisy sigh of delight seemed to fill the chamber. My heart pounded so that I could hear nothing else.

Gawain did not appear to breathe, nor did he seem agitated. He moved as languidly as if he had all the time in Christendom. His hands were steady as he coaxed the gem closer and closer to being entirely in his grasp.

It disappeared abruptly into his hand in the same moment that he stepped carefully away.

"Until later, my lady love," he whispered and blew Fiona a kiss. He turned to me, eyes gleaming in his triumph. I stepped forward, so anxious to claim my prize that I forgot the loose floorboard between myself and the bed.

It groaned so loudly that we both froze in horror. For a

moment, I thought it would pass unnoticed. Fiona frowned in her sleep and burrowed deeper into the covers. I dared to exhale in relief.

Then her hand moved to close upon the crucifix and my eyes widened in horror. Gawain glanced over the chamber in haste, and I knew he sought something of roughly the same size and shape to slip into her hand. He seized a small candlestick, but it was too late.

Fiona's hand closed upon nothing. Her eyes flew open. Her shock was evident when she spied us, but she bellowed with alarming speed and volume.

"Thieves!" She bounded from the bed, and shouted loudly enough to wake Fergus himself. "Thieves, scoundrels, and criminals! The murderers have escaped!"

Then she screamed fit to shatter glass.

The door of Fergus' chamber banged upon the wall of the corridor and boots thundered upon the stairs. Fiona screamed and screamed.

"Fool woman," I muttered.

Gawain winked at me, such a mischievous twinkle in his eyes that I knew he enjoyed the challenge before us. We lunged as one for the connected door to the last chamber on this level of the keep. We barricaded it behind us, dropping the latch, then slid the sole trunk in the room against it. I was breathless, but Gawain surveyed the small chamber.

The men burst audibly into the room behind us. The sounds of shouting and stamping and a woman raging carried easily through the door. I had a fleeting hope that we might make the stairs while the men were occupied with Fiona and reached for the door to the corridor.

"No," Gawain said in a tone that told me it was pointless

to argue the matter. He tightened his grip upon my hand and kicked open the shutters over the window.

I recalled all too well that he had once been cast through this very opening, and at my command. The lake glistened far below, looking cold and deep.

Was this his vengeance?

"No!" I cried, pulling back and fighting his grip.

Gawain released me readily. He stepped to the lip of the chamber and balanced on the balls of his feet, unafraid as he assessed the drop before him. The green forest canopy stretched into the distance, uncommonly vivid in first leaf of spring. He glanced back and the light of the dawn touched his features with silver.

He might have been of the fey, gifted with the ability to fly.

Gawain offered his hand to me without a word. He proposed that we leap together. He would not cast me into the abyss alone. But still, I quailed with fear.

"There must be another way." Even as I said the words, I knew my hope was not to be. Blows hammered on the wooden door behind us, then footsteps sounded in the corridor.

We were surrounded.

Gawain's gaze flicked to the lake once again, impatience touching his expression. "Now!"

"But . . ." The door began to splinter behind me. I caught a glimpse of Alasdair's fury through a widening crack and my heart nigh stopped.

I would never leave this room alive, if we did not flee.

I leapt toward Gawain as the men kicked the door with unexpected strength. His arm locked around my waist in the same moment that he stepped off into the void. The men burst into the chamber with a shout and Alasdair snatched at the air behind us.

Gawain spared Alasdair a jaunty wave of farewell.

I could not have cared. I screamed with terror as we fell, my arms locked around Gawain's neck. We fell and fell and fell, certainly to a fate far worse than the one that might have met us above. I knew we would perish immediately, rather than sometime this day. I screamed with all my might, screamed with the vigor of what was certainly my last breath.

XII

It was only when the cold water closed over us that I realized Gawain had been laughing as we fell. I was outraged by his cavalier manner.

I was more indignant that, not only did I not die, I was utterly graceless in the cold water. I began to sink, despite my struggles to reach the surface. To my relief and disgust, Gawain seized me by the back of my chemise—much as one would seize a wet cat—and hauled me toward the light.

I came up sputtering, cold, embarrassed and flustered. I spied the merry sparkle in his eyes and could have spit sparks.

"Do not laugh at me!" I huffed. "There is nothing amusing about our predicament!"

"Trust me, it is easier the second time," Gawain asserted with disgusting composure. His arms moved powerfully beneath the surface of the water and kept him afloat. His hair was dark gold, slicked back against his head, and he looked so at ease that he might have preferred to be in such a dilemma.

That was the sum of what I saw before I slipped under the water again. I fought for my survival and came up, gulping for air and probably looking like a landed fish as I did so. I took a great swallow of lake water for my trouble and nigh coughed up my innards trying to take a simple breath. In the meantime, I sank lower again, despite my wild attempts to keep my face above water.

"Can you swim?" Gawain inquired in the tone one might use to ask whether a guest would prefer venison or pork.

"No!" I shouted, then sputtered as I sank yet again. This time, a strong hand caught me around the waist and lifted me to the surface.

"Better?" he inquired as I coughed in a most inelegant way.

"I think sometimes that you try to ensure that I am disheveled in your presence," I accused.

Gawain laughed. "It is the only time you seem to have blood in your veins, Evangeline. When you bind your hair and lift your chin, you are like a woman wrought of ice." He winked. "And I confess to preferring fire to ice, even if it prompts your ire."

I could have dunked him then, but I was not so distraught that I forgot he was my sole chance of salvation. Something fell into the water beside us with a hearty splash, deluging us again. It was the trunk that we had used to barricade the door. It floated for a moment, then sank much as I had, its base so damaged that the water readily filled it.

We both looked up to see the silhouettes of our pursuers as they leaned out over the water. A mist of rain drizzled between us, disguising their features. They cast something else after us and Gawain adroitly pulled me from the way.

"Hang on this way," he counseled as I seized him in gratitude. He guided my hands to his shoulders and I am ashamed to say that I dug my nails into his flesh when I clutched at him. "I ask only that you let me breathe, Evangeline. It will be for the better of both of us."

With another confident wink, Gawain moved so that I was behind him, then he began to swim for the shore. He moved like an otter, his strokes so fluid and effortless, our passage so considerable that I was envious of his ability.

"I never learned to swim," I said, feeling the need to offer an explanation. "I was not allowed."

"Because it was feared that a fragile maiden would die of the cold in this lake?"

"I am not so fragile as that!"

"I know that, but there are those who make assumptions based upon gender alone."

"Indeed," I said, surprised to find our opinion of this practice in agreement. "Swimming was forbidden because it was not deemed a fitting activity for a lady."

"While I was compelled to learn, for the opposing reason."

"What was that?"

"When one travels often by ship, it is useful to be able to ensure one's own survival. My father's opinion was that men are fundamentally selfish and cannot be relied upon to serve any interest beyond their own in a time of crisis."

I could hardly argue with that. "I suspect he was right."

"More right than I knew."

"And what is that to mean?"

"That his edict applied also to himself." Gawain sounded grim, then said no more. As he was saving my life, I deemed it unfitting to annoy him with unwelcome questions. I bit my tongue and held on, my relief increasing as the shore drew steadily nearer.

"It is warmer than the last time I swam in this lake," he

mused, his good humor evidently restored. "Though still not warm enough for my taste."

"As in Sicily?"

"Indeed." I heard the smile in Gawain's tone. "So, you were prepared for your future as the lady wife of some barbarian by being forbidden to swim."

I took umbrage at his mockery. "You may not believe as much but Inverfyre is a rare prize in these parts. Its site is formidable, its lineage noble and its wealth has been considerable."

"And this despite the clime and the proliferation of ruffians in its locale and its hall. I profess myself amazed."

"We are not so uncivilized as you would imply!"

"I remind you, my lady fair, of that dungeon known as the Hole. It is one of the most crudely effective means of slowly killing a man that I have ever seen."

"But we are not without refinement. My mother was most concerned with bringing the charms of the king's court to Inverfyre. She was the daughter of a lord in Burgundy." I sighed in recollection. "By her command, I was not to run, climb trees, frolic with boys as I had for years or lift the hem of my skirts above my ankles. The celebration of my tenth birthday was a dark occasion in my recollection, for that was when all the rules changed and not in a way I appreciated."

Gawain chuckled as we drew nearer to the shore. "Let me guess—you were to embroider?"

"There was no time for such fripperies at Inverfyre. I was to spin, for there was never enough cloth to replace the threadbare garments."

"And yet you did not hesitate to leave Inverfyre without your drop-spindle," he teased.

"I was hopeless with the task. My mother finally allowed that I could watch the falconer."

"Not aid him?"

"That would have been inappropriate." I smiled in recollection. "But Tarsuinn's father let me feed the birds and sing to them, he even let me choose their feeding songs."

"You were lucky to have had such companionship."

"Indeed." I wondered then whether Gawain had been raised alone, without friends or family other than his father, whether that accounted for his desire to remain alone.

Had he ever been loved? Though my parents had had their harsh moments and I had oft felt unappreciated due to my gender, I had known without doubt that I was loved.

I appreciated that now as I never had before.

Gawain rose to stand in the shallows, his garments dripping. He helped me to gain my footing, my hands held firmly in his, then bent and kissed me so boldly that I no longer felt the chill. "I should have guessed that you were one to win your way despite the odds. I have an unholy affection for willful, charming women."

He laughed and I laughed with him, my heart sinking a little even as I did so. His words made it more than clear that I was but one of many, neither first nor last in his affections.

Oddly, I felt less appreciation for his honesty than I had before.

To my astonishment, Gawain's horse was tethered in the shadows of the woods, his pack and saddle at the ready. The steed nickered as Gawain offered me dry chausses, a chemise and tabard.

"My apologies, but I tend to not carry women's garb."

But I was still amazed that he had been so prepared. "You knew you would leave the keep this way."

"I guessed that matters might not proceed smoothly. Your people are somewhat inclined to take insult with theft." He patted his saddlebag as he tied it to the saddle, his expression so satisfied that I eyed it with suspicion. I touched it once I was dressed, knowing that round shape all too well.

"The *Titulus*!" I gaped at him, finding myself matching his triumphant smile with one of my own. "But how? But when?"

He flicked a playful finger across the tip of my nose. "I was here a day earlier than any in the keep knew. I had a matter to resolve before I declared myself to you."

"But . . ."

"I learned upon my last visit here that a hasty departure can be an asset." Gawain lifted his finger and I heard the distant groan of Inverfyre's gates opening. I met his gaze with alarm. "They saw us make the shore. I suspect the chase will not be readily abandoned."

"Not with Dubhglas so sorely injured. Alasdair will want blood for vengeance."

"Dubhglas." Gawain rolled his eyes. "How could a man be expected to live a life of any merit burdened with such a name? I would have done him a favor to have killed him."

"You do not mean that!"

He laughed merrily, clearly liking that I could discern the truth of his intent.

A roar of outrage carried to our ears just then, interrupting our jest. I leapt into the saddle, anxious to be gone. Gawain swung into the saddle behind me and gave the beast his heels. It trotted, cautious of its footing along the shore and I knew it had need of encouragement.

"There!" I declared. "There is a path through the woods to the road. It is narrow but passable. Lead the beast to it."

"I cannot discern any passage," Gawain said, pushing the reins into my hands. "You guide the beast."

I faltered for words, so surprised was I that he entrusted

his fate to my hands. The men of my life have insisted upon leading the horses or guiding the way, even when they knew not what they did or where they went.

"Surely, you jest," I managed to say.

"Surely not. You know the way and I do not." Anxiety tinged his tone. "I remind you that our lives hang in the balance, Evangeline. Do you mean to make haste or not?"

I laughed and gripped the reins with delight. I am no common rider, for I was fairly raised in the saddle. All the same, no man had ever trusted his fate or his horse to me.

Until Gawain. My heart thudded.

I nudged his feet out of the stirrups and half-stood in them myself, leaning forward to speak to the beast. I used my knees as I had been taught. The horse was well-trained, taking my command with ease. It quickly discerned the path I followed and increased its pace without much encouragement from me. It was sure-footed for its short stature.

"Praise be that you have such a steed," I said to Gawain. I cast a glance over my shoulder as we gained the road.

He smiled sunnily at me. His grip was firm upon my hips, but he seemed at ease. "I have developed a fondness for the creature's steadfast determination."

Determination it had, and speed as well. I cried out encouragement as the beast leapt to the dirt road, then dug my heels into its sides.

It ran like the wind, despite its double burden. I looked back to find Alasdair far behind us and laughed as I coaxed the steed to greater speed. We were escaping!

I was truly free! The wind unfurled my wet braid and ran its fingers through the length of my hair. The steed's muscles moved beneath me with vigor, Gawain held fast to my hips and I felt more alive than I had in all my days. We would not only survive this day, but we had the *Titulus*.

For the first time in many years, I felt invincible. I knew that I could restore Inverfyre to my hand, I knew that I could clear my name and bring the truth to light. I knew that Fergus' kin could not stop me—and I knew that I needed no man to aid my cause. I would resolve this myself and reclaim Inverfyre for my son.

Given that, I was in a mood to celebrate. I liked being with Gawain—it was his confidence in me that fed my confidence in myself. I liked his uncommon blend of ease and determination. I liked how bold and unrestrained I felt in his presence—indeed, I felt that I was myself solely in his presence. It was clear that my desire for him was returned.

But it was also clear that he was not a man who would undertake my quest to regain my family holding. He had relics to steal, maidens to ravish and pomegranates to savor in distant Sicily.

On this night, though, a widow would ravish him and give us both a memory to warm the flesh when we faced cold nights alone. I wanted to savor this last night with Gawain.

It was the least I could offer the scoundrel who had just saved my life.

It was falling dark when we spied the roofs of a village ahead. "Do you know it?" Gawain asked.

I shook my head. "We are too far from Inverfyre's walls. This must be the Comyn's land and one of their villages."

"Hide your hair," Gawain counseled. I tucked my hair into my tabard and pulled his hood over my head. "Remain silent and keep your head low."

"None will know me here, especially in such garb as this."

Gawain's lips thinned. "Indulge me." Then he gave me a squeeze. "And dismount to lead the horse, if you will. People will suspect if I tend to my squire and not the other way around."

"I will not be your squire!"

"You will if you mean to sleep untroubled this night and ride onward." He grinned then, enjoying my dissatisfaction too well.

I gave him a look fit to curdle milk as I did his bidding, for I suspected that he enjoyed himself overmuch. I trod before the tired beast, my head down and face hidden, and Gawain began to sing.

He feigned drunkenness with appalling ease, and the villagers spilled from their homes to look upon us. "Is this Edinburgh yet, lad?" he roared.

"No, milord," I mumbled dutifully. My sour mood did not last long with his antics and I had to fight the urge to laugh.

"Then, where in the name of God are we?" He stood in the stirrups and waved a hand at the village. Praise be that his steed was a sensible one—or accustomed to him—for it walked onward, oblivious to his behavior. "And where shall a man find a decent cup of brew? God in heaven, will we have to spend another night outside of the king's walls?"

"Yes, milord. I fear as much, milord."

"You!" He pointed at a man who seemed to stand slightly forward from the assembled people. "You look to be a man of resource." Gawain flicked a coin in the man's direction and it flashed in the last light of the sun. "Find me an innkeeper, or failing that, a soul with a keg of ale and an empty pallet for a guest."

The man bit the coin, his eyes widening slightly at the quality of the silver, then he bowed. "I shall host you myself, my lord, and in the same fashion as I would host the king, for another of these coins."

"Have you meat for your board this night?"

"Venison stew, my lord." This he said boldly, as if asserting his right to hunt deer. He had no such right, for it was one granted to the nobility alone—but only a nobleman could demand compense for the crime.

Perhaps this was why the man would seek Gawain's favor, to ensure that no penalty was demanded.

"It is said my wife makes the finest venison stew in all of Aberfinnan. And my stable has a loft filled with sweet straw. The structure is newly completed this very year and free of vermin."

Gawain, typically, was indifferent to minor crimes wrought against some absent or distant overlord. "Two coins it will be then," he cried gaily. "And a third in the morn if my boy and I awaken unaccosted. You will not find my coin if you try to steal from me in the night—instead you will find my blade in your back. Are we understood?"

The man stepped forward, his eyes narrowed. "You will find my blade in your back, my lord, if my daughters suffer a visit from you this night. Are we understood?" The villagers took a discrete step away from the man, their eyes wide at his boldness. Indeed, I was shocked that he would make such a demand openly.

"Are they beautiful?" Gawain demanded.

The man straightened. "As fair as a May morn."

"Then they may be the sole asset you own. Keep them as safe from others as you would from me." Gawain dismounted and winked at me, as if in warning though I could not guess what he would say. "And you need have no fear of my desires, my good man, for I ensure that my appetites will be met when I travel abroad."

And he grinned as he slapped me on the buttocks. I flushed scarlet, knowing full well that those before us thought me to be a boy.

The villagers were shocked and fascinated, no less that this visiting nobleman indulged himself with boys than that he openly admitted as much. The whispers began immediately, and I knew that I did not imagine that our host kept his distance as he took the horse's reins.

"It is splendidly sensible, you must admit," Gawain confided to our would-be host, as if he would talk more about his preferences.

Our host was disinclined to do so. "Of course, my lord." The man bowed and strode away, leaving me fuming beside Gawain.

"In this, you go too far . . ." I began hotly if beneath my breath.

Gawain waved away my objection, then leaned closer, his eyes gleaming. "And how else would I ensure that none glimpsed your gender this night? How else would I ensure that we had no curious parties visiting our lodgings in the night? I have flashed coin and I am thief enough to know that there are more of my own kind in every corner of every land."

"I see," I said primly, disliking that his tactic showed a measure of good sense.

"You will follow the steed and see it brushed down, like the dutiful squire that you are," Gawain continued softly, granting my ear a friendly cuff. "I shall take my meal with the family and bring yours to you, the better that you not be detected."

I was irked that he had matters well in hand, and that my part was so neatly consigned to the less amusing tasks that had to be done. I knew he was right and this only annoyed me further. A cup of ale and a bowl of stew before a warm fire would have suited me far better than brushing down a horse while my belly growled.

"I would suggest you do not defy me," Gawain said in a voice as smooth as fine silk. I met his gaze and found it piercingly green. He arched a fair brow, his expression making him look devilish indeed. "That murder that stains my blade? It was my own accomplice, in fact the boy who ensured that I escaped public execution. I could not have managed that escape alone, but he came to my aid most cunningly."

"But . . ."

Gawain's eyes narrowed. "Sadly, he was caught while we fled."

I stared up at him, holding his gaze and fearing what he would say.

"And as a reward for his devoted loyalty to me, I abandoned him." Gawain's gaze never swerved from mine and I knew he told me the truth. "The villagers were a bloodthirsty crowd and one denied a hanging by my escape. I am certain Michel did not survive the day."

"You did not go back for him?" I tried to swallow the lump in my throat. "You did not try to save him?"

Gawain smiled a chilly smile. "I saved my own hide instead. Indeed, I never looked back. There is honesty for you. There is the measure of the man with whom you have been allied. Do not forget this truth."

With that, he released my elbow and left me standing outside the village walls. He hailed our host and merrily made his way into that man's abode, noisily proclaiming the beauty of the man's daughters.

My heart sank with every step he took. I had been warned and I knew it well.

XIII

When Gawain came to the stable, the light had faded almost to naught, though I could see his silhouette. He paused on the threshold, then made his way across the stables with care. He stroked the horse and spoke to it, then peered up at the loft. "Are you there?"

"Have you drunk all the ale so soon as that?"

Gawain chuckled, untroubled by my tone, and climbed nimbly to the loft. He bowed low. "I bring an offering of peace, if the lady will hear of it," he teased.

"It had best be a fine offering," I said with a hauteur I did not quite feel. Indeed, my pulse already quickened at his proximity, though I knew I should heed his warning.

"Venison stew, bread and, remarkably, a cup of ale for your very own."

I fell upon the fare like a hungry wolf, unable to feign disdain before the prospect of a hot meal. The settling of food in my belly spread a heat that dissolved much of my resentment.

Gawain peeled off his clothes in turn, looking about himself as I ate. "This is not so barbaric as I feared."

"Was that why you lingered in our host's abode, to ensure your comfort?"

He raised his brows, then settled beside me. "To allay their suspicions, more like."

"By drinking their ale?"

"By spreading sufficient coin that they will feel no urge to gossip to strangers about us. It can make an alliance out of naught, the spending of coin."

"How much do you have?"

Gawain dug in his purse, as if concerned with that very matter. "Enough to see us to Ravensmuir, at least. And there, our ways shall part forevermore."

It was Ravensmuir that had been my destination all those months ago, Ravensmuir where it was reputed I could find the stolen relic that I sought. I had looked but once upon its forbidding facade and known that my mission would be a failure.

But the Fates had smiled and I had spied a golden-haired man riding south, riding with all haste away from Ravensmuir with a bundle beneath his arm. I had gambled on his identity and his burden, despite the years lost, and astonishingly, I had won the wager.

Or had I? I studied his shadowed features, this man who could be both tender and callous, and knew that my wager had brought me far more than I had expected.

"You will return to Sicily," I guessed.

Gawain nodded once. "My brother Merlyn can aid you in your petition to the king. His is an honorable soul—indeed, it could be said that all the good traits in our family were claimed by Merlyn afore I was conceived. You can trust Merlyn." He seemed untroubled by this, but I knew enough to suspect otherwise. He was too composed, his expression too carefully neutral.

"I thought he had killed your sire. That is the rumor."

Gawain shrugged, his manner yet cool. "Beyond that, Merlyn is honorable. As you are neither my father nor any soul associated with him, you should be safe at Ravensmuir."

"And you?"

He smiled tightly. "I shall leave, as you guessed."

I thought again of his earlier warning as to his foul character and wondered. I ate in silence, unable to believe that Gawain was as wicked as he would like me to think, but knowing all the same that we were not destined to be together.

Oblivious to my musing, Gawain completed his inventory of the coins. Amber glinted between the folds of leather and I swallowed my mouthful of stew.

"May I have the crucifix?"

Gawain flicked a bright gaze my way. "It would be safer here, for the moment." He secured it in his purse once again, then stretched out beside me.

"But I would like to have it in my own grasp."

"Fear not, I will return it to you at Ravensmuir." I near spilled the ale when he pressed a kiss to my shoulder, his eyes gleaming with devilry. "You have my most solemn pledge, Evangeline."

I regarded him, not knowing what to make of his playful mood. "You think me foolish to have a care for my family's heirlooms and traditions."

Gawain sobered. "I think you care more for what others have insisted you should desire than for what you might desire yourself."

"It is the responsibility of any laird's child to ensure that his legacy continues. . . ."

"What of your father's own failures? What of the deterioration of Inverfyre's fortunes, of your father's choice to lie to his people?"

"Do not malign my father!"

"I note only that the legacy he granted to you was a damaged one, that the fault of Inverfyre's state is not yours alone."

I straightened. "I have a duty . . ."

"To those who are dead and rotted, to those who have demanded too much of you." Gawain laid a fingertip across my lips when I would have argued with him. His gaze was solemn. "Perhaps I am too selfish, but you are not selfish enough. What do *you* desire, Evangeline? What do you wish, if you could pursue any path you chose, if you were unburdened by responsibilities and duties?"

"I am not so unburdened."

"If you were."

I looked away, fearing that he had glimpsed my unwelcome urge to journey far, that he had spied my rebellious urge to forget Inverfyre. "It is a foolish question. I am so burdened and always will be. I have no right to desire any path other than the one demanded of me by my birthright."

How odd that my voice did not resonate with the conviction it once had carried.

Gawain laid a hand upon my shoulder. "Your chance is here, Evangeline. Your opportunity has come to make what you will of your days."

I bit my tongue and looked to my hands. Gawain was wrong, though part of me yearned to agree with him. I knew my duties, I knew that nothing had halted my forebear Magnus Armstrong from achieving his dream and thus nothing should halt me. I knew that I must exhaust every possibility before abandoning Inverfyre to the MacLaren clan, even if I must die in the attempt.

I could not persuade a man like Gawain Lammergeier of the necessity of such a course, so I said no more.

Gawain spoke lightly then, as if he knew he had pressed too much. "I must admit, Evangeline, that I did linger at our host's board for longer than there was need to do so."

I glanced at him, wondering what jest he played now. "Indeed?"

"Indeed." Gawain grinned, mischief personified, and pulled off his tabard, leaving his hair rumpled. "The man told no lie. His daughters are gorgeous creatures, all long hair and sweet faces and breasts!" He shook his head as if marvelling anew, then cupped his hands before himself. "Breasts as round and ripe as . . . as pomegranates!" He winked at me. "Which reminds me—do I not deserve a reward for saving you from drowning?"

I cast the wooden bowl at him. "Cur!"

Gawain laughed. "Why not frolic abed until we make Ravensmuir, that we might better remember each other's charms?"

"There is no need."

"What if you have not yet conceived that child?"

"I have!"

"Let us be certain." He whispered something that made my ears burn. I could not imagine what ailed him, for he had never been so coarse of speech in my presence. Perhaps he showed his true nature finally. Perhaps I should be glad to know the ruffian he was.

I retreated across the loft. I was vexed with Gawain and did not trouble to hide it. "We both know that we have used each other for our own ends and no more. Let us be done with the lie of that. You do not need to couple with me to sate my pride."

Gawain's gaze flickered, and I wondered then if I had responded precisely as he had intended. He took his cloak without another word and bedded down on the far side of the loft. It was not long until I heard his breathing slow, though I lay awake, yearning for what I had denied myself.

The reckless side of me could have had the upper hand for one last time this night, for the demure and proper Evangeline would reign for the rest of my days and nights.

But it was too late.

Indeed, I could not help but wonder whether Gawain had contrived to annoy me to ensure that we did not meet abed.

But then, he would only have done as much if he had a care for something other than his own satisfaction, and I knew that was not the case. No, he was a knave and a scoundrel, as I had known from the outset, and he was simply confident enough in my presence to believe that I accepted him as he was.

I wished belatedly that he had not shared this view with me, that we could have parted with my illusion of his character intact, then reminded myself that I had been the one to request his honesty.

It was cold comfort that Gawain himself had warned me that I might not like what honesty showed. I thumped the straw of my makeshift pillow, tossed and turned, and tried desperately to sleep.

I waited until I heard the first goats bleating, my sense of purpose complete. Mercifully, Gawain slept even when I rose, so there was no need for an awkward parting. I stared down at him as I dressed, knowing that I could never change the manner of man he was. Indeed, I had no desire to do so—had he been a sober and solemn man of honor, he could never have unbridled my passion as he did. I would have his son and he would never see the child, never see me again.

What we had had would have to be enough.

I studied him as I refastened my garments, then leaned close to kiss his cheek. I could not bring myself to touch him, lest he awakened, so I took a deep breath of his scent to sustain me for what might be many years of solitude, or worse, dutiful coupling.

Then I repeated my original crime against Gawain—I stole his saddle and his horse, the garments he had lent to me and his saddlebag with the relic within it. I left him his purse, though I stealthily removed my mother's crucifix.

I felt unexpectedly heartsick as I rode away from Aberfinnan and the man who had awakened a passion I had not known I possessed. I rubbed away tears with my fingertips, but rode on, unable to deny my responsibilities.

All—my forebears, my kith and my kin, the villagers dependent upon me and my father before me—demanded that I grant my all to reclaim my legacy.

Regardless of the cost.

It was evening by the time I reached Inverfyre again, and the hills were quiet. Dark clouds gathered anew, threatening yet another downpour. I did not have much time to find the aid I needed desperately. I raced down the winding path I knew so well, turned the last curve and expected full well to find Adaira's hut.

But there was nothing there. I dismounted and retraced my steps, fearing I had taken a wrong turn even as I doubted it could be done.

I heard the falcons cry then and saw them circling above

me. This was no good sign. Indeed, as I listened with care, I heard a hunting party drawing closer.

The hills had been quiet because they were full of watchful eyes. I had foolishly assumed that all were busy elsewhere, but they were busy watching for me. I had been spied and I would be returned to Inverfyre's keep to face my fate.

I did not imagine that Alasdair would be merciful. Sweat ran down my spine at the sound of the hounds, barking and whimpering, crushing the undergrowth as they sought me out. They were close, too close.

Adaira could grant me refuge. I moved with haste, my gaze darting from this crooked tree to that bent one, to the oak that marked this turn to . . .

To the deep shadow where Adaira's abode should have been.

I turned in place, incredulous, but her hut was gone as surely as if it had never been. The shadows were deep and murky here, almost impenetrable. I peered into the forest and could discern the outlines of trees that I should not have been able to see for the hut itself.

I licked my lips as the men shouted, directing the dogs toward me. I could hear the horses now, their hooves pounding on the path. The dogs began to bark with renewed vigor and I knew they were upon my scent. I sent out a silent plea to the woman who had been my confidante, begging her to aid me.

But Adaira did not reveal herself.

The forest brooded, holding its secrets, every hare hidden deeply in its burrow, every bird silenced by the echoes of the hunt. I felt watched, observed by more than hawks and hounds, under the scrutiny of a hidden woman.

My pounding heart seemed to be the sole sound of the forest at this moment. I turned one more time, even as I knew it was futile, unable to understand why Adaira betrayed me.

Then my toe struck something.

Whatever it was glittered as it rolled. I fell upon all fours to pursue it, knowing it was not of the forest itself. I reached into the underbrush and seized its smooth coolness, my heart nigh stopping when I opened my hand before my own eyes.

It was the vial that Adaira had given to me and it was still full.

I eyed the forest with newfound understanding. As I had rejected Adaira's counsel, so she now rejected me. This was no accident. Her hut was not truly gone. I had always felt that her abode was neither in this world nor of it—to evade me, she had chosen to pull it and herself deeper into the shadows. She had disappeared beyond the veil between the worlds.

She had spurned me. I had betrayed her trust and thus my access to her was denied.

Fury burned hot within my chest that she could so abandon me. I straightened, closed my fist over the cold vial, then flung it with all my force into the shadows where her hut should have been. It collided with something and shattered, though I could not have said whether it struck a tree or a wooden wall I could not see.

"You are wrong, Adaira!" I cried, caring nothing if the hounds heard me. It was already too late to flee. "I will bear this child and we shall both live to tell of it."

There was no reply, but I had expected none.

I spun, shoulders squared and chin high, just as the first dogs broke from the cover of forest. They bayed with delight at the sight of me, the men and their horses thundering fast behind them. I stood like a woman graven of stone and waited.

When I spied Niall leading the hunting party, I felt that my plan had been blessed by a force greater than any of us. There was but one tale I could tell, but one wager I could make.

The seventh son had to be born legitimately to the Laird of Inverfyre to fulfil the prophecy. That my scheme would give Niall what he desired, as well as save my life and that of my unborn child, was no small thing. I folded my hands over my belly, tried to swallow the lump in my throat and stepped forward.

The hounds barked as they circled me, snapping that I not stray too far. Then the horses came to a halt around me, their heads tossing and nostrils flaring. Alasdair took the fore, Ranald beside him, but I turned my gaze upon Niall. Even I, who had no tender feelings for him beyond the legacy of affection from our shared childhood, had to admit that he was a fine-looking man.

"Evangeline," Niall said with clear disappointment. "You should not have tried to escape. Matters will only be worse for you now."

"I could do nothing else, Niall," I said, casting my voice so that none should miss what I said. "I could not let our unborn child be killed so easily as that."

The men gasped and exchanged glances. Alasdair's lips tightened to a grim line and he urged his horse forward.

"The heir to Inverfyre is cossetted in my belly," I declared boldly. "It is true that I took a lover while Fergus yet breathed, for Fergus yearned for a son. I took a lover with the blessing of Fergus, for he said that Inverfyre had need of an heir."

"But the stranger . . ." Alasdair began to protest.

I interrupted him, knowing that he would disavow my child's legacy if Gawain was known to be the babe's father. "The stranger was a convenient scapegoat, no more than that. My lover rides among you."

As they slanted glances at each other, I walked toward Niall. I reached up and laid my hand over his, willing him to support the lie I had to tell to save my child and my home.

"Wed me, Niall, and ensure that the child we have already wrought is not bastard-born."

An Unlikely Knight

Gawain

XIV

I awakened alone and devoid of the *Titulus*, yet again.

All that lingered of Evangeline was her sweet scent upon my chemise, the indent of her figure in the straw. I peered over the lip of the loft, not truly surprised to find my horse gone, as well.

Had I not warned her away from me? Had I not ensured that she was disgusted with my vulgarity? I know the look of a woman whose heart is softening to the point that she believes me capable of some misguided nobility—though I had never expected pragmatic Evangeline to regard me thus, she *had* done so after I pulled her from the lake.

It would not do for her to have tender feelings for me, the greatest rogue to ever cross her threshold. Matters had been acceptable so long as we made a fair exchange—my seed for the *Titulus*, for example—and indeed, I had admired her ability to consider amorous relations like trading agreements.

But that had ended when we escaped the Hole. Indeed, the admiration and gratitude in her gaze had terrified me. I knew myself well enough to recognize that I was not a man for whom she should care.

And I had shown myself sufficiently common to ensure my point was taken. It was remarkable, for I could have spent a pleasant night betwixt the lady's thighs, but had denied my own pleasure to protect her heart.

Chivalry, which I had long believed to be dead and gone from this world unlamented, had proven to be hidden in the most unlikely of places—it had been nestled in my very marrow, and had revealed itself at a most inconvenient time.

I saw now why I had always avoided noble deeds: I had slept alone, awakened alone, been relieved of my valuables, and all because of my own misguided urge to warn the lady away from me. Gallantry, in my opinion this morn, was of less merit than most men believed.

I dressed, then leapt from the loft to the stable floor. I opened the door, knowing I should depart, but leaned against the frame instead, letting the mist of the morning surround me. It was early, the sky faintly grey.

There was no sign of Evangeline, who was clearly long gone. I should have been pleased that she took my warning with such alacrity, but instead, a gloom was cast over my mood.

A rooster strolled the perimeter of this humble clearing, tilted his head to regard the sky, and decided to delay his summons. When I looked back over the hills, I could faintly discern the silhouette of Inverfyre's tower. I narrowed my eyes and watched the hawks circling that remote place and fancied that I could hear their distant cries.

There was no doubt where Evangeline had gone. I should have already been walking in the opposite direction, yet I lingered, watching the morning sun touch that cursed tower. A year ago—indeed, a month ago!—I would have abandoned both relic and woman, continuing upon my merry way. On this day, though, I hesitated to do so. Indecision was a novelty for me, so I considered both it and its import.

Mine was no longer a concern with retrieving what I considered to be my own. I had surrendered the quest for more valuable relics than the *Titulus* in the past when they proved less difficult than this to claim. My brother Merlyn was still alive, which contributed to my diminished desire for the *Titulus*. It was likely that Merlyn could be persuaded to part with other relics gathered by our father and myself.

Indeed, he had already done so. I had ridden south this winter and made a considerable trade with my brother's consent. Given that Merlyn had abandoned the family trade, there were relics of dubious origins that he certainly preferred to not have in his possession. I had no doubt that a few more trips would ensure that I still acquired my villa in Sicily.

I recalled all too well Evangeline's admission of why she had initially seduced me. It had been so dark in the dungeon that I had had only the tremor of her voice to assess her emotions. I had heard her uncertainty, and her hope.

I remembered too my own shiver of mingled delight and dread. A child! *My* child. Our child. In past times, I would have nigh climbed the walls of that dungeon unaided to avoid any news that I was to be a father. Such confessions oft were followed by expectations and obligations, responsibilities that I could live well enough without.

Revulsion had not risen in me, though, when Evangeline spoke. It was remarkable. Perhaps it had been that none might overhear her, perhaps it had been that the lady herself could not see my response, perhaps because Evangeline had had all that she expected of me. Perhaps one baby girl had opened my eyes to possibilities. She had been a cursed amount of trouble, that child, but her smile had made me forget much of it.

I reminded myself that Ysabella would not accept another child from my hands, convinced as she was that she already sheltered one of my bastards. Yet it was not any perceived obligation to that child, or even a desire to look upon it, that drew my gaze to Inverfyre's tower.

I closed my eyes, hearing Evangeline's protestations anew, aching at her naive insistence that justice must be served. She was new to the challenge of living outside the law and burdened by her own inability to see the wickedness in others. I had seen how shocked she was by her incarceration.

She would step directly into the fire, unaware of what she risked until it was too late. She would believe that the truth was of import. I shook my head at such folly.

For this time, Evangeline's opponents would not err. They would kill her immediately and before witnesses to ensure that she could not escape or foil their plans again.

I could not permit that to happen. I could not permit this lady of stalwart will to stumble so fatally.

Evangeline was the reason why I would return to Inverfyre. Make no mistake, this was no lasting change in me. The goddess Fate had merely mistaken me for a man of honor and, despite the odds, had persuaded me to make a chivalrous choice rather than a selfish one.

Indeed, I felt responsible for Evangeline's situation. Having made too persuasive an argument that I was an unreliable and heartless scoundrel, I had inadvertently convinced the lady to retreat to Inverfyre rather than continue to Ravensmuir with me.

I had long suspected that scruples were troublesome and

thus had always ensured that I not cultivate any. It was no consolation to find my suspicions correct.

My every instinct told me it was fool's errand to pursue Evangeline and that either of us would be fortunate to escape Inverfyre again alive. My gut told me that this was no longer my concern, that the lady could fend for herself well enough. My desire to survive, which had always served me well, told me to flee for Ravensmuir while I yet could and leave this land far behind me.

But I turned back to collect my few remaining belongings, knowing full well that I would not go to Ravensmuir this morn.

No, I and my newfound scruples would go to Inverfyre.

Evangeline, I was certain, would seek out this old woman in the woods, name of Adaira. So concerned was Evangeline with justice, so persuaded was she of its power, that she would collect the sole witness of her innocence before returning to Inverfyre's keep. No doubt, she would knock upon the very gates, the old woman's hand fast in her own, certain righteousness would reign supreme.

I strode a little faster at that chilling prospect. I would have much preferred to ride through the forest than to walk, but that choice had been made for me.

Forests, after all, are filled with dangers of a most human kind. People who live in the forests outside of towns are of two types: those who choose their abode and those who have the choice made for them.

It is the nature of our kind that some are wrought wicked, and also our nature when in groups to mercilessly outcast those whose presence is not of advantage to the rest of us. I make no judgement here, merely comment upon what I have seen. One cannot readily distinguish between the unfortunate and the lawless in the forest, as either may be maimed or scarred.

Neither is less dangerous. All people of the woods are suspicious beyond expectation and, shall we say, enterprising beyond belief. They will steal, even kill, without compunction for some trinket that might ensure their own survival.

They also know their abode better than any other stranger can. A person of the forest will be found only if he or she desires to be found—thus, I made no effort to find Adaira, but concentrated on remaining undiscovered myself.

Although Alasdair and his comrades would be delighted to retrieve one of their escaped prisoners, I doubted that I would enjoy the ensuing festivities. That they might be prepared to pay a bounty for my hide had me repeatedly glancing over my shoulder.

I moved with considerable haste, knowing that I could not match the speed of the horse. At least the path was sufficiently uneven that the horse could not set an aggressive pace. My sole hope was that Evangeline had found Adaira and that the older woman had dissuaded her from marching up to Inverfyre's gates.

Of course, the old woman might be mad. There was consolation!

When it fell dark, I slept in a tree, which I assure you is not pleasurable in the least, and leapt awake at every snapping twig in my proximity.

As a result of worry, discomfort and a decided lack of life's most meager comforts, I was not at my best the following morn.

My own growling gut awakened me at first light, and having nothing with which to sate it, I began walking again.

Greenery erupted from its winter slumber on all sides of me. I had no doubt that some of what I could see was edible, but one has only to make a single bad choice of mushroom to cease foraging forever.

I know nothing of mushrooms, nor other plants, so chose to go hungry.

Thus, I was in somewhat of a sour mood—walking toward my certain demise, damp and tired and hungered—when someone tapped me upon the shoulder around midday.

I nigh leapt for the sky, so startled was I.

I spun and found a wrinkled old woman before me, chuckling to herself as she leaned upon a stick nigh as gnarled as she. She tilted her head as if to regard me, but I noted the blue haze across her eyes and knew her to be blind.

Then I recognized her.

"You are the alewife!"

"And where is the child I entrusted to your care?"

"I am not Connor MacDoughall." I stepped closer, intending to see matters straight upon one matter. I was more angry with her than even I expected. "You erred gravely in thinking that I was that babe's father. . . ."

"I knew you were not Connor," she scoffed. "You did not answer my query. Where is the child?"

"That child might have died! I know nothing of the care of children, but you, you should have known better than to force her into a stranger's care, into *my* care." I scoffed in my turn. "Now, you fear for her survival. What if it is too late?"

"You did not kill her and you are not so fool as to not ask for aid."

"You know nothing of me."

"I know that you are a man to see to his own advantage. It can be no advantage to be burdened with a dead child. You do not have her with you and did not when last you came to Inverfyre, which means that you have found a home for her. Where is it?"

"I have no obligation to confide in you."

She laughed then, a wry cackle that seemed to weaken her knees. "Do you not then?" She turned with unexpected speed and began to stride through the woods.

In a heartbeat, I realized that she would fade from view before I could catch her. Her homespun cloak already seemed to disappear at the edges in a most curious way, blending with the forest so that only her whitened hair could be spied.

If she but lifted the hood, I would lose her utterly.

"Halt! I will tell you!"

"I am blind, not deaf," she said without slowing her pace.

"You need not fear for the child. A couple have taken her in, upon my entreaty." She paused. I scrambled closer, and smiled my best smile though I knew she could not see it. "You will enjoy that they think the child to be my own bastard."

She snorted. "Where?"

"You cannot retrieve the babe or visit her. You no longer have a claim upon her, not now that you have surrendered her welfare so heedlessly."

"How far?" she demanded. "I care not where but only how far."

I considered her, then realized that she might not wish the child to return to her one day. "No one knows of your tale but me, and I will tell none."

"How far?"

"More than four days' ride."

She nodded and turned to the forest, chomping her lips together as she evidently thought about this. "It may be enough," she muttered. She strode into the forest again and it was only as she nigh disappeared that I came to my senses.

"Wait!" I lunged after her, finding a muddy puddle that she had neatly evaded and miring my boots. She did not so much as pause, so I began to run. The mud sucked at my boots, the branches slapped my face. The ground was uneven and I had a hard time meeting the old woman's pace. "Wait! I beg of you. Do you know Adaira?"

She halted suddenly, as if her feet had taken root.

I hastened toward her, disregarding the brambles that scratched my flesh and the rocks that tripped me. I came to a stumbling stop beside her, my breathing heavy. "Do you know where I might find Adaira?"

She slanted that odd milky blue glance at me, as if she could indeed see, despite her cataracts. "Why do you seek Adaira?"

"I seek the lady Evangeline, in truth, but she has gone to Adaira. She has been accused of murdering her lord husband, Fergus, and Adaira is the sole witness of her innocence."

The old woman pursed her lips.

"The lady's life could rest in your hands," I added, hoping that none in these woods held any grudges against Evangeline.

"The lady's life rests in her own hands," the alewife said firmly. "So it is with all of us." She began to march away again, but this time, I was fast behind her.

If she spurned my quest, then all the forest dwellers would do so. I have learned that they act with more cohesiveness even than those within towns—it is not merely their safety at stake, but their very lives.

"You must have some fondness for her, as you burdened me with that babe at her bidding."

The woman snorted. "The lady knew nothing of the child, nor indeed of what aid I granted to you."

"Then why did you aid me, if not by her command?"

"Because I chose to do so," she said with unexpected ferocity. "Just as I choose now to *not* aid you."

It was not my imagination that she moved more quickly then, barely stirring the leaves of the forest as she passed. She might not have been of this world, for she seemed suddenly less substantial, more likely to vanish if my gaze slipped from her. She lifted her hood, turning her entire figure to the same hue as the forest, and I despaired.

I had heard that hunger begat whimsy and now I knew that too was true.

"Do you feel no compassion for her fate?" I dodged a tree, managing to keep reasonably close behind the old woman.

She laughed. "In the great scheme of things, there are matters of more concern than the fate of any one of us. I have learned that lesson well enough myself."

"Do you not care that Evangeline is innocent?" My ire rose when the old woman shrugged. "Do you not care that she is so trusting of others that she will declare herself before her opponents? Do you not care that her husband's family will be more than pleased to kill her that they might secure their grip upon Inverfyre?" My words might have been more misty rain for all the heed she granted them. "Do you not care that this woman will die needlessly and her unborn child with her?"

"Ah, you know of the child."

"I fathered the child!" I roared.

Her step seemed to falter, but she recovered so quickly that I doubted what I had seen. "So, you would save the lady to ensure the survival of your get?" Her low opinion of this was most clear.

"No!"

She turned a corner so quickly that I was compelled to leap over a rock to pursue her. I landed upon a scree of rocks, which then tumbled. I fought to gain a footing and found one in a burrow, turning my ankle painfully in the process.

"For the love of God!" I shouted, my patience well-expired. "Can you not take me to Adaira and let her decide whether she would aid me?"

The old woman began to cackle. She laughed so hard that she nigh bent in half. She sat down upon a rock when she apparently could not support herself, not while in the grip of such mirth. She braced her hands upon her knees as she hooted and guffawed.

So, she was mad.

That was a perfect outcome, well-suited to my fortunes in this sorry land. Indeed, she would likely be of no aid to me at all. I tested my ankle and found it could bear my weight, if only just, then turned to limp away. I would seek Adaira without whatever assistance this one might choose to grant.

"And why do you leave?" she asked, probably hearing my footsteps on the stone. I glanced back, intending to make some cutting remark, but she lifted her hands and turned her palms up. She smiled just as a shaft of sunlight pierced the leaves high above and landed upon her face. She looked suddenly younger and less gnarled, and I could have sworn that her clouded eyes twinkled with mischief.

"Why do you leave, Gawain Lammergeier, just when you have found the Adaira whom you seek?"

I gaped, for I do not take kindly to surprises. "*You* are Adaira?"

She smiled with all the innocence of an angel, then inclined her head in acknowledgement.

I propped my hands upon my hips. "How did you know my name?"

Her peal of merry laughter was apparently the sole answer I would have. I was irked, if you must know, certain that I had been made to look a fool and not at all convinced that she was Adaira as she claimed.

She rose to her feet, grasped her walking stick and beckoned to me with a twisted finger. "Come. I will feed you and tell you some of what you wish to know."

Some, not all. I swallowed my foul mood and followed the woman, intent upon charming more of the tale from her lips than she intended to tell.

Her abode was a hut, buried in the deepest shadows of the forest. It was wrought of wood, but not in any fashion I knew. The builder had used salvaged timber, perhaps trees that had fallen in storms, for entire branches were netted together to make the walls and roof. The shape of the dwelling was irregular as a result, the walls far from flat or of consistent thickness. The spaces between the branches were filled with dead leaves and moss.

It was as if Adaira had wrapped the forest around herself like a cloak. Much of the moss was growing, to my surprise, and the walls were alive with small creatures when one truly looked.

I chose not to truly look.

There was a hole in the roof at one end and a hearth in the middle of the hut. A great flat stone made the base of the hearth, the fire kindled atop it and contained by a ring of smaller stones. There was a band of carving upon the big stone that looked like knotted cords, its relief dark with soot.

Adaira had left a fire burning low, the amount of stone evidently allowing her to have no fears of the fire spreading. I sat upon the bench she indicated, surprised at the comfort to be found here. It was not only dry within these walls but fragrant.

Tied clumps of plants hung from the ceiling to dry and a cauldron simmered upon the embers. I could spy an array of bowls in the back corner and various implements, including a drop-spindle. Two rabbit skins cured in the corner, notable because they were the sole things within these walls wrought of dead creatures.

The pottage she offered to me contained no meat, solely onions and wild leeks and some kind of legume stewed to softness. It was flavored with herbs and hot and perhaps the finest fare I had eaten in years.

Hunger, as it is said, is the best sauce.

She gave me some dark bread as well and a cup of her ale. I ate with inelegant haste, but my manners did not seem to trouble her.

Sated, I set the bowl aside and thanked her most graciously. She inclined her head, but said nothing, her gaze seeming to be fixed upon the fire.

"You said you would tell me some of the tale," I prompted.

"Perhaps I lied."

"Perhaps you do not truly care for the fate of another."

She tilted her head. "Is that not what is said of you?"

I stood. "I thank you again for the fare, but I will not trouble you further. It seems that you will not aid Evangeline . . ."

"Will you?"

"Of course."

"For the sake of your unborn son?"

"You cannot know the babe's gender. Evangeline is not even certain that she carries a child."

"The lady does not heed the signs of her own body. She bears your son, upon this you can rely. I ask again: is this why you would aid her, to ensure that your son is born?"

"No." I would have halted there, but she watched me, a curious smile upon her lips that prompted me to say more. "She trusts overmuch and that trait will be her bane."

Adaira's smile broadened. "Why would you care what fate awaits the lady?"

I felt my color rise in a most uncharacteristic way and my words faltered. "I know that she does not understand what she does, yet I know that her intentions are good. I know that she places too much trust in justice and truth, and I would not see her suffer for it."

"You sound to be a man besotted."

I halted and stared at the old woman. She poked the fire with a stick. Every defense that rose to my lips sounded like something another man would say. It is not like me to behave honorably, and yet, here I stood, intent upon saving a lady from peril and unable to claim my intent so clearly as that.

"I am fond of her," I managed to admit.

Adaira smiled and said nothing more.

Mortified that I had confessed as much as I had, I turned upon my heel to leave. I would not humiliate myself further by begging an old madwoman for crumbs of information. I reached the portal before she spoke.

"What do you know of Gilchrist of Inverfyre?"

I halted, blinking. "Who?"

"The lady's father."

I glanced back as I shrugged. "Nothing, beyond the assumption that she had one."

Adaira sighed. "You can know nothing of Inverfyre without knowing about Gilchrist, even less without knowing of Magnus Armstrong, the forebear of all the lairds of Inverfyre." She gestured imperiously to the bench I had vacated. "Sit."

I hesitated, then driven by a curiosity I had not known I possessed, I sat.

XV

As I settled myself, Adaira began to murmur beneath her breath. It was a rhyme of some kind, though it took me a moment to discern the words.

When the seventh son of Inverfyre,
Saves his legacy from intrigue and mire,
Only then shall glorious Inverfyre,
Reflect in full its first laird's desire.

It was clearly a prophecy. "Gilchrist was the seventh son of Inverfyre?"

"No. He was the sixth."

I settled my elbows upon my knees, intrigued beyond expectation. "I have not heard that Evangeline has any brothers—does she?"

Adaira smiled.

For a long moment I thought she would not respond, but then she did. "One of Gilchrist's many flaws was his ambition. He would do any deed to enlarge his holdings, to grow his power, to broaden the repute of his name. He cared for little beyond prestige—and the sating of his own desires. He had inherited his own father's lust abed."

"The laird whose wife had the trapdoor constructed that her husband's courtesans might be cast into the lake," I said, remembering.

Adaira nodded, "Gilchrist's lust was why he came to me." I must have recoiled, for she smiled. "I too was young once, and not so hard upon the eyes. I suspect, though, that part of my allure was that I was from one of the few serf families left at Inverfyre. Gilchrist owned me, and he savored that."

I looked away, uncomfortable with such intimate and unsavory details.

"And so, he had his son, but the boy was a bastard and thus not acceptable to his sire." She cocked her head. "Worse, he was a bastard with the taint of his father's ambition in his blood."

I was intrigued by this detail, though could not guess its import. "What happened to your son?"

"Why do you think I live in the woods?" Adaira asked. "Gilchrist had no qualms against killing to see his ends achieved. He feared both me and the child I bore—and I refused to be rid of my babe. I chose not to suit the convenience of the man who had used me and discarded me."

"So, you raised him here, in the woods?"

She laughed. "Gilchrist was not so timid that he would not come down from Inverfyre to his own forest to hunt the babe! I bore my son here, it is true, and when his gender proved to be as I had feared, I gave him away. It was vengeance enough for me to have Gilchrist tormented with the possibility of the boy's return one day."

"To whom did you give him?"

"To strangers. He could not fare worse than the fate I offered him at Inverfyre, and I dared not leave Inverfyre."

"You feared to leave your master, even knowing he might kill you?"

"There was another reason, one of no interest to you. I cannot leave Inverfyre, not for long. I left once and only once, only to carry my babe three days to the north. I left him on the steps of the monastery in Glenfannon. I thought it far enough." She seemed to find this amusing, though I could not guess why.

"And?"

"The monks sent him back to Gilchrist, unaware of what they did." Adaira laughed bitterly. "The monks thought such a hale child better suited to a life of warfare, and every soul for miles around knew how Gilchrist wished for a son. The monks thought they showed compassion for an orphan and gained the boy a fortune that might suit him better than a life of prayer."

"But they, however unwittingly, unfurled what you had tried to do."

"We cannot challenge the gods. I have tried to thwart their schemes a hundred times, I have tried to avert tragedy and wring kinder solutions from the elements at hand over and over again." She lifted her head and I fancied that she looked into my very thoughts. "I have lost, every time. The gods will not be thwarted. Any deed can be twisted to their purposes; any mortal intent can be undone."

Her shoulders sagged and she appeared more ancient than she had all along. It struck me that she would not live long, perhaps not long enough to see what came of what had begun.

I had to know more while I had the chance. "But what became of the boy?"

"He was raised at Inverfyre, for Gilchrist was not adverse to another warrior in his hall and he knew nothing of the child's origins. I said nothing, for I still hoped to see matters resolved for good."

"And when he grew, the boy chose to stay?"

"If you were a young and valiant warrior fostered by the laird, would you leave a holding that lacked an heir?" Adaira shook her head and answered her own query. "Not if your father's ambition burned in your veins. No, you would fight for the chance to make that holding your own, to have yourself declared heir." She arched a brow as she turned to face me. "You might even demand the hand of your laird's daughter as your bride."

"Niall." I breathed the man's name in sudden understanding.

"No man of merit would let his son and his daughter become man and wife," Adaira said, poking the fire with her stick, her expression grim. "Gilchrist, for all his faults, was a man of merit. I had no choice but to tell him the truth once Niall's intent was clear, and Gilchrist acted with honor."

"Niall and Evangeline are siblings."

"Half-siblings: Evangeline wrought in the marital bed, Niall wrought where you sit."

I leapt to my feet, not having desired that particular detail. "But do they know?"

"Niall knows. Gilchrist had to grant a reason when he refused Niall's request for Evangeline's hand. I would have preferred that Gilchrist lied and the secret be left a secret between we two, but the revelation from me came too soon before their meeting, too soon for Gilchrist to hide his disgust from Niall."

"But Evangeline does not know."

Adaira shrugged. "She cannot. Their nuptials will be celebrated on the morrow."

I felt my jaw drop. "What is this?"

"The lady confronted Niall in the forest and demanded they be wed. She declared that they had been lovers and that she would have their child born in legitimacy."

"I am that child's father!" I declared, more irked by Evangeline's deed than I could say.

Adaira smiled. "The prophesied son must be born legitimately to the Laird of Inverfyre. No doubt, the lady thought that both she and Niall would win their desire with this wager."

"Why would she do this?" I raged.

"They have long been friends," Adaira said mildly. "Doubtless, she thinks Niall her sole ally at Inverfyre."

I frowned at the floor of the hut, disliking the web that seemed to be tightening around me. I knew Evangeline had been stung by Niall's refusal to take her cause before Alasdair and now I knew why. Her annoyance with his lack of faith made sense if they were old friends—while his ambition explained why he was intent upon being shown to be a just lawgiver.

But if Evangeline bore a son, that child would be the obstacle to Niall's ambitions. Indeed, he could only assert his claim to the lairdship if there was no other seventh son to compete with his claim.

I feared suddenly that Evangeline's child—my child!—would die very young. Babes died in childbirth very commonly and none would ask questions if another failed to draw its first breath.

I stood, impatient to do some deed to aid the lady who stumbled unwittingly into a nest of vipers. "How ruthless is your son?"

"As ruthless as his father." Adaira turned and presented a vial to me, one that exuded menace even as it lay cradled in her palm. "As ruthless as his mother."

I disliked the look of the vial's dark contents. "What is that?"

"A remedy I granted to Evangeline and one which she refused."

I stared at her, horrified. "An abortifacient. You favor your son's cause! You too would ensure that this child never sees light."

Adaira licked her lips. "Understand that I have a fondness for the lady, but I know my son as few others do. She will find that there is a price to be paid in trusting to the goodness of others. She has seen only the sunshine in Niall's heart, not the shadow."

"But . . ."

"But there is more at stake, far more. The lady bears her heir too soon. This soul returns too early. Trouble will come of it, trouble far worse than a child dying in the womb. My solution was the more kind one." Adaira turned aside, but our conversation was not finished. She mused as she fingered her herbs. "Can you guess how often a seed takes root but never ripens to fruition? It is common, appallingly common." She paused and pursed her lips, as if considering whether to continue.

"The choice is not a mortal one to make," I retorted. It seemed that the priests had found an unlikely champion in me.

"What if the child threatens the mother's survival, solely by occupying her womb?" Adaira turned to me, her milky gaze seeming to hold mine. "Recall that until a child looses its first bellow, its survival depends solely upon the survival of its mother. It may be simpler, to the thinking of some, to be rid of both mother and child lest the lady later conceive again."

My blood ran cold as I understood her warning. The matter was more urgent than I had realized. Evangeline would die, by some supposed accident, so Niall would never face a challenge to his claiming of Inverfyre. Indeed, she might not survive her wedding night.

Unless I aided her.

Unless I ensured that she knew the truth and avoided such a fearsome error. The terrifying import of that was not that I held responsibility for Evangeline's fate in my hands, but that I knew without a shadow of doubt that I would risk even my own life to ensure her safety.

In my urgency to flee that realization and my uncommon confidante, I forgot to ask her about Magnus Armstrong.

Later that evening, as the sounds of merrymaking rose from the hall below to serenade me, I reflected that it was not the first time I had lain in wait in an unsuspecting lady's chamber.

I sincerely hoped it would not be the last.

I possess no superstitions, but it simply is not good sense to return to the scene of a previous theft. To return once and escape relatively unscathed is splendid good fortune. To return twice to the same locale and escape would be a success inconceivable.

Yet I lay in the dark upon Evangeline's bed, my boots crossed at the ankle and my weight propped upon my elbow.

It was not a reassuring situation, despite all my careful preparations. At least, every soul in Inverfyre celebrated in the hall, unaware that I had climbed to the lady's eyrie from the forest below. My desire for haste had been misguided— I had even had time to explore the meager treasury, left in what had been Fergus' chamber and protected with a ridiculously simple lock. There had been one or two items of interest within it.

You are surprised? I cannot change my nature any more than a leopard can change its spots. Indeed, I was more at ease while on the prowl. I heartily disliked my growing sense that I was cornered in the chamber while I awaited Evangeline. There was nothing for it, however, as I would have no other opportunity to speak with her alone.

I had to tell her what I had learned, even if I could not predict her response. Memories of our last night together here assailed me with the scent of the lady's perfume, distracting me from my purpose. I shifted my weight restlessly and eyed the darkening sky as circling falcons cried out to each other. Why did Evangeline delay her retirement?

I would have swung to my feet to pace, but there were sounds in the corridor at that very moment. So, I lounged, belying my concerns with my posture.

Evangeline opened the door.

She was alone, Fiona having been banished precisely as I had anticipated. And she was, of course, heart-wrenchingly beautiful.

This was despite the fact that the lady was dressed as primly as she had once been in the chapel. The deep plum hue of her kirtle favored her coloring most well and the tight laces showed her curves to advantage. Her magnificent dark hair was braided back tightly, instead of loose as I preferred it. She did seem to be more pale and certainly moved with less vigor.

She held a flickering oil lantern and was intent upon not spilling the oil, her concentration so complete that it made me smile with affection. I dearly loved how she gave the smallest matter her utmost attention. Indeed, the reminder tightened my chausses, for she spared her greatest concentration for matters savored abed.

If I considered that overlong, I should forget my noble mission. I cleared my throat softly lest I sully a fine moment with base desires.

Evangeline jumped. Her gaze flew to me and her eyes widened slightly as she halted upon the threshold to stare. Her ruddy lips parted in surprise and I began to rise, thinking to reassure her with tender kisses.

But Evangeline schooled her features and closed the door with resolve. "You!" she said with heat.

This was neither the lusty greeting nor the relieved embrace that I had hoped for. I hid my disappointment quite well, considering the circumstances.

"Me, indeed." I patted the plump mattress beside me and smiled with all my charm. I am not so readily deterred as that. "Come to bed, Evangeline, and let us make merry once again."

"I will not." She set the lantern down with such vigor that I thought she might shatter the earthenware. Then she folded her arms across her chest and regarded me, her expression highly unwelcoming. "Why are you here?"

I leaned back to watch her, folding my arms behind my head and reclining against her pillows with leisure. "Perhaps you summoned me in your dreams, so great was your desire for another stolen night abed."

Evangeline rolled her eyes. "Perhaps you fancy yourself more than any other soul could do."

"You enjoyed our nights together. I ensured as much."

"As did you. But they are past and you are not welcome here." She fixed me with a quelling look. "You offer no pleasures in which a sensible woman would indulge for long."

I was insulted by this estimation, though found myself in agreement with her claim. It was somehow unseemly that she had stated the truth aloud. I smiled. "But you have indulged several times already—what damage once more?"

The lady was unpersuaded. "What brings you back? I thought you long gone to the south."

"I heard that there was to be a wedding. I considered that it would be remiss of me to not extend my felicitations to the bride."

Evangeline arched a brow. "The bride accepts your kind wishes. Now, leave my chambers. I can risk no scandal on this night and I have need of my sleep." She dismissed me with a glance and moved to place the lantern upon a chest. She was cool and composed, so remote that once again I feared that my Evangeline had a twin.

I felt foolish for reclining upon the bed to greet her. I remembered belatedly that I had acted churlishly in the stable to warn her away from me. "I returned to save you from a grievous error."

"You?" A smile touched her lips though it was not overly warm. "*You* undertook a chivalrous deed? I cannot believe it."

I swung to my feet, irked that she was so prepared to think poorly of me. "You should believe it. You cannot wed Niall, not if you value your life."

Her sidelong glance was skeptical. "I will wed Niall precisely because I do value my life."

"Why?"

"I must wed someone who could have fathered my babe. Thus, it had to be someone who was here that night the *Titulus* was shown."

I could not refrain from a wry comment. "I thought every man in this part of Scotland was here that eve."

Evangeline impaled me with a glance so frostily blue that I could not catch my breath. "It had to be someone I could *trust*."

I smiled despite myself at the irony of this. "You trust Niall?"

"I have known him most of my life."

I sauntered closer, not yet prepared to tell her news she would not welcome. "How fares the babe?"

She shrugged. "I was resoundingly ill this morning. I suppose if he can make such trouble, he is well enough." She cast a sharp glance my way. "Perhaps if he is so inclined to make trouble, he favors his sire."

I feigned innocence. "But I have never made trouble for a lady. Perhaps I am not his sire, after all." I leaned back against the bed and regarded her with amusement. "Perhaps he is a she, and she favors her mother's ability to challenge expectation."

A light flickered in Evangeline's eyes that I should have missed if I had not been watching her carefully, so quickly did she dismiss it.

"It is a boy, and your son." She nodded briskly. "Indeed, I am glad that you are here. You must vow to me that you will never tell another the truth of it. It would injure Niall's pride to have the paternity of his son a matter of gossip."

I was annoyed, if you must know, that this was the sole reason that my presence could be accounted to be good. "And we must ensure that dear, dear Niall is not insulted."

Evangeline's eyes snapped with anger in a most reassuring way. I had awakened the slumbering passion within her, and she was a demure, dutiful maiden no longer. I much preferred her with fire in her eyes and her words, even if it meant we must disagree.

"What right have you to mock a man? Niall is a good and

noble man, a man of honor." Her implication that I was not such a man was clear, but I could hardly take issue with such a fundamental truth.

"He is ambitious, Evangeline, and ambitious men are the most troublesome kind."

"Nonsense! Niall and I are well-suited. Our match will be a good one."

"Your match will be horrific from beginning to end, for no man takes well to being cuckolded afore his nuptials, particularly a man of scrupulous honor. He will have his vengeance from you for your lack of chastity, upon this you can rely."

"You do not know Niall," she scoffed.

"Nor do you."

"You are oddly certain of your claims."

"I have seen much of men in my days. Few men have as much to lose by the birth of a son as Niall, yet still you choose him." I shook my head with undisguised disgust. "You cannot complain that you have lived a fettered life, Evangeline, for at each opportunity you choose your irons anew."

"How dare you say as much to me!" She marched after me, a warrior queen intent upon slaying me with her bare hands. "What would you know of honor and duty and ensuring a legacy? You care only for what you can *steal*, and that only because the sale of it puts coin in your purse! You are your father's son, just as I am the daughter of mine—a noble and good leader who took care for those beneath his hand!"

I jabbed a finger through the air toward her. "Your father made but *one* choice that made sense, though I know that he did not do as much for your sake."

She folded her arms across her chest, her expression

skeptical and her lips a taut line. "And what was that, since you seem suddenly to know so much of Inverfyre?"

"He forbade Niall to wed you."

"There is no mystery in his reasons for that." Evangeline's smile turned wry. "Before he lay dying, my father thought no man good enough to be his successor."

"No?" I waited for a heartbeat, wanting my revelation to have the might of silence before it. "Not even his own bastard son?"

If I took triumph in surprising others, Evangeline's reaction would have delighted every fiber of my being. She gaped at me, stunned to silence, yet I felt a wretch for burdening her with this truth.

When she began to shake her head in disbelief, I plunged on. "Niall is Gilchrist's son, Evangeline. That is why Gilchrist forbade Niall to wed you, for you are half-siblings. He told Niall as much."

"No, this cannot be true."

"Did I not vow to never lie to you?" I flung out my hands. "Here is a truth, Evangeline, a truth that I risked my own life to bring to you even though I doubt it is one you desire. Niall is the seventh son, though not legitimately born. He will not suffer the challenge to his ambitions that fills your belly!"

Her mouth worked as she held my gaze, her own incredulity slowly melting away before my certainty. "Who told you of this?"

"Adaira. Your father got Niall upon her. She sent the babe away, but he was returned to your father's court as a gift, for the monks of Glenfannon believed him wrought to be a warrior."

Evangeline caught her breath and turned away. "No one told me of this blood link!" she whispered, then paced the width of the chamber with haste. She frowned and I expected her to seize her cloak and demand we leave immediately.

But she halted before me and locked her gaze with mine. "I thank you for these tidings. All the same, I will not abandon my legacy without a fight."

Now, I was the astonished one. I met her steely gaze. "But surely you will not wed Niall?"

"I can and I will." She lifted her chin. "He is yet the best choice."

"But . . ."

"But I shall simply have to ensure that Niall and I do not conceive another child." Evangeline spoke firmly, then looked me in the eye and offered a polite smile. "I thank you for bringing me these tidings, Gawain. Do you not have a villa awaiting you in Sicily's sun?"

It took me some time to summon a word. Evangeline's indifference astonished me to silence, which is a rare feat. "But such a match is against law of both church and king!" I finally sputtered.

Evangeline smiled with a serenity the situation did not deserve. "*You* are concerned with this? I confess myself surprised."

I felt flustered and uncertain, which did not please me well, no less because I could not readily identify the reason for my lack of indifference. "Can you not see sense? You cannot remain here!"

"I cannot bear this babe out of wedlock if he is to claim his legacy," Evangeline explained, as if I were a stupid child myself. "This is my sole option. Niall would not have agreed to my proposal if he were concerned about the matter for, as you say, he knows the truth. Together, we shall rebuild Inverfyre's fortunes."

I gaped at her. "But how will you do such a deed?"

She lifted a finger and I heard a bird's cry. "The name of Inverfyre will again be associated with the finest falcons in Christendom."

"But the birds are barren at Inverfyre."

"Then we shall hunt further afield." She smiled, her manner cool. "I have retrieved the *Titulus*, I have conceived the seventh son and he will be born legitimately to the Laird of Inverfyre. I have done all that is mortally possible to ensure success, and now can only have faith that divine favor will follow."

My mouth opened and closed, as if I were a fish hauled from the river and cast upon the shore.

A serene Evangeline pivoted and turned to her bed, pulling down the linens and plumping the pillows. "I would appreciate if you would leave me that I might be well rested for my nuptials in the morning."

I strode after her angrily. "Evangeline! Do you not understand? Niall may wish to be laird, but he cannot want you to bear another man's son, especially as that son will usurp him as laird."

"Not for fifteen or twenty years, Gawain." Her manner was so mild that I yearned to shake sense into her. "The babe must grow to a man to be fit to rule."

"But if Niall is ambitious, then he could plan ill for your child. . . ."

Evangeline began to laugh. "Niall? You see threats where there are none. Begone, Gawain. Save your fretting for some soul in need of it."

I seized her elbow and fairly did give her a shake. "You are in need of my aid, for you refuse to see the threat to you and our child!" I growled, so annoyed was I by her calm smile. "I should steal you away from this place!"

She lifted a dark brow but spoke with fervor. "And I would despise you for it."

I shoved my hand through my hair, knowing she was right, and paced the chamber's width.

Evangeline folded her arms across her chest as she regarded me. "Gawain, your part in this is over. There is no need for you to pretend that you care about my fate, or that you have concern for the child you sired. There is no need for you to try to save me from my nuptials in some misguided bout of gallantry. You are free to go." She yawned elaborately. "Indeed, I wish you would do so that I might sleep before the morrow."

This was not how I had expected matters to proceed. Indeed, I glowered at her. "You cannot imagine that there is no darkness in a man's heart, simply because you have not witnessed it."

"I clearly have no need to imagine anything at all, for you have imagined enough for both of us."

I took a shaking breath, hating her bemused smile for it hinted at indulgence undeserved. "You cannot forget that Fergus' murderer is still unnamed and likely still in these halls. How can you abide here without knowing who killed your spouse?"

"But I do know who killed him. Alasdair clearly thought that he could claim the lairdship easily, and he truly would be one that Fergus would never suspect of malice. Niall will drive Fergus' kin from the gates as soon as he is made laird, upon this we have already agreed, and that will be the end of the matter."

Evangeline patted my cheek in a most infuriatingly maternal way. "Go to Sicily, Gawain. Have a pomegranate in memory of our nights together. I shall go to sleep, the better to dream of my nuptial mass on the morrow."

She turned her back to me and began to untie the laces of her robe, as if I were an old woman who posed no threat to her desired chastity on this night.

It was intolerable to be dismissed in this way, especially after all that had passed between us.

I could not leave the matter be.

XVI

"Do you love Niall? Is that why you embrace this folly?" I regretted uttering the question as soon as the words passed my lips, just as I knew I wanted to know her answer.

Evangeline spun to face me, her eyes wide. "Why?"

I shrugged with an indifference I did not feel. "I thought ladies wed once for duty and thence for love, that was all."

That sobered her so promptly that I felt a knave. "Then, I shall wed twice for duty," she said with a tired resolve. "Inverfyre's succession must be assured."

"How noble of you."

Evangeline sobered as she studied me. She marched across the chamber then and seized my hand, fairly hauling me to the window. "Look over these hills," she commanded, encompassing their shadowed sweep with a gesture. I could barely take in the view, so deluged was I by the scent of her, so betrayed was I by my desire for her.

"Look at Inverfyre. How can you not love the curve of these verdant hills, the touch of the mist upon them, the sparkle of the streams? How can your heart be untouched by its beauty?"

I stared out the window into the moonlit night and let myself be lulled by the music of the lady's voice.

"I love this land, love it with every fiber of my being. Its contradictions are a part of me, indeed, I am not convinced I could survive elsewhere. I know the sounds of the forest, I know the calls of the falcons when they hunt and when they return to feed. I know which bubbling streams carry the blessings of the fey, which glades are enchanted.

"This was my mother's chamber when I was a child, and I grew up with this view before me. I grew up knowing how Magnus Armstrong had come from the south and chosen this site for his abode, how he had wrought a keep from naught and built a fortune from the bounty he found in the land he claimed. I grew up understanding my lineage, my birthright and my responsibility. I grew up certain of who I was, why I had been born, what I must do before I die."

I watched her, noting her passion, aware that I had never had such a sure sense of my place.

Indeed, I felt a measure of envy.

Evangeline spread her hands as she talked, her love of Inverfyre weighting every word. "I learned as a toddler how Magnus brought law to these lands, how he offered justice and protection to the people living here and how they welcomed his suzerainty. They are of me, as well, every one of them, however humble. I learned my duty to these people, these stalwart souls who show such kindness to strangers even when they themselves are beset."

She turned slightly to look up at me, raising a fist to her heart. "There is goodness here, Gawain, goodness that needs protection to survive, goodness that I dare not permit be ground beneath the heel of misfortune."

Tears came to her eyes. "I am the last of my lineage. Though there have been times that I resented the burden of my obligation to Inverfyre, I cannot imagine forsaking it." Her voice turned husky. "Can you not see? I would rather die fulfilling my destiny than flee for my own safety. I would be ashamed to admit my own name if I showed such cowardice. That would be no life for the last descendant of Magnus Armstrong."

She held my gaze for a long moment. I not only saw the depth of her conviction but loved her for it.

Yes, I loved this woman. I loved the myriad hues of blue in her eyes, I loved the passion that oft lit her features. I loved the vigor of her convictions and the magnitude of her compassion. I loved the fire that drove her deeds. I loved how she met me touch for touch abed, how she stepped back from no foe, how she was prepared to fight for whatsoever she believed. I loved the nobility of character that was hers, a nobility utterly alien to me.

Indeed, Evangeline made me yearn to be a better man. Evangeline awakened a side of me that had slumbered for long years. Yet fast on the heels of the realization of my love came a second realization and one less welcome: I could not stay.

Because of the ilk of woman she was, because I loved her, I would leave Evangeline forever this night. I knew that a man like me could only disappoint her one day. I feared seeing the warmth in her gaze inevitably fade to disappointment. I knew I would break her heart, I knew that the sight of that would break mine.

We were best without each other, Evangeline and I, and the sooner we parted the easier that parting would be.

It would be most merciful to never tell her what was in my heart.

* * *

Evangeline, unaware of my thoughts, leaned closer, her eyes bright. "Have you never loved anything so much, Gawain, that you would sacrifice yourself to ensure its survival?"

A lump rose in my throat for she knew not what she asked of me. I shook my head all the same and spoke with a levity I did not feel. "The very opposite, in fact. As you recall, I easily sacrificed Michel when the choice was his life or mine."

Evangeline studied me with such intensity that I feared what she might discern. She took a step closer, then raised her hand to lay her fingertips upon my cheek. She spoke with quiet fervor. "But if you were there again, in that very place in this moment, would you still make the same choice?"

I knew the answer she wanted of me. Indeed, I felt as if my very mettle was being measured by this woman. The word she desired rose to my lips, but I dared not utter it, I dared not encourage her to hope that I was what I could never be.

Breaking my pledge of honesty was the lesser crime.

I jerked away from her. "People do not change, Evangeline. It is only in the tales of the bards that love brings enlightenment and change. Indeed, admiration bestowed is not always returned, as they would maintain, though a scoundrel might cultivate the *appearance* of reciprocity." I smiled at her, coyly.

Evangeline blinked quickly and looked away, stung.

I was not done. "Indeed, love oft blinds the thinking person to her own folly."

She spared me a glance but said nothing.

"What you do here is folly, perhaps wrought of love for Niall, perhaps wrought of love for your father's aims."

"My father . . ." she began hotly, but I granted her no chance to continue.

"How do you imagine that you shall rebuild this land and undo years of neglect? You will have no tithes from starving peasants and no taxes in kind from untilled fields. There may be no eyasses, even further afield. It is a fool's errand you accept here, Evangeline, and one doomed to failure."

Her lips set stubbornly, but I persisted. Perhaps there was one gift I could give her.

"I warn you because I know how it is to be cheated of reward for loyalty to one's sire. My own father profited heartily from my skills for years untold, and always he pledged to leave his wealth to me."

A flicker of interest lit her eyes. "But he did not?"

"My father lied to me. I returned a dozen times to Ravensmuir after his death, hoping to find the *Titulus*, the minimum due that he owed to me. I was certain he had hidden it in some corner known only to the two of us, that he had secured it for me, that he had kept his pledge."

She bit her lip. "You never found it."

I shook my head. "He left all to my brother Merlyn, my brother from whom he was estranged, my brother who murdered my father."

Evangeline inhaled sharply. She stepped forward and laid a hand upon my arm. "Then how did you come to have the *Titulus*? How did you gain your inheritance?"

I held her gaze, knowing my own was hard. "I stole back what was rightfully mine own."

A grudging smile touched the lady's lips and her grip tightened on my arm. "Just as I stole it from you."

I could not fully halt my answering smile. I felt that bond betwixt us again, that strange sense of commonality that so beguiled me.

Then Evangeline shook her head. "I am sorry that you were cheated, but your father's deceit is of no import to me."

"It is of every import to you!" I argued. "I know all that is needed to know of the old deceiving the young to achieve their own ambitions. I would warn you that you do not consider the matter dispassionately, that you sacrifice yourself to no good end. How much will you surrender to sate your father's ghost?"

"What would you have me do?" she demanded, flinging out her hands. "Abandon my legacy because *your* father proved himself a thief to the end?"

"Think of our son!"

"I *do* think of our son." She tapped my chest with a fingertip and her voice fell low. "Would he not be as angry with me for denying him his birthright as you are with your sire for denying you your inheritance?"

I turned away, seeing then that she would heed nothing I said. I fumbled with the lace of my purse, then presented her with a token I had retrieved earlier this night, one I knew I could no longer take with me. "Take it," I said roughly. "You will need it for your ill-fated nuptials on the morrow."

Evangeline stepped to my side, her fingers brushing mine as she accepted her mother's crucifix once more. I refused to look at her, so heartsick was I, but she touched her fingertips to my jaw. I turned beneath her touch and found her smiling at me, her eyes filled with tears.

"Thank you," she said softly, then reached to kiss my cheek.

It was too much to be offered such a chaste kiss when I desired so much more of her. I caught her chin in my hand before I thought better of the impulse, then I kissed her soundly.

Evangeline resisted my touch for the barest moment, but

I poured my heart into my embrace. In a trio of heartbeats, she melted against me, her hands sliding around my neck to pull me closer.

There is a force between Evangeline and I, a desire that pulls us closer just as the North Star pulls the lodestone. It cannot be denied, nor can it be ignored. I have never felt the like of it, and each time I step into her presence, I am shocked by its vigor.

I cannot dismiss it, and I suspect that she too finds its allure undeniable. I will never forget its power.

Indeed, when I kissed her, the fire raged between us as always it did and I could feel her pulse matching mine. I might have continued longer, but Evangeline abruptly broke our kiss.

She planted both hands upon my chest and pushed me away, despite the fact that her lips were swollen and reddened by my kiss, despite the glimmer of desire in her eyes. Her cheeks were flushed, her hair disheveled in a most fetching way.

"It is the eve of my nuptials," she said, her words endearingly husky. "I beg you, leave me."

"You are wrong about Niall," I said, sounding like a grumpy man who foretells doom for all who spurn his advice.

Evangeline shook her head. "You do not know Niall as I do." She turned her back upon me, so still that I knew she was yet aware of my proximity.

I wished then, with uncommon ferocity, that I was not the man I was. Evangeline awakened this urge in me, though I knew not what to do with its demand. My heart in my throat, I lifted her circlet from her veil and put it aside.

The lady swallowed but did not step away. I slipped my

hand beneath her sheer veil and eased it aside, baring her neck to my gaze.

She averted her face and closed her eyes, her dark lashes fanning against her fair flesh. I could see the ripple of her pulse at her neck. I landed a fingertip upon her nape, where the dark tendrils of hair had escaped her braid, and traced the line of her spine.

She shivered in a most promising fashion and her protest was breathless. "You had best be gone. None will be kind if you are found within these walls again—know that it has been decided that you killed Fergus."

"But I did not."

"I know. Go, all the same. You have been banished from Inverfyre and any soul has the right to kill you on sight, so long as he brings your head to the laird himself."

I ignored her counsel, so pleased was I that she feared for my survival, so desperate was I for more of a taste before I left. I touched my lips to her flesh. She caught her breath and tipped back her head. I removed one of the pins that held her braids coiled against her head. She raised a hand to deter me.

I smiled, catching her hand in mine and pressing a kiss to her palm. She shivered, as I had hoped she would, but parted her lips to protest.

I laid a fingertip upon her lips and her eyes widened at my caress. "I apologize for my vulgar speech when last we were together," I said softly, no doubt surprising both of us.

"Breasts like pomegranates," she said with unnecessary precision.

"I feared that you came to care for me," I admitted.

Her gaze brightened, then her lips slowly curved with what might have been affection. "Did you truly intend to protect me from a knave like yourself?"

I felt the back of my neck heat and could not summon a

word to my lips. This is the difficulty with gallantry—it leaves a man with little coherent to say. "I know what I am," I said, more harshly than I am wont to speak. "And I suspect that I know the manner of woman you are."

Evangeline's smile broadened and her eyes began to twinkle. "I too know the ilk of man you are," she said softly. "But I like you, all the same, Gawain Lammergeier."

I was ridiculously pleased by this claim. Indeed, a tightness seized my chest and a foolish smile touched my lips. "How improbable."

"Indeed it is."

I am base enough to be encouraged by a lady's smile. "You have no maid. I would aid you that we might linger for a few moments. You said yourself that you had need of your slumber this night and I would not keep you overlong from your bed."

She swallowed, her questioning gaze fixed upon mine. The chamber seemed to heat, even more so when she whispered my name. I lifted her veil away, letting it drift to the floor like a gossamer web. Her breathing became quicker than it should have been, her breasts rising before my very hands.

The flame of the lantern gilded her features, making her look younger and softer than I knew she was. She was wrought of steel, my Evangeline, as steadfast as a warrior and as true as a finely honed steel blade. An unexpected tenderness squeezed my heart and nigh stole my breath.

This would be the last time we were together.

I drank in the sight of her, flooding my mind with fodder for memories. I removed the pins that held her coiled braids against her head. The braided hair fell heavily unto her shoulders, coiling around her neck like a lover.

"I can manage the rest," she said with unseemly haste. "Begone, Gawain, I beg of you."

"Indulge me," I whispered, my voice husky. "But once more, my Evangeline, indulge me." I bent, inhaled of her beguiling scent, then kissed the sweet flesh beneath her ear.

Her breath caught and she closed her eyes. "You know that I cannot resist your touch, though on this night of nights, I must do so." Her smile was sad. "And I fear that I am weak enough that I would not be able to halt at a mere kiss. I have to survive through my nuptials, Gawain, and the investiture of Niall as laird if I am to survive at all. If you are found here—worse, found in my bed—neither of us will see the morning sun."

My very presence put her in peril yet I was still loathe to leave. We stared at each other, the chamber filled with the heat between us and the thunder of our heartbeats.

Perhaps I feared overmuch. Perhaps Evangeline did know her people better than I did. Perhaps her way would triumph—indeed, I had seen before that she was a skillful strategist and she had the will to force many matters to her way.

I had no right to endanger her further with my presence.

I stole one last kiss, a kiss that would have to warm me all the way to Sicily's sun. It was salty with the lady's tears and I knew that our hearts were as one, even if neither of us dared to say the words.

That kiss, and those we had already shared, would have to be enough. I pivoted and lay a hand upon the rope I had knotted over the sill. Rope is easily found in a town occupied by falconers, and not missed when those falconers do not climb to the high nests any longer.

"Untie the rope when I am gone and let it drop," I counseled Evangeline. "I shall gather it from below. There will be no accusations made against you for my deeds."

The lady nodded and a tear splashed again upon her cheek. "Go," she said, her voice catching on the word. "Go while yet you can. I could not bear if you were caught here this night, if you suffered for coming to warn me."

My heart clenched, as it had so oft of late.

I leapt over the sill then and climbed down into the protective darkness of the forest. The rope fell not long after I reached the forest floor, tumbling like a great snake from the height of the lady's window.

The tie between us was severed for all time.

And I, I was bereft.

I glanced up as Evangeline was briefly silhouetted in the window. She raised a hand in farewell, though she could not have seen me, then shuttered the window against the night.

I closed my eyes, saving my last sight of her, trying to ensure that I would remember the sound of her voice. My heart felt as a stone in my chest, cold and weighty.

I should have turned and walked away then. I should have accepted the lady's assurances and put Inverfyre behind me. I should have agreed that her fate was not my concern.

But I could not compel myself to go.

It was a mercy that I had never cared for any soul before, for the deed certainly addles one's wits. I could only hope this madness was as fleeting an affliction as lust oft was.

I feared that it would not be.

I watched a hawk circle high above me, its cry sending a thrill through me. It landed upon some high eyrie, folding its wings as it settled. The sky was streaked with the hues of the sunset and I had a sudden impulse to seek out the bird's nest.

It was not so ridiculous a notion as that—such a perch

would be high and remote, thus beyond the sight of bloodthirsty locals anxious to collect the bounty on my head. I could not journey sufficiently far this night to matter—thus, I found a reason to do precisely what I desired to do.

Perhaps I would attend Evangeline's nuptials on the morrow, to ensure that Niall's intent was true. Perhaps I would be able to leave once I knew her to be safe and well pleased with her circumstance.

I doubted it, but I climbed the cliff beneath the bird's resting place all the same. Darkness and cold wrapped their embrace around me. I had the sense once again—it was increasingly familiar in this haunted land—that I entered another realm than the one with which I was familiar, a place wrought of dreams in which any deed might happen.

I glanced back to find the valley below me filling with mist, the heights of the peak above me lost in the low clouds. The air was moist with impending rain, as cool as a balm. I peered up the cliff face as the way became less clear, then down into the shrouded abyss below.

I might not survive the climb, or if I did, the bird on the precipice above might take my liver as her toll. But I could not remain still, and I could not leave Inverfyre. Indeed, in a curious sense, I welcomed the challenge of scaling this rock.

It might well be conquerable, unlike a certain woman who had tied my heart in knots.

You should understand that I would not normally have undertaken such a climb. That I did so seems to have been a symptom of my sense that I dreamed with my eyes open. In dreams, the impossible oft is easily done. In dreams, one can fly, or scale cliffs, or change form so readily that it seems unremarkable.

In waking life, I am leery of unhewn cliffs, although I do

not think twice about scaling an edifice wrought by men. Walls are smooth and straight, embellished with useful cornices and nooks. There is always some saint or cherub which one can seize. There is always a rationality to what is wrought by men, and few surprises for any soul who considers his path with care. Even Inverfyre's steep walls I had scaled without too much difficulty. A hook and a rope are all a thinking man needs.

Cliffs, on the other hand, are unpredictable, irregular, ridden with crumbling ledges or as smooth as glass. The structure of cliffs is not solid and eternal; it shifts constantly, even as one climbs.

I find them troubling.

As troubling, perhaps, as standing alone in the forest surrounded by falling snow. Perhaps it is the quietude of these places, and the invitation that silence extends to thoughts I would prefer not to think.

I should not have been surprised when I heard the haunting voice again. I grit my teeth as a young boy called my name, seemingly from high above me. I knew that I was tired and hungry, thirsty and in a distraught state that might leave me prone to visions, just as I had suspected that I would not endure this climb without such visitation.

Michel had loved to climb, after all. He had been at ease when he climbed, no matter what he scaled. And he had mocked me for my uncertainties with a boy's confidence.

"Gawain!" The phantom boy cried again, and this time I noted the change in his voice. His voice was filled with laughter, not with anguish. I looked up, but there was no one above me.

"Gawain." Again my name, again that familiar, teasing voice.

I halted, and therein lay my error. By stopping, I lost my

rhythm and then could not spy a handhold above me. I clutched the rock face and peered above me, seeking a grip that eluded me. My heart was pounding, more from the spectral cry than a fear of heights.

Which said something.

My heart seized when the small rock ledge began to give beneath the weight of my boot. I desperately shoved my toe deeper into the cliff face, scrabbling for a better grip with my hands.

Suddenly, a considerable chunk of stone broke away and fell far beneath me, leaving me with one leg swinging in the air.

I managed to get my boot onto a gnarled tree root. Relief flooded through me and sweat trickled down my spine. I was panting like a dog in the summer's heat.

I swallowed at how long it took the stone to crash through the leaves of the trees and finally hit the earth with a dull thud. I had come far, perhaps too far. I might have wiped the sweat from my brow, but I would have had to relinquish my grip to do so.

I clung there, panting.

I licked my lips and glanced down at the canopy of leaves. Indeed, I could not spy the forest floor. I was too high to jump without killing myself in the deed. The cliff below me was arrayed with jutting tree roots and crumbling stones, of small plants clinging desperately to small precipices.

If I fell, I realized, I might be so battered by the time I hit the ground that I would not care whether I lived or died.

I was trapped. I could not even discern how I had managed to come this far. I looked up and saw only smooth stone rising before me, the plants having lost their tenuous hold at this height. To the left and the right of me was more smooth stone.

This, it appeared, had not been one of my better plans.

XVII

Even as I thought as much, the root holding my weight began to crack. My palms were sweaty as I ran one hand across the stone, desperately seeking some niche that would save me.

"There," whispered a boyish voice into my ear.

Through a haze of panic, I saw a ghostly vision of a boy's hand, the knuckles grubby and scratched. Those plump but agile fingers were painfully familiar, and I would have recoiled had the root not cracked more loudly. It began to shift and my weight slipped. I snatched at the grip the ghostly hand indicated, too relieved to be surprised that the rock was warm when I grasped it.

As if another hand had just abandoned it.

I pulled myself up and watched for Michel's guiding hand. I dared not consider why he haunted me now, why he might choose to save me when I had not done as much for him. Memories assailed me of a young boy laughing as he tried to teach me to climb stone cliffs.

It was the sole deed he had done better than me, and he had loved to torment me about it. A lump rose in my throat.

"Here." I heard his voice, bubbling with merriment at my incompetence, and saw his phantom hand above me once again. His eye was as sharp as I recalled.

As I climbed with phantom aid, the mist rose from the ground, its chilly fingers surrounding me like a shroud. There was only me and Michel's ghost and a seemingly endless façade of stone.

This might well be a reckoning, but I did not care. A reckoning was long overdue. If not for his parents' untimely demise, Michel might have had an honest trade; if not for my untimely abandonment, he might have yet been alive.

That was not an attractive truth, but I faced it squarely.

Michel's father had been a falconer and the boy had learned young to climb to the eyries of gyrfalcons and peregrines. He had learned thievery in an honest trade, for stealing chicks from wild birds is not counted as a crime by men.

The birds, though, keep their own reckoning. Michel had been fleet-fingered because he had to be. A peregrine deprived of her offspring will hunt the offender as diligently as she hunts a partridge. She might not manage to kill whosoever assails her nest, but she will have her due in flesh and blood.

It is no accident that kings and queens prefer to hunt with the female, the peregrine, for her bloodlust is more fierce. Michel had had a scar across his temple, a reminder of a poorly calculated assault upon a nest.

I was destined to recall this detail shortly. As I drew nearer the lip overhead, I saw that it was not the summit of the cliff. The rock face stepped back and continued upward, though that had not been discernible from below. This was but a ledge—and a falcon was perched upon it.

The peregrine turned her cool gaze upon me as I hauled myself over the edge of the precipice. Her nest was a mere hollow scratched in the dirt and rock. She was herself no larger than a crow. These are remarkable birds when seen at close proximity, all dark feathers and sharp angles. They seem wrought for fast flight and for killing.

I glanced back to find a carpet of fog, sealing me from the world of mortal men below. There was no way, even with ghostly aid, that I might find my way down again. I was bone-tired from my climb and more than willing to share the ledge amiably.

I knew that the peregrine might not share my perspective.

Indeed, she surveyed me coldly. I smiled, for though it seemed foolish, I doubted it could hurt. Then I recalled that peregrines are said to despise the sight of a man's face.

I froze there, braced upon the weight of my hands, my legs dangling into the void, my smile like that of the corpse I might soon be. The peregrine did not so much as blink, though she ruffled her feathers in agitation.

Perhaps she sat upon eggs and was loathe to leave them. I did not dare to breathe, so fervent was my hope that her desire to shelter her eggs would outweigh her lust to protect them.

Night had fallen fully now and from this perch, the sky was awash with a million stars, the valley cloaked in silvery fog. We might have been the only two souls left in this world. My arms ached, though I dared not move quickly lest I startle the bird.

"Gawain, here!" My head snapped to the right at Michel's cry of delight.

The precipice was not so small as I had originally believed. It curved around the face of the cliff, albeit somewhat narrow, and clearly offered a respite to the right, out of view of the nest.

If I could get out of the peregrine's view without incident.

When I looked back at her, she had risen to her feet with purpose. I saw the four eggs beneath her, gleaming like great pearls in the moonlight. Creamy white they were, smaller than those of a chicken, and speckled.

Eggs! Had Evangeline been right about the effect of the return of the *Titulus*? I would not have credited it without this sight before me, but four eggs there were.

I dared not admire them long. The peregrine's pupils had widened, as if she spied prey, and her gaze was fixed upon me.

My heart nigh stopped.

I heard the cry of another bird far overhead and guessed that she would hunt me once her partner was returned. The tiercel screamed at closer range and there was no more time to linger. I eased my knee onto the precipice, not averting my stare from hers.

With painful slowness, I eased to my feet, hoping my knees would not buckle from my exertion, hoping that my greater size might deter her. She settled back upon her nest cautiously, as if she considered an alternative plan for being rid of me.

I did not intend to give her the chance to create one. I stepped swiftly to the right, moving with the silent ease to which I was accustomed, knowing that stealing myself away from this huntress would be among my greater achievements. Her head swiveled as she watched me, and I did not know whether I imagined that her manner eased slightly when I was more distant. I slipped around the curve, releasing my breath.

There was no echo of pursuit.

The tiercel landed with a piercing cry and the female cried lustily in answer. I glanced back at the rustle of feathers and realized that I had been momentarily forgotten.

He had brought fresh kill, a bird of some kind by the look of it, though it had already been mostly deplumed. The pair fell upon it greedily, scattering feathers, breaking bones, shredding flesh. There was blood on their talons and mandibles and a ferocity in their manner that nigh curdled my blood.

But they were too busy to trouble with me.

To my great relief, there was a crevice not far along the precipice that I could reach with care. I would be less exposed there, and I recalled with relief Michel's certainty that falcons are clumsy unless aloft.

They would not pursue me into a darkened nook. Much reassured, I darted into the hiding place and only felt then the cold sweat upon my back. I slid down to sit against the wall, my legs straight out before me, and closed my eyes in relief.

I swallowed at the press of another beside me, a smaller soul, curling close for warmth. A ghostly hand slid across mine. I felt its weight on mine but did not look.

No, I dared not look. Instead I recalled an orphaned boy to my mind's eye, a boy with tousled hair and an engaging smile, a boy who had been rewarded for his trust with betrayal. Michel had saved me from my own folly on this night, I knew not why, save that his loyalty and friendship was undiminished by either death or my own faithlessness.

I did not deserve such loyalty and I knew it well. Regret filled me then as I faced the fullness of my deeds. Evangeline had guessed aright—confronted with the same choice on this day, I would never abandon Michel, even if it meant my own demise.

But on that day long past, I had done so and I had never forgiven myself. In the black solitude of that refuge, I finally allowed myself to weep for what I had done.

* * *

I awakened to the screaming of the falcons, my neighbors evidently dissenting over some matter. My eyes were crusted with sleep and I ached from head to toe. The sky was rosy with the light of dawn and the mist had not yet begun to thin. My belly growled, though it would have no morsel soon.

I crept to the opening of my hiding place and took a breath, then peered around the corner. A falcon flew overhead, some bloody prize clutched in its talons. It was the male, for it was smaller than the female—one third smaller, as the name "tiercel" does imply. The peregrine on the nest flapped her wings in annoyance, and rose to her feet as she screamed. Her partner ignored her, concentrating upon his struggling prey.

With a mighty beat of her wings, the impatient peregrine took flight and pursued the tiercel. This time, he seemed disinclined to share his prize. She flew after him, crying outrage.

Aloft, their grace was peerless and a curious joy lifted my heart just watching their flight. I recalled Evangeline's pleasure when she loosed the gyrfalcon and felt a commonality with her in this sense of wonder.

A scrabbling upon the stone drew my gaze back to the precipice. To my astonishment, a man's head appeared at the lip of the ledge. He hoisted himself up the cliff and braced himself upon his elbows, sparing a glance skyward to the birds.

It was Dubhglas. I blinked, but it was certainly he. I retreated and took refuge in a shadow that I might watch him unseen.

Dubhglas glanced furtively to the left and the right, then hauled himself upward with a swift movement. There was a sack upon his back, which he slipped easily to the ground. He looked again at the feuding falcons, then promptly wrapped the four eggs in cloth and put them into the sack.

In the blink of an eye, the nest was empty and he was gone. I heard the scrabble of his boots as he descended with haste, and understood with sudden clarity what had ailed Inverfyre's falcons.

They were not without issue: their issue had been stolen afore Inverfyre's falconers came to gather their young. It was no curse that visited Inverfyre, no loss of divine favor or retaliation for poor guardianship of the *Titulus*.

It was deceit.

I imagined then that some ancient keeper of scores had compelled me to remain at Inverfyre, even to climb to this eyrie, that I might learn the truth.

I had to tell Evangeline.

First, though, I had to learn precisely what Dubhglas planned for the eggs, and gather some evidence to support my charge. I needed to know whether he had allies within Inverfyre or whether he acted alone. I had to be certain, lest I endanger myself with an untimely revelation.

I peered down the cliff and saw to my dismay that Dubhglas had nigh disappeared. I fairly leapt over the lip of the precipice in my haste to not lose him, ensuring that I kept to my side of the jutting face that would hide me from him.

Meanwhile, the falcons fought over the meat high above me, unaware that they had been robbed. They would not be pleased when they returned to their nest.

And the peregrine already knew of my presence. I had no doubt who she would blame for the thievery.

It is amazing how terror can add to one's agility and speed. Indeed, I had not a single fear of falling on the descent as I had the day before on my ascent: my sole concerns were stealth and escape.

*　　*　　*

I wrestled with the question of whether I should disguise myself to enter Inverfyre or not, but I should not have troubled. There was little fear of my being recognized in Inverfyre's keep on this day. The gates thronged with merrymakers, come on short notice to attend the lady's nuptials. The square was glutted with peasants and petty nobles, warriors and even a few whores. I pushed my way through the throng, my hood over my head, and headed for the keep proper.

It was there that Evangeline would most certainly be.

A maiden pressed a braided garland of spring flowers into my hands and I bestowed a kiss upon her fingertips in return, my gallant gesture making her laugh. It was a day of celebration, to be sure.

I entered the hall without much subterfuge, and noted that it was too congested for me to climb to the solar without being noted. I had promised Evangeline not to sully her reputation so close to her wedding. This tale would be worth that, but I doubted I would survive any attempted ascent of those stairs.

Mercifully, I spied two familiar figures already seated at the board. I claimed the seat beside Fat with a flourish so that he glanced up. Dour glared at me from his seat opposite.

"You!" Tarsuinn whispered and began to rise to his feet.

I laid a hand upon his arm and pushed him back to the bench so firmly that he could not resist.

"Connor MacDoughall is the name," I growled, sparing a stern glance for each of them. "I come solely to celebrate the laird's wedding feast, and to warn you of a traitor in your own ranks."

You are surprised, perhaps, by my choice of moniker. The name had brought me such foul fortune that I assumed matters could only improve with its continued use. The wheel of Fortune turns, after all, and persistence in a course marked by bad fortune often results in remarkable bounty.

It could not hurt.

"Aye, he sits opposite me," Dour retorted.

"He sits at the head table," I asserted. "You can aid your lady and the memory of her sire by heeding what I have come to say."

"But . . ." began Tarsuinn's protest.

"Would I risk my life for no good cause?" I demanded.

Both men watched me warily, though Dour gave a minute nod of acknowledgement to this point. Tarsuinn eased back into his seat, his expression confused. He stared at the empty trencher before him, then seized his ale and drank it all.

"Courage, my friend, is not to be found in a cup of ale." I surveyed the company and discovered—not to my surprise—that neither Niall nor Evangeline were present.

Dour snorted. "You are no friend of ours, upon that you can rely."

"Am I not?" I accepted a cup of ale from a serving boy with a cursory smile, then sipped at it carefully. Either it was less foul than was typical or I developed a taste for the fare in this land.

There was an unsettling prospect.

"And who would be your friend? These men of repute?" I gestured with the cup to Fergus' three kin who now entered the hall. Alasdair, who was dressed most richly for a mere guest, surveyed the hall with the look of a man with a scheme. Ranald kept his devoted gaze upon his older cousin. The youth, Dubhglas, appeared smug to me.

They tried to take seats at the high table but were turned away, much to their evident dissatisfaction. A brief argument ensued which was abandoned at Alasdair's word. The three sat together at a table close to the high table and called for ale.

"They are no friends of ours," Tarsuinn said. "Indeed, I am surprised they chose to remain for the nuptials, for there is nothing at Inverfyre for them now."

"They will not linger long," Dour predicted, drinking of his own ale. "They wait only to ensure that the wedding occurs."

"I would not rely upon that," I said. Both men glanced at me with curiosity, then shook their heads.

"Niall will see them gone if they do not leave of their own volition," Tarsuinn insisted.

"And why is that?"

"Because they covet Inverfyre, everyone knows as much." Tarsuinn smiled amiably as a woman from the kitchens brought a steaming bowl to our board. Tarsuinn fairly licked his lips at the custard therein and ladled a goodly serving onto his trencher.

"Custard? At this hour?" Dour made a face, but the woman shrugged.

"Fine fare for a fine day," she said, then thumped a similar bowl on the next table before returning to the kitchen.

I cleared my throat. "What of Fergus' family's own lands?"

"The lands of the MacLarens were claimed by the crown some twenty years past," Tarsuinn confided between bites. "The MacLarens have become tenants instead of lairds, by the king's own decree."

"So, they would claim Inverfyre instead," I mused.

"Not now," Dour said with resolve. "Not now that Niall will take the lairdship. He has long suspected their scheme and will see them banished from Inverfyre. Fergus was indulgent of his kin, but Niall will not be so."

Tarsuinn gestured to the custard. "It is good, thick with raisins. Indeed, I doubt that we shall have Fergus' favored dish oft after this day, and all the worse the fare shall be for its lack. You should eat, Malachy, you should savor this treat." The other man grimaced and clung to his ale.

"Indeed, you should eat," I said, leaning back to sip of my own ale. "With every bite, you ensure the MacLarens' plan comes closer to fruition. Eat, eat so that Inverfyre's fortunes never recover."

They both regarded me with new suspicion.

"What is this?" Malachy demanded.

I leaned forward, tapping my finger on the board. "What if I could prove to you that Inverfyre's fortunes have failed because the MacLarens planned its downfall, that they ensured the estate was weakened so that they could claim it more readily?"

Tarsuinn shook his head and shoveled custard into his mouth with gusto. "The root of the matter lies with the falcons. No man can plan that wild birds become impotent."

"But any man can ensure that eggs are not allowed to hatch. One does as much with chickens all the time." I nudged the bowl of custard. "Who could tell if these were the eggs of falcons or of chickens?"

Malachy gasped. Tarsuinn dropped his spoon with such a clatter that several of the men at neighboring tables looked our way. He flushed and made a fuss about reclaiming the utensil. "So clumsy!" he said with a smile that might been born of embarrassment. "I have need of more ale this morn!"

The other men laughed and turned away, then both Tarsuinn and Malachy leaned close to me. Their eyes gleamed with curiosity.

"Are you certain?" Tarsuinn asked.

"Can you prove this assertion?" Malachy demanded.

"Show me where the refuse of the kitchen is tossed and you will see the truth of it," I said. They exchanged a glance, then nodded agreement as one. I drained my ale, knowing that such sustenance would be welcome in the job ahead.

I have never had a fondness for sifting through kitchen waste, but that was the sole source of evidence in this instance. I dearly hoped that my suspicions would be proven right. I needed the aid of these men to ensure that proof was found by witnesses Evangeline could trust. I needed the MacLarens to be fool enough—or confident enough—to have grown careless with hiding their scheme.

I like risk as a rule, though in this case, my teeth were nigh on edge. The initial waste was discouragingly benign, so I insisted that we dig. We were knee-deep in rotting peelings, blackened pits, bones and enough grease to make a dog die happy when Malachy cried out.

"It is true!" He held half of an eggshell in his hand, a shell of creamy white adorned with speckles.

Tarsuinn's eyes widened in horror. The pair dug with new fervor, unearthing an enormous cache of falcon eggshells. We made a pile of them, a pile which grew with every passing moment.

"Enough!" Tarsuinn groaned. "There are so many that there can be no doubt." He sat down and put his head in his hands. "This has been happening for years!"

"Fergus favored eggs at every meal," Malachy concurred. "He brought his own cook to Inverfyre so that there would be a complicit soul in the kitchens. He must have begun this travesty afore he came to our gates, knowing he and his chickens would be welcomed." He spared a shocked glance for his companion. "It is true! We have eaten Inverfyre into poverty!"

Tarsuinn turned away from us, his expression dismayed, then vomited the custard he had recently consumed. Fortunately, we stood in refuse and none would comment upon the mess.

"What a scheme," Malachy said sourly. "Indeed, one must admire how clever it was."

"And mourn how gullible we were," Tarsuinn added.

I recounted my tale of Dubhglas' deed to them and they nodded grimly. "Niall must learn of it," Malachy said with resolve.

"And afore the nuptials," Tarsuinn concurred.

"No, there must be no nuptials," I insisted, and both turned to me in surprise. "Evangeline and Niall are half-siblings."

Now, Malachy looked green, while Tarsuinn's lips tightened in disapproval. "This is why the old laird forbade them to wed all those years ago."

I nodded.

"Does Niall know?" Malachy demanded.

I nodded again.

Malachy exhaled with a frown, his gaze trailing over Inverfyre's high walls. "Niall sees nothing beyond his own aspirations," he said with a shake of his head.

"And the lady?" Tarsuinn asked anxiously.

"She knows now for I told her. She says she has no choice, and that she must wed Niall to save herself and her child and her child's legacy."

"She would say as much," Tarsuinn said.

"She is the spawn of her sire," Malachy agreed. The pair nodded solemnly for a moment. "The old laird must be rolling in his grave at this travesty," he muttered, then turned and offered his hand to me. "I am Malachy and my loyalty is pledged to the old laird, and thus to the lady Evangeline, his sole get. If you aid the lady, you may rely upon me to aid you, as well."

"And I am Tarsuinn, similarly pledged. If you know how we might save the lady Evangeline, our aid is with you."

I was as astonished as any to realize that I had enlisted the aid of two others—me, who always worked alone, had willingly sought out assistance. I had little time to reflect upon this oddity because the chapel bells began to ring, merrily summoning all to the nuptial mass.

"First, we must halt the wedding!" I said.

"We must hasten!" Tarsuinn cried and the three of us moved as one.

Despite our desire for haste, there was little progress to be made. The village square was thick with peasants come to celebrate the wedding. Indeed, their merriment was as likely due to the prospect of the feast the laird owed them on the day of his nuptials than any joy for the match itself—they were painfully thin, each and every one of them.

I was not surprised that after fifteen years of hardship, they looked so ravaged: I was surprised by how angry it made me that innocent people had suffered for the sake of the MacLarens' land lust.

I pushed my way through the throng with new vigor. I had no other plan beyond stopping the nuptials, indeed, I was not certain what could be said to make a difference.

Evangeline waited on the steps of the chapel, her lips tight and her countenance pale. My heart leapt at the sight of her, tightly bound into the same plum-hued kirtle embellished with pearls. Her hair was not to be seen, pulled as it was beneath her veil and circlet. The amber crucifix gleamed upon her breast, the purple hue of her garb showing the golden stones to advantage. Her hands were knotted tightly together and I knew then that she was not as content with this match as she would have had me believe.

I was so focused upon her unhappiness that I did not realize immediately that something was amiss.

"Where is Niall?" Tarsuinn demanded. "How dare he keep his bride a-waiting?"

It was true. There was no sign of the tall warrior. The priest looked impatient and Evangeline's expression could have been one of vexation. The assembly began to whisper, more than one glancing over the crowd. Evangeline's color rose.

When Alasdair stepped forward, garbed so richly that he might have known he would be the center of attention on this day, a horrible suspicion filled my thoughts.

"Since your knavish bridegroom does not deign to greet you, I offer myself in his stead," he said, then bowed low over Evangeline's hand. "Indeed, no man of honor could let such a beauteous bride come to the altar in vain."

She visibly recoiled, but Alasdair gave her no chance to reply.

"It is only fitting that a man wed his brother's widow, to ensure that his niece or nephew is raised with appropriate care." Alasdair's tone turned chiding. "Had you made your state clear sooner, I would have offered immediately for your hand."

"My hand is not for you to claim," Evangeline snapped, then pulled her fingers from his grip. "I will wait for Niall of Glenfannon."

"You will wed the man who will become the Laird of Inverfyre," Alasdair declared coldly. "And that man will be me." He seized her hand and turned her to face the priest. A murmur passed through the crowd. Evangeline struggled for release, then abruptly froze.

"It is Ranald," Malachy whispered, but I had already seen that deceptive snake slither into place. "To the lady's left. Did you see the flash of his blade?"

I nodded. I did not like it. The blade was too close to Evangeline for us to risk an assault. Tarsuinn grimly fingered the hilt of his own dagger. Dubhglas too was near the chapel steps. They could not win this day simply by proximity!

"The blade is against the lady's ribs, if I do not miss my guess," I whispered. "Do nothing, lest we risk her survival."

They acquiesced with a nod, clearly unhappy with this state of affairs. I looked again for Niall as the barely cooperative priest began to bless the couple, but he was not to be found.

These MacLarens surely offered a greater threat to the lady's survival than even Niall might have done. Indeed, there was an ease in their manner—as if they were unsurprised by the groom's absence—that made me wonder whether they had ensured that Niall could not attend his own nuptials.

I had no time to ponder such treachery. I had to act.

"Evangeline!" Every head turned at my cry, but I strode forward with a smile. "I do apologize for my tardiness on this day of days. Details took somewhat longer than anticipated."

The assembled peasantry parted before me in astonishment. I bestowed a confident smile upon them and strode forward, delighted that Tarsuinn and Malachy followed directly behind me.

"How charming of you to offer to wed the lady in my absence," I said to Alasdair, taking advantage of his surprise to pull Evangeline to my side. Tarsuinn slipped with remarkable agility between the lady and an open-mouthed Ranald, while Malachy elbowed Alasdair away from my side with a disarming smile.

"You cannot do this!" Alasdair argued. "You are a thief and a man with a price upon your head! Is no man in this company brave enough to claim that bounty?"

"My crimes are petty in comparison to yours." I spoke with such resolve that the men who might have seized me fell back in confusion. Tarsuinn and Malachy flashed their blades to deter the others. "For I never did aspire to steal Inverfyre."

The assembly gasped.

"You cannot make such a charge without evidence," Alasdair said.

"Oh, there is evidence aplenty." I smiled confidently at the company, who gained a better entertainment on this day than any might have hoped. "You and you and you," I said, pointing to peasant boys near the steps. "Fetch the buckets left by the kitchen door, by the portal that leads to the refuse pile." They ran off as the crowd watched.

"You cannot usurp the nuptials of the Laird of Inverfyre," Alasdair insisted.

"You claim to be the Laird of Inverfyre?" I spared him a glance. "Show me the seal. The laird always has the seal in his possession, does he not, Father?"

The priest began to smile as he nodded.

"I do not have the seal," Alasdair admitted through gritted teeth. "Not as yet."

"Does anyone have the seal?" I cast an eye over the company, knowing full well that no one could have it in their possession. I evaded Evangeline's gaze for I feared her silence to be a poor portent of her reaction.

"I demand that you halt this folly. . . ."

"If you do not hold the seal, then you cannot be the laird," I interrupted Alasdair firmly. "And if none are prepared to invest you with the seal, then you will not be laird soon. Thus, your command is of no import to these proceedings."

"My lady Evangeline," Alasdair growled. "Where *is* the seal of Inverfyre?"

I turned my back upon him, seizing the lady's hands within my own. "Since there is no Laird of Inverfyre, but there is a Lady of Inverfyre, her nuptials should be of our greater concern. And as the child in her belly is of my seed, I would think that we should be wed with considerable haste. Do you not agree, Father?" I dropped my voice, daring to look into the lady's eyes only then. "Do you not agree, my lady Evangeline?"

To my relief, she smiled, a twinkle lighting in the blue depths of her eyes. "You are a reckless scoundrel," she whispered, laughter underlying her words.

I laughed and bowed slightly. "But I am a reckless scoundrel at your service, which is more than can be said for your other choice of spouse on this day."

I glanced over my shoulder at Alasdair's grim countenance. "Indeed, I am a scoundrel arrived, I think, not a moment too soon." Evangeline smiled fully then, her eyes filling with warmth. I captured her hand in mine, my heart thumping with vigor. "Will you wed me, my lady fair?"

Endgame

Evangeline

XVIII

What was I to make of Gawain's deed?

I was thrilled to see him again, more delighted than I knew I should be. I had spent the night trying to wring some conclusion from his return of my mother's gem to me, even knowing that I should not make much of what he probably thought inconsequential. I had envisioned him heading determinedly south, in the ports of London, perhaps, or Southampton, negotiating for his passage with ease and charm.

But Gawain was here, just as Niall was not, and his very presence addled my wits. When he kissed my knuckles with a flourish, his eyes twinkling with merriment, I could scarcely summon a thought to my head. A yearning took hold within me, perhaps an unhealthy one, but an undeniable one all the same.

This was the father of the child I bore. This was the man who accepted me as I was. This was the man whose very presence made my pulse quicken. Surely, there was but one reply I could make.

I smiled and inclined my head. "I should be delighted to exchange vows with you, Gawain."

The assembly hooted and stamped, some evidence of our ardor apparent to them. Indeed, Gawain grinned, then scooped me into his arms and swung me high. I laughed, feeling unburdened for the first time in years—nay, decades.

Alasdair stepped forward, his scowl fierce. "I will not permit this match!" he shouted, then pointed at Gawain. "This man is an outcast from this holding, by dint of his thievery and deception, and unfit to usurp the place that should be mine."

"Usurp you?" Gawain asked, arching a fair brow. "And what of the intended bridegroom, Niall of Glenfannon? Surely, none could have anticipated that he would not arrive here—save a man who had ensured Niall would be absent."

Alasdair's lips set and his voice dropped low. "Do you make an accusation? If so, state it clearly, Thief. We shall have truth between us on this day."

The assembly seemed to hold their collective breath, indeed, I scarce breathed myself. What did Gawain know? What had he dispatched the boys to fetch? In the weight of silence, one sound carried to our ears.

It was the voice of a woman, a woman singing.

She sang an old Gaelic funeral song, a tribute to a nameless fallen warrior. I turned to look toward the gates, then caught my breath at the sight of Adaira. I had not seen her since her betrayal of me, and indeed, could find no reason why she should have contrived that I appear guilty of Fergus' murder.

But this was not the time to demand such an answer. Adaira was more crooked and bent than I knew her to be, burdened by a weight of grief. Her keening carried as clearly as a mountain stream and drew every eye to her. She walked beside a horse and a man was draped across the horse's back, a man who was either asleep or dead by his limp posture.

I saw the fallen man's stature, I saw the dark tangle of his hair, I saw the armor I knew so well. I murmured a prayer, but to no avail. There could be no doubt whose corpse she brought.

Adaira's daughter had died in birthing a babe abandoned by its sire, and now her son died young as well.

"Niall," I whispered, wishing it were not so. Gawain's expression had turned inscrutable, while Alasdair looked wary. Every soul seemed to have turned to a pillar of salt, so still had each become.

I left the church steps and the silent crowd parted before me as I strode to meet Adaira. She looked up at the sound of my footfalls. "My lady?"

"It is, Adaira."

"I have brought the bridegroom to his nuptials," she said, her voice thick with unshed tears. "You had to know that only foul play could keep him from this ceremony he desired more than life itself." And she lifted Niall's head, cradling his dark curls in her gnarled hands, turning his face to me.

I gasped at the crude slash across his throat, still wet and fresh. Indeed, I stepped backward so hastily that I tripped on the hem of my gown. The crowd murmured angrily.

"Who did this deed?" I cried.

"Who knew that Niall would not reach the chapel steps this day?" Gawain asked, more calm than I.

Alasdair flushed. "Do you call me a murderer?"

"If he does not, I do," Adaira shouted. She left the horse and clambered up the chapel steps. "You and your kin are all murderers and thieves, all determined to possess what should not by rights be yours, no matter what the price."

Alasdair rose to his full height. "Fergus was right in banning you from this keep," he said. "You are no more than a madwoman of the woods, and only nonsense falls from your lips. Begone, begone to your hovel in the forest and plague us no longer!"

Adaira began to laugh. "Nonsense is not why Fergus banned me from Inverfyre. The truth was what he feared, not nonsense."

"You do not know what you say!"

"I know precisely what I say."

"What whimsy is in this old woman's reminiscences!" Alasdair scoffed. "We have assembled for nuptials and a feast, not foolish tales."

Gawain raised a hand to silence the other man. "Do you fear what she might tell? It seems you must, for all others are intrigued."

"We shall listen," I insisted. "For no good choice can be made with only part of the tale."

Alasdair fell silent with obvious reluctance.

Adaira gestured to me. "My lady, who tended your father at the end of his days?"

"You did. All were forbidden from his chambers," I informed the company. "All save Adaira, my mother and I, for this was my father's demand."

Adaira nodded. "But I slept one morning, after Gilchrist had a long and troubled night, while the ladies slumbered themselves. It was early, for even the goats had not begun to bleat."

The assembly eased closer, their attention complete. Adaira nodded, as if lost in the memory of that day. "I was in the corner, in a shadow, which must have been why Fergus did not note me when he crept into the solar. I noted him, though, for my hearing has long been sharp. I knew it was him, though I was fool enough to think Gilchrist's fears were no more than the ravings of a dying man much enamored of his own authority.

"I heard Fergus approach the bed. I heard him whisper to Gilchrist that the time had come to pay his due. Then I heard Gilchrist struggle to breathe. The sound of him was muffled, just as it would be if something was held over his face, as if something kept the breath from filling his chest."

"You know nothing!" Alasdair said with scorn. "You insult the memory of Fergus MacLaren, the last Laird of Inverfyre!"

"While you insult the memory of the last *true* Laird of Inverfyre by refusing to acknowledge his untimely death," Adaira snapped. "I have no doubt of Fergus' guilt, and indeed on that morn, I did not dare to move from my corner lest a murderer cast his gaze upon me."

The crowd murmured, but Adaira held up a warning finger and her voice became more resonant. "I will tell you this—Gilchrist pledged nothing to Fergus, he had neither the chance nor the desire. Fergus' claim to Inverfyre was based on nothing but his own lust for the holding, a claim he could make as there were no witnesses of Gilchrist's last moments."

"Nonsense!" Alasdair laughed a little too loudly. "Gilchrist made Fergus his heir! We all know as much."

"He never did," Adaira said with resolve. "Fergus lied to steal the suzerainty of Inverfyre. He embellished that lie further to fetch himself a pretty bride. Gilchrist promised him neither Inverfyre nor his sole daughter. Fergus lied to better the circumstance of his own sorry kin. You arrived shortly thereafter, for you knew in advance of his plan, just as Fergus knew in advance of his arrival that our fortunes were failing. You all ensure your success by treachery aforehand."

A furor erupted in the crowd. A few raised their fists and

began to shout for blood. It seemed that I was not the only one to have wondered how my father could have made such a choice of heir.

Sadly, we questioned it too late.

"If what you say is true," Alasdair scoffed, "if Fergus were truly as wicked as you suggest, then he would have seen you silenced."

"He was never certain what I knew," Adaira asserted. "And even he dared not risk too much. He forbade me from Inverfyre, banishing me to the forest where I prefer to be at any rate. I daresay I have eaten better than most of you beneath his hand."

"This is madness!" Alasdair appealed to the crowd with a charming smile. "This accusation is made upon nothing but the word of a sightless woman known to be ancient and addled."

"You think you are safe from the word of a blind woman," Adaira sneered. "You think I do not know your smell, the sound of your footsteps, the rhythm of your breathing, the echo of your voice. You think a man can be identified by sight alone, and in this you are wrong." Alasdair took a step back but Adaira pursued him. "You think that because you cannot hear another in the forest, that there cannot be another there, that another cannot hear you."

Alasdair paled, as Adaira tapped his chest with a gnarled finger.

"I heard you argue with Fergus," she said. "I heard you tell him that his scheme to possess Inverfyre took too long. I heard you accuse him of cowardice."

"Lies! These are all lies!"

"You stood outside the gates of Inverfyre, awaiting your hunting party. Fergus sent his squire on some errand, to ensure that the two of you were momentarily alone. You were restless, your words strident. You told Fergus that he took too long in fulfilling your family scheme, that it was time he named a successor and retired to his hunting."

"I did not. . . ."

"You told him that if he were man at all, he would step aside. You told him that the MacLarens appreciated all he had done, but that the time had come for action. He told you to learn patience, but still he was goaded and angered, precisely as you intended. I *heard* you, Alasdair MacLaren."

"This is a tale, composed for the entertainment of all!" Alasdair argued, but I could see the fear in his expression.

Adaira barely paused for breath. "And so, when the boar plunged into the woods, the dogs fast at its heels, Fergus spurred his horse to pursue it. He rode with folly, anxious to prove his virility, desperate to assert his courage by the killing of a boar. Instead, you separated him from the boar and killed him."

"A boar is not so readily diverted as that, old woman."

"I have no doubt that you had aid," Adaira said with resolve, then turned her milky gaze upon Ranald and Dubhglas. The boy fidgeted, but Ranald stoically stared at the blind woman.

She held up her hand and counted off the crimes. "Fergus killed Gilchrist to claim Inverfyre with a lie; you killed your own brother to claim Inverfyre in your turn; and on this day, you killed my son, Niall of Glenfannon, to ensure that he did not contest your claim. Your ambition to see yourself made laird cannot be swayed, for you do not care how many you must kill."

To my surprise, Alasdair shrugged. "You have no evidence to support your accusations. Why would Fergus kill a man who favored him, and concoct some tale of what he would have rightfully been granted at any rate? You see tales where there are none!"

"Do I?"

"What if I do wish to see Inverfyre more competently ruled? I am not alone in this desire—there have been many to argue with Fergus of late, including the man whose corpse you bring this day. I did not kill my brother, but I am content to repair the holding he ruled."

Alasdair turned to the assembly, appealing for their support with a confidence unexpected. "Who among you can yearn for more of poverty and illness? Who can imagine that the state of Inverfyre is a good one? Who among you is not tired of an empty belly every night and cold feet every winter?"

The assembly rumbled at this truth, and nodded to each other.

Alasdair took strength from their uncertainty. "Who can argue that Inverfyre has need of strong leadership? Who can argue that it is time to put aside what does not work and begin anew?"

Gawain pursed his lips. "Perhaps only those responsible for Inverfyre's current state."

Alasdair turned upon him. "Thieves, perhaps?"

Gawain smiled. "Yes, thieves. Thieves of an unexpected kind." He turned to me with easy confidence. "Tell me, what fare was offered in the hall this morn?"

I struggled to recall. "A custard, wrought with raisins on account of the day's festivities."

Gawain's smile broadened. "Wrought, too, with eggs."

I was puzzled. "Of course. It was a custard."

Gawain turned to the assembly. "And how many of you ate heartily of this treat?"

Most of the people gathered there nodded, many smiling in recollection of the rich fare they had enjoyed.

"Every one of you who ate of this dish contributed to the poverty of Inverfyre," Gawain asserted. Confusion crossed many a face, then anger. "All know that Fergus brought chickens to your gates when Inverfyre starved for lack of eyasses and for lack of trade. But who knows how long Fergus lingered in Inverfyre's forests, ensuring that those eyasses did not come to be?"

Adaira drove her thumb into her own chest. "I knew! I knew there was malice in my woods. I knew he lurked there, though I knew not why. Not then."

"But how?" I demanded. "No man can affect the mating of wild birds."

Gawain smiled. "Not their mating, but how many of their eggs are hatched. What a fancy the court of Inverfyre has for eggs."

A horrific conclusion came to me. "No!" I cried in dismay. I lunged to the steps again and seized Gawain's sleeve. "Tell me that there were not falcon eggs mixed with those of the chickens!" I saw from his expression that he would not do so, that I had glimpsed the depth of Fergus' deception too late.

"I saw this morning a most interesting sight." Gawain indicated Dubhglas and the boy's face turned even more red. "I saw this boy steal four falcon eggs from a nest. He did not see me, thus I know that you all need evidence of this deed."

"Four eggs does not fifteen years of impotency make," Alasdair sneered.

Gawain smiled coolly. "If there are but four egg shells to be found outside the kitchens, then you have naught to fear."

The three MacLarens paled and said no more. The villagers cried out in rage, even as the boys who had been dispatched earlier returned. They carried pails, and poured the contents at my feet. One after the other, the pails were emptied of eggshells, some rotted nigh to oblivion, some fresh.

They were speckled eggshells, precisely as peregrines lay, thousands upon thousands of them, dispatched from our own kitchens for fifteen years.

"Malachy and I aided Gawain in his search of the kitchen waste earlier this day, my lady," Tarsuinn said with a bow.

I fell to my knees with a cry of anguish and lifted broken shells in my hands. I knew the size, I knew the shape, I knew the markings. I knew that Gawain was right.

"It is true," I said clearly to my people and held up the evidence. "We have been eating our own fortunes, though we have done so in innocence, never guessing the deception in our own hall." I spun and flung a handful of shells at Alasdair. "We never guessed the treachery of the MacLarens!"

Anger erupted then in the crowd. Furious cries rent the air, fists were shaken and feet stomped.

"We showed them compassion and gave them shelter while they planned our downfall!" Tarsuinn cried. "The MacLaren clan has ensured that your bellies were empty, that we had naught with which to trade, that Inverfyre's fortunes dwindled to naught—all the better that they might steal Inverfyre."

Alasdair stepped forward, his manner unexpectedly composed. Indeed, he smiled. "This is all terribly interesting, and truly, I do hope that the falcons prosper in the first year of my lairdship. The treasury of Inverfyre has dire need of the coin."

"But you will not be laird!" I said, marveling at his audacity.

"Of course I will be," Alasdair insisted. "Inverfyre will be mine and you will all be the richer for it." He offered his hand to me. "Here is your last opportunity, Evangeline, to be the

Lady of Inverfyre, as you were born to be. Wed me on this day—save yourself and your child."

"Never!" I shouted, much to the approval of the villagers. They began to stamp their feet and to hoot.

"A most unfortunate choice," Alasdair said with a sad shake of his head. He stepped back, then lifted his hand as if to beckon to someone. I feared suddenly what preparations he might have made.

His kin had shown, after all, a tendency to prepare for all eventualities. I pivoted in time to see scores of armed men slip from huts and shadows, pour through Inverfyre's gates, appear seemingly from every corner. They were men I did not know, men garbed for war, men who unsheathed their swords and began to slaughter the peasants who had come to see me wed.

The square of Inverfyre filled with blood as I began to scream.

I was knocked from behind and fell on the stone steps, barely curving my arm beneath my belly in time. The battle swept over me, spattering me with the blood, then moved on. The wind was knocked from me and I lay there for a moment, watching madness unfurl in my home and powerless to do anything about it. I had solely a small eating knife hung upon my belt, no match for swords and daggers of these men. I had lost track of the people who had stood alongside me, and indeed, it was difficult to pick out individuals in the slaughter that confronted me.

The fallen, however, were almost all the people of Inverfyre. I was sickened. They had been betrayed by surprise as well as a greater arsenal of weapons. As I watched, several of the assailants shoved torches into the huts of Inverfyre and the village began to burn.

Panic rose within me at the ease with which the flames spread. I could not stay here, indeed any soul would be fortunate to escape alive. Just then, one of the monks who sang the offices in our chapel fell heavily before me.

He was dead. Before I could avert my gaze from this travesty, I spied the brass key tied to his belt.

I knew then what I must do. Indeed, the key glinted in the sunlight, daring me to do what I must. If I survived this day and my son survived, he would have need of one item to prove his birthright.

I would not leave without the *Titulus*.

I rolled until I lay against the stone wall of the chapel, beside the dead monk. I surveyed the mayhem through my lashes and saw that I had been momentarily forgotten. I lingered there for a moment, ensuring that I was not observed, then seized the key. I leapt to my feet and lunged through the chapel doors, the key held fast before myself. I bolted them behind me and leaned back against them in relief.

It was dark and cold in the chapel, quiet as only a sanctuary of worship could be. My gaze trailed over the stones in the floor, stones marking the tombs of my forebears. Magnus Armstrong lay beneath my very feet, his six sons laid head to toe before him. My own father lay closest to the altar, with but one spot left betwixt his stone and the high table itself.

I took a step forward then, reassured by the embrace of silence, then took another and another. I moved more quickly toward the reliquary with every pace until I was nigh running. I fumbled with the brass key, a key brought to the chapel only that the *Titulus* might be lifted high for the celebratory mass of my wedding. I rounded the altar, lifted the key and a gloved hand snapped out of the darkness to seize my wrist.

I gasped even as Alasdair smiled. He unfolded himself

from his hiding place behind the draped altar, his grip upon me relentless.

"How accommodating of you to bring me the key," he whispered, his eyes gleaming. "Unlock the reliquary, Evangeline, and surrender the prize of Inverfyre to me. We shall celebrate our own investiture of the lairdship afore you die."

I gaped at him, my heart racing. "Then the accusations were all true."

Alasdair smiled without regret. "Open it."

My hand was shaking, my thoughts spinning, as I lifted the key to the lock. "But what of the child I bear? You yourself said it was your duty to provide for your brother's get."

"That was before his widow was proved a liar, before I knew for certain that the child was a bastard." Alasdair shook his head at me. "You cannot bargain for your life, Evangeline, not now that you have declined your sole chance to survive. And do not imagine that you can delay the matter—if you take overlong to surrender the *Titulus*, then I shall dispatch you and take it myself."

I regarded him for a moment, letting him see how I despised him. I then turned the key in the lock with resolve, flung open the door and reached for the *Titulus* within. My hands closed over its familiar shape as Alasdair watched avidly.

"It is oft poor judgement to leave a captive with no hope," I said quietly.

"I shall take the chance," he said, not disguising his conviction that he feared nothing a woman might do.

I moved with haste then, hauling the relic from its sanctuary, and jabbing Alasdair hard with my elbow in the same moment. He cried out and tried to grab me, but I darted backward. With the relic in both hands, I brought it down hard on his head.

There was a resounding crack. I hoped for the blink of an eye that I had dealt him a fatal wound, but the *Titulus* fell in two fragments in my hands.

And Alasdair snarled as he snatched at me. "Whore!" he shouted.

I ran, but stumbled over my full skirts. He caught the end of my veil but I let it tear, spinning out of his grasp for a hopeful moment.

But Alasdair was taller than me and faster than I had hoped. He lunged after me and caught the back of my kirtle, his expression cruel as he hauled me back toward him. I struggled and twisted, I tried to escape his relentless grip, but to no avail.

He tore away the last of my headdress and flung it aside, grasping my mother's crucifix. He coiled the chain around his gloved fist and held me captive before him, the gold biting into my throat. I panted in my desperation but there was naught I could do, even when he drove his knife into the soft flesh beneath my chin.

"My lady?" came Tarsuinn's cry from the other side of the chapel doors. I cried out and the son of my father's falconer tried to force the doors. A hammering began as Tarsuinn was joined by another.

But the lock was doughty, I knew it well.

Alasdair smiled. "What foresight you showed, Evangeline, to ensure that we could not be disturbed."

I closed my eyes and looked away, heartsick at the fullness of my failure. Here before my slumbering forebears I lost the estate they had labored to build. There could be no greater disappointment to any of our ilk.

They might witness that I was doomed, but they also would see that I fought valiantly to my last breath.

"Do your worst," I told Alasdair. "I regret nothing. I will

never endorse your suzerainty. I would rather be dead than see you on Inverfyre's high seat."

"You are almost too proud to kill so secretly," Alasdair had time to say before the stained glass above the altar shattered into a thousand pieces.

We both looked up in astonishment as Gawain leapt through the space. He landed on his toes with untold agility, a dagger gripped in his teeth. He plucked the knife from his teeth, twirled it and grinned.

I know that I smiled, so delighted was I to see him here, so reassured was I by his confident swagger.

"How fortunate to find you here, Alasdair," Gawain said with cocky ease, sparing a conspiratorial wink for me. "I have a missive for you that must be delivered afore you die."

"You have no missive for me," Alasdair snarled.

"Indeed I do," Gawain said amiably. "This dagger—" he twirled it so that the blade flashed silver and I recognized it with astonishment "—commands me to avenge its owner."

"You speak nonsense."

"It is Niall's blade," I said breathlessly. "My father granted it to him when Niall pledged his loyalty to Inverfyre. It is an old blade, a blade that belonged to my grandfather."

Gawain arched a brow, no doubt surprised that none of us had guessed why my father granted it to Niall. "And this family blade calls for blood in vengeance. It calls for *your* blood, Alasdair. Niall of Glenfannon may have been many things, but like his father, he was a man of honor, a man who demanded that justice be done."

"Lies!" Alasdair roared.

While Alasdair's attention was diverted, I drove my knee into his crotch. His grip loosed on me even as his eyes bulged. He swore, but that instant was all I needed. I leaned toward him so that the chain fell slack, then ducked my head through its loop. My mother's crucifix remained locked in his fist, the chain swinging empty, but I chose to live without it.

Tarsuinn pounded on the chapel doors with renewed vigor. I raced for the back of the chapel, my heart quailing at the clash of steel on steel behind me. I gathered the *Titulus* pieces against my chest with one hand and opened the latch with the other.

The doors were cast open with such vigor that I was flung back against the wall. I caught my breath, certain that I had aided Gawain as best I could, then gasped in horror at what I had done.

It was not Tarsuinn who thundered into the chapel, nor indeed was it anyone I knew. Four of Alasdair's troops ran down the aisle, their mail clattering and their blades held high.

"No!" I shouted in dismay.

The mercenaries bellowed as one, ignoring me as they joined the fight. I had a fleeting glimpse of Gawain when he glanced up at my cry and saw the multiplied number of his opponents.

I had betrayed him!

But Gawain cast no accusing glance my way. His lips set with such resolve that I knew he would fight to the most bitter end. Indeed, the sunlight gilded his hair as he leapt to the altar and swung his blade in a battle he was destined to lose.

XIX

"My lady!" Tarsuinn hissed.

I spun to find him on the threshold on the chapel, blood running from the shoulder of his sword arm. He was pale, but he relinquished his grip upon his wound to offer me his hand.

"Come, my lady, we must seize this chance to flee."

I glanced back as a man groaned and fell. It was Alasdair, Niall's knife lodged in his chest. Gawain must have no blade! I took a step just as Alasdair lunged to his feet with a snarl.

"No!" Tarsuinn seized my hand and pulled me back.

Gawain kicked Alasdair in the chest and Alasdair fell, hitting his head and moving no more. Gawain seized Alasdair's sword without hesitation and spun to face his assailants.

"The specter of Niall of Glenfannon demands vengeance!" Gawain cried with wicked glee. I was fascinated and thrilled by his boldness. "How fearless are you now, my friends?"

"We must leave," Tarsuinn urged.

"A man gives his life to ensure yours," Malachy insisted. I turned to find the smaller man panting with his own exhaustion, blood spattered across his face and garb. "Do not make his sacrifice a worthless one, my lady."

I looked back, torn, to see Alasdair's men fall upon Gawain with renewed vigor. They quickly obscured him from my sight.

Tarsuinn tugged my sleeve anew. Only the knowledge that my babe relied upon my survival made me turn. I would save myself that I might save Gawain's child—had I not carried the fruit of his seed, I would have aided him, even died without remorse.

But I could not think only of myself. I took Tarsuinn's hand, my vision veiled with tears. They cast a cloak over me, these men so loyal to my father's hand, and led me nigh blind through the market square. I could see little with the hood of the cloak pulled over my face, but knew that if I were recognized, I would breathe my last.

I put my trust in these men who had earned it time and again.

We nearly tripped over the fallen, our cloaks were singed by the flames that swept through the village. A shout echoed when we drew near to the shadowed gates. Tarsuinn and Malachy flung me ahead of them, but I could not abandon them wholly. I cast back my hood to better defend myself just as Dubhglas dove toward me.

I buried my eating knife in his eye. He fell back, screaming. My companions dispatched their attackers and we turned to flee, just as the portcullis rope began to groan.

"Run!" Malachy cried.

His cry prompted half a dozen men to turn. A shout rose from the square behind us, the iron gate began to lower toward the earth with relentless speed. We raced for the narrowing portal, and I saw that the gate descended too fast.

"Roll!" Tarsuinn shouted. Malachy tripped me and I fell behind him, tumbling through the narrow aperture. For a heartstopping moment, I stared directly upward into the descending spikes, fearing I would not be through in time. Malachy seized my hand and tugged, and I pulled my legs through. Tarsuinn rolled through the space behind me.

The points of the portcullis buried themselves in the ground with a resounding thud. Tarsuinn gasped, for the points had barely missed his flesh and pinned his tabard into the ground. We pulled upon his hands, I heard cloth tear, but we ran, not a one of us looking back. The mercenaries gathered shouting at the gates, demanding that it be raised with haste.

Indeed, we ran as if the hounds of hell were behind us, scattering into the welcome haven of the cool green forest.

When we crested a distant hill, the forest holding us in its embrace, I dared to look back. I groaned when I saw that Inverfyre burned with unholy vigor. The blaze was as bright as a beacon, the flames consumed hut, village and wall.

My legacy was lost.

As I watched, the roof of the chapel was devoured by flames. The cross upon its roof was illuminated with a corona of fire, then it tumbled along with the crumbling roof. It fell burning into the chapel and the ground seemed to shake with its impact even where we stood.

My heart sank at the sight. Even if Gawain defeated his foes, I could not imagine that he would escape the chapel alive.

My love was lost. I knew this to be the truth as soon as the thought came to me. I loved Gawain, loved him as I could never have believed a woman could love a man. Without him, without the prospect of hearing his laughter, without knowing that he plundered and pillaged abroad, without knowing that the man I loved lived boldly somewhere, my own life was as dust in my mouth.

I had realized the truth too late to share it with him.

At Tarsuinn's urging, I turned reluctantly away from the scene of destruction and we began to put distance between ourselves and Inverfyre. I did not know where we went, I did not care. I but followed their lead and grieved.

I wept at the blood that stained my slippers, blood of the people I had failed. I wept for Niall, who had been killed because I sought his aid. I wept for the forebears I had failed, for my parents whose pledges I had broken, for my son whose legacy I had lost. And I wept for Gawain, a man who professed to care for nothing or no one but who had died ensuring my survival.

I had failed in every way that mattered, failed in ways that I had not dreamed existed. I could not imagine how I would continue in the face of these facts. I walked with these two loyal men, respectful of my turmoil in their silence, and gradually my tears spent themselves. The air cooled, the screams faded behind us and the shadows of the evening began to fall. We walked until we could walk no more, then Tarsuinn touched my elbow.

"There is a glade here, my lady, a sheltered hollow that cannot be readily discerned by any who might pass. I would suggest that we halt for the night."

"I can walk to Edinburgh," I said, though the exhaustion in my bones belied my words.

Tarsuinn smiled. "I do not doubt it, my lady, for you have your father's strength of purpose. Think of the child you carry, though, afore you tax yourself too much."

I did think of the child, for I wished to put a thousand miles betwixt we two and the ambitious MacLaren clan who assailed Inverfyre. All the same, there was some merit to Tarsuinn's argument. We could not get so far this night, and Tarsuinn needed care for his wound. I realized how tired these two men must be and found the truth of it in their faces.

I smiled in my turn. "Forgive me, both of you. In my haste to be away, I have forgotten the battles you have faced this day."

"Not only us, my lady," Malachy said quietly. He raised a hand, though did not touch my throat. I was aware suddenly of the burn upon my flesh and raised my hand to the welt wrought by the chain of my mother's own crucifix.

I refused to dwell upon the fact that I had lost that, as well. "Let us halt then, as you suggest. You must have your wound tended, Tarsuinn."

There was a tranquillity in this glade, a caress in its welcoming shadows. It seemed our hearts were lightened even as we stepped within it, as if this place belonged out of time. The hues of green seemed richer here, the burble of the stream more merry. The cool shadows embraced us, a light breeze coaxed our cares away. Tarsuinn took a deep breath and seemed to drop a weight from his shoulders; even Malachy seemed less dour.

"There is no balm like a place with old bones," Tarsuinn said, then cupped his hands and sipped of the stream trickling there.

"You know this place?" I was surprised, though I supposed we had not come that far from Inverfyre.

Tarsuinn colored. Malachy chuckled. "Many know it, my lady, though I am not surprised that you do not. It is a place where lovers oft come to meet, a place where they forget the cares of the world of men."

"It is said that the old goddesses walked here, trailing their skirts upon the ground and leaving flowers in their wake," Tarsuinn confided. "It is here the peasants come to leave prayers to the Lady of the Waters."

I looked and saw a few rags tied in the trees, their ends trailing in the water. It is an old charm to journey to a holy fount, to pray, then to leave a token behind. The rags were old and I suspected that this place had lost its allure as a place to beg favors, at least of a divine feminine.

I had no doubt that the old goddesses would have approved of mortals making love in this glade so fond to them. I smiled that they might smile upon those who trysted here.

"And you should know such a detail," Malachy teased his comrade. "Given your many encounters with the ladies."

Tarsuinn colored more deeply. "Do not blame me if you have poor fortune in matters of the heart," he said gruffly. "Your own tongue is your worst enemy."

I glimpsed a side of these men I had never seen before and watched with welcome amusement.

"While your insistence upon showing gallantry even where it is undeserved has won you untold hearts," Malachy said, then grinned. "Even those you do not desire."

"We need not speak of this. . . ."

"Tell me, did ever you bring *Fiona* to this place?"

Tarsuinn shook a finger at his friend. "You promised never to tease me about this matter again! I cannot help an old maid's folly . . ."

"Fiona?" I echoed.

"Tarsuinn was kind to her, which was his sole crime." Malachy barely restrained his laughter. "He has paid for his foolhardiness ever since." He laid a hand upon his chest and fluttered his lashes. He then pursed his lips and offered a parody of a kiss to Tarsuinn before mocking a woman's voice. "Oh, Tarsuinn, Tarsuinn, *take* me!"

Tarsuinn dove after his friend with a growl of frustration and they tussled good-naturedly. Malachy rolled on the greenery, laughing that Tarsuinn was so outraged.

"What of your wound, Tarsuinn?" I asked.

"Aye, his heart is broken now that he is parted from his beloved Fiona," Malachy managed to mutter. Tarsuinn tussled the smaller man to the turf, Malachy's defense much impeded by his helpless laughter. He whispered "oh Tarsuinn!" at intervals, until he was breathless with laughter.

Tarsuinn abandoned the battle, returning to me as if affronted beyond belief. "No doubt you are jealous, for you desired to court her yourself," he cast these words over his shoulder, his manner smug.

"Me?" Malachy sat up, leaves in his hair.

"Oh, I have seen the eyes you make at Fiona across the hall," Tarsuinn insisted. Now, he laid his hand over his heart and tried to look like a man besotted. "I have heard you catch your breath when she enters the hall and I have heard you whisper her name in your sleep."

"Me? Never!" Malachy bounced to his feet. "That is a lie!"

Tarsuinn leaned closer to me, his manner confidential. "It is a sly rogue, my lady, who pretends to care nothing for the woman who has seized his heart forever."

"Fiona! There would be a sorry fate!" Malachy grimaced, his expression so eloquent that I began to laugh. The pair exchanged a glance, then began to chuckle themselves. They embraced and tussled a bit more, then Tarsuinn winked at me.

"It is good to see the lady smile."

My smile broadened that they had such a care for me, and I thanked them before beckoning Tarsuinn that I might look at his wound. He amiably peeled off his tabard, then pulled back his slashed chemise, revealing the gash in his shoulder to me. He sat down as I indicated, his back to me, a last beam of sunlight touching the bloody gash.

"How bad is it?" Malachy demanded, peering over my shoulder.

"It is deep but cleanly wrought, at least."

"That will teach you to face a dozen men at once," Malachy chided with affection.

"They would have finished me, were it not for your timely arrival."

"Ah, now he is sentimental with gratitude." Malachy rolled his eyes, then winked at me. He fetched some water at my request and I rinsed out the wound until the blood ran clear, ignoring the two's bantering accusations. Malachy finally waved off his companion's teasing with disgust and stomped into the woods, probably to relieve himself.

"You should stitch it closed," counseled a woman behind me.

I jumped even as Tarsuinn did the same beneath my fingertips. I turned to find Adaira standing there, and marveled that she had approached so silently. She reached for Tarsuinn's shoulder, her twisted fingers feeling along his wound, even gently probing its depth so that he flinched.

"Fiona is dead," she said afore any of us could summon a word. "She died as she lived, grasping for what was not hers to have."

Tarsuinn glanced back, a query in his expression, and Adaira nodded. "She tried to raid my lady's chamber when the flames rose around the keep. She was trapped there and, despite her entreaties for aid, none would risk their life to save hers. She perished there."

Tarsuinn frowned and looked away.

"Do not mourn her or her kind," Adaira said gruffly. She gave his wound another prod, then nodded. "Yes. It must be stitched to heal aright. Have you a needle?"

I finally found my voice. "What brings you to my side? What trouble have you yet to wreak?"

She tilted her head to regard me, as if puzzled by my manner. "I come to aid in healing, as always."

"You healed nothing in pressing those arrows into my hands, for that ensured that I would be considered guilty of Fergus' demise," I said hotly. "And you healed nothing in offering me a means of killing the babe in my womb."

Adaira shrugged. She produced a needle and eased me out of her way as she set to stitching Tarsuinn's wound. He grunted as the needle bit into his flesh, but she passed her hand over his skin and his tension eased. "It will not take long," she told him. "And treated thus, it will heal with only the barest scar."

He nodded and bent his head, surrendering to her ministrations. She ignored me as she worked, her fingers showing a familiar grace in this task that my more youthful fingers would have lacked.

"Why, Adaira?" I asked when it was clear she would say nothing to me. "Why did you try to incriminate me?"

She pursed her lips. "There are greater forces in this world than the life of one unborn child, greater matters to be resolved."

"Not to me."

"Understand, my lady, that I knew you would never be found guilty of this crime you did not commit. The desired end is more likely achieved in any situation when there is more than one path leading to it."

"I do not understand. You wished for me to be imprisoned?"

Adaira frowned as she concentrated on her stitching. "There are many ways to be rid of a babe—you spurned my potion, as I anticipated you might. The shock of this charge and whatever response was wrought from those in Inverfyre's court could well have induced you to lose the babe, as well."

My hand curled protectively over my belly. "Why would you desire me to lose my babe? How could you do this ill to me, to him?"

Adaira knotted the last stitch and bit off the thread, in no haste to sate my curiosity. She threw back her head then and recounted that old rhyme.

When the seventh son of Inverfyre,
Saves his legacy from intrigue and mire,
Only then shall glorious Inverfyre,
Reflect in full its first laird's desire.

"No doubt you do not know the whole of the tale," she said.

"I have heard all of the verse."

Adaira smiled. "Ah, but the meat of the tale was never included in the verse you heard."

"Why not?"

"The troubador who wrote the *chanson* put no credit in the truth. It is common for men to despise what they cannot hold within their hands, to disbelieve what cannot be proven in their own experience. The tale was an uncommon one and he, like many others, was too much the skeptic to grant it credit."

"What truth is this? And what has it to do with my child?"

"Patience, my lady, patience." Adaira took a seat upon an old log and sighed as if tired. Her features seemed more lined and I recalled that she had found her son murdered on this day. My heart twisted in sympathy, though still I could not face her with the same warmth as once I had.

She cleared her throat before she spoke. "There are those who believe that the tale of Inverfyre begins with Magnus Armstrong's arrival, but they are wrong: the full tale began long before. Even the tale of Magnus himself, who was called thus solely in that time, began long before. Magnus did not come to this place by choice or by chance, he did not find his home at Inverfyre by accident. No, he returned to Inverfyre by compulsion. He may not have been aware of what he did, not at first, but his soul knew the site of Inverfyre and the debt he was pledged to pay there. The soul keeps a reckoning that cannot be denied."

"You talk in riddles," I said with some irritation.

"The truth is oft like that." Adaira gestured in the direction of Inverfyre. "These woes are not new. Inverfyre, under all its names, has long been a contested land, and the combatants of each epoch have oft had much in common with the combatants of the past. It is a place of some witchery, a place that casts a light into the heart of all those who pass its threshold, a place that condemns many of them to return again and again."

Tarsuinn nodded. "I have heard of this, my lady."

"I have not!"

Adaira smiled. "You have been protected from the truth

of your birthright, as all noble ladies tend to be. Gilchrist called it whimsy but he could not abandon Inverfyre either."

"I do not understand."

"One hears of ghosts in this land, of souls condemned to haunt a locale or rest uneasy. This is a tale of ghosts, if you will. Two souls I speak of, two souls whose fates are entwined like two plies of a rope. And like the plies of that rope, neither can be strong or complete without the other."

I sat down, compelled despite myself by this tale. Tarsuinn turned to watch Adaira, something in his expression hinting that he had heard part of this tale afore. Malachy came out of the woods, his hand upon the lace of his chausses and halted to listen.

Adaira nodded. "Magnus Armstrong was drawn to Inverfyre to meet his fated partner, to lay an ancient crime to rest, to release their souls. It is the fate of these two to return time and again to Inverfyre. By divine compensation, they have the chance to set an old wrong to right, to seek each other anew each time their souls don a cloak of flesh."

She shook her head. "But the gods are not kind. No, they are tricksters, each and every one of them. They give with one hand while stealing with the other. The chance of winning eternity together was what they offered, but memory of the tale was what they stole. By the time Magnus understood the price of his own ambition, he had betrayed his destined lover yet again and lost her companionship for yet another mortal life."

I had an inkling of what she would tell me, but I held my tongue, content to wait for counsel I doubted I would like.

Adaira tapped her fingertip on my arm. "Your son is Magnus Armstrong in new guise, as well as all the other men Magnus was afore. The wheel turns, the soul takes flesh again, and each course through the world is destined to teach some morsel of a higher truth."

"But if this is fated to be, why do you try to stop my child from taking his first breath?"

"Because he comes too soon!" Adaira hissed, then rose to her feet. She flung her arms skyward, looking virile and powerful. "Magnus comes too soon! Aye, the gods will have their jest—they will ensure the failure of these fated lovers solely to entertain themselves with mortal folly."

"You tried to aid this couple by delaying my conception of a child," I guessed.

Adaira sighed and glanced about herself, as if surprised to find herself here. "I tried only to grant them some small chance of success. I tried to serve the greater good—the cause of love immortal, if you will—but I have failed. You will bring Magnus to the world, though I fear he is destined to fail again."

I felt a quickening within me, the babe shifting within my womb. It was almost as if he heard her tale and would endorse it, as strange as it was.

Adaira's milky gaze fixed upon me, her expression grim. "My efforts have been futile, though they have cost me dearly." She sighed again, and shrank, her shoulders slumping and her head bowed. "I have paid more than my due in this battle."

"But you cannot see all of the future, Adaira," I said. "What if this child is not Magnus?"

"I told you that you wove a new thread into the warp of Inverfyre and I did not lie. You would have conceived no child, not for another decade, had you done as you were bidden."

I folded my cloak around myself. "I am not sorry to carry this child."

"I know." Adaira shook her head and seemed to shrink again. "And despite myself and all I know, I cannot mourn that Magnus will return to Inverfyre sooner than I believed."

I rose to my feet, wanting only to console her, but Adaira abruptly drew up her hood and wrapped her cloak about herself. She turned away from my touch and walked briskly into the woods. She faded with every step until she had disappeared so surely that she might never have been among us.

Tarsuinn shivered and Malachy shook himself as if waking from a dream. I rubbed my upper arms, suddenly chilled. We exchanged glances, then spoke as one.

"You knew this tale?" I asked Tarsuinn.

He shook his head. "I heard another. It was of Magnus Armstrong, but far different in its details."

"The one your father told," Malachy said with a nod. "That the peregrines permitted Magnus to take their young because he was one of them."

"What is this?"

Tarsuinn smiled a little sheepishly. "My father insisted that Magnus had lived as a man by day and flown with the falcons by night, that he had an agreement with them that saw to the prosperity of all."

"It is the manner of tale a falconer would recount," Malachy amended. "Though it is reputed that Magnus had an uncanny ability to find eyasses just as they left the nest."

"There is an interval of but a day when it is ideal to capture them," Tarsuinn said. "And Magnus was said to be infallible." He shrugged. "I always thought it a fable, concocted to explain his expertise as more than human talent."

"And similarly, the tale of his lost love trapped in the guise of a peregrine."

Tarsuinn nodded. "An explanation for the fact that he

took a wife late and for duty solely. It was well known that there was only a cursory affection between Magnus and his bride, that their nuptials were conducted that Inverfyre might have an heir."

I marveled, for I had never been told these tales.

Tarsuinn touched my arm briefly and I looked up to find his gaze filled with understanding. "Your father believed these tales to be fictions, my lady, and further, to be malicious hints of sorcery in his lineage. It is no surprise that you were spared them."

I smiled for him, for he spoke aright. All of us proved anxious to forage for a bit of food, all of us wanted to search alone. But as I plucked mushrooms and shoots, I wondered. What had I set awry in my decision to seek out Gawain?

And what fate awaited my son?

XX

I slept like a corpse, so exhausted that I did not care whether or not we were found. Indeed, I knew not where we would flee, where we would find sanctuary. I could not even think of possibilities in my state.

I awakened with the dawn's first light, noting immediately that Tarsuinn and Malachy were still both lost to dreams. I rolled over, planning to consider our situation, and yelped to find that I no longer lay alone.

Gawain clapped his hand over my mouth. There was soot on his face and mire in his hair, blood on his tabard, but his eyes gleamed with his usual devilry. He winced at his quick move, then sighed most eloquently as he lay back with feigned weariness. "Truly, I grow too old for this trade."

"You are alive!" I managed to say, knowing that he delighted in having surprised me so thoroughly.

He grinned and released me, propping his weight upon his elbow with enviable ease. A shock of hair fell over his brow as he looked down at me, a familiar twinkle lit his eye.

"Ah, but I could not die, my lady fair, not without knowing precisely who Connor MacDoughall was."

I laughed then, laughed with a joy I had never thought to feel again, uncaring who I wakened with the sound. I fell upon Gawain, rolled him to his back and kissed him with vigor, my heart singing at his presence. He parted his lips beneath mine and I tasted him thoroughly, loving how he caught his breath, how he closed his eyes, how his tongue danced with mine.

We parted breathless, me lying atop his strength. I caressed the singed tips of his hair, ran my fingers across the bruise rising on his brow, touched my lips to the scratches upon his neck. He sighed, his hands fitting around my waist, and permitted me this exploration. There was a gash on the back of his hand, beads of dried blood lining it like jewels, but he shrugged when I touched it gently.

"It is nothing."

"But how did you escape? There were so many besetting you."

He winked. "My will to survive is a powerful one."

I swatted him, not content with this easy explanation, then seized the sleeves of his chemise in sudden recollection of my fear. "I saw the roof of the chapel fall, I saw it burn. I thought, I feared . . ."

Gawain kissed me swiftly, silencing me, and his arms tightened around me. "Some fled when Alasdair fell, others when the chapel roof began to burn. It was then that a trio of your own men came to my aid and we routed the last of them. We fought in a band to the portal."

"But where are they? What fate befell them?"

Gawain held my gaze. "Niall's corpse was yet there, as was the horse Adaira brought him upon. I could not believe the beast held its ground, but it seemed overwhelmed by its fear. We rallied around it and made our way to the gates, gathering men all the way."

"You saw them all escaped," I said beneath my breath.

Gawain shook his head. "Not all. Too many fell at Inverfyre, that much is certain." He took a deep breath, the memory not easy even for him. "We managed to get the portcullis open, then those of us still standing escaped Inverfyre. The gatehouse caught fire behind us, the rope burned and the iron gate fell, sealing those within forever." He gave me a squeeze. "They were mostly MacLarens or those already dead, Evangeline."

I shuddered and buried my face in his shoulder. "And those you escaped with?"

"They went to bury Niall, for they could not leave him without a tribute. They said they would await your return in the forest."

"So few," I whispered.

"There were MacLarens in the woods as well," Gawain counseled quietly. "There may be fewer men living on either side by this night."

I sighed and felt again the weight of my failure.

"And what is this?" he asked, touching the welt upon my neck.

I winced but did not evade his gaze. "Alasdair seized the crucifix to hold me captive. I had to abandon it to escape him."

"It was a small price to pay for your life."

I blinked back tears and buried my face again in his shoulder. He smelled of woodsmoke, of fire and devastation, but beneath that was the alluring scent of his own flesh.

Gawain stroked the back of my neck, his lips touching my brow. "Treachery is the hardest villain to guard against, Evangeline. You cannot blame yourself for the price ren-

dered by your father's choices. He was the one who welcomed Fergus. He was the one who accepted Fergus' cook
and counsel."

He cupped my chin and lifted my face so that I met his
gaze. He smiled at me so gently that my heart lurched. "You
tried to fulfil the expectation of your parents, and indeed you
achieved far more than any could have expected. You hold
yourself to a higher standard than any other would dare,
Evangeline. Credit yourself with what you valiantly
achieved, and do not condemn yourself that there was a
more formidable force arrayed against you."

Something awakened in me as I held his compassionate
gaze, something made me yearn to couple with him more
boldly than ever we had. I had always held some measure of
myself back when we met abed, I had never abandoned
myself fully to our lovemaking. Now it seemed to me that
restraint and decorum had served me poorly, that doing as
was expected of me had borne no good results.

I was yet alive. I yet had a chance to live with vigor. A
boldness claimed me then, a determination to live each
moment to its greatest potential.

Gawain kissed me then, his touch kindling my newfound
desire. I stretched to meet his embrace boldly, twining my
fingers into his hair and urging him closer. I welcomed him
with an enthusiasm I had never unleashed. My heart sang as
he met me touch for touch, and truly, the heat between us
burned with the bright vigor of the sun. I savored every
moment of our powerful coupling, and that I regretted no
deed I had done.

Indeed, on that morn on the forest floor, I soundly
seduced the man who was not the scoundrel he would have
had me believe.

*   *   *

"So?" Gawain demanded when we were sated and yet entangled with each other. I felt languid and warm, and the baby stirred deep within me, awakened perhaps by our activity. My belly was rounding now, not too much but more than ever it had done, though Gawain did not seem to find it unattractive. He trailed his fingers across it, tickling me playfully when I protested.

Our garments were unlaced and there were leaves caught in his hair after our lovemaking. My hair was unfurled and probably a ruin of knots, though I did not care. The unmistakable scent of desire tinged the air as I nestled closer to him and nibbled upon his neck.

Gawain caught his breath. "What of this Connor MacDoughall?"

"I suppose if curiosity was solely what kept you alive, I should tell you," I teased.

"I suppose it would only be fitting." Gawain kissed the tip of my nose.

"If I tell you, will you immediately expire?"

"I shall endeavor not to do so."

"Connor was a scoundrel of no account," I said, smiling all the while. "A rogue and a troublemaker, a seducer of innocents and a deceptive selfish cur."

"Ah, a man with whom I share certain common traits." Gawain arched a brow before I could argue this. "What happened to him?"

"He was killed in a brawl in a tavern, ironically one in which he had no stake. He was simply in the wrong place at the wrong time, as it is told, and rose to his feet with unfortunate timing."

Gawain's expression turned thoughtful. "It seems a hazard of this land for a man to find himself in the wrong place at the wrong time."

"How so?"

He held my gaze steadily. "If I had not left Ravensmuir precisely when I did, you would not have been able to follow me to York."

"And we should never have met in truth." I braced my weight upon my elbow to stare down at him, unable to guess his mood. There seemed a coolness between us suddenly, as if he raised a barrier though I could not guess why. "Do you regret your timing?"

Gawain toyed with the leaf he pulled from my hair, avoiding my gaze. "Adaira said that Connor fathered the child of her daughter."

I rolled my eyes, dismissive of this detail that took our conversation upon an undesirable path. "Connor sired many a child, for he was not hard upon the eyes and he could show a ready charm to a woman he desired." I tapped a finger upon Gawain's chest, determined to seize this chance to resolve matters between us. "I once thought that you and he were two of a kind, but you may be assured that I have learned the error of my conclusion."

Gawain grimaced. "Perhaps you see only what you wish to see, not what truly is."

"Perhaps I saw what you chose to show me, perhaps I now see the truth of the man behind the mask."

Gawain looked up, his gaze cool. "Perhaps you have been deceived, as the women seduced by Connor were evidently deceived."

I thought that he warned me away from him again but I was not inclined to accept such counsel. I shook my head with vigor, and leaned down to brush my lips across his. "Not so. I have seen the truth. I love you, Gawain Lammergeier, I love you for the man you are."

I might have expected some sweet reply to my confession, but I was to have none. Instead of replying in kind, Gawain abruptly eased my weight from atop him. He was on his feet so swiftly that we might never have lain together, so occupied with lacing his chausses that I might not have still been in his presence.

I felt soiled then, soiled like a whore dismissed after her services have been savored, and I was not amused.

I leapt to my feet in my turn and seized a handful of his chemise. I gave him a shake but he spared me only the merest glance. "Answer me!" I demanded. "I said that I love you, just as you are."

I had never seen Gawain so agitated, this man who always showed such cool poise, but he laced his chausses with unholy haste.

"You should not," he said, his voice hoarse.

I felt my eyes narrow. "Nonetheless I do."

Gawain granted me a quelling glance. "Then, cease to do so."

"What is this?"

"You are too clever a woman to make such a mistake."

I straightened, indignant. "I make no mistake. . . ."

"You do. If any should know the truth of it, Evangeline, it is me and I say that you err."

"It is you who err, you who would conceal your own feelings." I was outraged that he should hide the truth from me. "Do you think I fail to see the import of your killing Alasdair to save me?"

"Alasdair is dead by Niall's blade," Gawain said through gritted teeth. "And even if you doubt that Niall's ghost drove my hand, you cannot know whether I raised my blade to save you or to save myself. I am not a man that any woman of sense should love."

I must have looked skeptical, for Gawain shoved a hand

through his hair. He stepped back toward me, his gaze steadily fixed with mine. He spoke with quiet urgency, though he kept a distance between us. "Heed this, Evangeline. My mother loved my father with all her heart and soul. Perhaps he even loved her at one time, I do not know, but it was of no import in the end."

"You see?" I said with triumph, but Gawain shook his head.

"I do see," he retorted. "For the truth of my father's nature came to the fore: he left his honest trade in silks to trade in religious relics of dubious origins. He preferred the wealth and fame he found more easily with such trinkets, and did not care that he lied and stole to win it. That wealth drove him to greater and greater excess."

"You are not your father."

Gawain swallowed. "But I am his son. And you yourself have noted that I share traits with him." He raised a fist between us, his gaze burning with rare intensity. "I watched him destroy her, Evangeline. I watched his sins weigh heavily upon her. I watched her try to change him, a thousand times in a thousand ways, but he was what he was, and even love could not change the truth of it." His gaze bored into mine. "He ruined her, Evangeline, he fairly killed her. She loved him but that love brought her only torment."

I was momentarily at a loss for words, a fact Gawain used against me.

"You are seduced by the reasoning of the heart," he said harshly, "but as my mother learned, the heart gives unreliable counsel. Its advice in this matter will only bring you grief."

"This is why you put no credence in marriage."

Gawain shrugged and looked away. "She could have left him, if they had not been wedded. She could have wrought a new life for herself on some other shore, she could have even found happiness with a man who appreciated her for who she was. My mother was not an unattractive woman, nor was she bereft of charm. If anything, she loved too fully for her own good."

I closed the distance between us. "If she loved your father truly, I doubt she would have left him, were they wedded or no."

Gawain studied me and his features set with resolve. "Then love is a folly, if it makes a person disregard his or her own survival."

I caught at his sleeve when he might have strode away. "And what of you? What have you done? You return to aid me time and again, regardless of the risk to yourself. You counsel me against pretty words and pledges, but your words always hold a warning that I should not rely upon you."

"Because you should not."

"But can you not see, Gawain? You are the sole person upon whom I *can* rely. You are the sole person who has never failed me."

He looked at me then, and I saw the alarm in his eyes. "It is only a matter of time, Evangeline. I will spare myself the sight of you learning precisely the ilk of man I am."

"I know the ilk of man you are," I insisted. "I know that there is honor within you, though you have learned to hide it well. I know that you care for me, just as I see that you fear what might come of declaring as much."

"You see what you desire to see," he argued. "I am no knight come to save you from your fate, Evangeline."

"While you ignore what you do not wish to see. This is no ending, Gawain, it is a beginning. We could wed. We could reclaim Inverfyre. You could live a life of honor. . . ."

"Why? Why would I do such a thing?"

I straightened and held his gaze. "Because my love and companionship is worth the exchange. Because we would be happy together." I thought for a moment that he was torn, that he might step forward and take my offer.

"How? How could you be happy without Inverfyre? I could drag you across Christendom and watch you pine for your birthright—that would ensure our match was fine."

I ignored his sarcasm, for I knew it unwarranted. "Love will find a solution."

"Perhaps you would prefer that we squat in the ruins of your home, perhaps even attempt to rebuild it. Even with success on your terms, you could watch me wither and fade for lack of adventure." His words were bitter and his gaze was sharp. "Would that be fair compense to you for my father's crimes against your father?"

I stepped forward and laid my hand upon his arm. "I love you and that is not so worthy of dismissal as you would imply."

Instead of coaxing Gawain to my side, my words made him abruptly turn away. He tore his sleeve from my grip. "Then you are a fool to cling to such whimsy. There is nothing I can do to save you from yourself."

I was so shaken by his coldness that I could not think of a protest in time. His gaze darkened, then he turned his back and stepped out of the shelter of trees to gruffly greet Tarsuinn and Malachy.

I was left in the forest's shadows, devastated that I had offered my all to Gawain and it was not enough.

We walked then, walked to Ravensmuir. We had no other place to go and Gawain insisted that his brother would offer us protection. It was a long walk, and our sole consolation that the weather was fair. It was almost unseemly how robustly the land burst forth in spring's garb, how lush and green the countryside became.

I remembered Inverfyre burning and knew no spring would come there this year. Indeed, we saw the dark cloud of smoke rise behind us for four days and wondered who was beckoned to see its origin. The destruction of my home and birthright was echoed by the yawning emptiness in my heart.

But Gawain and I spoke no more beyond a minimum of cordial civility. What else could be said?

We turned our backs upon the smoke from Inverfyre and walked. We avoided the road, uncertain whether we might be pursued, though there were no signs of it. When we begged for food, only Malachy or Tarsuinn showed themselves. I remained hidden at all times, at Gawain's insistence, while he hung back after my warning that his height and fair hair would be readily remembered.

Matters were so strained between us that I abandoned any hope of a tender glance that would reveal the contents of his heart. If he loved me, he would give no sign of it. If he loved me, it mattered no more to him than his father's love for his mother had mattered to either of them.

Perhaps my mother had spoken aright, that the Lammergeiers were cursed by their very name. Scavengers and bonebreakers, she had called them, but even knowing what I did now, I could not hate Gawain.

In a strange way, I respected him, for he knew what he was and accepted it. He knew that his essence could not be changed and he would deny the simple solution because it would prove less than adequate in the end. I could respect the nobility of his thinking, even knowing that he was wrong, even knowing that there was nothing I could do to shake his conviction.

We trudged east for fourteen days, and with each day, the land became more softly contoured, more welcoming, more cultivated. We saw more villages, more mills, more monks. We skirted Edinburgh with difficulty, for all roads led to its gates. We slept less as the signs of habitation became more numerous and took to walking all night, napping during the days, hidden in some copse of trees. Our course was not a direct one, thus took longer than if we had walked openly.

At Edinburgh, we debated the merit of approaching the king, but Gawain counseled that none would heed us in our current ragged state. Better, he advised, to continue to Ravensmuir and make our appeal with Merlyn's endorsement. I suspected that he spoke aright.

We followed the south coast of the Firth of Forth, passed the royal docks at Queensferry, circumvented the salt flats maintained by the monks, and had porridge from the nuns who fired tiles near North Berwick. When the coast turned south, the Firth having opened to the sea, the wind offered an invigorating bite.

On the fourteenth morn, when we halted to sleep, I could see a dark keep in the distance, perched on the lip of the sea. I did not sleep that day, merely rested, my gaze fixed upon Ravensmuir.

Upon sanctuary.

Twilight claimed the skies that night with a leisure that infuriated me. Gawain was restless, unhappy with the open stretch of land we had to transverse and the fullness of the moon. The skies were clear that night, adding to his displeasure. He insisted that we wait until night reigned fully, and hesitated even then.

"We cannot stay here all the night," I said finally. "Look—Ravensmuir is but there! We shall arrive no sooner for not beginning."

"I do not like it," he said, frowning as he shook his head. "Something is amiss. I can smell it."

"What you smell is the salt of the sea and the dung of the cows."

"No, Evangeline, my instincts tell me that danger is near."

I heaved a sigh, well aware that our two companions watched us closely. "My instincts tell me that a soft pallet and a hot meal are near. We gain nothing by the waiting, Gawain."

With that, I lifted my hood and strode out of our hiding place. They followed, of course, for they could do nothing else. Gawain quickly overtook me to lead the way. We moved quickly, though there seemed to be no one abroad but the four of us. It rose to my lips to tease Gawain that his instincts failed him and indeed I tapped upon his shoulder to do so.

But when he glanced back, I saw in his eyes what was happening afore he shouted.

No!

"We are assaulted! Run!" Gawain flung me ahead of him even as he pulled his sword from its scabbard. I stumbled at the vigor of his push and glanced back.

Six horses rode towards us, their riders' cloaks flying in the wind. I saw the glint of steel and my heart quailed.

"Run, Evangeline!" Gawain shouted. "Run!"

Tarsuinn seized my elbow and urged me onward. I picked up my skirts and ran, sparing only one glance back.

Gawain stood silhouetted behind me, Malachy fast at his side. Their feet were braced against the ground and their blades held high.

"Run!" Tarsuinn insisted. "Do not look back!"

I ran, his heavy footfalls beside me. I ran to the sound of swordplay, I ran as hoofbeats echoed louder. I ran as a man cried out in pain, I ran as one man, then another, fell hard to the earth. I ran as a horse shied and whinnied, recoiling from the scent of blood.

I ran faster when Ravensmuir's gates were thrown open, ran towards that haven. I heard the hoofbeats of the horses behind me and feared we should not make the gates afore they overtook us.

I ran when Tarsuinn was snatched away from my side. I heard him fall, I heard both horse and rider fast behind me. I glanced back and stumbled even as Tarsuinn shouted for me to hasten. I was sickened by the carnage behind me, my throat choked with tears.

But I ran.

Hope lit like a flame in my heart when a great brute of a horse burst through Ravensmuir's gates. It reared and its rider bellowed, hauling on the reins.

I glanced back as Gawain rose from the ground, his fair hair gleaming in the moonlight. He swung himself into the empty saddle of one of our attackers' horses and gave the beast his heels. I dared to hope that all might come aright, then I saw the dark rider betwixt Gawain and I.

The steed was turned in my direction and I knew that I was the target, the reason, for all of this. I held my belly tight, my skirts bunched in my grip and ran.

The hoofbeats pursued me. They gained upon me, my heart thundered, my chest was tight. The rider from Ravensmuir would never reach me in time, though he stood in his stirrups and coaxed his horse to greater speed. I felt the breath of the horse, so close was it. I glanced behind me.

I saw Ranald's smile of triumph.

I screamed in terror as he brought his shining blade down. I felt the cold bite of the steel sliding into my back. I had a moment to marvel at how readily, how treacherously, the smooth blade slipped between my ribs, and then I knew no more.

XXI

A haze engulfs me, swallowing me in pain as red as rubies, as merciless as flames. I burn, dimly aware of shadows beyond my pain. I am cognizant of shadows and whispers, silhouettes and commands.

From this world or the next? Do I wake or sleep? Live or die? I cannot say. I do not care. The pain consumes me, makes me bare my teeth, cup my hands around my swelling womb, weep and wail.

"It is not so fearsome as it appears." A woman's voice, pitched low and soothing. She sounded competent, someone who could be relied upon.

"The risk will be infection." A man said this. His voice was low and his words slow. It reminded me of the sea, dangerous and mysterious. His accent, though, was like Gawain's, foreign but not exotic. His voice was shadow to the sparkling laughter of Gawain's, more like the roiling shadows of the sea than a merry brook dancing in sunlight.

"She cannot remain here," he said.

"She cannot depart, not with such a wound," Gawain argued.

"Of course she can, if well tended," the woman argued firmly. "To remain is to die for certain, to depart grants her the chance to live. The infection will come or nay, regardless of where she slumbers."

"You do not know their number, Gawain," counseled the man. "And they know now that the lady is here."

"I thought the walls of Ravensmuir unassailable."

"You thought wrongly." The man cleared his throat. "The *Melusine* is loaded to sail on the tide. Take her, take the lady, take my goods south."

"You invite me to steal from you!"

"I invite you to partner with me."

There was a pause, then Gawain spoke with resolve. "The life of reputable trade is not for me."

The other man chuckled. "You think there is no thievery in the silk markets? You think there is no theft in good haggling? You think there is no adventure in cheating the sea time and again? I predict that you will be better at this than ever I was, Gawain."

Silence. A bustle of activity, a plethora of shadows, stabbing pain in my back again. Soothing sounds when I cried out, a hand upon my brow. I feared suddenly for my child, for his future, and an urgency seized me.

"The babe," I managed to say, uncertain of my coherence. "The babe must be named Niall."

"She is pregnant?" The woman. Surprised.

"Since January." It was Gawain, his words uncharacteristically hoarse. I reached for him, but someone placed my hand back on my chest, rolled me to my stomach with a firmness I could not fight.

Water ran in my wound.

"You need not fear for the babe," the woman said with authority. "You will heal."

"Fortune has already smiled upon you," added the deep-voiced man.

"Niall," I said again as a needle bit into my flesh. The pain swelled within me once more, screaming, protesting, pushing everything out of my thoughts. "Champion."

I heard footsteps, fading footsteps as I succumbed to a descending veil of dark slumber.

"He is curt this night," the woman said. I struggled to remain conscious, that I might hear what she said of Gawain.

"He has killed three men, chère," replied the man. "No man of merit puts such a deed readily behind him."

Three?

"Is he changed, or am I deceived anew?"

A smile in the man's voice. "He is again what once he was, before our father put his taint upon him. Do not marvel that he is so surprised. And do not marvel that you see the change in him—you are as good a judge of a man's measure as ever."

Then darkness and pain claimed me again.

I am at Inverfyre then, impossibly balanced upon the summit of the roof of the chapel. A glistening half moon pours silver light over the land I have loved all my days. My birthright and legacy, my responsibility and obligation. It is green yet, leafy and untouched by fire, complete as it is solely in my mind's eye.

A peregrine cries, the shadow of her outstretched wings passing between me and the moon. I turn to watch her flight, taking joy in the beauty of her white wings against darkest night.

"A gyrfalcon," my father murmurs, his voice beside my ear. "The noblest of birds, the consort of kings and emperors alone."

I turn and find my father not rotted, but a shadow clothed in quicksilver. He is there but not there. His affectionate smile is so familiar that it brings a tear to my eye.

"Thus wrote Frederick II, who knew so much of falcons and their ways," he says. "They sewed the eyes of eyasses closed to train the birds until he advised the use of the hood. He saw further than most from his court in Sicily."

He smiles, holding my gaze. He turns then, as regal as I recall, and lifts a fist as he whistles an imperative. I remember now his three-note whistle, how every falcon in the mews turned at its sound. And I see now a tracery of feathers in his shadow, a hint that there is some commonality betwixt us all.

The gyrfalcon lands with a cry upon the fist of my father's specter, so beautiful and white and wild as to stop a heart with joy. My father lifts his face to her, something in the crook of his nose echoing her beak, something in the brightness of his gaze echoing her stare.

And when he launches her again, I feel something rise within my breast as if I could fly with her.

The impulse is forgotten when my father kneels before me, this man who bent his knee only to king and archbishop. He bends and looses the jesses I have only now noticed upon me.

They are wrought of leather and fastened about my ankles, tethering me to the roof of Inverfyre's chapel just as falcons are tethered to their perches. I *even wear a bell as the falcons do, a massive bell which sits behind me on the thatch, the bell which ensures that strays can always be found by the falconer.*

My father casts my jesses aside, then stands anew. He frames my face in his hands, kisses my brow and releases me with tenderness in his smile. "You have done more than a man could expect of a daughter, more even than one could hope from a son," he says, then offers me all of the sky with an expansive gesture.

An urge claims me and I impulsively spread my arms, raise and lower them in a move that is instinctively right. I part my lips to speak but a cry comes from my lips.

I take flight effortlessly, unfettered by obligation and birthright, free as I have never been free. I cry out with delight at this gift, I soar joyous in my new agility, and then I fly so high as to touch the stars.

It is there that I turn my gaze back upon the earth, then that I spy a lone man standing on a peak so distant as to be foreign. The moonlight touches his hair, gilding it, and I know my destiny with a surety all should envy.

I awakened once, lulled by some unfamiliar rhythm. I did not know the chamber but I knew the man opposite. Tarsuinn was in the midst of shelling a boiled egg. He smiled when he saw my eyes open and lifted the arm below his wounded shoulder. "As good as ever, my lady." He stretched out the arm and flexed his fingers. "A fine job, my lady, and a service for which I am most grateful to you."

"Peregrines," I whispered, my dream clouding my

thoughts, my memories of Tarsuinn's father mingled with the sight of him.

Tarsuinn's face crinkled in a smile as he held the egg aloft. "Fear not—it is pigeon, not peregrine." He winked, buried the shelled egg in a dish of salt, then ate it.

I closed my eyes, exhausted beyond belief, confused.

"You knew as much." Tarsuinn nodded when I opened my eyes again, chewing as he studied me. "But what of peregrines? Ten years is my wager, my lady, ten years for the peregrines to recover their numbers at Inverfyre. Twenty would be better. Is this the query you have of me, the falconer's son?"

I could not summon the strength to reply, but closed my eyes again, troubled.

I dream of hunters and prey, a vague dream of shadowed threats and veiled dangers. A cool touch lands upon my brow, something wet and soothing pushes my fears away as a candle will chase the shadows back to the corners.

"Ranald is dead," Malachy says softly. "Alasdair is dead. You have nothing to fear from the MacLaren clan, my lady, not here, not now."

But Dubhglas is not dead. He is blinded, blinded by me, and I feel his lust for revenge reaching out to snatch me from my sanctuary. The shadows loom high, rising over me like an ocean wave, then fall, sealing me alone in darkness and despair.

I awakened to the sense of being rocked in a cradle. I felt well enough, restored and rested, if somewhat hungry.

Intriguingly, I was not anywhere I had been before. The wooden walls were unfamiliar, the strange curved shape of the chamber unknown to me. I certainly did not recognize the young woman who nursed a babe on the far side of the chamber.

And surely, she could not hold my son? How long had I slept? I felt my belly, but it was still barely round.

She smiled at my alarm, then bobbed her head. "Good day, my lady. My name is Anna and it is my duty to serve my lord Gawain's daughter." She changed breasts then, showing me the healthy babe with some pride.

"But I have borne no daughter. . . ."

Anna flushed. "This babe was wrought of my lord Gawain's seed, so said my lady Ysabella after he brought the babe to Ravensmuir." She swallowed but did not seem to take a breath. "And thus she said that he must have a care for what he had wrought and that if he left Ravensmuir, he must take his child with him. And thus it is that I am here, for my lord Gawain is possessed of no milk to feed the babe, nor indeed of the knowledge of what she needs."

Anna fell silent abruptly and turned a brighter hue of red, as if fearing she had said too much.

But I leaned back against the pillows in understanding. This was Adaira's granddaughter, whose mother had died in labor and whose father was the unlamented Connor MacDoughall. This was the child Adaira had pressed upon Gawain and that he had brought to his brother's wife at Ravensmuir in desperation.

If Merlyn's wife Ysabella believed the child to be Gawain's own, her insistence that he see to the child's care made sense—especially as Ysabella was the woman Gawain had deceived to steal the *Titulus*.

I imagined that he would have done well to escape her annoyance with him so simply as this and smiled despite myself. "May I see her?"

Anna finished nursing and fastened her chemise with haste, willingly bringing the babe to me. She was a lovely cherub of a child, all fat cheeks and good health.

"She is a beauty." I touched a fingertip to her cheek and the babe smiled, dimpling in a delightful manner. Her eyes were so blue that she could have been mine own. I felt a desire to hold this fair-haired child close.

Anna seemed to sense as much, for she was quick to offer the child to me. With some effort on the part of both of us, I was propped up a bit more, the baby girl nestled in my embrace. She burped mightily once she was settled, prompting Anna and me to laugh.

"Indeed she is lovely, my lady. I fear that if she also has my lord's charm, she will lead an interesting life."

I laughed aloud then, for I could do nothing else. "No doubt you speak the truth, Anna."

Anna cleared her throat and shuffled with anxiety. "But my lady, no one will tell me this child's name. My lady Ysabella said she had none, but that is not natural." Her sweet face tightened with concern. "You must know her name, do you not?"

"Of course, I know her name," I said with an ease I did not feel. Adaira would not suit, for it would identify her grandmother too readily. Adaira's daughter had been Annelise, so that would not do either, and Anna was a servant's name. I seized upon the first pretty name that came to my thoughts. "She is Rosamunde, of course."

"Rosemunde." Anna leaned over us, cooing the name to the babe. The babe smiled and fidgeted, managing another belch that left a milky froth upon her lips. "Is that a manner of flower, my lady?"

I smiled. "Of a kind. It means the rose of the world and implies that she is beauteous indeed."

Anna nodded, well content. "And so she is." She tickled
the babe's chin and Rosamunde chortled. "I am delighted to
meet you, my lady Rosamunde Lammergeier."

I opened my mouth to correct Anna, but the words froze
on my tongue. Connor MacDoughall was of no more use in
death than he had been in life to the child he spawned. His
name was of no merit and would bring the girl no advantage.
Indeed, she might be poorly served to be known as orphan,
bastard and commonborn.

What harm to give Rosamunde a protector in name as
well as in duty?

"Rosamunde Lammergeier," I echoed, lying with a
bravado that I might have learned from a certain rogue. "It
is a name truly fitting for a great lady."

We smiled as Rosamunde yawned fit to swallow both of
us, then endeavored to fit both fists into her mouth. Anna
began to sing softly and I rocked the child, even though the
chamber itself seemed to rock.

Rosamunde's lashes landed on her cheeks, so dark
against the fairness of her skin that I caught my breath. Her
little hands were so tiny, the finger of the hand locked
around my own finger so impossibly perfect. She dozed
finally and I peered about myself with new interest, feeling
a pain in my back when I moved too much.

"Oh, you must not stir yourself, my lady! I forgot! Your
wound is only just closing and my lord will be most irked if
the stitches tear again." Anna lifted the child from me and
saw to my comfort even as she cuddled the babe close. "You
had such nightmares when first we left Ravensmuir that I
thought the flesh would never heal."

A hundred details made sense to me suddenly. I remembered that flight to Ravensmuir with clarity, and some snip-

pets of conversation as well as a haze of pain. "What of my child?"

"Lady Ysabella said you would ask. She bade me tell you that it is hale. She told me to tell you not to fear for its welfare, for you alone took the blow."

I leaned back against the pillows again, reassured.

Anna perched on a stool beside me as Rosamunde drifted to sleep. "It was most curious, my lady, for you and Lady Ysabella are each nigh as ripe as the other. Had you stayed at Ravensmuir, your children could have been milk-siblings as well as cousins!"

We had left Ravensmuir, then. I caught a whiff of sea salt and heard suddenly a creak from overhead.

"Are we on a ship?" I demanded.

Anna smiled. "Yes, my lady. The *Melusine* it is and a finer ship I have never seen. My lord Gawain undertakes a journey for my lord Merlyn. . . ."

"An honorable mission, if you can believe as much," Gawain interjected wryly. He leaned in the portal, looking hale and healthy. His flesh was tanned to a rich golden hue again. He wore a white chemise and dark tabard, dark chausses and boots. His hair seemed to have captured more of the sun's glint, but his gaze was guarded.

My heart leapt in painful fashion at the sight of him.

"Merlyn would renew his former trade in silks and thus seeks my aid. He is disinclined to leave Ysabella while she carries their child."

"It seems you have developed an affection for such noble missions," I said.

"A fleeting fancy, no doubt." He crossed the room with long strides, his very presence sending Anna scampering from the chamber, her face as red as carmine. "A skittish woman, but competent," he muttered, then studied me carefully. "How do you fare?"

"It seems I shall survive." My attempted jest did not sound as one, not with my voice so breathless as this.

Gawain studied me for a moment, then sat upon the stool Anna had abandoned. "Merlyn and I decided that it was too dangerous for you to remain in Scotland. You can bear your son in exile, where the MacLaren clan cannot hunt you."

"A respite," I said softly, welcoming this chance. I was tired and wounded and unprepared to continue the fight for what was mine own.

As yet.

"Indeed," Gawain agreed. "And one beyond harm's reach. Even Merlyn does not know precisely where we will go, no less where you will chose to linger and bear your child."

"Sicily," I said with resolve.

"You declined to journey there afore," he said carefully.

"You offered once to take me there, to show me the land you so loved," I said, my heart in my throat. "To share your bed for so long as we both should please."

He watched me, his eyes bright. "You said you would be no man's courtesan, for you feared the day you would be cast out."

I smiled, fearing that he would refuse my bold proposition. "You will have no chance to cast me out. I shall stay but a year, long enough to bring our son safely to light and regain my strength."

"Then?"

"Then I will return to Inverfyre," I said with resolve, "that I might seize again his rightful legacy."

Gawain arched a brow. He winked, then pulled a small chamois sack from his tabard and offered it to me.

I gasped in recognition, then lifted my gaze to his. "How can you have this?"

His wicked grin nigh made me smile in response. He shrugged with the insouciance I knew so well and his eyes twinkled. "You were late to retire the night that I came to warn you of Niall's intent. I had to do something to pass the time."

"But the treasury was always locked. . . ." My words faded, for I guessed what he had done.

Indeed, Gawain scoffed at this flimsy obstacle to his curiosity. "I took it on impulse, but now my instinct has proven aright." He opened the sack and removed the seal of Inverfyre, placing its weight in my hand. "You need not fear for Inverfyre, Evangeline, for no man can rule it in the absence of that seal. No man can make law, no man can pronounce justice, not without the laird's seal."

"The king could make another and grant it where he would."

"Merlyn and I have written to him, telling him of the treachery of the MacLaren clan and informing him that you are beneath the care of the Lammergeier. We wrote that you will bear your child in exile, then return. Merlyn believes the king will heed our counsel, for he has enough woes in his court."

"You guessed my desire," I whispered with pleasure.

Gawain smiled as he closed my fingers over the familiar seal. "Consider this a gift from father to son, that his legacy might be complete." Our gazes locked for a dizzying moment, then Gawain pushed to his feet.

"You have no need, Evangeline, to seal our wager or secure your safety with what you can offer abed." He turned and left me there, fingering the seal, distressed that there was yet a wall betwixt us and no way to remove it when he refused my overtures.

Our journey south was long but fascinating. I was glad beyond belief that I was not ill with my pregnancy, nor made ill by the sea, for once I managed to leave my bed, I could not see enough of the marvels of the world. I stood at the rail when the weather was fair, transfixed by the endless coasts unfurling before me.

I meant to make the most of this year's respite by ensuring that my taste for journeying was sated.

Indeed, I had never imagined that the world was so very large, nor that there were so many souls within it. Gawain was indulgent of me, putting into port whenever I saw something that fascinated me, or we came to a town of which I had heard.

We paused at the Templar docks at LeHavre, so large and bustling a port that I turned and twisted like the country girl that I was. The streets echoed with the sounds of a thousand languages, languages that I had never guessed existed. I found it exciting that the world was bigger and more varied than I had known and a lust to explore all of it burned within me.

We halted again at Saint James de Compostela and attended a mass at the cathedral there, its golden altar bright enough to blind the faithful. The devout had come from all corners of Christendom and the assembly was nigh as fascinating as the building itself. I crawled on my knees to mass with the others, I prayed with equal fervor and I wept in that golden shrine at the miracle of the host.

I ate olives for the first time there, sipped wine as red as rubies, tasted oranges and lemons and almonds and glorious foods of which I cannot even recall the names. Gawain bought me a pilgrim's lead cockleshell, evidence that I had been to this great shrine, and offered it to me with a sly smile.

"A genuine relic?" I teased.

He laughed aloud, the first time I had heard his laughter in weeks. "A cheap trinket, sold for many times its value," he said. "But a token of a momentous journey, all the same."

We then sailed around the coast of Spain. I shall never forget my first glimpse of the marvelous blue hue of the Mediterranean. I felt that I had been viewing the world from behind a veil and only its removal had revealed the bright hues before me. The sun was just as Gawain had foretold, warm enough to drive the memory of winter from my very bones. Shades of gold and red and blue unknown at Inverfyre sparkled on all sides, shades never seen at beloved Inverfyre with its thousands of greens and greys and blues.

Through it all, Gawain was courteous and gallant but distant. He never came to my bed, though he was most solicitous on those rare occasions when the babe made me ill.

I told myself to be content that Gawain shared what he knew of the world with me. He was always ready to explain some marvel, or to tell me what he knew of any place, or to buy an exotic fruit for me. Our pace was leisurely, a concession to my curiosity, and I loved him all the more for so adeptly understanding that what I desired most was time.

I watched him in my turn, noting how his swagger gained its former confidence. I watched him turn his charm and skills to win better terms in legitimate trade, caught more than one triumphant wink when he left a stall. He feigned horror at a price with such believability that the price was oft lowered on the spot. The merchants enjoyed him, the bartering they made was akin to a game. I watched

Gawain awaken to the gift his brother had given him, and saw him accustom himself to it.

Indeed, I saw him learn to revel in it and I knew that Merlyn had spoken aright—Gawain would excel at this trade in silks.

I was glad that he had found his place, even as I knew I would return all too soon, alone, to my own. The prospect was less tempting than I knew it should be. I could have persuaded myself to forget Inverfyre, but not for the company of a man who had no care for me.

Indeed, I then could find myself discarded by my lover in a strange land, with no friends or family to aid me and a child suckling at my breast. It was the very prospect I had feared and I would not choose it willingly, foolishly.

No, never such a fate for Evangeline of Inverfyre. I had told Gawain of my love and he had refused it and its import. One year only would I linger in his company.

Though my heart would break, I knew, on the day we parted forevermore, I also knew that I had no choice.

Those of the line of Magnus Armstrong do not beg.

XXII

We reached Palermo on the north coast of Sicily some three months after we departed Ravensmuir. I was round with child, ripe with my lord's seed, and losing confidence in my footing. Thus, I was anxious to feel the earth beneath my soles again, though Gawain rowed off alone, with nary an explanation. He bade us only to remain aboard and wait.

I followed his bidding, if impatiently.

Three days later, Gawain returned to the ship with a dozen men who set to moving ashore every trinket I had bought or brought. He said nothing in explanation, so I knew there was some matter of import bearing upon his thoughts. Indeed, I sensed a test afore me though I did not know its form. He took my hand and led me through the crooked streets of Palermo, behind the agile porters. He offered to fetch me a donkey, but I wanted to walk again.

The road inclined slightly, hills and cypress trees on every side ahead. When I paused for breath, I glanced back at the blue of the sea cradled in the arms of the harbor.

"It is beautiful here," I said and Gawain smiled slightly, politely.

We passed a cathedral, the darkness of its interior pierced by candlelight. The streets smelled of cooking, of lamb over the spit, of bubbling stews, of ripe fruit and wine. Though the cobblestones underfoot were warm enough for their heat to be felt through my slippers and the sun shone warmly on my back, I heard the trickle of fountains and glimpsed lush gardens behind walls and gates. I had the sense that a thousand paradises lurked just out of view.

I was enchanted.

Eventually, we climbed beyond the city walls and passed through a green space. Gawain said it had been a hunting park reserved for royalty. It was wilder here and quiet. I was more at ease amidst a forest not unlike the forests I had known all my life at Inverfyre. Cities intrigued me but I found them overwhelming. Though I enjoyed their charms, I knew I was not destined to live within their walls.

I like to hear the wind.

We strolled through the forest to the calls of distant birds and the rustle of leaves. I could have walked forever in that dappled sunlight, but soon I saw a building ahead, perhaps a small palace. The men halted at Gawain's signal, even Tarsuinn and Malachy and Anna waiting while we two entered alone.

Gawain and I passed through a fortified gate in the wall that surrounded the building and skirted a pond of breathtakingly deep blue. Golden fish flickered in the water's depths, and the fruit trees surrounding it were reflected in its still surface.

I halted to stare at the trees, for they bore not only round green fruit, but round fruit ripened to a reddish orange hue.

Creamy white blossoms adorned the trees as well, and the air was redolent of their sweet perfume.

"Orange trees," I guessed, turning to Gawain with pleasure.

His smile broadened. "And so you see, they do indeed exist."

I laughed, marveling that they were precisely as he had told me.

The walls were wrought of reddish stone, or perhaps stone painted red, and their hue was reflected in the surrounding pond as well. The walls were thick beyond belief, but when we passed through the portal, the air within was delightfully cool.

The entry was in the side farthest from the harbor, around the back, which seemed humble until we entered the hall. Then I halted, stunned by the view spread before me. The hall was as large as the house itself and open entirely to the harbor side. The view of the sea and city below was framed perfectly by the arches of the house, the red of the cathedral visible, the gold of the town, the vivid blue of the sea.

The hall itself was paved with marble, and empty save for two staircases that wound their way upwards at the back. In the midst of the hall was a fountain, the water bubbling from the north wall. The fountain split the room in two, the water dancing and chortling as it fell over steps in a great runnel and finally spilled into the pond before the house. The runnel was lined with tiles painted white and yellow and blue in fanciful designs that shimmered beneath the water.

I turned to Gawain, letting him see that I had guessed where we had come. I knew, too, why we were alone. My reaction was of import to him. This was the test I had anticipated. Gawain showed me the secrets of his heart anew, as he had the first night we met and he had spoken of this place.

I smiled, to show him he had nothing to fear. "The house you yearned for?"

"It is mine, as of this day." Gawain inclined his head slightly and could not help a quick glance of pleasure over his prize. I looked again, fiercely glad that he had won the objective he sought, that he had done so without the *Titulus*. That relic reposed in my trunk along with the seal of Inverfyre, broken but in agreed trust for our son.

The walls were tiled in mosaics, as well, with a curious border running around the entire room. It might have been adorned with script, but I could not read it. At my inquiring glance, Gawain lifted a finger to one corner.

"It is Arabic, the language of the Moors, and it is read from here."

"What does it say?"

"'This is paradise on earth'," Gawain read, progressing from right to left. "'Here dwells he who desires glory and this is the 'Aziz.'"

"The 'Aziz'?"

"It means magnificent or noble palace. All in Palermo call this place 'la Zisa.' It was the summer palace built by the Norman kings, who retired from the city in the summer months."

"To hunt," I guessed, knowing the ways of monarchs well.

Gawain nodded. "It had fallen into disrepair but was recently fortified by the Chiaramonte family."

"It looks empty."

"They decided that it was not suitable to them after all. They like the sounds of the city."

"And they agreed to sell it to you."

He shrugged. "My mother was kin. Merlyn and I spent some time here as children and he has traded much over the years with the Chiaramontes. I have felt welcomed here in my life, accepted for both what and who I am."

"It is your home." At Gawain's nod, I bowed my head. "I accused you once of not knowing what a home was, but I was wrong. I am sorry."

Gawain narrowed his eyes and surveyed the view of the city spread before us. "Sicily is not a place that many would find welcoming," he said with care. "It is a place where passions run high. The people are not above rebellion or violence to ensure their voices are heard. It suits me well to be slightly outside the turmoil that can seize the city, but close enough to see and to hear its vitality."

I smiled to myself. "No doubt you would argue that their passion is honest."

"I would. No wound can fester here, no secret grows in darkness unobserved. No soul is afraid to utter what is in their hearts, nor to partake of the joys life offers to us all. It suits me here, suits me better than any other place I have been. I like to know where I stand in the hearts and thoughts of those surrounding me."

I stared into the vivid green of his eyes and understood that only in a place of such forthrightness could Gawain Lammergeier feel at home. There was a question in his gaze, as well, a query as to whether I could accept this place along with his affection for it. I understood now why he had been wary, for he had wanted to see my reaction to the house he so desired.

I thought it marvelous and exotic, though alien to me in a way I could not explain. I removed my slippers and let the cold of the floor claim my feet. I moved to the fountain, aware of Gawain's watchful gaze, and dipped my hands in its delightful coolness. I glanced up at the aperture through which the water flowed into the house and a polite query about its origin froze upon my lips.

The opening was surrounded by a tiled mosaic depicting a falcon, the spout of water spilling from its mouth, its wings spread high behind it.

"Frederick II hunted here," Gawain said softly. "And is said to have written his treatise about falconry here. We can visit his old mews, if you so desire, though they are ruined as yet."

A lump rose in my throat that I should tread the same land occupied by the king and falconer so revered by my family. This was a land of legend and one filled with the history of the birds I knew as well as my own blood.

I thought of my dream and understood something I had missed. Like a peregrine, I had traveled far to find my true home. Like a peregrine, there could be only one mate for me, and I was content to be wheresoever he was content to be. I had journeyed to find him, and what was of import was that we be together, for wheresoever we were together would be our home.

I turned to Gawain, my heart nigh bursting, daring him to see the truth of my love for him. "I have chosen a name for our son," I said. "And I hope you will agree when you know the reason for my choice."

"I know you favor naming him for the champion Niall," he said tightly.

I shook my head and crossed the distance between us. I halted before Gawain and held his gaze. "I thought to name him Niall, it is true, because the name itself means 'champion.' "

"You would not name him for Niall of Glenfannon, your lost love?"

"No. Niall and I were friends." I smiled. "I covet only his

name. Our son will need the strength and the cunning of a champion to reclaim the legacy that is rightfully his own." I shook my head then. "But that is not the name I favor now, for I have thought long upon the matter."

Gawain said nothing.

I laid a hand upon his arm. "I would name him Michael, in memory of another boy who deeply touched the heart of my son's father."

I thought I glimpsed a glimmer in Gawain's gaze, but he turned away from me.

I pursued him, though this time I did not touch him. "I have realized something else, as well. Perhaps an illness has its merits."

Gawain glanced over his shoulder at me, his eyes dark.

"I have done all that I will do for the sake of my forebears," I said quietly. "The rest remains with our son. No doubt, if he resembles his father, he will savor the challenge of making what he desires his own. I will aid him in reclaiming Inverfyre, when he chooses the time."

Gawain seemed uncertain what to make of this. He shoved a hand through his hair, his composure slipping. "What will you do? Where will you go? Where will you make a home for yourself?"

I smiled with a confidence I did not quite feel. "I would remain abroad, to raise our son in exile. Tarsuinn recommends two decades for the birds to recover their numbers and our son will need that long to grow to manhood and learn what he needs to know of lairdship."

Gawain watched me in silence, his gaze dark with intensity.

"There is an old tale that the Armstrongs of Inverfyre are part peregrine," I continued softly. "And I can see some truth in that. There can be only one partner for a peregrine, only one tiercel with whom she will consent to mate. They mate for life and return to each other, regardless of the obstacles between them."

"Like Aphrodite, the gyrfalcon you released," he said.

I took the last step between us and placed my hand upon his jaw. My touch seemed to soften his resolve and I felt the tension ease from him. "You killed to see me live," I reminded him. "I know the import of that."

"Three I killed that night," Gawain admitted with a shuddering breath. "And Alasdair as well. Still it was not enough." He touched my cheek. "I feared you lost, my lady fair."

I turned and kissed his palm. "But I am found and I am here."

"Will you stay here?" he asked with uncharacteristic urgency. "Will you stay, Evangeline, if I pledge to return to Inverfyre with our son twenty years hence that he might claim his legacy?"

I fought against my smile. "You seek the challenge of stealing it from whosoever might claim it in the interim."

Gawain smiled, then sobered anew. "It would be unfitting for a man destined to be laird to sully his hands with any dark deeds. I will do this for him, that he might nobly claim his birthright. I will do this for you, that you might fulfil your parents' expectation of you."

I cupped his face in my hands and leaned against him, well content with what he offered. "I accept your wager, Gawain, but you should know the exchange in full."

"What is this?"

"Wheresoever you dwell, Gawain Lammergeier, there is my home. In claiming my heart, you are entrusted with it for all time."

"I believe I can accept your terms." Gawain grinned mischievously, then cupped my chin in his hand. His voice dropped low, his eyes gleamed with affection. "Will you always challenge my expectations so?"

I laughed. "I hope so."

"As do I." He bent to kiss me then, all the confirmation of his own love resplendent in his kiss. Our wager was sealed, and I was well content.

Or perhaps matters were not as fully resolved as I thought. Perhaps my beloved scoundrel had yet one more surprise in store for me.

I awakened when the evening's cool air touched my brow. The silk curtains around my bed fluttered in the breeze, their gold and red hues shimmering in the light cast by a dozen candles. The windows were open to the wind and that curious warmth of a southern night. I rose from my bed, drawn to the window by the sound of women singing, and looked out upon a sea of stars.

No, not stars, candles. I looked again and saw the faces of unfamiliar women, all touched with the gold of the candles that they carried. There were hundreds of them, their lips curved in smiles, their burning candles and glowing faces reflected in the pool beneath the palace windows. I could not discern their words, but their joy was evident.

I turned and spied a length of cloth that shone with the same shimmer as my bedcurtains. Something gleamed atop the array of sapphire silk and a note was perched there.

I called out but no one answered, the house silent but for the singing of the women beneath the window. I crossed the chamber and caught my breath to find my mother's amber crucifix glinting in the light. Gawain had claimed it, for me, before leaving the chapel. God in heaven, but I loved this man!

I read the note, my heart in my throat.

> *There is a matter left unfinished between us, my lady fair.*

I glanced back to the window, to the gem, to the note, and smiled in understanding. I donned the silken dress, feeling as resplendent as a queen, put the crucifix around my neck and wrapped a golden veil over my hair. I slipped on the fine stockings and leather slippers of red leather, arranged the folds of silk over my belly and took a deep breath before I left the chamber.

I descended into the sea of stars. The women laughed and smiled, catching at my hands. We did not speak the same tongue, but it was no obstacle between us. They led me down the hill like a tide that cannot be denied, their jubilation making my heart sing.

A lump rose in my heart when I saw Gawain, waiting with the priest on the steps of the cathedral. Tarsuinn and Malachy stood beside him, beaming with pride; Anna bounced Rosamunde; the rest of the crew stood in ranks on either side.

I had eyes only for the man I would wed. His hair was golden in the candlelight, his tanned features glowed with vitality. He was garbed richly, in black and gold, like a man attending great festivities.

He offered his hand and I laid mine within his palm's warmth, loving how his fingers closed over mine with surety.

"It is tradition here that women escort the bride to her nuptials with song and candlelight," he informed me quietly. "My mother was escorted thus, and it is a custom that I find most enchanting."

"As do I. This is magical."

Gawain bent and kissed my hand. "Wed me, my Evangeline, as you agreed to do once before. Wed me and we shall ensure together that our son fulfils the prophecy of his birth."

The babe stirred within me then, as if he too agreed with this scheme. I seized Gawain's hand and pressed it over my belly that he might feel his son's activity as well. We shared a smile, marveling at what we had wrought, then Gawain sobered anew.

"I love you, Evangeline. I love the vigor with which you greet every challenge afore you and I would share my days and nights with you for all time."

I leaned closer to him. "I love you, Gawain, though you are less a scoundrel than I had believed." I pressed the seal of Inverfyre in its chamois sack into his hand and smiled when his eyes widened in surprise. "One might expect as much of the Laird of Inverfyre."

He snorted even as he tucked a tendril of hair behind my ear. "Only a lady wrought of surprises such as you could have awakened a slumbering nobility within me," he teased, "though in the end, it is you, Evangeline, who have proven to be the more agile thief."

"Me?"

Gawain chuckled. "Yes, you, for you have stolen the heart that no other even guessed I possessed. That was a feat indeed."

I might have laughed but the priest cleared his throat, recalling us to the celebration at hand. We exchanged our vows hand in hand, stars above and candles around, our hearts filled with a glorious variant of the song that filled our ears. We made our version of tradition, as I guessed we oft would in years ahead, and it was far, far better than ever I might have hoped.

And when Gawain kissed me soundly, setting a thousand fires alight within me, I knew those thousand fires would burn through all eternity. This love was the fate I had been born to feel, and I welcomed it with all my heart and soul.

the nobility of his making; even knowing that he was

Dear Reader

How do you reform a scoundrel? I couldn't resist Gawain—especially when everyone who had read THE ROGUE was aghast that I could imagine there was anything heroic about Merlyn's brother! There's something about a man with a twinkle in his eye and confidence in his swagger, isn't there? I knew that the best way to find his vulnerabilities—if Gawain even had any—was to toss him into a trying situation. What better than a challenge from a woman every bit as clever as he? Evangeline was the only woman I knew who could catch Gawain's attention and hold it fast. I enjoyed their battle of wills, and the changes they wrought in each other, and hope you did, too.

What drives a man to thievery? What makes a man abandon his morals—and what drives him to reclaim them? You've read a bit already about the prophecy regarding the son of Evangeline and Gawain, and that son is the hero of my next book, THE WARRIOR. Join the adventure as Michael returns to claim his hereditary holding of Inverfyre, only to learn that old wrongs are not set to rights as easily as that. You and I both know that love holds the key—how long will it take Michael to realize the truth that his true love is trying to tell him?

Visit my website to find up-to-date information on upcoming releases, to enter my biweekly contest (win a book!), and to join my listserve. Château Delacroix, my

virtual home, can be found at http://www.delacroix.net.
You can also write to me at:

Claire Delacroix
P.O. Box 699, Station A
Toronto, Ontario
Canada M5W 1G2

Until the next time, happy reading!
All the best

More
Claire Delacroix!

❧⤜⋆⤛❧

Please turn this page
for an excerpt from
THE WARRIOR
a new Warner book
available in paperback
in Spring 2004.

Chapter One

Inverfyre, Scotland—November 1390

His father had been right.

Every step Michael took into the forests of Scotland made it more impossible to evade the astonishing truth. He had always assumed that his father's tales of Scotland had been whimsy, heavily embellished with a nostalgia that his mother would find appealing.

But they had been true. The land was so beautiful as to leave him breathless—but it could be mercilessly cruel, as well. What made it exceptional though was his growing sense that these lands were not quite earthly.

There had been frost this morning when they awakened, and all the trees were etched with silver filigree. The sky was a blue so bright as to hurt one's gaze, but the shadows in the forest yielded their secrets to none. Michael eyed the surrounding trees, unable to dissuade himself of the conviction that he was being watched.

And not by mortal eyes.

Certainly not by friendly eyes. What madness did these northern woods awaken within him? He thought of his father's tales of ghosts and fought to dismiss such nonsense.

Michael trudged onward, fighting to ignore the oppressive feeling that the forest disapproved of his intrusion. He was the seventh son of Magnus Armstrong, the heir of Inverfyre, the warrior destined to fulfil an old prophecy, and the son of the greatest thief in Christendom besides. Fortune would not dare deny him his due.

At least, he was not alone. Tarsuinn had been invited to join this journey, his sister Rosamunde had not, but they both trod behind him all the same. A dozen stalwart men from his father's household and ship comprised the rest of the group that had sailed north.

He had commanded the crew to drop anchor at the Lammergeier stronghold of Ravensmuir to seek the counsel of his uncle, Merlyn. But Merlyn and his wife Ysabella had been away—in lieu of Merlyn's counsel, Michael's cousin Tynan had insisted upon accompanying the party to Inverfyre, along with his trio of squires. They were nineteen in all, with a dozen horses between them, but the sound of their passing was almost naught.

The young squires had ceased their chattering as soon as the shadow of the woods closed around them. By the time Stirling had fallen into the forgotten distance behind them, none of them dared to make so much as a whistle. It was as if they trod close to a sleeping demon and dared not awaken him.

Yet something surveyed their progress. Michael halted suddenly and knew without glancing back that the rest of his party stopped behind him. Stillness settled on all sides, the shadows seemed impenetrable, the cold of pending winter chilled his marrow. The forest breathed on all sides, watching, waiting.

Michael shivered involuntarily. It seemed suddenly to be tremendous folly that brought him here, that he could never accomplish his objective, that he had made a fatal error.

Nonsense! He would not be defeated by silence!

"Are there wolves in these woods?" he demanded of his cousin.

Tynan shrugged. "There are wolves in all the forests of Christendom. They are not more numerous here."

"Are they more malicious?" Rosamunde asked as she eased her steed closer to the pair.

Tynan snorted. "Have you amiable wolves in the south?"

Rosamunde flushed but did not look away. "Are they especially vicious in this barbaric land?"

"All predators are vicious, particularly those willing to prey upon men." Tynan turned to scan the forest and Michael did not miss the glare that Rosamunde cast at their older kin. Tynan was some eight years their senior, tall and dark and given to dismissing Rosamunde in a manner she clearly did not appreciate.

"What observes our progress, then?" he asked.

Tynan smiled crookedly. "I could tell you a thousand tales of ghosts and specters, each and every one of them purportedly true. One seldom feels alone in our woods, though I never have felt another presence so strongly."

It was on Michael's lips to ask whether they should continue by this way or choose another, when a cloaked figure stepped out of the forest ahead of them.

He blinked and looked again. Indeed, he could not have said that this soul truly stepped from anywhere—it was more that the figure had appeared where it had not been before. He might have thought that he imagined the figure, but Rosamunde whispered a prayer and crossed herself. Tynan lifted a hand to stay his cousin, suddenly as watchful and silent as a predator himself.

"Do you shirk what you cannot see, heir of Magnus Armstrong?" the figure shouted, her voice revealing her gender. "Or is the blood of Magnus' lineage so diminished that his heir has not the boldness of a babe?"

Tarsuinn gasped. "God in heaven, it cannot be."

"Who is she?" Michael demanded in a whisper.

"An old crone of the woods. I thought her dead years past." Tarsuinn peered at the distant figure, shaking his head as he marvelled. "But it is she. This one was of aid to your parents once, though she is unpredictable. I advise caution, my lord." He eased his steed forward and raised his voice. "Adaira? Do you yet occupy these woods?"

"Tarsuinn Falconer," she replied haughtily. "I would know your voice in any land, though the birds have spoken of your pending return."

This made little sense to Michael, but before he could ask, the crone lifted one hand. She pointed a gnarled finger toward the clouds and birds cried overhead as if she had summoned them. Their distinctive silhouette made the company gasp.

"Falcons!" Tarsuinn whispered in awe, craning his neck to follow the course of the birds. Another trio followed, crying as they flew. One had a fresh kill and the others tormented it, trying to steal the meat. Tarsuinn smiled, tears shining in his eyes. "How many, Adaira? How many have returned?"

"The falcons are plentiful in numbers at Inverfyre again, Tarsuinn Falconer, and await your hand."

Tarsuinn's delight was nigh tangible. "My lord, this is the finest news for which we might have hoped. . . ."

Adaira's voice hardened. "I have no business with you on this day, Tarsuinn Falconer, and the falcons have not waited so long that they cannot wait longer. It is the boy I have come to greet."

Michael felt the hair rise on the back of his neck when she pointed a calloused finger at him. Tynan and Rosamunde eased their steeds to his either side, but Michael raised his hand to stay them. He urged his destrier to step forward alone.

The old woman's eyes seemed to glow within the shadows cast by her hood. "Aye, boy, I come to parlay with you." When he did not move further, she cackled with laughter. "Are you afeared, boy? You will not recapture Inverfyre if you cannot even speak to an old woman!"

One of the squires snickered, but Michael was already swinging from his saddle. He cast his reins aside with impatience and doffed his gloves. Tynan said something but Michael strode away from his cousin, making his way directly to the crone. She was smaller than he had guessed, the top of her hood below the middle of his chest. She watched him approach, her eyes gleaming, though he only saw why they shone so oddly when she suddenly cast back her hood.

Her gaze was veiled with the pale blue sheen of cataracts. Her tanned skin was as wrinkled as old leather, her features so shrunken that the flesh was tautly stretched over her bones. Her teeth were gone, her hair as white as fresh snow, her pose defiant. He recoiled and she laughed beneath her breath.

"What is your name, boy?"

"Michael Lammergeier, Laird of Inverfyre."

She chuckled. "You are not laird yet."

"I have the seal and the bloodright. . . ."

"And there are others who occupy your keep, others who are not creatures of the forest."

"Do you come to curse me?"

Her smile softened, as did her voice. "Not I, Magnus. Not I."

Michael shook his head, thinking her wits addled. "I am not Magnus, but Michael, as I just told you. . . ."

Adaira interrupted him. "You are Magnus Armstrong, just as you are the seventh son born in succession from him. Make no mistake, Michael Lammergeier, the spark of Magnus resides within you and his debts sit upon your shoulders."

"I do not think so." Michael took a step back from this woman who was obviously mad. She granted him a look so quelling that he halted, then she beckoned.

He found himself leaning closer, almost against his own volition, half-certain she would tell him something that would be of merit in his quest.

Instead she caught the back of his neck in her hand, her gesture quick and her grip strong. Before he could protest, she pressed her ancient lips to his in a parody of a kiss. Her tongue was between his teeth before he knew her intent, its invasion as skilful and revolting as that of a snake.

He made to pull away but froze when a curious sense overcame him. He was remembering, remembering events that were not his to remember. The scene of a richly appointed hall unfurled in his own thoughts, himself garbed like a king, a glorious maiden seated at his left. Her hair was of chestnut hue, her complexion was creamy, her waist narrow and her eyes a fathomless blue. She turned to him, her gaze filled with adoration, and smiled so sweetly that his heart nigh broke. He recalled raising a hand to her nape, pulling her closer, kissing her deeply.

That kiss melted into this kiss and he realized what he did.

Michael tore his lips away from the crone's and felt himself trembling. "What witchery is this you do?" he demanded, his words hoarse. To his horror, the crone's smile was tinged with his recollection of the sweet smile of the maiden, the blue of her clouded gaze reminded him all too well of the maiden's clear loving gaze.

He wiped his lips with disgust and made to step back, but her hands were locked around his neck. "Release me, witch!"

"Again," Adaira whispered, her voice as low and velvety as a ripe maiden's. Indeed, he knew that if he closed his eyes, he would err again, he would think this crone the maiden he remembered.

But he had never known a woman who looked like that maiden, he had certainly never loved a damsel with such vigor that his heart ached so at the very sight of her. This was sorcery! Michael fought Adaira's wickedly strong grip, but her lips closed over his all the same.

And the witchery worked its darkness again. He tasted the sweetness of honey and the tang of wine on the lips of his maiden, felt the ripeness of her naked breast beneath his hand. He saw that he and the demoiselle had retired to a richly draped bed, a bed unknown to him. Her hair was unbound, hanging thick to her waist, her flesh was fair, her nipples rosy. She was perfection, she was his love.

"Magnus," she whispered with awe as her playful fingers closed around his erection. She giggled when he caught his breath, as merry a sound as he had ever heard and he thought his heart would burst with the fullness of his love for her.

For a woman he had never seen before.

Madness!

Michael broke their embrace with an effort and glared at the old woman. "You are a sorceress, bent on driving me to madness," he accused in a low voice. "Why? What accusation would you make against me?"

Adaira smiled. "You will remember, Magnus, in time."

"I am not Magnus. . . ."

She turned then, her head lifting suddenly like a doe who hears the hunter. Then she seized his hand, her other hand fumbling beneath her cloak. He struggled to break free of her merciless grip, but she had an unholy strength.

"It was not my intent to betray you, Magnus, never that," she declared in a low voice. "Still I love you, with all my heart and soul, as I did centuries past, as I loved you on the night that you betrayed me."

"I have never . . ."

"Still I love you," she insisted, then lifted an ancient dagger high in her hand.

Michael cried out and took a step back, thinking the madwoman meant him ill. He fought her grip with renewed vigor, but to no avail.

"What do you fear of me?" she whispered. "I offer you aid, no more than that. You will need this." She turned her hand, offering him the blade, even as two arrows tore into her chest. Her body jerked as she fell back, her grip upon Michael's hand loosing only now.

"No!" Michael shouted. "She meant me no ill!" Later he would marvel at the root of his certainty, but in that moment, he knew without doubt.

He heard the members of his party running closer, but he cared only for Adaira. He caught her in his arms as she collapsed and watched helplessly as the blood flowed from her. The dagger tumbled from her feeble grip and she raised a trembling hand to his face. Her odd gaze seemed fixed upon him, nay, it seemed she could see directly to his soul.

"Remember me well, Magnus Armstrong," she whispered. "It was not my intent to betray you, though I feared matters come to this. The gods will have their jest, after all." Tears began to run from her eyes. Her fingers traced the lines of his face as if she would know the look of him despite her blindness. "I love you, I love you for all time."

He saw her die, he witnessed the moment that life left her being. Indeed, Michael could have had no doubt of it. Just as the old woman's eyes closed and her lips stilled, a light seemed to flood her face and he saw again the features of that young beautiful maiden.

On impulse, he bent, compelled by some nameless urge to press his lips to the maiden's lips one last time, then the vision abruptly faded and he saw only the crone dead before him.

Michael laid her on the ground and took an unsteady step back. As he stared at her, a tumult of memories loosed in his mind that he was certain were not his own. Throughout them all rode that maiden, her smile tightening his chausses and making his heart pound. He looked at his companions, seeking some hint that he was not the only one affected, but they regarded him with uncertainty.

He bent and claimed the dagger, shoving it into his belt, as he sought the words that would return matters to how they had been.

He did not have long to think, for the forests were rent

suddenly with shouts. A tattered army of vagabonds leapt out of the shadows, blades flashing. They were assaulted on all sides by a nameless and innumerable foe.

Tynan roared and unsheathed his blade, the horses neighed. Rosamunde drove her dagger into the face of an assailant. Michael was the slowest to draw his blade, then he fought with vigor. He bellowed and his men formed a circle around him.

Blades swung and blood flowed, the watchful silence of the forest shattered by the warfare of men. Michael had no doubt that this was but the first of many battles he would fight to regain his legacy. They were upon the soil of Inverfyre, he could feel it in his very feet, just as he knew he was destined to triumph.

Aye, the maiden smiled benignly in Michael's new-found memories, encouraging him, loving him, welcoming him. He knew he would never forget this beauty, a conjured dream who claimed his heart without saying a word. Indeed, in time, he would recall that she was his destiny.

It would be eighteen years before he glimpsed her again, eighteen years of memories and yearning. She would be taller, more fair, but with the same blue eyes and the same mysterious smile. And Michael would be convinced that he dared not to leave any chance for her to evade him again.

Michael would steal the sole prize he desired, as befitted the son of a thief he had always been and the ruthless warrior he had become.